Praise for Amanda Dykes

"Moving between a contemporary setting and the early nineteenth century, Amanda Dykes has written a sweeping split-time novel, in turns mysterious and adventurous, mythical and romantic. Filled with magic, wonder, and gorgeous writing, *Set the Stars Alight* is a stirring gem from a gifted author."

—Julie Klassen, bestselling author of *A Castaway in Cornwall*

"Amanda's lush tale took me to another time where her subtly crafted scenes left memorable impressions of the mysterious expanse of faith, hope, and especially love. Timeless love. I hope you'll linger over the pages. Hidden in the carefully crafted words is an invitation to share the rare gift of a sense of wonder."

—Robin Jones Gunn, bestselling author
of the HAVEN MAKERS SERIES
and Christy Award Winner

"The stars align beautifully in this latest tale from Amanda Dykes. A split-time search for light both in the past and present, brings the reader on a poetic journey to find belonging and hope. Misted with sea water and lit by the moon, the words on every page of *Set the Stars Alight* become integral to the reader's own journey, and the ending will resonate long after the last page has been closed."

—Jaime Jo Wright, author of *On the Cliffs of Foxglove Manor*
and Christy Award-Winning novel *The House on Foster Hill*

"An absolute gem of a debut! With her breathtaking prose and captivating setting, Amanda Dykes weaves a tale of utter charm along the rugged coast of Maine. *Whose Waves These Are* transcends to the highest level of fiction. The author has paused to see humanity at its most real and precious, leaving the reader to tuck this one among the classics. It's a novel that wraps around the heart, breathing of hope and light in every scene. Equal parts relevant and nostalgic, this is a novel for the ages."

—Joanne Bischof, Christy and Carol Award–winning author
of *The Gold in These Hills*

"This is the book everyone will talk about all year—lyrical, lovely, full of heart and heartache, secrets kept and revealed. These characters, this town, and their stories will seep into your soul and leave you wanting more. A novel of hope and reconciliation you won't forget for a long time, probably not forever."

—Sarah Sundin, bestselling and award-winning author
of *When Twilight Breaks*

"With a gorgeously inimitable voice, Dykes sets herself apart with a debut novel as timeless as its themes of redemption and everlasting love. I dare you not to be swept into a yarn of age-old tales and seaside secrets deftly penned by a lyrical pen that pliantly shifts between contemporary and historical frames. Romantic, spellbinding, and wonderfully unique, Dykes's sense of setting and emotional resonance is nearly unparalleled. A book world to be savored and returned to again and again."

—Rachel McMillan, author of *The London Restoration*

yours is
the night

Books by Amanda Dykes

Yours Is the Night

Set the Stars Alight

Whose Waves These Are

NOVELLAS

Up from the Sea from *Love at Last: Three Historical Romance
Novellas of Love in Days Gone By*

From Roots to Sky from *The Kissing Tree: Four Novellas Rooted
in Timeless Love*

yours is
the night

AMANDA
DYKES

BETHANYHOUSE
a division of Baker Publishing Group
Minneapolis, Minnesota

© 2021 by Amanda Joy Dykes

Published by Bethany House Publishers
11400 Hampshire Avenue South
Bloomington, Minnesota 55438
www.bethanyhouse.com

Bethany House Publishers is a division of
Baker Publishing Group, Grand Rapids, Michigan

Printed in the United States of America

Library of Congress Cataloging-in-Publication Data
Names: Dykes, Amanda, author.
Title: Yours is the night / Amanda Joy Dykes.
Description: Minneapolis, Minnesota : Bethany House, a division of Baker
    Publishing Group, [2021]
Identifiers: LCCN 2021004780 | ISBN 9780764232688 (paperback) | ISBN
    9780764239274 (casebound) | ISBN 9781493431465 (ebook)
Subjects: LCSH: World War, 1914–1918—France—Fiction. | GSAFD: Historical
    fiction. | Christian fiction.
Classification: LCC PS3604.Y495 Y68 2021 | DDC 813/.6—dc23
LC record available at https://lccn.loc.gov/2021004780

Cover design by Kathleen Lynch/Black Kat Design
Cover image of poppies by Trevor Payne/Trevillion Images
Map illustration by Najla Kay

Author is represented by Books & Such Literary Agency

21 22 23 24 25 26 27   7 6 5 4 3 2 1

To Ben,
my beloved.
The "boy born in a barn."
What a gift to travel this road with you.

And to the four million men who served in the
American Expeditionary Forces of the Great War.
Your journey was harder than we can know,
your lives more meaningful than we can say.

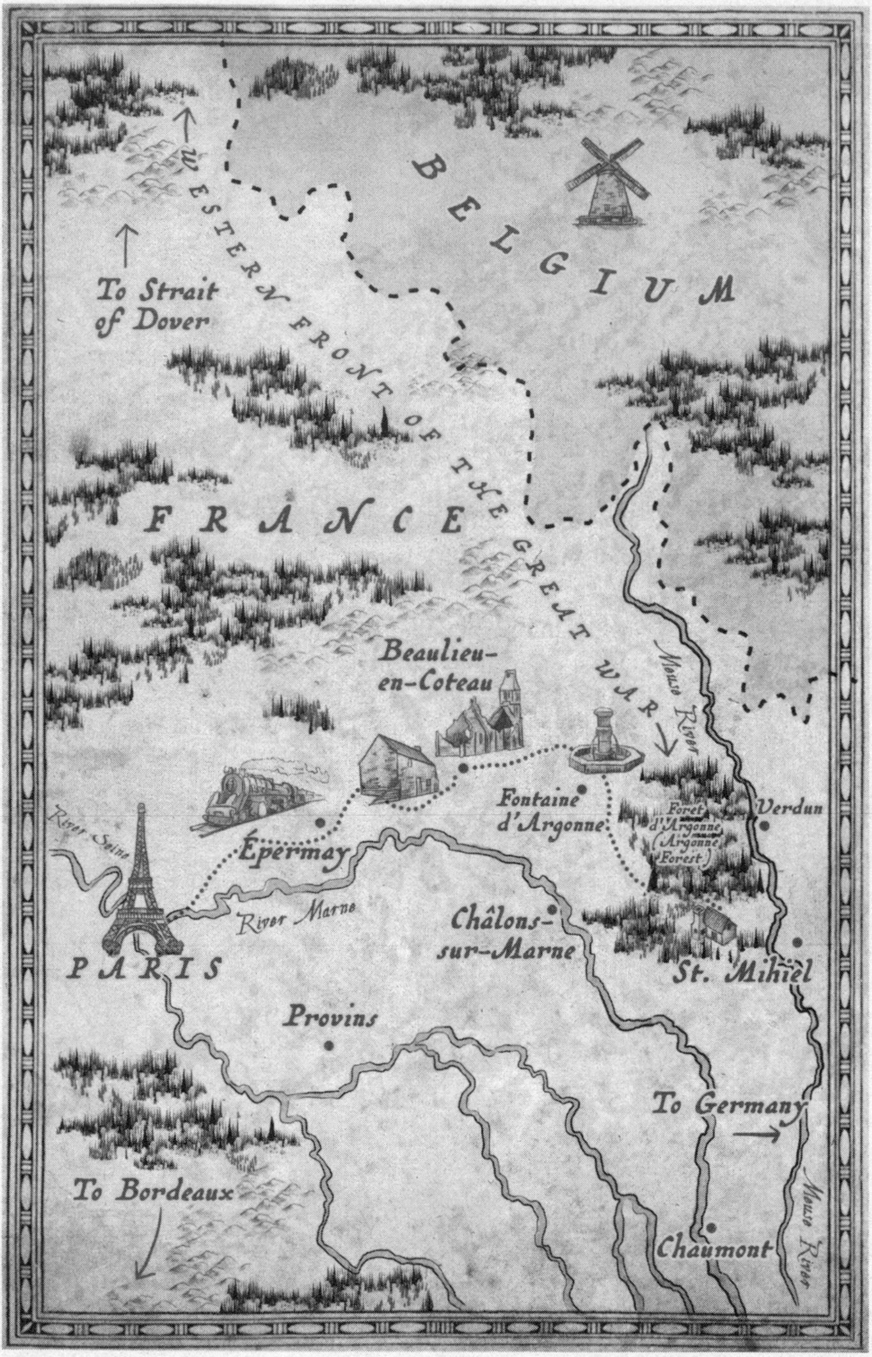

BELGIUM
WESTERN FRONT OF THE GREAT WAR
To Strait of Dover
FRANCE
Beaulieu-en-Coteau
Fontaine d'Argonne
Foret d'Argonne (Argonne Forest)
Verdun
Meuse River
River Seine
Épermay
River Marne
Châlons-sur-Marne
St. Mihiel
PARIS
Provins
To Germany
To Bordeaux
Chaumont
Meuse River

"The day is Yours,
the night also is Yours . . ."

Psalm 74:16

prologue

October 24, 1921
Chalons-sur-Marne, France
Ceremony for the Choosing of the Unknown Soldier

There are days you live over and over again, for as long as you live. October twenty-fourth of 1918, just days before the unending war ended, was one of mine. I went into a forest of darkness that day, never imagining how that place would claim me. Four years ago, to the day.

And four caskets before me now.

There were four of us, then, who took a journey. Armed with bayonets and canteens and a mission we had no idea how to accomplish, bumbling fools that we were. A mission of greater import than we realized at the time. One that would change us all.

I watched now from the outskirts of the solemn ceremony as a man in uniform gripped not a bayonet, but a bouquet. A grip of roses—white. Pure. Absent of the scarlet we'd all seen too much of. Slowly, he walked down the line of boxes that held the remnants of so much life. Nobody knew whom the boxes held. And yet everybody knew a thousand soldiers, brothers, friends whom they might hold.

We were no different. I stood shoulder to shoulder with two of my brothers from that time. We'd seen it all, then. We'd seen each other at our best and our worst. We'd scorned one another and needed one another and had left that battle-gouged land with battle-gouged hearts. We'd left one of us behind, in that forest, and though we would never know who lay in these caskets, every one of us wondered: *Is it him?*

11

The man before us now would walk this line. He would place that spray of roses on a single casket. The casket would be taken back across the sea, to our nation's capital, to the soldier's homeland, to be entombed there. Guarded, always. Kept safe from war, from loss, from all the atrocities he had faced. And in this . . . he would bring something to a nation. Something we brought out of the forest that day, a lifetime ago.

Hope.

This is our tale.

May we never forget.

Matthew Petticrew

1900
Greenfield, New York

Rules:

1) Keep off the racetrack, you dolt! That's what Mr. MacMannus says. He says if Maplehurst Stables is the crowned jewel of thoroughbred racing, then "that dirt you think you can just run on any old time is good as gold."

2) Feed the hens and horses between the hours of four and five, and if you finish early, stay out and play. Do not come back to the caretaker's quarters before that. And don't run on that gold dirt.

I looked at my old notebook, with these two rules scratched inside. I was five—almost six—and I had written them down with the help of Mr. Haggerty, the gardener, so I wouldn't forget. When I forgot, bad things happened. He'd looked at me a little funny when I told him what they were, but he wrote down the hard words for me before getting back to pruning his roses.

The rules weren't so bad. The rest of the green rolling hills of Greenfield Springs, New York, were mine for the taking, and most of the racetrack, too. But tonight—tonight there was one more rule.

"Stay with Mrs. Bluet, tonight," Mother had said. "You know the way?" She'd smiled and winced at the same time, cradling her swollen belly before reaching out to ruffle my hair. I was not the smartest boy around, but I could tell something was different. Her breath came quick or sometimes not at all, like she'd been the one caught running around the racetrack and not me.

Her hand was stiffer than usual, and her smile so tight. It wasn't right. Her smile always went deep and wide, probably the deepest, widest thing I knew.

So, I packed a clean shirt like she told me to right after she'd kissed me on the top of my head. But I tucked myself under her window outside instead of heading to the cook's quarters at Mr. MacMannus's house. It sat just on top of the hill, looking down on our little house, the way hawks look down at field mice. I didn't like it there. It was called Maplehurst too, just like the stables. It sounded sweet like the syrup, but for all its fancy rooms and people coming and going in suits and dresses, it felt awful cold and un-sweet to me. I accidentally called it Maple*hurts* once when I was there eating a molasses cookie in the kitchen. Mrs. Bluet looked at me with flour on her face and her eyebrows raised and said, "Well, young Matthew, if that isn't about the rightest thing I ever heard."

I did not wish to go there that night. I didn't want to be near Mr. MacMannus and his rules and the big, cold house. I didn't want to be away from my mother. She needed me. I could tell.

Only once did I peek inside the window, where an oil lamp glowed so dim I could barely see her there on the bed. Her face was so pinched up that it hurt me to look at her, and her cheeks were wet with tears.

That was the night I first felt the Flame. I called it "the Flame," for it burned in my chest, right where Mrs. Bluet said my heart was. I once saw them set off dynamite at the quarry over the hills. The way the spark chased a cord to the place it would explode—that's how I felt. A spark hot within me, a cord running between me and Mother, but I was not allowed in, not allowed to let that spark rush in and explode inside the little house and chase her pain away.

Two ladies came and spoke together so quietly I couldn't hear. Mother always said that hearing was my gift because I could hear things others couldn't. Even so, strain as I might, I couldn't make out what their concerned tones were saying. One woman kept coming and going, bringing cloths and boiling water, while the other one stayed with Mother and said things to her and held her hand while her cries turned into the sort of moan that could dig into your insides and hollow you out. What was wrong?

The groans grew louder and longer until the spark inside of me was gone, smothered by a blanket of fear so heavy I didn't know whether to run or stay.

So, I prayed. We always prayed on Sundays. Mother would tuck her white blanket around my shoulders and read scriptures to me at our table beneath the very window I now crouched under. She baked something very special on those days, like an apple cake just my size, which she gave completely to me, or vinegar pie, which we shared. I felt like a king on Sundays, wrapped up in that blanket like those red capes that kings wear, only mine was so old and had been washed so many times, it was much softer than any king's.

But for the rest of the week, she was quiet and troubled most evenings, her only prayers silent, and mine, too.

That night was a Tuesday. I prayed aloud on a Tuesday for the first and only time I could remember, that night. The shortest prayer—it did not rhyme or sound very right, but it was the truest prayer I had ever prayed.

"God in heaven, help her." I pressed my eyes shut so tight it must have sent my prayer higher, louder. It had to. I rocked myself back and forth to the words and said it again. And again, and again, and again, my words mingling with her cries until her cries grew quiet and were replaced by another, smaller cry. That of a baby.

Something strange happened, then. I have never felt it since that moment and maybe never will again. But as I rose to my knees and clutched the windowsill, my fingernails caked with dirt, and peeked inside that golden-glow room, I saw something perfect.

Mother, happy. A baby in her arms, all wrapped up in the old king's cape blanket and her smile once again so deep and wide.

That was the last time I saw her. I did go up to Maplehurst after that, and when the morning came, I awoke to Mrs. Bluet sitting beside me and holding my hand. She looked like the whole world had cracked open overnight. And when she spoke, I found that it had.

Mother was gone. She had died in the night, gone to the angels and God above. Leaving behind one tiny angel in her place, and both of us without a mother or a home.

2

1914

The world was going to pieces at war, way across the sea. But at Maplehurst, the earth erupted every day at twelve o'clock sharp. It started as a rumble. A tumbling, trembling sound that burrowed through the soil like it burrowed through my veins. And then it grew louder, the current separating into rhythm, the rhythm pulsing into force, eclipsing the tick of the clock on the stable wall.

I looked down the corridor. I'd pitched hay, mucked stalls, and pounded horseshoes since before dawn. I'd known little else in my nineteen years, but it was a good life. My work was done—almost. And the pulsing called to me until I obeyed, leaving the home stable behind and letting my own pulse sink into it as I ran out the big white doors, up the pasture hill, over the ridge until I could see the cloud of dust rising, like it was reaching up to see me. My own feet pounding back into the earth in response: *I'm coming.*

I knew each one of those beasts like my own always-smudged face. From the time Mr. MacMannus discovered me and Celia squirreled away in the old loft rooms over the stable, where Mrs. Bluet and Mr. Haggerty took turns smuggling us food and staying with us while we were still small, he'd looked at us grim and silent and said a few words—powerful and unhappy words—to our unlikely caretakers. They'd said a few words back—quiet and strong ones—that seemed to silence his anger, or at least send it deeper inside of him, away from us. Ever since, I'd been the resident stable hand, and Celia a small seamstress at the ready, mending blankets and garments for horses and humans alike by the light

17

of our one window. She sewed, and I worked shoulder to shoulder with the best thoroughbreds in New England. *"The finest in the country,"* Mr. MacMannus liked to tout to his visitors.

It was not a bad life. We had a home. We had food. We had the gruff humor of Mr. Haggerty, who gave us a garden plot out behind the barn and liked to call me "the boy born in a barn!" *Stable*, I'd correct him with a laugh, even though we both knew neither was true. I only lived in a stable, and Celia was closer to being born in one than I had been.

Still, something in me rather filled up with a sort of pride when the gardener called me that. At times, it felt like it must be true, this tale of my being born in a barn. For this was what I was born *for*. Mr. Haggerty started saving the funnies from his Sunday edition of the *Herald*, slipping it my way so I could read "The Escapades of the Rough Riders." It was a comic strip, but nothing was comic about it at all. I followed the daring deeds of Theodore Roosevelt, Jasper Truett, and the rest of the men, wondering why I hadn't been born two or three decades before so that I could've been valiant alongside them.

Mrs. Bluet, whenever she sensed either of us was feeling sad, would bake a blueberry buckle before the sun was up and sneak it our way. It was a consolation, but also an omen of sorts. I always got a sinking feeling when I smelled the sweet dish in the air, for it meant something difficult was afoot.

We had good work to do. We had a surly overseer in Mr. MacMannus, who'd tanned my hide a time or two when he'd discovered footprints on the track. I couldn't tell him who they really belonged to. But for the most part, he ignored us, so long as we did our work and didn't raise a racket.

Celia had inherited Mother's deep and wide smile, and she loved to hear me tell of it. She'd soaked in the stories of vinegar pies and Sunday scriptures like a person starved for air, especially during the long nights bedded down with a sick mare or struggling foal. She was drawn to them, then, a better sickbed attendant than I, and would stay up all night asking for stories and tending to the horses, with a knack for soothing a worried animal. Stitching its wounds, healing both fear and hurt.

And Mr. MacMannus kept away. I only ever saw him across the track, when I arrived in time to see them running the horses in practice heats, those daily rumbles that summoned me. I watched for years from the shadows, but slowly, over time, I found a spot at the fence, obscured slightly by a nearby tree, where I could drape my arms over the rail and taste the dust as the horses drove with all their might toward the finish line.

So much purpose, they had. I watched the singular, fire-hewn focus in their animal eyes. I could almost hear them, in the steady pounding of hoofbeats, drill the one truth into me that Maplehurst had taught me: *Make a plan*. With every disaster, make a plan. For every uncertainty, make a plan. The hoofbeats and the words drilled: *Make a plan. Make a plan. Make a plan.*

I didn't have two pennies to rub together, or much educating in my brain, but I could at least be ready for anything.

"Matty!" Celia's voice sailed up the hill behind me now. "Matty, wait!"

My feet urged me on but something inside slowed, and suddenly I was stuck in the middle of a tug-o'-war. "Yeah?"

I turned to watch her, her gait carrying a lilt with the way her left foot limped. Some folks thought it made her a spectacle. But I knew it gave music to her movements and matched something inside of her, the way she was always coming at things from an angle, seeing more than everyone else.

She was fast, too. We'd made sure of that, she and I, in case she ever had a run-in with the man who'd left more than a few scars on my back with his horsewhip. There'd been too many close calls already, though Mr. MacMannus hadn't come anywhere near us since his first wife died a few years back and he'd brought a new wife home three months later.

The first Mrs. MacMannus had simply ignored us. The new Mrs. MacMannus liked to turn her nose up at us like we were vermin discovered in her mound of jewels, which by all appearances was a heap bigger than the Adirondacks. Apparently, she didn't like to be reminded of her husband's . . . well. Let's just say I'd grown up pretty quickly after our mother died and learned fast what happened to a widowed caretaker's wife trying to earn her keep by darning socks and trying not to lose the only home she'd known. The owner came around during the hours of four and five o'clock most days, that's what happened.

I was born a year later, and then Celia. Everyone knew it to look at us; I had the blue of his eyes and Celia the gold of his hair. But he'd never acknowledge that, not in a million years. And word all over the manor was that the new lady of the house was already fashioning a nursery upstairs, in anticipation of the children she would give him. Heirs to Maplehurst.

And we continued up in the stable loft, happily living in our little wood-slatted, sun-shafted kingdom, and choosing not to hear the talk.

Celia drew up beside me now quick as a wink, her face pained.

"You okay?" I asked, forgetting the pounding river beneath us for a minute.

"No," she said, her features drawing deeper. I stopped entirely, then.

She gave me a pleading look, her green eyes big.

"C'mon, Celia . . . we're getting too old for that." I was closing in on twenty—she was fourteen. We'd carried the roles of adults for more years than we could count. Still, I knew what she wanted. She'd ridden around on my back since she was six and I was eleven, whenever her leg gave her trouble. "Let's just go home."

She tipped her head in a silent plea.

I stooped, crouching so she could climb up.

"Gotcha!" she cried, pulling right on past me. A smile spread across her face as her feet pealed across the ground. "Race you!" She was a mystery. Sometimes acting eight—like right now—and sometimes spouting words that made her sound wiser than an eighty-year-old.

"No, you don't," I said, and ran to beat the band.

We both stopped at the rock wall, catching our breath and watching as the clouds dissipated into the sky.

"How much you want to bet it's Poseidon?"

"We shouldn't bet, Celia."

"How much you want to bet the food on Maplehurst's table is paid for by betting?"

I gave her a look. She knew as well as I did what a lost bet could do to a man, to his family. We'd seen it as much as we'd seen the sunrise, growing up at the stables and just a stone's throw from Saratoga Springs Racetracks, where MacMannus thoroughbreds were often crowned with wreaths of roses.

"Anyway," I said, "it's not Poseidon."

"How can you tell?"

I could no sooner have explained it than I could explain my own pulse. "Listen."

And we did. To the thrumming, pounding beat. "It's Gulliver. That's a horse that was born to run."

And I was born for this, I thought once again. For the smell of the hay, the slick of the mud on a fresh-rained track, the click of the starting gates harnessing oceans of strength. For that single moment, when the gate flies open to the crack of the pistol—and life, life, life beats into the ground. Going somewhere.

And I knew—I could stay right here, watching all this "going somewhere," for the rest of my life.

But knowing something doesn't make it true.

We arrived at Maplehurst's practice track out of breath. I'd been right—it was Gulliver rounding the bend, his jockey feeling the curves of the track, leaning into them. Gulliver's hooves pounding while the sounds of birds singing, a saw working, and hammers hammering all struck up a background chorus. A crew of men were building a new grandstand for the MacMannuses' upcoming private race. *The social event of the season*," Mrs. MacMannus had been saying for months now.

It was just five days away, and the track was in a flurry with preparations. Gardeners, groomers, builders, jockeys, guests who'd arrived days early to stroll the estate with their parasols and canes. New uniforms for the entire staff, both house and stable, were another innovation of Mrs. MacMannus. Her idea of garbing the staff in a way that made them look like accessories to the track she was attempting to elevate to the status of the Waldorf.

Celia and I hadn't received ours yet, but she'd hear no complaints from me on the matter.

The evening before, she'd hosted a fancy dance for her guests at the big house. I'd seen from our windows, looking up into theirs. The glow of all those lights, Mrs. MacMannus fluttering a silk fan with the vengeance of a thousand flies, a string quartet playing.

A pang had struck my chest, then. Nothing to do with wanting inside. The farther away, the better, in my view. But as those couples danced around, my hands suddenly felt very . . . empty. The thought struck me, unbidden—*what would it be like to have someone lace their fingers into mine?*

Ridiculous thought. I shook it off immediately, filling my hands instead with Gulliver's reins for a midnight ride out in the pastures. It had been a good ride. Maybe I'd do it again tonight.

As we arrived back at the stable, I climbed the stairs in jovial spirits for the first time in days, Celia on my heels, chattering about making a loaf of bread for supper. Just as I was ready to turn the dented doorknob to let her step in ahead of me, I froze. I knew that smell.

Blueberry buckle.

Either this was consolation for the past days of Mrs. MacMannus's flurries . . . or something bad was about to happen.

I had my answer when I saw Mrs. Bluet sitting at our wobbly table, eyes rimmed in red.

"What is it?" I rushed in past my deadpan words, spoken in cold dread. "Are you alright?" She didn't seem to know what to say. I felt the Flame rising up in me, ready to defend her if someone had dared to hurt her. Mrs. Bluet had once cautioned me about the Flame when I'd chased down the pack of kids who had raided her garden for strawberries when I was twelve years old.

"That burning justice is a gift, Matthew Petticrew. But you be sure and save it for where it's needed. Some battles aren't battles after all."

I stood ready to fight this battle for her, if needed.

"There's no easy way to say this, young Matthew." She had always called me that, and the name took on a gleam in her eye the year I turned twelve and overtook her height in spades. "You're— you're to leave here. The two of you." Her voice caught.

My jaw twitched. Anger flared. I tamped it down. This was not Mrs. Bluet's fault. "Who . . . who wants us to leave?"

"Well, that's just it, my loves." She put on a smile. "They say the new groom—Hector—will be needing these living quarters."

"He has living quarters."

"Yes, and Mrs. MacMannus is bringing in a new caretaker who'll be needing those."

Hector was to have our home. A caretaker—whose role I had been filling for years now, with no compensation or dedicated living quarters—was coming. Taking Mother's old house.

And we were to leave.

"Where will we go?" Celia spoke for the first time, her eyes round. She had made this place a palace, fashioning curtains and couches from castoffs.

"Now, there's a piece of good news. Mr. MacMannus has found you both good positions. At a hospital for you, Celia," she said brightly. "In the city. With a boardinghouse for young women just next door. And as a groom at the stable of Harvard University for you, Matthew."

Celia hung her head. "We won't be together," she said quietly.

"We will," I said. "We'll find a way."

A silent word hung heavy over us all, and it was Celia who had courage to speak it. "When?"

Mrs. Bluet hung her head and wiped her eyes. "Today."

And it was done. Maplehurst, for all its imperfections, had been our whole world for our whole lives . . . and it was closed to us now.

We packed what little we had and were on trains headed in

separate directions that very afternoon. As we left Maplehurst for the last time, I cast one last look at it. There, in a window on the third-story landing of the great stair, and hawk-like as ever, was Mr. MacMannus.

I could have been mistaken, but at a distance, he appeared to hang his head . . . and then he vanished. Walked away from his gabled window, away from us. A cloak of remorse about him.

It would be the only gift I was ever to receive from my father. I used to wonder what it would be like to have a father who would fight for you. Not the sort that would attack or ignore you. I imagined the Rough Riders, whose courage and daring I read of in my youth. Theodore Roosevelt, and the kid who rode with him all those years ago—Jasper Truett, who embodied courage. What would it have been to have a father like that?

But that was not for me to know. What I did have, in this moment, was the realization that perhaps, all along, he had been watching us from a distance. He had seen that a hospital would make Celia thrive, her caring spirit meant for such a place. And whether he knew it or not, that arrangement he made for me at Harvard—it was to change my life forever.

3

Mira

1914
Forest of Argonne, France

The sun awoke as a kaleidoscope, pouring in the window of our small kitchen. It was old fabric that made it so, hanging there in front of the glass in colorful strips sewn together. Today, I imagined they were once a part of a beautiful lady's ball gown. I had read many times of balls in the book of fairy tales on Grand père's shelf.

We did not have such balls here, but why should we not? It would be nice to meet people, or at least to see them. They might like to have a ball among the trees. When I was younger, I always lingered on the same tale in those same pages: the tale of a girl and the road. She left home to discover great treasure, and what adventure awaited her on her journey! I used to pretend, as I went about my chores, that I was the girl on that journey. Pursuing great treasure. Perhaps someday, I would find it.

Grand-père teased me back then, so often was my nose glued into that volume with its blue spine and gold letters. *Volume II*, it said, and I asked him once if there were others. I loved his smile when he answered. Yes, a whole set of them, from when he himself was a boy. And he'd read them to my own Papa when *he* was just a small thing toddling about. *"Where are they now?"* I had asked once. He had grown a little sad, then. *"I could not bring them when we came here, Mireilles. But I can tell you the tales they held.*" And so he had. Stories of matchsticks, mermaids, cinder girls, and poison fruit.

My thoughts still full of balls and fine dresses, I slipped out the door into the morning air to milk Antoinette and bring in fresh blackberries. I set the berries aside for Papa, for tradition stood that whoever had slept upon the floor the night before got the berries. Papa and Grand-père squabbled every night over who would get the lone bed downstairs and who would sleep on the floor in our little chalet. I had the bed in the loft room above, always, because they would not take any argument on that matter.

Papa always insisted Grand-père take the bed, saying, "*What son on God's earth would force his father to sleep on the floor?*" Grand-père always fought back, claiming his son was "*getting old, older than the dirt of the woods, and must take the bed.*" If what he said was true, then it meant he himself was getting older, too, but he ignored that. It was the same every night, a grumpy lullaby. Their own fond way of expressing their care for each other, squabbling as Papa knelt by the hearth and pulled out his matchbox and filled our home with warmth and light.

I fell asleep to that grumpy lullaby smiling, for I knew what I would find each morning: Papa gone early in the morning, while Grand-père snored upon the bed until the sun awoke him. "*Let him sleep, Mira,*" he had told me once. "*He has earned it. Your grand-père has led a remarkable life.*"

When I returned from the milking, the man with the remarkable life was wide awake, sitting at our small table.

I told Grand-père of my theory about the curtain.

"A fine lady's skirts, is it?" he said in between spoonfuls of boiled oats. He ate them slowly, for they must stretch. He would not leave our land of trees for the journey to market for another two weeks yet, and we must have more walnuts and carvings to trade by then. Perhaps his oats would work magic, like Jacques's magic beans, and make my idea true. I plunked two berries in his oatmeal, a bribe.

Grand-père's forehead wrinkled, but his eyes twinkled. "You might say that. It would not be untrue, *ma petit cheval*." He called me this, always. *Little horse*. It was silly, I knew, now that I was fifteen and did not know if I fit in the land of fairy tales or in the land of true ball gowns. I supposed my life, odd-shaped as it was, just fit where it fit—which was right here in the Forest of Argonne. A tight and funny fit, like one of Papa's wooden puzzle pieces, its curves and gaps just so, never to be bound for another place.

I smiled, remembering how I used to give the toothiest grin I could to live up to the name *petit cheval*. He would lift my chin to gently close my mouth, tug my braids, and say, "*You have all the majesty of such a creature, and all the strength too, hiding inside of you. But none of the bad smell. Most of the time.*"

It was not the name that stopped me now, but his words. "*It would not be untrue.*" Never had he said such a thing to one of my stories of the colorful curtain.

I spun my way through feeding the chickens and wringing the laundry and pinning it up to dry, moving to the steady beat of Grand-père's ax falling upon firewood behind the chalet. This was their way—Grand-père chopped the wood, Papa laid the fires, inviting me to help him kindle and grow the flame. When it was time to bank the coals or stir them up, he would grip the old fire poker and make three rotations, raking it through the coals in circles. The three of us made a complete fire; the three of us made a whole life.

Grand-père's words from earlier set my fingers to the nimble work until they seem to tap out the song of them. *It would not be untrue.* Was it truly a lady's dress, once upon a time? I thought of the village we sometimes traveled to, and of the dance I had seen in the street there one evening. There had been a musette player, letting his arms push his accordion in and out and releasing magical music into the air as his fingers pranced over white and black keys.

If I tried hard, now, I could hear it. Reaching to the village with my memory, gathering that song into the woods, through my veins, out through my feet. I remembered how the couples had danced—men in caps bowing to girls in their cleanest frocks, and how the girls would reach out and take the offered hand. I opened my fingers, but no hand was there to hold. Perhaps one day . . .

But one day might very well not come. This I knew, and so I must soar on that music and hold fast the knowledge that the music was alive and the dance so real, partner or no.

When I reached up on my toes to unclip a sun-dappled bedsheet from the line, a shadow fell upon it from the other side.

"Papa!"

He smiled that quiet smile of his and bowed. I blushed to have been caught humming again. He would know I had been daydreaming. Perhaps he would even see what I was imagining, with the fine ladies and gentlemen dancing among the trees of this wild wood. He knew me so and had guessed my thoughts many times.

"May I have this dance?" He bowed, holding out a hand. I blushed—feeling again the heat of being caught at such a girlish imagining, when I knew I should be thinking on serious things, real things, the things of a young lady. For I was nearer that than I was a child. But what did a young lady think on? I did not know.

I laughed, and he folded my hand into his. It was not as small as it once was in his blistered one, but it felt just as safe. I curtsied and hid my smile as he drew me into his embrace and swayed me this way and that. He smelled of spiced tree sap, and his hands were rough but strong and kind. His satchel flapped against my leg, empty.

I cleared my throat. "Was it not a good day in the woods?" His satchel was often full to bursting of walnuts and other foraged items.

His smile did not fall, but it changed. It looked like one of Grandpère's creations, carved into wood.

"No walnuts today," he said. "But every day the woods are good to be in."

I tried to match the gravity in his voice. "Because we are safe here," I said, echoing what he had told me so long. Papa had always said it was so. *La maison vous attend toujours.* And it is true—home waited for me, always.

He said we are safe here, but there were things that did not make sense. Why, if we were safe, did Grand-père set traps in the ground long ago, before I was even born? Why did he sometimes stop in the middle of speaking, as if he had just heard something, and pin his eyes on his rifle upon the wall?

"Yes," Papa's words said. *No,* said his eyes as they darted around our patch of home, to the edge of the green trees all around. They hugged our home, wrapping us up like the way Papa tied a small box with burlap for me, the ends in a funny bow, every Christmas.

I had not seen this look before, him so wary.

"Papa," I said, feeling safe in his arms. But the question did not come. I tried to pull it out, as I had every day back to when it first planted itself deep. Years ago, it was. But it was the sword Excalibur, stuck in stone.

"Papa," I tried once more. He sensed it was heavy, this question, for he held me close.

I closed my eyes. Pulled hard on the question. Forced my voice around it. And Excalibur came loose.

"What is it we are safe from?"

He stopped. Eyes searching mine, hands on my shoulders.

"Much," he said. And I heard in the sorrow of his voice that there *was* much, though I knew already he would not speak it into shape. "But . . ."

I held my breath. Perhaps he would tell me, after all.

He opened his mouth.

"Franz!" Grand-père hollered from the door, and the glass castle of that almost-truth shattered into a thousand pieces. He summoned us in, and the shards were left there to vanish.

They argued again that night. But it was not over who would sleep upon the bed.

Tonight . . . tonight there was desperation in their voices, not fondness. Desperation sprung from deep feeling, dropping words off when they could not continue. They believed I was asleep.

That I did not hear whispers shot like arrows. Talk of unspeakable things, of German armies marching into villages in Belgium and turning them into wastelands before heading toward France. Of the human hearts and lives that were destroyed far more than the crumbled stone buildings left in their wake. Of things I would never forget, though I wished to. Things that Papa could barely speak, and when he did, his voice cracked like clay.

Grand-père did not believe it, that they snuffed the life out of these places—and did worse, too. Things so terrible, he lowered his voice to a whisper and I could no longer hear.

But well did I hear Father's next words.

"I must go."

I scrambled to see through the knothole in the wall, made myself silent and invisible, though my chest pounded: *No. No. No.* Along with my wild heartbeat, just so.

Grand-père protested. Called him a fool, hissed a question— "You would leave this place? The last refuge in the world?"

"Why do you think I must go?" Papa snapped, his shoulders rising and falling fast. He picked up the fire poker to stir the coals, and this time the old three circles came fast, with a jab of frustration at the end.

"*Absurdité.*"

"They march for Paris, Father."

I watched Grand-père sit, drop his head in his hands. "Again," he said, so ragged it sawed through my knothole, made me draw back. "All of this . . ." He swept his hand over the room. "Only for history to repeat. Will that city never be safe?"

Silence billowed.

"When?" Grand-père said, barely scraping the word out.

"Now." Papa sat beside Grand-père. His voice sad, but kind once more. I do not know how, but in the stretch of wordless sea, with the fire snapping inside and the wind shuddering the walls from the outside, the men understood one another.

When the sunlit kaleidoscope awoke the next morning, it was upon Papa that it fell. He had slept on the bed, across the room, and I imagined a battle for the ages must have waged after I'd fallen asleep to make it so, with Grand-père emerging as the victor. Papa sat on the edge of the bed, looking into the colorful light.

I made myself silent as I approached. I wanted to see him, hold his hand, keep him always. I did not want him to disappear like Mama.

But beside him sat a lumpy satchel, all drawn up for travel.

I tripped. Un-invisible. He turned and his eyes were red.

"*Mon papillon*," he said. A name he spoke to me every day but never like this. Never like he meant to cradle my whole self, for always. "You keep the fire lit now, yes?" He slipped something into my palm. His matchbox, the wooden sticks inside rattling around inside just like my shaken soul.

It was thus that he left. Quiet words exchanged with Grand-père outside, a solemn wave, a sure and steady gait carrying him away.

When my senses caught up to my sorrow, I ran after him, hollering. "Papa! Papa!"

He paused at the edge of the clearing.

I looked to the matchbox in my hand and then at him. "I will," I said, holding up the box. "I will light your way home."

He fixed his eyes on me as if he were etching me onto his very heart. I was doing the same of him. And then, with a nod and a few steps more, the trees swallowed him up—and he was gone.

I watched for him. I took his forest satchel and gathered walnuts as he used to, every week venturing farther east, in the direction that he had gone. I only hoped for some small glimpse of him, perhaps waving at me from across the valley, a promise that he was well. From the edge of the Argonne I could see the winding blue of the Meuse meandering though green fields but not a hint of Papa. I always stood there a long time, in case he should come up over the rise and find me.

One day, when he had been months gone, I fell asleep waiting. It was spring, and the grass was softer than my own mattress at home, sun warm upon my face. A songbird trilled and a breeze blew sweet with the scent of lilac. In this world, this moment, I could hardly believe the things Papa had spoken of. This "Great War," as the people at the market in the far village called it.

And so I fell asleep thus, with sweet smells and bright things as my lullaby. Perhaps we were closer to a fairy tale than the horror of nightmares, after all. Perhaps . . .

When I awoke, it was with a jolt, dread deep down. Something was not right. I stayed as still as I could, listening. Feeling. A rumble, as if the ground beneath me had come alive.

"Papa?" I listened. "Papa!" Flipping over on my belly, I soaked in the rumble, the sound of homecoming. A vision of a hero from one of the old stories, riding home upon a steed—victorious after battle—filled my head.

I inched my way to the top of the rise, ready to pop up and surprise him, waving with all my might. But as it grew louder and closer, my smile melted. That was not the sound of a horse. But . . . what, then? The river, breaking through a great dam, somewhere? About to flood? Or a plow, perhaps, if a mule were pulling it very fast indeed. I had not seen farmers hereabouts, but perhaps they were venturing farther to find fertile land.

Or—a recollection of one of the girls at market, pointing me to something called an auto car. A wealthy landowner of one of the vineyards had got one and it stood shiny and black on the cobbled street. She described to me how it sounded like the wind coughing up gravel when it was running.

It seemed more farfetched to me than all the tales in Grand-père's books, this notion of a carriage with no horse. But perhaps they used them in this war. Perhaps Papa had got one too, and it was bringing him home even now. If I had not been petrified I would have laughed, picturing the man of the woods, wrangling a metal steed with an engine instead of a heart. I would never see such a thing, I was sure. The Argonne was no place for the auto car.

Clutching the earth until dark soil crammed beneath my fingernails, and clutching hard the last shred of hope that perhaps it was Papa, I peeked over the rise.

My eyes flew open and I stumbled back, all thought of stealth replaced by sheer shock. My pulse pounded, telling me to run. *Run*.

And I did. It was not an auto car. It was—it was—I could not fathom what it was, hovering above me like a great metal dragon about to descend. As if someone had taken an auto car and removed its wheels and given it great revolving belts instead that dug into the land and spat it out like bullets, climbing down crevices and up ridges as if they were nothing. Preparing to squash forest girls as if they were nothing.

I am nothing, I thought, wishing it might be true. *Invisible. Please, make me invisible*, I prayed, running and running and running all the while and not looking back until I reached the wood's edge. I hid in a stand of trees that surely could not be taken by such a creature and watched. The great metal dragon lumbered toward me and then turned, skirting the woods and going south.

It would be hours before my breathing slowed and my heart landed back inside my chest from wherever it had run off to during our great escape. "Our," because it leapt so far out of me that it became a separate being. It returned, though I had doubted it would. I told Grand-père of it, ready for the censure I would receive for venturing so far from home.

But I received no such censure. Only deep, deep sadness in his eyes. "It is here," he said. "The war has come."

4

Captain Jasper Truett

1916
Plattsburg Training Camp, New York
One Year Before America Enters the War

The sun rose again. I had half a mind to point the artillery at it and let her rip. But these green-gilled college boys need light to figure out which way is up, so here we went again.

They came in spades to Plattsburg, those Harvard and who-knows-where kids, lining up with eyes wide as dinner plates to register. Part of me wanted to lift their caps up and see what was inside their university-stuffed brains, what they were thinking. Maybe all that studying had choked out their common sense. But part of me wanted to clap them on the back and say "good on you" for showing up, and honestly, too. It was better than I'd done when I was near their age. Sure, I'd "showed up" back then—all the way from the rails I'd made my home, down to Cuba with the Rough Riders—but I'd lied to do it. Said I was eighteen and thought it was convincing. Maybe it was—maybe a life like mine ages a kid quick. Kid or not, I thought I knew a thing or two back then. Turns out I still don't know a thing or two.

Go easy on them, I reminded myself. Having dinner-plate-wide eyes wasn't a crime. Showing up to volunteer for training even when no one thinks we'll enter this war wasn't a crime. They were here. No one made 'em be here. Good on them. My job was to make sure they were ready for what they couldn't even imagine.

They had a long way to go, it was plain to see. I had a mental checklist of what a good officer should look like if he was to be effective in warfare:

Constantly aware of his surroundings
Keen insight into geography and terrain
Calm in a crisis
Able to command respect without belittling his charges

The list went on, but even these four items had me looking around at the trainees and trying not to get swept under in the sea of hopelessly naïve faces. We had our work cut out for us, that was certain.

One of them kept craning his neck toward the stables like he was a giraffe and thought he maybe belonged over there, too. Out of habit I pulled my compass from my pocket and ran my thumb over its not-so-smooth-anymore surface. Like it might help him find his way.

"Barracks are that way, kid," I said. He had the good sense to nod and veer off that direction. Some of them laughed and joked like the Plattsburg training camp was child's play. That one, the one with the stables set in his crosshairs, seemed to at least understand the gravity of all this. There was a war raging, and though America at large thought we'd have nothing to do with it, the tightness in my belly told me otherwise. I knew it was just a matter of time . . . and time was ticking.

He hesitated, looking back at the stables. Most of the boys made a beeline for the white-peaked tents of their barracks, the closest thing to home they'd have while here. They'd paid for the privilege, after all, right out of their own pockets. Preparedness, preparedness, preparedness at any cost—even when the country was not funding its own training for the army we'd need if—*when*—we jumped into this war.

So here we were, training anyway.

Except for him. He seemed . . . lost.

"Hey, kid," I said. He straightened, as if his whole body saluted me. I could at least point him to his unit's barracks.

"Orders," I said, holding out an expectant hand.

His jaw twitched. "I—" His vision sought my uniform, trying to find a name. A horse released a powerful neigh from the stables, and he jerked his attention in that direction. This one would need all the help he could get. I should've been brought low that these were our prospects for an officers' training camp. *Officers*, for Pete's sake. But something in him harkened to the old me, the clueless kid who'd battled at San Juan all for the chance to ride a horse into history.

"Son," I said. "Captain Truett. If you'll show me your orders, I can point you where to go."

His eyes snapped back to mine, alert and alive. "T-Truett?"

I checked my pocket watch. "Yes, and if you'll—"

"Captain Jasper Truett." He spoke again and gulped. I looked at him. He gawked. "You—you're Captain Truett."

"Seems so. Now, son, you've got to get to your barracks or you'll miss your own company commander's orders. If you'll show me your orders . . ."

He shook his head quick, to pull himself out of his stupor. "Sorry, sir." He had a fierce gaze, when it wasn't muddled by whatever had claimed him five seconds earlier. That sort of gaze—the kind that could pin a man fast and cut away any nonsense—was the kind that would serve him well in commanding privates. If, indeed, he was to be an officer one day. Stranger things had happened.

"I don't have orders," he said at last.

"You have orders," I said. "When you registered for the training camp, they sent them to you."

He hung his head, breaking eye contact for the first time. "I'm not registered."

As if in reply to this revelation, a sudden clatter sounded, startling the whole camp. All the men near us froze and looked to the west, where the deafening blow seemed to originate.

36

But the one before me looked the other way. To the east. And he took off, vanished from my sight in a split second.

My eyes were on him, my feet pounding fast to catch up. He was either extremely dense or extraordinarily sharp, and I would find out which. After the disaster at hand, which was presently pounding directly at us.

The clatter had come from the stable area, where a fallen gate, half entombed by rising earth and still sliding, clanged again as it collided against a panel of metal paddock.

A horse bolted straight toward the barracks with the whites of its eyes flashing, panic infusing each hoofbeat with terrible strength.

The creature would tear right through the tents, tear them down, trample anyone inside without even batting one of those wild eyes.

Men dove in frantic escape, making way like Moses and the Red Sea. And still the other one ran straight into the fray until it was just him and the horse. Soon it would just be the horse. It would pound him to a pulp.

"Move!" I shouted. "*Now!*"

He did not move. He stood fast, locking eyes with the mad creature. He held up his hands as if in surrender. Slowly, steadily.

The horse did not slow.

"Whoa," he said, moving his hands back and forth.

A split second more and he'd be trampled if he didn't dive out of the way like the others had.

Move, I wanted to shout again. But something stopped the word in my throat. Something in the kid, the way he stood with eyes wide and stance firm.

Every instinct told me to slam into him, pummel him out of the way. But just as my muscles poised like springs to lunge, the horse veered. Reared. Hooves large in the air, the mass of the creature huge as it hung above us and released a trumpeting neigh before landing again to a cloud of dust. It pawed and grunted, eyeing the kid as he stepped to the side of it, hands still raised.

He gave it a clearance that made no sense to me. Dive in, grab its lead, get that maniac fenced in and quick, that's what made sense. I made to do so. But at the first sight of my movement, the horse skittered to the side.

The kid moved one of his upheld hands toward me, slowly, his message clear. *No.* Calm, steady, but assured. *No.* And I felt it, hanging in the air with the smell of horse and sweat and dust: *Not yet.* He kept his eyes fixed on the beast and waited.

The whole camp watched with bated breath. The kid held an entire platoon of officers and trainees in the calm authority of his silence—and more than that, in his unflinching, singular focus.

He took one step. One. And the horse lifted its head, wary. He took another, this time edging toward the back of the horse—and waited.

The horse turned his head, fixing its eyes on the kid, as if realizing its life in this moment belonged to the only one in the camp who approached when all others fled. Belonged, safely.

The kid patted his leg softly, drawing nearer and nearer to the beast, speaking in slow, low tones . . . until the severed rope of his lead was, at last, in his hands.

Palpable relief washed out and over the sea of men from the epicenter of the kid and horse.

These men would train and test and we would separate wheat from chaff over these summer months, all so we could see the mettle of each one. Who would withstand, who would not. Tests, every moment, drilling or resting. This horse—it had put this man through the gauntlet of tests all in the space of seconds.

I narrowed my eyes, watching him run roughened hands over the creature's twitching coat, his dark hair tousled but his stance sure.

I approached.

"Everyone else looked west when the gate fell," I said. I let my question hang unspoken, another test. If he would answer without my having to spell it out, all the better.

"Sounds ricochet," he said simply. "I looked to where it had to have come from." He shrugged one shoulder. "There is no metal in that direction. The tents are canvas. There's plenty of metal over there"—he lifted his chin toward the horse pens—"and the hill beyond the tents acts like a wall to bounce the sound off of."

Aware of his surroundings—check.

Keen insight into geography and terrain—check.

Calm in a crisis—check.

Able to command respect without belittling his charges—check.

I looked closer at him, taking in his appearance. Sleeves rolled down, buttons fastened. Trousers laced and shoes shined—though there was little shine left in them. He had all the markings of a soldier whose uniform represented duty, honor, and country. Head up, shoulders square. All textbook markings of a man who'd studied up on how to bear himself as a man in uniform.

But he wore no uniform. Those sleeves had been cleaned, but that cleaning hadn't been enough to scrub out the markings of a life hard-lived. Those trousers were laced, but that did nothing to hide their threadbare knees. These were civilian clothes.

"You say you're not registered?" I asked. If that was the only issue, that was solved easy enough.

He shook his head. "I'm only here to deliver a few of the horses," he said. "Up from Harvard, with some of the fellows from there."

"So, you *are* a Harvard man," I said. Most of the boys here were. Recent graduates bound to be bankers, editors, businessmen, spending their summer training. Putting in the work to make sure America would have officers if the time came. "If it's a matter of needing to register, I can point you to—"

"I'm just the groom."

And I was sixteen again, standing in front of Theodore Roosevelt himself, alongside athletes and cowboys all vying for their place in his volunteer cavalry. They'd rattled off cities. Names. Events. All manner of escapades that had readied them to be part of the Rough Riders. Then he'd gotten to me and all I could tell him was I'd ridden the rails. A rail-car rat, homeless and too young at sixteen. *"Maybe I'm just a kid,"* I'd admitted. *"But nothing's beat me yet, and I'll make sure it stays that way."*

I could kick the young me, speaking to T.R. like I knew something, like I was somebody. But whether from a fleeting lapse in judgment or something else, he'd let me in and I'd never looked back.

Even when I should have.

"Just the groom," I repeated the kid's words. "What's your name, son?"

"Matthew Petticrew, sir." He swallowed. "Captain Truett."

He made himself taller when he spoke my name. Like he knew me and cared, for some reason, what I thought.

Truth was, I didn't know what to think, other than that we needed good men and I had been dead wrong about this one on my first impression of him. This guy had what we needed. A bit muddied beneath the surface, maybe, but we could bring it out in him. That's what Plattsburg was for.

"Do you want to join the training?" I asked, narrowing my eyes.

He swallowed. "Yes, sir."

"Well, then, let's make that happen."

I turned on my heel and took three steps, registering quickly that he did not follow.

I turned to face him. His face was beet red, but he held his head high. "I can't pay, sir."

I studied him a second or two. I wasn't letting this one get away. He belonged here, as much as I belonged all those years ago with T.R. in Havana.

"Follow me, Petticrew. I'll pay."

His already-round eyes grew a few sizes. "But you can't—"

"'*Yes, sir*,'" I said. "Get used to saying that."

A half smile, and he caught up. "Yes, sir. Captain Truett, sir."

I stifled my own smile. Couldn't let the men see me smile, not for at least another two months. A good dose of fear and trembling was what they needed to ready them to lead, to step into this role themselves.

"Will there be cavalry?" he asked. "Sir?"

I twitched my mouth to the side to lace my answer with some

element of compassion. "Afraid not, son. Not from here. The war started out strong with cavalry, but horses in battle are sitting ducks now, with all the tanks and trenches. Machine guns, barbed wire—horses over there at this point are more used for transport."

He nodded. "Transport." He spoke as if to fix the word as his destination. But I had a feeling . . . this one was destined for more. Transport was important, no question. But a calm in the storm like he had just shown, we'd need that in the trenches. This one would be no private. This one would be no transport officer.

Matthew Petticrew got registered that day, and it both boosted my hope and weighed down something else inside of me. When they all retired to the barracks after taps that night, I heard snatches of laughter and voices float from different tents. And despite the fact that they should be adhering to strict curfew and I should be putting them in their place, I thought—*good*. Let them be green-gilled and let them laugh as long as they could. There'd be time enough for the rest, later.

As for me, my sleep came late, as it always did. And with it, like always, visions of my Amelia. At the edge of every thought buried beneath ice-thin sleep, with those blue-as-sky eyes. Might be one of these young fellows here would've caught her eye. She'd have been about that age by now.

Maybe they weren't all bad.

The sun would climb up again tomorrow, and those blue-sky eyes would peer at me from the shadows where they were not, again, and maybe I wouldn't want to swivel the artillery at the sun so fast.

Maybe I'd be a better man.

Tomorrow.

5

George Piccadilly

1917
Two Months Before America Enters the War

"Foster, scare up some olives and tell the orchestra to play another, will you?"

"I did not think clergy were in the habit of . . . carousing," Foster said. "Sir."

I shot him daggers. He knew as well as I that I would never darken the door of a church, much less shadow a pulpit from the place of a preacher, despite the collar that declared the contrary. A collar I'd left in my room at Harvard for the summer, heaven be thanked.

"Olives are grown in the Holy Land, Foster. Very pious and all that. Nothing could be more fitting."

He bowed, then disappeared through the tent flap.

The whole thing was a riot, really. A manservant in a tent. A hooligan—yours truly—thrice removed from the ancient British institutions of Oxford, Cambridge, and *the* Imperial College of London, in that order, and thence sent to America to earn a divinity degree, all as part of an elaborate scheme perpetrated by the further-ups (Mother and Father, primarily Mumsie) to avoid the to-do on the battlefields of France. Clergy are exempt from the war, after all, and America will not touch the war with a ten-thousand-foot pole. A double measure of safety for my mother's son, or so she believed when she cooked the sparkling scheme up.

If she could see me now.

One must make the best of one's circumstances, and so here we are.

It wasn't my fault that I lost a bet at a game of cards. It was the luck of the draw, I say! I plead innocent. Quite innocent, for I had no money on the table, so truly it could not even be said that this student of divinity was gambling. But the stakes were high, it seems, as the fellow I was playing with had a bee in his bonnet for recruiting fellows for this training camp. I wagered, I lost, and so here I stand. Ready to train for a war I shall never see, under the guise of training for a life in clergy, which I likewise shall never see.

But I could rally the boys here. I could rummage up olives and a Victrola, and some dance partners too. Not to boast, but many-a-girl has carved a special place in her heart for George Piccadilly, and I for them.

In the meantime, I'd made a chum, his name being Maxwell. Or Matthew. One or the other, not that it made much difference. He walked around looking as if every step was a mission that might rescue the world at large or like he was searching for something with the fire of a thousand suns, poor chap. Nearly incinerated this whole place. I tried to do my bit to lighten the fellow up. He wasn't a bad fellow. Just seemed to have a ghost at his back, or a hole in his heart, or one of those timeless literary struggles Professor Milton was always pontificating.

Anyway, he was a good fellow to know, even if he was a bit on the serious side. Wouldn't even take a bet I placed with him to have the loser break rank and do a jig during drills. He was the reason we needed olives and music. He embodied the human struggle! The plight of the world! He needed merrymaking. Or marrying, though I couldn't imagine what girl in this wide world would sign on for a lifetime of his solemn-faced looks. Maxwell, Matthew, whatever his name may be, I'd help the fellow out. Anyway, they'd have us calling each other by surnames soon, I shouldn't wonder. Seems the military thing to do.

Military! Clergy! and Me! The unholy trinity! Well, they said all this war talk would come to nothing. Soon I'd be headed back to jolly old England. Unscathed, un-warred, and with a belly quite full of olives.

Until then, we'd conduct our drills. I might don my collar. They might call me chaplain, if they wish. I might even be able to muster a prayer or two, from the old Psalter they had us memorizing at the Imperial College, before the porcupine incident got me booted.

And further until then, I'd do as the song said. It spoke of war and it included mention of jam, so that sounded smashing to me.

> As soon as reveille has gone
> We feel just as heavy as lead,
> But we never get up till the sergeant
> Brings our breakfast up to bed
> What do we want with eggs and ham
> When we've got plum and apple jam?
> Form fours! Right turn!
> How shall we spend the money we earn?

By George (that's me!), I've got it, I thought. In answer to the sage song's question: I henceforth would spend my *money* on bets, rather than betting promises. Things like "Certainly I shall enroll in the training camp!"

And I would keep my eye on Maxwell-Matthew. He seemed to know a thing or two about surviving this place. Which is all that shall be needed, as this country refuses to enter the war, anyhow. It shall all come to nothing, mark my words.

6

Mira

1918

4 Years Since the War Has Come to France

The last refuge in the world.

So Grand-père has called our home, always. And always, I have promised it would be such to Papa when he came home from the darkness. He disappeared into the woods four years ago now.

Four years is many days. It is also 807 butterflies passing through our woods—and those are only the ones that I saw and counted. I told each one, "When you see him, tell him we are waiting. Tell him I will leave the lantern out for him. Tell him his papillon will fly him home."

And so I do. Though I have not ventured to the eastern edge of the woods since the day of the metal beast, still I keep a vigil for Papa. Every night at dusk, for so many days that I have left girl-hood far behind, the fairy tales darkened and dim, I have hung the lantern on the arch tree. I have lit it, watching my little matchbox grow emptier each time, willing my hope not to do the same.

I extinguished the flame only when the sun lit the sky the next day. Sometimes, to save matches, I lit it the next evening with a twig pulled from our hearth fire, which is kindled with leaves and grasses I find, and with steady dedication from Grand-père's weathered and weary hands, which work with vigor to spark warmth from sticks. In this, he finds purpose. A flicker of joy upon the face of a father whose son has gone away and whose life, in the missing of him, is aching, aching, so very much.

But we press on. It is our part, Grand-père says. Ours to carry on, because to carry on is to hope. I have taken over Papa's rounds through the woods, gathering what I can. And the two of us, we have gone to market once a month. Two days' journey there and two and a half days' journey back, for we always stop to fill our empty satchels with apples from a grove of wild trees along the way.

But much has changed. A year ago, we no longer had empty satchels on the way back, for the village people no longer bought our goods. They looked upon us with kindness but sadness. They had nothing to buy with, nothing to trade. They had had a scare— nearly been overtaken by the Germans. And it was then that we knew how close the war had come. It was on our doorstep, just as Papa had feared.

Still, I hung the lantern every night. For if the Germans were near, perhaps Papa was, too. He could come home, even if for a night. I imagined it a hundred times: I would make for him his favorite—*tarte aux pommes*. Golden buttery brown batter bubbling up around apples sliced and laid out like sunlight upon the water, in waving rows. It would tempt him to stay longer, but he would be valiant and go, I know.

And then came the true reason to wish him home: Grand-père fell ill. As the thunder tearing through the skies grew closer from the north, his heart grew sicker, and his mind wandered. He spoke to me now in ways I did not understand, as if he had slipped into the pages of his old fairy book. Only the things he spoke of, I could not find traces of in the book's pages. If I could, I would read it to him. Perhaps then, he might have some relief. He spoke of a glowing city, of a grand ballroom, of a great wrong. Of never returning, lest the city be swallowed again. It tormented him, and though I tried, I could not ease his anguish with any of my words, nor my singing.

This night, I did not put the lantern up, for I did not wish to draw attention. The sounds were too fierce, the shadows moving through our woods did not belong here. I ventured far from the cabin with the old rifle in hand, tracing the sounds. I became as a shadow, so that the voices would not see me, if indeed they had eyes.

They were men, uncoiling wire. Digging, speaking words I did not know that sound angry. They turned this land into a field of weaponry, laying traps for their enemy. Barking at one another, "*Nein! Nein!*"

Some of them looked so cold in their eyes. I wondered what those eyes had seen to make them so lifeless.

But by the sadness I glimpsed on the faces of some of them, I wondered—are they not their own enemy? For they looked defeated and hopeless. Just as I felt.

But these . . . these are the men Papa went to fight. To keep them far from us. These are the men who cast a shadow over our friends in the village.

And yet—so many of them, they are just boys. Younger than me, even. If I had a brother, he might look like them. What do they know of life? What do *I* know of life? Perhaps we know more than our fair share, and in that, I wish I could give them something. Take away the sorrow. Send them to their homes, to their mothers and sisters and sweethearts.

But what have I to give?

I slipped back into the darkness, back to our home. The last refuge in the world. I drew every window curtain, snuffed out every candle, and listened all night to the sounds of Grand-père's labored breathing, carried in spats by the sound of guns in the distance.

Help would not come. I knew this now. It was only me. The stories and tales that had spun in sun-shafts around me all my life . . . they had long fallen silent.

The sun awoke the kaleidoscope through that ancient kitchen curtain. It pooled in colors and light that made my soul ache, for the color had gone out of this world. Grand-père . . . he slept upon the floor, just where Papa used to sleep. Leaving the bed open for the son who would not come.

I took the kaleidoscope scrap of fabric down and hung it on my waist, for my apron had worn out long ago. There would be no more pools of colored light . . . and there was work to be done.

7

Matthew

Saint-Mihiel, France
September 13, 1918

When I looked back, the moments lined up like stairs, one step to the next: that night on Mother's porch, Celia entering the world. Our home above the stable, the goodness in a simple barn. The new Mrs. MacMannus sending toxic looks our way, packing us off. Me arriving on the steps of Harvard University, all its ivy-clung walls pointing me to the tack room at the stables there. I was allowed to sit in on classes and learned quick to bathe first, so that I didn't fill up the lecture halls with "horse stench," as the Brit said, shoving my shoulder like we were best friends. Still, I stood out, with my worn tweed suit, there among the others whose mounts I would kneel before to excavate muck from horseshoes.

A pack of the students began running regularly, training for the war we would not enter. I watched them from afar at first, and then the pounding of their feet rumbled down the rise and into my own feet until I was there too, running with them. Hearing of a training camp back in New York.

And so I arrived at Plattsburg and Captain Truett—the one whose tales of heroism had stood in the gap when a real father was absent—found me a place there for one summer, and then another. Letters flying between Celia and me all the while, as she made her way through her medical training and I made my way from camp, to school, to camp, to school—passing right past Maplehurst each time. I was stuck in a vortex. It was enough to drive a man mad, make him feel caged at the starting gate, awaiting the sounding bullet for his race.

Then it happened. America—the unswervingly neutral country in this war of the world—declared war. All because of unseen weapons beneath the sea, submarines attacking our ships. Our president asked Congress for a declaration of war . . . and then he went home and wept.

But this was it. This was what I'd been waiting for. A way to break out of this cycle, out of this gate. To do something that *meant* something.

Boats and trains and marching till my feet bled, then till I no longer knew whether I had feet, all feeling lost. Jostling rides in trucks that broke down yet transported me and a thousand other guys across the world, where we trained more and waited. Finally, we were called up to the front.

The front. It had a fabled draw about it, lighting up fellas' faces as if they were about to see the place they would meet their own courage.

The first night on the front, I dreamed of Gulliver, the horse back at Maplehurst. When Celia and I were younger—and perhaps even more recently than that, though I'll not be the one to say it—we would lay on our bellies beneath the old grandstand at Maplehurst and pull out a ruler we'd salvaged from the fire barrel in back of the barn. It only went up to 11.38 inches, because Poseidon had bit off the end when a reporter tried to measure his teeth. But it was perfect for us, a treasure to measure the explosions of sand made when Gulliver landed his hooves on the track.

It's amazing what you see when you lower yourself down and just wait. Every fall of the hoof for that horse was earthen fireworks. One thousand pounds of thoroughbred strength searing air and pummeling ground, dust flying upward. I used to close my eyes around that image—to see each particle, the way the dark soil soared into sunlight in her wake. If you didn't close your eyes, isolate that moment, it'd be lost in a dirty cloud.

And now, here I was. Lowered into the earth, peering over the edge of a trench. And do you know what I saw? Thousands of pounds searing the air, pummeling earth. Launching earth into air, dirt swallowing sun. As if an army of invisible horses—giants— were galloping through no-man's-land, the middle stretch between enemy trenches. Only these horses were not Gulliver. They were not horses at all, unless they were the sort that would carry the four horsemen of the apocalypse. They were weapons—metal falling, shells colliding. And the spray of earth from their unseen hooves would have crushed Poseidon's ruler to bits. There was no measuring the uprising debris, not here. Eleven inches or eleven miles, it mattered not. It swallowed everything around it into a colorless, lifeless landscape.

A kid called Chester trembled with anticipation beside me. His full name was Chester Hasenpfeffer—surname meaning some sort of rabbit stew. But it was the name that was a mouthful for us, and in a language none of us were too keen to be caught speaking in the trenches just now, so we all called him Chester, though he was earning his rabbit-y name now. Bopping up and down to see over the top and vibrating energy from every part of him, right down to the pinky finger that he kept tapping on top of his rifle.

"Wonder when it'll be us," he said. I shrugged the first three times he asked. The fourth, I answered.

"They say there's more wire out there than they've seen anywhere in the war," I said at last. "We won't get far till the first wave goes in and cuts it. And they won't get far till the shells and planes drive back whoever they can before that."

I said "drive back," but we both knew it meant "drive down," more truthfully. We just didn't want to think about that. Nor the fact that the Germans were doing the same to us.

Night fell, and with it, the rain and thunder. The shelling was so bad by then that I couldn't even hear Chester's chatter, though he was two inches from my ear and giving it all he had. I shook my head, trying to tell him talk was useless—but he kept on. I kind of appreciated it. The kid was undaunted.

For a moment, the shells were distant enough that I could hear him, and he told me of his parents, his two sisters and kid brother. "See?" He reached into his jacket and pulled out a picture that I couldn't make heads or tails of in the dark. "Hold on," he said, and pulled out a matchbox, removing a stick and making to strike. My hand clamped down on his, hard.

"Owww!" He yanked his hand back and shook it out, shooting daggers of a glare at me. "What'd you do that for? If you don't want to see the picture, just say so! You don't have to take my arm off."

"You light that match, it's not me who'll take your arm off." I jerked my head up and back, gesturing toward the German line.

Chester's face morphed from anger to horror. "Oh," he said. "Right." He stuffed the matchbox away but kept the picture out. I felt bad for the kid. A few yards down, I spotted a small light, cold and familiar. Some of the men had a jar of glowworms. It was a trench trick—enough minuscule light that it would let them see a map or a sweetheart's picture. Enough light to give them hope for the next moment but not enough to get them killed.

I closed the gap between us and asked if I could borrow it, bringing the little creatures back with me. Chester was duly impressed with the soon-to-be-beetles, the someday-lightning-bugs like the ones Celia and I used to capture back at Maplehurst.

He showed me his picture, worn almost away. The kid talked a lot of courage—and I could tell he had it, too—but the soft wear of this portrait told the tale of a boy who missed his family something fierce.

He returned the jar to the other men and walked back, shaking his head like an old war hero. "Oh, the tales we'll have to tell someday, eh?" he said, elbowing me. "Once we go up and over?"

I glanced at him sideways. "Maybe." Not the sort of tales he'd be eager to tell once he lived them. But I didn't want to dampen his spirits.

"The ladies will think it's somethin' else, eh?" he said, grinning. "But—and I hate to tell you this—you might need to lighten up your countenance if you want them to take note."

I had to hold in a snort. He looked hardly old enough to be out on his own, and he was apparently the expert.

"Yeah," he said, assessing me very seriously. "You'd have to travel the world over to find a girl for you, I think."

Good gravy, the kid was wearying. I opened my mouth to silence him—but then came the whistles, our signal to prepare.

"This is it," Chester said. "I've waited fifteen years for this. We'll be heroes today, you and me."

All fell silent as we awaited our command. But I couldn't look away from him. "*Fifteen* years." I'd heard wrong.

Chester nodded, his helmet wiggling back and forth on his head. "My whole life."

"Your whole life?" I hissed the words. He was fifteen? Fifteen. He'd always seemed young, but hearing this, with the deafening blows as a backdrop, sank heavy dread into my stomach.

I was twenty-three. Eight years older than him, and still I felt small in the face of this. But I was platoon sergeant, thanks to Captain Truett and reasons I couldn't comprehend—who was I but the boy in a barn, grown up? Still, I exceeded Chester in both years and rank. So I gave the private a dry and reprimanding look. He was three years younger than Celia. If we'd had a kid brother . . . I wanted to clock him on the head and deliver him to safety, all at once.

"What?" he whispered. "I told them my age when I signed up. They told me to step outside and have two or three birthdays and come back. So I did."

"And how long did those 'birthdays' take?" I could hear the anger in my voice.

"About seven minutes."

"Each?"

"Total." Chester raised his head over the top again.

"On my command, private!" the patrolling captain hollered, and Chester ducked back down to salute.

"Yes, sir!"

"Fix bayonets!"

A mechanical chorus echoed obedience.

Chester resumed his stance of preparedness like the rest of us while my mind scrambled to reconcile the information. Fifteen. What had I been doing at fifteen, but mucking stalls, failing at algebra, running a racetrack in the dead of night, and clawing for hope in the dark? And here was this kid, staring down Hades and grinning.

The whistle blew.

We were over the top, the outcry of all of us rallying each other, propelling our feet forward when our brains would have us stay.

I tried to imagine I was back at Greenfield Springs. *I was born for this. The smell of the hay, the slick of mud, the click of starting gates harnessing oceans of strength.*

But the second we were up, I saw it too clear: The smell here was not of hay, but of expired death. The slick of mud was not that of a racetrack, but that of an in-between land more cratered than the moon, where mud could suck you in and eat you whole. And the click was not of starting gates, but weapons. Weapons, and weapons, and weapons—again and again and again. Firing straight into an ocean of men.

Back home, the gate flew open to the crack of the pistol and life beat into the ground. Here, the floodgates flew open to the sound of the whistle and the ground beat the life out of us.

Moments ceased to exist out there. I could no more account for the timeline than fly us all to the actual moon. But I can say it was a mess of cold, wet, mud, and blood. Barbed wire. Famished craters made of our own artillery, gulping us down. Billowing curtains of grey smoke and dust arising out of nowhere. Wires lashing us as we passed, our own cat-of-nine-tails slicing flesh, as if to urge us on at the hand of a ruthless master.

So we went. Dodging gunfire, shellfire, machine gun nests. *Nests.* I remember thinking how odd, how ridiculous, to find nests out here where there were no birds. But these were not that sort of nest. Not even close.

The battle cry scattered, becoming less strong and being peppered with other cries—pained ones. I did not want to think what the shrinking chorus of voices meant. There was no time for thinking. Only acting. Chester harnessed all his youthful zeal into a dogged focus I had not seen the likes of nor thought him capable of. He was a dart, dodging and ducking, bending and leaping, falling to the ground at just the right moments. As if he, too, was made for this.

And yet in my own dodging and ducking and sliding, all I could see was the grin of a kid, the ruddy cheeks of someone who did not know the horror of war.

But I saw it find him. And it was not gentle in its approach. I saw him take in the sights and sounds, how it slowed him. Grew his eyes wide, horrified. Made him trip. Made him careless.

I looked at Chester over my shoulder, making sure he was still with us, and saw in the drawn desperation of his face a symbol of every one of the soldiers out here.

That was when it hit us.

One shell impacted to the right. Another to the left. One in front, boxing us in—and then one of our star shells, lighting the sky like lightning amidst all this thunder—and I heard the fourth one coming.

"Chester!" I yelled his name with a force that shook, and still could not hear my own voice.

He stood, shocked. Frozen. Unmoving, as the coming shell seemed to slow in my vision. I could see it, and for all that failed algebra, I knew exactly where it was headed.

I lunged. Grabbed him, tossed him into the crater to our left, the one that had been meant for our demise, and landed hard on top of him.

That shell . . . we did not see it land, our faces buried as they were.

But we felt it. To our bones and beyond, until I was sure we had no bones any longer. Only dust.

I do not know how long we laid there. I did not know if Chester lived. I, surely, was dead.

But a muffled sound broke through somewhere in our would-be grave, a sound unfurling into the *pound, pound, pound* of my own heartbeat.

I lifted my head.

Chester, beneath me, lifted his, and wriggled out, rabbit-like again. He said something. Two syllables, each silent.

"What?" My ears rang.

"Let's go!" I saw the words, more than heard them.

He clambered to get out of the crater. Jumped at the wall of it, jumped again. Looking more cricket than man. *Or boy*. I rolled myself up and slogged through the cloud to get to him, everything trembling before me. Whether from the world shaking or myself—I did not know.

I crouched and wove my fingers together, creating a sling under his foot. He looked down at me over his shoulder, eyes wide with excitement, and nodded. I gave a silent count with small nods—*one, two, three*—and launched him.

He was out. And off. Stupid kid forgot all about me. At least I hoped that was the reason his face didn't reappear. I felt a burn coiling up inside. The Flame—my old friend and foe. But it would do me no good here. I tamped it down and focused.

Knocking my soggy boots into the muddy sides of the hill, I tried to make footholds but found only mudslides. Backing up, I gave it a running start, ignoring a burn in my left calf. I failed, slicking to the ground. And failed again on the next try, with more running start, more burn. On the third try I nearly mounted the newly-born mud cliff—and just as I felt gravity about to take me down again, a hand appeared and grabbed mine, pulling me up.

I emerged to a sight I can never unsee: dawn rising over Armageddon. Shells piercing so deep they kicked up dust where there should be only mud, which also flew with impossible force. Tanks and horses painted a picture of two irreconcilable worlds, and among men in every state from living to dead—one muddy, fearsome face stared back at me.

Captain Jasper Truett. He'd found me at Plattsburg, set me on my feet there. Gave me a place to stand and belong. I hadn't seen him since the training camp, a world and a lifetime away. . . . And now here he was. Somewhere behind the grime, ice-blue eyes pierced the bleak landscape and landed on me.

He was talking. What had he said?

I stared, dumbly. He lifted his bayonet and picked up my hand from my side. "You'll be alright," he said. Muffled, the words made no sense. Until I saw my hand, the unnatural bent of two of the fingers and how they hung like broken things while the rest of that hand trembled. And as I watched, as the sensation of the uncontrolled shaking crept its way up my wrist, my arm . . . my body seemed to reawaken.

"Let's go," Captain Jasper Truett said.

And we did. We went, and we went, and we went, and I lost him pretty quick along the way in the madness between taking that first German line and liberating the village behind it, where the people would not come out. They did not even know America had come to France; they had no idea who we were, other than "*fou*." Crazy. Insane. And well did we fit that description.

But perhaps our barbaric charge and apparent fearlessness served us. For as I spotted one German emerge from a dugout, I mechanically marched to him. He registered the sight of me and disappeared back into hiding. I shot painfully, aimlessly into the dark with my useless fingers, expending my last bullets and not even caring. I had not the energy nor strength to care that I was unarmed. And perhaps to my shame, I prayed that the bullets did not hit their mark. It was my duty—but I did not want to do it. What had I against this man, who so easily could have been me, and I, him, but for the countries we were born into?

Perhaps God was in that godless place after all—for the man emerged, unscathed. My prayer, answered.

And then another emerged. Hands up, like his comrade, at the sight of my pointed, empty rifle.

Another.

And another.

And another—until a dozen Jerries lined up before me, hands raised, me the lone firing squad who could not fire.

"Please," one said, his words shaped by his accent. "Shoot don't. Shoot don't."

"Don't shoot," I mumbled, interpreting for myself.

"Yes."

"Yes?"

The man's eyes flew open wide, panicked at my misinterpreting his confirmation. He raised his hands higher, wincing. "No!"

"No?"

"No shoot!"

These men were as done in as I was. Jabbing my gun deep into my shoulder to show I meant business, they fell into line quick as ants. I ignored the numb throbbing in my hand and blessed the dusty fog that hid my crippled abilities from them. Could I have shot them, even if I'd wanted to? Even if I had ammunition? I did not know.

They allowed me to march them back to our lines in a bedraggled zig-zag skirting our fallen comrades, theirs and mine, and came back to a reception of clicking rifles emerging over the top of the trench, pointed at them . . . followed by a command.

"Hold your fire!" a voice said from below.

I came to the front of the line, and the men erupted in cheers as the Germans were ushered into captivity with the rest of the sea of them we'd captured that day.

"Three cheers for Petticrew!" a boisterous voice proclaimed. It was Chester, who remembered me well enough now.

"No thanks to you," I mumbled as I passed him.

"What's that?" He grinned, exultant at the reality of simple survival.

"Nothing," I said, shaking my head.

"You should be more careful," he said, pointing at my misshapen hand. I nodded. And hated the kid's naivety so much that I loved him for it, too.

"Look." He held up something dimly metallic. "You brought in a string of soldiers, and I brought something in, too."

I narrowed my eyes and stopped long enough to lean in to view the brass cylinder. "Whatcha got?"

"Shell casing. Pulled it out of the hole we fell in."

It was too absurd. I dropped my chin to my chest and laughed.

"What?" Chester brushed dried mud off of his prize in rhythmic repetition.

"You pulled that out of the hole."

He nodded. "Pretty great, right? Sort of like a trophy from my first battle."

"You had the presence of mind to pull out a spent shell casing but not your platoon sergeant?"

His hands froze. He lifted his eyes to mine and the mortification spread over his whole being as realization set in. He started to stammer, but I held up a hand to stop him. He looked so very young, so wide-eyed, there with his treasure in his hands. Better he pull something out of the war than the war pull something out of him. It was a wonder he still held spunk, some sense of innocence, after what we'd seen today.

"Listen, it's okay," I said. "It's chaos out there."

He looked ready to cry, chin trembling, and he clamped down, drawing his stature up to fight it even as he hung his head. There was no mistaking the cloak that draped him, ready to snuff the life out of him: shame. It was a powerful thing. And one thing he did not need to carry.

"Here," he said, thrusting the casing at me. "Take it. You deserve it more than anyone."

I shook my head, indicating he could keep it. It meant the world to him, clearly, and what use had I for an empty casing? They were a dime a dozen out here, even if I ever had need of one for some unknowable reason.

"Please," he said. "It's—it's the least I can do. I'm such a good-for-nothing—"

I reached out and took his offered prize, realizing it might be a mercy to him, a way to ease his torment and perhaps help him learn, too. "Thanks," I said, holding it up slightly. "I'll take it, if you'll take something from me."

His head snapped up. "What's that?"

"A promise. I won't forget you on the battlefield. I'll come for you, any time I can."

His shoulders relaxed, his relief and hope billowing so that they might've filled the trench. "Thank you, Sergeant." He nodded gravely. "Thanks."

I walked on, leaving behind the kid who'd lied his way into the war, knowing he had been refined today. That he was of the mettle, or well on his way, to being the sort of soldier himself who would never leave a brother behind.

A chorus of *hoorah* sounded as I left our interchange and made my way down the trench lined with cheering soldiers, someone tossing my name up in some mangled nickname. "Petticrew? Catch-a-crew, more like!"

And so I went to bed that night in a hole in the ground. Slicked with mud and blood. Labeled a hero, with a mangled hand and a mind that could not un-see what I had seen that day. I stared at the hardtack Chester had brought me—his own meager rations— and could at least find an almost-smile at that. He was trying to redeem himself. Good man.

I closed my eyes against it all and willed that dream to come. The one of something good and true and simple. A horse, running with all his might.

But my dreams were not of Gulliver that night. Indeed, I had no dreams. I had no sleep. And would not, for a long time to come.

8

Henry Mueller

September 1918
The Front

For column "Your Boys, America!"
WAR NOTES UPON ARRIVING AT THE FRONT.
AUGUST 1918. SUBMITTED FOR PUBLICATION TO THE
WASHINGTON WORLD.
By Hank Jones (or Henry Mueller)

This reporter comes to you with hat in hand, asking that you bear with him for the duration of this war. I have been tasked with accompanying a certain battalion (I cannot say which, for their protection) and reporting to you, as truthfully as I can, the happenings of your soldiers, here in France.

I do not take this duty lightly. These men are your husbands, your sons. It is their lives, held in the sticks and spaces of these words. And who am I but a farm boy who stumbled his way into journalism quite by accident, by fault of a missed streetcar and a sick cow? To honor them, and you, I give you this brief history, that you might know whose hands are working to record your loved ones' lives here.

I hopped a train into the city when I was nineteen, leaving our family's hundred head of cattle to my younger brothers and sisters to milk. One of the cows was sick, and I'd heard of a two-hundred-year-old journal of another Virginia farmer who had unconventional ideas for tending sick animals. Nothing had ever induced me to make that two-hour ride into our nation's capital before, but Daisy, the Jersey, was in a very bad way. So I journeyed to the library where this journal was kept.

There's an entire story of that farm kid trying to find his way to the library, including lots of wary looks from strangers when they saw his suspenders, worn trousers, rolled-up shirtsleeves, and they looked askance at him when he asked about the whereabouts of the library. But I'll skip those details and the saga of the streetcar bungle trying to get there, and tell you that when I finally stood in front of the library—what I had expected to be a building big enough to house a handful of old journals and books—I must've looked like Jack staring up at the beanstalk. It was called, officially, the Library of Congress, and how I was supposed to find one page of two-hundred-year-old notes from a farmer somewhere in that domed white palace of a place, I had no idea.

Three men in hats and dark suits and a handful of spectacles spoke to each other with great passion nearby as I stood outside dumbfounded, but their words were muddled as I took off my hat to wipe my brow and tell myself to get in that marbled building, for the cow's sake.

It was then, in my moment of dumbfounded glory, that the suited men's voices grew quieter but broke through my thoughts.

"What we need for our correspondent, gentlemen, is an everyman. A young fellow. Someone everyone trusts right when they see him. With that farm boy air of integrity about him."

"Fresh-faced, but bookish," the next replied.

"Smart. Clever. A bit of a blank slate we can shape for what we need. Uncle Sam needs a nephew, so to speak."

"Hear, hear! We need the face of the nephew. Brother to the soldiers. Beacon of hope to the mothers. Give him one of those holes on the side of his face when he smiles. You know, an indent. A whatchamacallit."

"A dimple!" the second man said, raising his cane in concurrence. "A spark of life in his eye. That's who we need. Someone approachable.

62

Who'll write to America like she's his sweetheart. The boy next door. That's who we need."

They fell silent just as I stepped forward, ready to go to battle against the books within for Daisy. A gust of wind tumbled down the vast white steps of the building, snatching my hat from my head and depositing it at their feet. I lunged to retrieve it, nodding in apology. "Gentlemen," I said, and turned to go, hat clutched in my hands.

A current of whispers followed me. Then a chorus of shuffling. They were following me, en masse. I quickened my steps.

"Son," one of the men said.

I froze. Some instinct told me not to smile—lest they see the "hole on the side of my face" that my mother used to kiss when I was a boy. I turned to face them.

Those men—editor, owner, and advertising man at the Washington World, I would soon learn—followed me into the library and became Daisy's own entourage, guiding me to the notes I needed. Enthusiastically jabbing their fingers at agricultural field notes of yesteryear while positing their own theories of cures for Daisy (they suggested molasses, fresh air, and the soothing strains of Vivaldi, respectively), they also filled my farm-clad mind with lofty ideas of the written word. "Hope in hopeless times," they said, speaking of how I could be the vessel of truth to the masses.

Reader, I owe you truth, and so I own this now: I was ready to hop the train back to the farm that moment and never look back.

That is precisely what I did. But a letter arrived the following week from the paper's owner, reiterating his invitation to "be a part of the making of history." As I looked out my attic bedroom window at the humble forty-eight acres of farm that barely fed our family and kept our small dairy business in enough milk to supply the local neighbors, I knew this was the way I could help. Help my parents, help my country. I was, and am, what my schoolmates called "bookish"—cramming my head full of pages of books when they were all out playing baseball. I tried to join them once, and they sent me back inside to "go finish reading about all the dead kings." It was a book about the French aristocracy in general, not really about kings at all, but I didn't correct them. The point is, when that letter came from the newspaper, all I had to offer was the pen and truth. But that was all that was needed.

We had not joined the war yet. As you may know if you have followed this reporter's humble offerings thus far, I have had the honor of reporting the journey of America's entry to this Great War, "the war to end all wars." And now I come to you from France herself and stand shoulder to shoulder with your boys. They are doing you proud already, and I promise to hold their stories, and yours, with the care and honor they deserve.

The warmth of the French people has overwhelmed us all, as we've marched and ridden to the front. From village to village, we've been met with eyes hungry for hope. People remove their caps and wave them in the air. Bakers bring out what meager supply they have and stuff our soldiers' pockets with rolls for the journey. There is great thirst for hope here, and hope is what America is delivering.

But along with the good, there is the bad. The hard. The heart-wrenching, to tell the truth of it. France has become a keeper of souls. We call them "casualties," but she holds them close in her earth, and each cross we pass that marks a grave reminds us that many have paid the greatest price. That we may do the same.

We saw it for the first time this week, at Saint-Mihiel. Your boys, America . . . they went over the top like a flood of courage, shedding their own blood to protect that hope. You should've seen the way the lightning ripped the sky in two, as if it, too, wished to crack straight down the middle of this war.

While this is sobering, while the sound of shelling reaches our ears even now from miles away, it also awakens a sort of urgency in the men. Your boys, America—they are standing for all that is good: Justice. Truth. And someday . . . Victory. They stem their fear with courage, and the whole land is palpable with it.

They are perched on the precipice of triumph. I feel it. All of France feels it. Your boys . . . your men . . . they are heroes already.

I tapped the last of the article over the wire from the dugout beneath the ground. It boggled my mind, that words could travel like miniature soldiers, lined up in invisible letters through a wire that runs deep through this earth, past the shelling, under trains and thousands of feet marching, beneath ocean currents where fish swim in peaceful oblivion, arriving at a news office in Washington in little dots and dashes. Where they will be transcribed, printed, rolled into newsprint, and tossed onto front porches to bring hope to anxious families and courage to a country. And where I fear the dots and dashes will, as they almost always are, be changed by editorial, censorial hands eager to protect the public from fear.

I understood the way words can shape hearts. Evade the creation of mobs and fear, and instill a home-front army of citizens armed with hope. And I understood that the words published must protect our soldiers, too. That they must cloak their movements while reporting them at the same time. To inform our own and pull a potato sack of blindness over enemies scanning our papers, eager for intelligence to get ahead in this never-ending battle.

And yet, where, in all of this, did truth lie? They will make me out to be the "face of the army, the voice of the men." Uncle Sam's nephew. *Hank Jones*, they call me, to make me feel like "the all-American fellow next door." But what about the farm kid, Henry Mueller, who spent his life elbow deep in mud and straw up until now? Sure, his name is much too German sounding to be related to Uncle Sam. Sure, he's just a gangly bespectacled guy, a vehicle for the words behind the face of this fictional character the paper has created. Still . . . I hoped plain old Henry Mueller might have a voice in this, too. I hoped he might be brave enough to report truth, always.

The men here deserved it. The people deserved it. And then, some blessed day, I'll go back to milking cows.

9

Captain Jasper Truett

September 1918

"Rot." I slammed the newspaper down on the makeshift table in our dugout. A light bulb swung above like a pendulum powered by the distant explosions of shrapnel.

"What's that, Captain?" Sergeant Steerforth yanked his head up from a map.

I jabbed a finger at the newspaper so hard it should've snapped my knuckle. "That. Makes the war out to be one big parade."

Steerforth picked up the newspaper and read aloud.

"'YOUR BOYS, AMERICA, issue 8. AMERICA A BEACON TO THE FRONT—WASHINGTON WORLD—SEPTEMBER 1, 1918. By Hank Jones.'" He read on a bit and then got to the part that made us out to be one collective savior. Nothing of the hardships of war, the flies that buzz over fields of wreckage and the birds that have fled the same. The writer seemed bent on declaring a syrupy version that made himself a hero.

"'The warmth of the French people has overwhelmed us all, as we've marched and ridden to the front. From village to village, we've been met with eyes hungry for hope. People remove their caps and wave them in the air, bakers bring out what meager supply they have and stuff our soldiers' pockets with rolls for the journey. There is great thirst for hope here, and hope is what America is delivering.

Your boys, America, they are standing for all that is good: Justice. Truth. And someday . . . Victory. They stem their fear with courage, and the whole land is palpable with it.

Your men are heroes already.'"

My jaw twitched.

Steerforth shuffled his feet, squinting at the paper. "I . . . don't know that I see the problem, sir."

"The problem?" I raised my brows, feeling the old anger simmer. "The problem is that if the families who read this are to be receiving death notifications any day, we'd do best not to raise their hopes higher. They'll fall all the harder for it. America is going to suffer enough as it is." I knew too well what it was to get a death notification. Knew too well the way it carved itself, word for word, on a person's very bones, marking him for all of time.

I knew it from long ago, and too many back home were learning the same every day this war went on. I would not stand by and let their blow be made even crueler.

Steerforth gulped. The heat of my words, lacking anyone else to land on, snaked around him.

"Who did you say wrote that?"

Steerforth studied the paper. "Jones. Hank Jones. Embedded with our battalion, sir."

I'd have to find a place for Jones, where he'd find something less glamorous to shine his words on.

"Bring Jones here. And a couple of others, too."

"A couple?"

"Two or three."

"Anyone in particular?"

A sea of faces swarmed my thoughts. This Jones needed exile. The shame of it. And one tortured face—the wide-eyed shock of Matthew Petticrew back at Saint-Mihiel as he gripped my arm from that shell hole—needed it, too. *The mercy of it.* We would need him and his leadership again soon. Best to have him rested, restored, as much as a man could be out here, for the next battle.

"Bring Petticrew."

10

Matthew

Meuse-Argonne Region
The Front

We were men. It was why we were here.

And then we were uniforms. Bearing them proudly, morphing into one force. Bent on saving humanity.

And then, finally, we were ants. Tunneling earth, shoveling graves, running with speed and conviction we did not feel, past diseased mud and stench we could not forget, through networks that were more lifeblood to us than what ran through our own veins.

I closed my eyes against it. *We are men*, I reminded myself. *We are human.* I leaned back against the cold sandbag wall and lifted my face to the sky. Nearly night, and the clouds promised rain.

Yes. Please, God. Rain.

The sky opened, but it was shrapnel and dirt that fell. I remembered then what one of the officers had said—that a trench is just a grave with the ends kicked out.

I closed my eyes and drowned out the sound of that memory. A trench was also the way a field was watered in Greenfield Springs, a bringer of water. Green grass. Life.

I reached into this truth to remember what life sounded like: the song of birds and the lift of gates and the pounding, always, of hoofbeats. Majesty unleashed. It had come to the point that if

I didn't do this—if I didn't carve a place in my mind for a trench to mean life—I would die. And, more than that, hope would die.

"Petticrew!" Sergeant Steerforth hollered and my eyes flew open. I stood tall. The first day in here, I hunched over, afraid my height would not fit entirely into the safety of the trench. I needn't have hunched, as it was redundant on two counts—the trench was deep enough, and the trench was not safe to begin with.

"You're up," Sarge barked. I stood straight.

"I'm going over the top?" Something flopped inside me and I rallied it back up. I could do this. I'd done it before. But the images of that day were engraved in my mind . . . and they were not the sort to bolster a man. I knew, now, that I could do it—but I felt myself slipping into some mechanical, detached place, preparing.

"In a manner of speaking, sure. You can call it that."

I leaned in, not understanding.

"You're on lumber," he said. "Trench fell a quarter mile south. Mudslide from all the rains."

Rains? They were getting rain, a quarter mile south. Water from the sky instead of shrapnel. My rain. The rain that only came to us as drainage downstream in the sickly trickle at our feet, carrying with it vermin and worse. Things unfit to think on, let alone speak of.

"We need trees from the woods," Sarge said. "Lumber to shore up the trenches, if your hand is up for it."

"*Lumber*," I muttered the word like it was a dream. Lumber—a trip out of this place—sounded too good to be true. "Yes," I said. "All good," I raised my hand to show it was ready. It had its . . . issues. But they would cease. I was sure of it. "Thank you."

"Good. You and Jones."

"Jones?" George Piccadilly piped up, suddenly there. He was always suddenly there. Popping up like a dog at a banquet table, begging for crumbs. Only the way George carried himself, you'd think this particular dog presumed he belonged at the head of the table. "When you said 'Jones,' did you mean 'Piccadilly'?"

"I meant Jones."

"Or possibly Piccadilly?" Piccadilly was indefatigable. And he wasn't even a soldier.

Steerforth was losing his patience. I spoke up before he could, hoping to avoid a blow dealt to Piccadilly. He wasn't terribly . . . thick-skinned. Just incredibly oblivious.

"I don't think chaplains get lumber duty," I said.

"Come on. What can Jones offer that I can't? He's a reporter. If a reporter can go, a chaplain can go. I'll find the holy wood. Surely you want the pious sort of lumber."

Steerforth was near fuming.

"Take me," he said, drawing himself up with a grin that he appeared to believe sparkled with the light of the noonday sun, rather than rotted with trench breath. I stifled a gag. "If Jones gets to go, I get to go. You'll want George Piccadilly on this troop, mark that."

Sarge laughed. "Get to? I've got half a mind to send you just for that. They're going into the Argonne." He named the forest we'd heard tales of. Thick tangles of lumber both living and dead. Terrain that rose as fast as it dropped, ground that would shift from solid to quicksand without warning, sucking men up to their knees in muck. And dark. Not a light to see by, or to trace any Jerries, come night. The Germans were in there, we knew. Somewhere.

"Right," George said. "And I have extensive forestry experience. Send me in, Sergeant Steerforth."

Steerforth shook his head, looking at George dubiously. "You, Chaplain?"

George was looking at the sky overhead, hand to his domed helmet as he surveyed something up there.

"Chaplain?"

"Eh?" George looked around, then seemed to register that he was the chaplain being spoken to. "Me?"

"I don't see any other chaplains about. Might do you some good, get your head out of the clouds."

George laughed. "You know what they say, mate—"

The sergeant shot him a look, reminding him there was such a thing as rank.

"Pardon me," George said. "You know what they say, Sergeant."

"No," Steerforth said dryly. "Can't say that I do."

"Too heavenly minded to be of any earthly good," George said, tapping his helmet with a finger. "It's a high calling, but I am here to serve." He looked back up at the sky, his attention wandering again.

"True," the Sergeant said. "And you versus the Argonne . . . that's a battle I'd like to see. Alright. You'll go. Fetch Jones."

George disappeared around the corner, stopping to read a plank that had been stenciled with a name. It was one of the things that had struck me as odd when first we came to the trenches. That they had names, just like the streets in a city. Some named for places, to remind the boys of home—*Manhattan Lane*. Others dubbed with foreboding names, meant as both a warning and a joke, the way men often treated death down here. *Death Valley. Suicide Corner.* George lifted a hand to slap the sign as he passed it, this one reading *Piccadilly Circus*. He paused to give a jubilant look and point a thumb at his chest.

Yes, George, I thought. *Your name. And a circus, to boot. Very fitting.*

"That one's a little mad, isn't he?" Sergeant Steerforth watched after George Piccadilly. "Well, madness looks different on every man," he said, shaking his head. "We'll all go mad out here, I think. It is not a question of whether, but when. But we carry on best we can."

"Yes, sir," I said, trying to reconcile the weight of his words with the casual tone in which he said them.

And then I heard it. The approaching whistle of a shell.

My mind marched orders to my body, shoving back the revolt of bile that came with every explosion now. "Incoming," I said.

"What's that?"

"Incoming!" I screamed. My voice had taken on heights I never knew it could, before coming here. Sarge and the men nearby threw themselves on the ground none too soon—and there I stood like a stupid pole. My hand trembling as bits of mud and rock showered down upon us, fireworks of mud and clay.

My vision darted in every direction. Everyone was fine. Everyone was fine. Everyone . . . a man lay with his face turned away, still as a board. I rushed to him, rolled him over. He rubbed his eyes and spat angry words at me. I'd woken him up from the few winks of sleep he would be able to manage before his next two hours on.

"Petticrew." Sargent Steerforth was at my back, turning me to face him.

"Sorry, Sergeant. I saw him laying there and thought—"

Sarge drew out a patch of gauze. "Your face, Petticrew." He gestured, and shoved the gauze into my hand.

I lifted it, hating that tremor in my hand and how I could not hide it in this moment. The injuries from Saint-Mihiel had been healing. The medic had relocated my fingers and set them to reinforce. When the splint had come off, this trembling remained—and it went deeper than the bones. Its source further in, like some hidden part of me even I could not unlock to stop, when the shelling came.

Pressing the gauze beneath my eye where Sarge gestured, I drew away and saw it soaked in blood.

"Go on," Sarge said, his face serious as he studied me. I could well imagine his thoughts. *Fool wakes up a soldier, doesn't even know he's the one hurt.*

But he spoke different words. "You, Jones, and the Brit." He wasn't the only one who'd taken to forgoing George Piccadilly's name. "Get to the forest. It'll do you good. Take the night. And take care. The Boche get over there sometimes and try and take us from behind our own lines. Those woods are like the promised land to them." I could picture it, silhouetted German soldiers crouched behind the trees we were to bring back. I gulped.

"But, uh . . ." he hesitated. "It's quieter there," he said, looking at my hand. "Might be good."

He gave the rest of our instructions and we were off. We snaked our way through the maze of trenches, soggy footprints sliding to a stop in the muck.

It was strange work, the felling of trees only to bury them again in the ground from whence they came. I imagined their roots reaching out for them, searching, finding them in their new home where they held back soil and sludge and allowed men to live.

To reach them, we passed men digging holes. I tried to tell myself they were trenches, but I knew the truth. We all did. They were graves. I looked away from the empty graves, and then I hated myself for it, and looked back. This—the seeing of the sacrifice—was the very least they deserve, the souls who'd left the bodies soon to be placed within. We all knew, though none of us spoke it, that it could be us next.

The tree line rose above us like a fortress—but it was impossible to say which side it kept safe. We stood, the three of us side by side, looking up at the black silhouettes of the trees against the dark night.

"Jolly lot, aren't they?" George finally said.

"Jolly or not, guess we'd better get in there," Jones said dryly. He stopped to scribble something on a notepad, then put it back in his jacket pocket. He was a journalist, I knew, but I wondered what tale there could be here.

We entered. The air cooled, wetter and heavier than on the outside. Blindly we strained to see and feel for trees large enough to give strength but small enough to cut through quickly. It was easy at first, until the supply grew thin and we ventured farther in.

Hank Jones and George Piccadilly set to sawing a thick one down, each of them taking an end of a saw. The metal began to protest as it wobbled and bent.

"You ever even used a saw before?" Jones asked.

"*Use* one?" George said. "I was *raised* by one."

Jones stopped sawing. Even in the dark, I could hear the look he gave George. "What does that mean?"

"Nanny Matilda," George said. "She *saw* everything!"

Jones's silence stretched, and I could picture him giving a deadpan stare.

George thwapped him in the chest with the back of his hand. "Come on, mate, only trying to lighten things up."

Jones folded his arms over his chest and stepped back, nodding at the saw embedded in the thick trunk. "Be my guest," he said.

They were well matched, George's nonsense with Jones's dry-humored ways. He'd grown up on a farm, Jones had, if I remembered right. He knew his way around a toolbox. Their bickering went on and I didn't know what was louder—their back-and-forth, the saw's grating, or my hissed attempts to shush them. It was a hopeless prospect, attempting to sow peace between a bull and a pillar. I took myself away to find another tree, each footfall carrying me farther from the splintering of air, deeper into darkness.

At some point—and I cannot pinpoint precisely when—I entered another world. There was no mark of it—no creaking of hinges, no fall into a rabbit hole, no flight unto a second star to the right. More of a gradual mist of quiet, where the pleasant smell of decomposing leaves and pine washed away the smell of decomposing flesh. Where the air rose clear and high, and did not hang in a veil of sulphur.

Even the trees seemed to take on a different sort of life here, one of them growing up and over, into the form of an arch. Another, farther on, dipped to the right at middle height, giving the impression that it had grown into the form of a bench for passersby, or a swing, suspended in wood, before continuing its upward climb. And on, near a steep incline, grew a great thick beast of a tree, towerlike. Its trunk hollowed out into a gaping entrance that made it appear it was a deep yawn. I had half a mind to crawl inside and see if it might hold the secret to sleep—the rest-filled sort of sleep, not the nightmarish trap that snapped at me whenever I let myself drift off in the trenches.

Here, in this world I'd entered . . . was life. And signs of life, too. Snapped off at intervals were boughs of pine, their freshly exposed tree flesh bright against the dark. Someone—or something—had done this. At nearly the same height, never more than a branch from any given tree, until I traced its path to a smallish clearing.

I lingered long there. Near a clustered stand whose thin trunks held round knots that made them look like members of a choir, mid-song, I found a lone tree a stone's throw away and timed my ax-falls to coincide with the distant explosion of shells. I could not believe any enemies traversed this ground—it was so peaceful here. But then again, hadn't all of Belgium, the idyllic land of creaking windmills and fields bursting into flower, thought the same until Germany ravaged them?

A footfall sounded. Not close, but close enough.

I froze. Senses alert. But nothing came. "George," I whispered. "Jones?"

Only silence. I resumed my work, wincing a prayer that the tree, when it finally fell, would not bring a company of Germans upon me.

I repeated the work, felling three more trees, getting lost in time until I realized my night-seeing eyes could no longer see anything, not even the hand in front of me. Something had passed over the moon above, blocking out light. Closing me in.

And that's when it came.

Slow, at first. A voice, distant. Soft and breathy in a low, constant tone that tiptoed up, and up, and down, and down. A melody—burrowing through the underbrush in minor notes, emerging from the bracken to lift its fair head into the air with major notes.

It was—it was a woman. The effect of the forest was such that I could not place the direction of the voice's source, with branches snatching pieces of the song and trunks echoing them back. But oh, did I strain to find it. Turning this way and that. Eyes upward to that dark sky. Hearing the rustling of leaves above, twigs clattering to carry that tune to the heights.

A lullaby.

My very being stood at attention with every lift and drop of that voice. The words were soft, but when I could catch them, they came in French. Whatever their meaning, their theme was clear: Peace.

It stopped, or rather faded as it journeyed away from me. I remained there, unmoving, for too long. Willing the sound back. But it took itself away and left me only with a hollow feeling at my back that I had entered some haunted land.

"Nihtgale. Old English. It means 'night songstress,'" Celia had once told me from a book she was reading. *"It sings in the dark, when all the other birds have gone to sleep."*

Was that what I'd heard?

I shook my head. This was . . . something more. Human, light as air, somber but sweet. She didn't sing when all the others had gone to sleep; she sang when all the others had gone to war.

I had imagined it, surely. There were no birds here. They were long flown, driven by the things that occupy a war-torn sky. There were no women here. Not for miles and miles and miles.

"We will all go mad. It is not a question of whether, but when." And suddenly, I saw something more in Sargent Steerforth's face as he told me to get lumber. It was a mission of mercy, I understood now. To get me away from the trenches, even if only for a night. He recognized it in me, madness encroaching, and sent me away to find my grounding.

But if madness sounded like what I'd just heard . . . I wasn't sure I wanted to find my grounding. It was a deal kinder, that sound, than the incessant yelling, shelling, shredding of my eardrums back in the trenches.

But that was reality. And what I'd just heard—it had to be imagined. I would not let myself slip into a dreamland, only to escape the things my compatriots were now facing.

Lashing the felled trees together and harnessing them to myself like an ox with his cart, I dragged them out of the depths of that place and back to where I'd left George and Henry, expecting to step right back into their war of insults.

But they sat side by side on a log, silent.

"You fellas okay?"

They just looked at me. Looked askance at each other, then each of them fixated on something in the opposite directions. They looked like I felt.

"Did you . . ." I began.

If I finished that question—*hear a siren singing in the middle of the woods*—they'd know what I'd heard. They'd have to report me, surely. And aside from hearing things, I was certain I could still perform my duty.

"What?" George said, standing. Looking at me accusingly. "Did we what? Do our work? Jolly if we didn't. Look at that. What do you call that?" He pointed at a pile of saplings, as if revealing lost treasure.

I nodded. The sound still haunting me, still at my back. Hank Jones narrowed his eyes, staring at me. "You heard it, too."

I gulped. Stiffened. "I've heard a lot of things."

George shot to his feet, pointing at me with far too much joy on his face. "Ha! See?" He whacked Jones in the chest with the back of his hand. "Told you we hadn't lost our marbles. You heard her. You *heard* her."

"Her . . ." It was the first time any of us had spoken of the voice in human terms.

George shook his head, mouth open, as if I were stupid. "The Angel of Argonne."

I stared at them, then back at the woods. Feeling I'd lost something, in this knowledge that they had heard the voice, too. I turned and started the march back to the trenches. "Let's go," I said.

George ran to catch up, his rifle slinging against his side, while Jones dragged the saplings lashed together behind him. "Come on," he said, his voice jostling the words. "Admit it. You heard her, and you're all in a knot that it's true."

I clamped my mouth shut over any response, hoping against hope that George, geyser-like as Old Faithful, might see fit to cease talking.

Back behind our lines, we passed the graves once more. Filled in, now, and quiet. Even the two bickerers fell into a reverent silence. And just as we were about to pass them, I saw something that made me stop in my tracks. I squinted, sure the pale light of dawn was fooling me. But there, on each of the graves, was laid a wreath. Boughs of pine so fresh I smelled them, threading through the cloud of sulphur, dust, and stench. The same spiced smell that had lured me into the woods, into the place where branches had been snapped off of trees for some unknown purpose.

The hands that had taken them, it seemed, had known just what they were for.

Back in the trenches, it was hard to believe any of it had happened. The three of us ate an early breakfast of canned corned beef, cooked over a fire so small it would not give off enough smoke to tell the Germans where to aim.

Hank Jones reached into his pocket and pulled out what looked to be a newspaper clipping. Giving it a disgusted glance, he crumpled it up and added it to the dying fire.

"What?" George said, around mouthfuls of beef. "Looks like your story!"

"Yeah, you'd think," Hank said. "One or two of the words are mine, I guess." He looked at it burning and seemed satisfied. George shrugged, jabbing his fork into Hank's can, who jerked it away promptly.

George wolfed the rest of his fare down and spoke around his last mouthful. "I'll tell you who it was. It was the Angel. Some fellows up the line spoke of her, said that she came some nights to sing. That many have heard her, but none have seen her."

"Sounds like trench tales to me," I said. The men were known to pass hours by making up all manner of fables. Often they'd involve some sort of woman. Thousands of weary men in these trenches, pining for mothers and sweethearts and wives.

Hank Jones pulled a pencil out from behind his ear and a notebook from his pocket, scratching words down. "What else did they say about her?"

George contorted his face. The act of mental exercise appeared to be an excruciating one for him. "They said . . . she walks the front with bare feet, leaving tokens for fallen soldiers and song for those who live. She is the mother to a thousand lost boys, these men who would give anything for a home-cooked meal in the safety of their own mothers' kitchens."

"Like Wendy," I said.

"Right-ho!" George raised a finger in agreement. We'd all grown up on *Peter Pan*, all envisioned ourselves adventurers to take on a mighty foe when we'd brought the brand-new book home from shiny bookstore windows or library counters. We'd just never figured that adventure would look like this.

I shook my head. "It's made-up," I said. Partly not believing it myself, but mostly not wanting to acknowledge that others had heard a song that had felt so distinctly personal to me. It was selfish, but I could be a selfish guy. "Besides. If no one has seen her, how do they know she comes barefoot?"

George gawked at me. Jones scribbled some more. "Have you seen this place? Mud!"

"Footprints?" I said. "And why has no one followed the footprints, then?"

"They have." George stabbed his fork into my can of beans, spearing the last lone legume. "They hit the edge of the forest and *poof*—" he circled his fork in the air. "The footprints disappear." He made his fork disappear back into his grubby mess kit, for emphasis. "By George, what I wouldn't give for a full English breakfast right now. Sizzling egg, crisp bacon, sausage, the whole lot."

Hank gawked at him. "How'd you even end up in this battalion?" he said. "Shouldn't you be with the Tommies?"

George waved him off. "I missed my chance to fight alongside my countrymen when I dodged it all to come to America. So? You lucky blokes get me instead."

My stomach rumbled and my mind protested as the conversation moved on. I wanted to hang on to that image of the Angel of the Argonne. But George prattled on with endless breakfast foods of toast and tomatoes, tea and coffee.

"That's right, you heard me, tea *and* coffee, both. Maybe together. Mix it all up and spoon it down, I'll take it all. Marmalade, mmm . . ."

He was soon asleep, doubtless dreaming happily of rivers of golden butter and honey. And I . . . I tried with all my might to etch that song onto my memory.

My hand shook, and my eyesight blurred for want of sleep. But I knew it wouldn't come, not more than a few minutes. Sleep had become an act of tiptoeing until my subconscious stumbled over trip wire and clashed against the sounds very real around me, jerking me out before I could go into that dream realm. I feared it. I knew where it would take me, and I refused to go there.

I rummaged around my kit for something—anything—to set my hands to. What I wouldn't give for a book, or a radio, or even a sheet of paper to write Celia.

The tops of my fingers, in their jittering cadence, brushed over something cold. I pulled it out—Chester Hasenpfeffer's empty artillery shell. His trophy, hollow as could be.

I'd seen men in the trenches make things of them before— etching designs upon them, engraving the names of salients and other battle places they'd been. They'd take them home to give to sweethearts as vases, or perhaps use them to stow pens or some such—a souvenir of this "grand adventure." Maybe they, too, knew how to push the nightmares away.

I turned the brass in my hands, that song weaving through my mind. I'd give anything to keep the notes, the melody, forever. To trap up inside this shell the swelling peace both mournful and hope-filled and cap it, bury it somewhere safe. Not that I had any use for a vase. I had no wife, no sweetheart, nobody to even wonder about a future with.

I had only a song. I pulled out my pocketknife and began, slowly, to carve. It was clumsy work—I was no artist. But it was something, and with every chink in the metal, that song burrowed deeper into my soul.

And so it went, for the next many days. The three of us fell into a rhythm. The sun fell and rose. I chiseled and engraved during the day when the others slept. Darkness came and we felt our way into the woods. We'd fell trees, sometimes together and sometimes apart. Three times I ventured back to that place that had felt so otherworldly that first night . . . but it felt empty, each time. The spell of it had fallen away.

None of us heard the Angel of Argonne.

I listened hard from the trenches the rest of the time. For her, but also for the shells, as always. Straining in the silences for that approach from nowhere. Knowing I had mere seconds, if that, to determine the direction of the incoming whistle before it splintered land and exploded upward into a volcano of dust and fire. It had become my job, once Captain Truett had figured out about my ears, the way they picked up on things quicker than others. So I would listen, and bark out a warning, hoping to save a life.

Captain Truett clapped me on the head once when I dared to suggest that I might not be doing much good in that way. *"Get some sense in you, son,"* he'd said. *"And let your ears do their work. Like it or not, you're making a difference."* Truett rarely offered a compliment, and when he did, it almost always snuck past, unrecognized in the cloak of an insult. But still, it lit a fire in his men to press on.

But behind and beyond and in between and above that—I listened for her, always.

As did every man. One night, when all was quiet, I spotted George sticking his head up over the top of the trench—in the wrong direction. I tossed a pebble at his helmet.

"Get down," I hissed.

"Ow! What's all that for?"

"Better me with a pebble than a Jerry with a bullet," I said. We caught on quick at the front to the terms used. Not "Germans," but "Jerries" or "the Boche." Not Brits, but "Tommies." And us Americans were the doughboys, named so for the way our buttons resembled doughnuts. Cruel and unusual punishment, this constant reminder of food. Edible food. *Real* food.

I felt in my pocket and pulled out a hard biscuit. Chiseling a chunk off, I tossed it at George and whistled in time for him to look up and catch it.

"Thanks," he said.

"What were you doing up there?"

He tore a bite out of the biscuit and shrugged. "Listening for my lady love," he said. The three of us had heard something out there—but if hundreds or more lonely, forlorn soldiers heard the same, I didn't want to even begin to imagine the riot that might ensue if they learned we'd been close to her. Every man would be clamoring for lumber duty.

A soldier raised his head from where he'd been resting his chin on his chest, legs stretched out on one of the driest pieces of trench. "You and every other guy down here," he said.

I shoved the rest of the biscuit back in my pocket. "You heard her?" I tried to sound disinterested.

"You didn't? You coulda heard a pin drop, right out here in the muck. We all thought we'd gone crazy. Shell shock, all of us at once. But when two hundred guys hear the same song at the same time, you know you ain't the crazy one."

I nodded. And knew then that I *was* the crazy one. Me, thinking that song was intended, somehow, for my ears. I knew enough of sound and distance to know that these men and I must have heard different parts of the song . . . and part of me argued that maybe at least that small part, deep in the woods, was just for me.

But such thoughts would do none of us any good.

It was this I carried with me that night into the woods. I determined to stay with Henry and George, to remind myself I was no different from the rest. But when they kept shooting me looks that told me I was in the way, I set off on my own. I pointed my feet in the opposite direction of the otherworld, that quiet place. Venturing instead away and closer to where the Germans were rumored to have been spotted some weeks before. I took extra care, knowing I could trigger trip wire or entangle myself in barbed wire at any moment.

And then it happened. Not the voice, but the heated whistle of a shell approaching. It impacted a hundred yards away, just outside the edge of the wood. I hit the ground, pulse slamming. Another one followed, this one closer.

They were aiming for the woods.

Before I could think, I was up and running. Hollering to Henry and George to get down as I neared them. They did—and then they made for the trenches. I followed—but twisted to a halt in the mud as a third shell impacted deeper into the woods. Into the land where the branches had been snapped off for wreath-making.

And I followed it.

My breaths coming short and urgent, I ran beneath the arch tree, past the swing tree, beyond the great yawning tower tree.

A breeze came, and light flickered beyond a screen of branches before me. Was that—a lantern? Shoving the branches away, unheeding of their scratching ways, I confirmed it was. Yes. Golden and glowing, out here in the middle of nowhere, a lantern hung from a tree.

Where was she?

The shelling stopped.

I froze.

In the silence, I listened hard for sound of her, or sound of shells, and heard neither. Before me stood the stand of trees that I'd thought so resembled a choir, with their straight postures and wide-mouthed knots. Only tonight, their open mouths looked shocked and fearful.

"Where is she?" I spoke it low and told myself I wasn't actually speaking to trees. I hadn't lost my senses quite that much, yet. *We all go mad.*

Mad enough to chase after a phantom, fancying myself some sort of guardian. But the choir trees answered me anyway, with their blank unknowing stares.

And then came that sound of metal. Rhythmic but slow, the ring of a shovel. I followed it, chest pounding in tune to the slide-and-lift of the metal. I traveled on as the sound grew louder, the frequency less. And when it stopped—so did I.

I will never forget that moment, my hand pressed to the rough bark of a pine, seeing—for the first time—the Angel of Argonne.

She stood beneath a tree so large and wide it looked to have tapped into the stores of ancient time, somewhere down under, with its roots. I willed my breath to come quiet, every muscle frozen at the picture before me. White moonlight crowned the girl so that her hair, wild as the wind and dark as the earth she now stood upon, shone like a tangled halo. Unlike any angel the lore of the trenches could have produced. She was breathtaking. And, wonder of wonders, the legends had got one thing right: she wore her feet bare, white against the dark soil.

She was a question mark, there in the dark. An air of rugged innocence that bespoke childhood, but the figure of a young woman, willowy yet strong. She began to speak. Words soft, but certain, mangled with the choke of sorrow. My feet—clumsy things with a mind of their own—took a step, recognizing the voice that had stopped them in their tracks on that first night.

She whirled, hearing the sound of that footfall. Eyes ablaze and shovel held out like a bayonet ready to spear. She had seen me. She had to have, for the way she trained that shovel handle in my direction, unflinching. And yet her gaze did not focus on me. Perhaps she had only heard, and I had a chance of remaining hidden.

I didn't move.

Not an inch.

The breeze tumbled through the clearing, sending the branches above her clattering, setting her shoulders at ease once more. And with a wary glance around the clearing, she lowered her shovel again.

She knelt, uttering a prayer in all the rolls and rises of French. Though I did not know the words, I knew the voice: grief.

This was a grave. And she, the one who laid wreaths upon countless graves of soldiers unknown to her, was now the gravedigger. The thought tore at me. There were none, perhaps, but me, who knew the source of the wreaths. It tied me to her, drew up a sense of duty to honor that fact.

I watched as she laid down on the earth beside it, drew her knees up in a hug. Her shoulders rose and fell ever so slightly, again and again, peppered with shuddering trills intermittently— the aftermath of those tears. At last her grief-laden breathing fell into a rhythmic repetition of sleep. The voiceless sounds struck me. Even in sorrowful slumber, she sang.

I watched too long, I knew. I had wood to cut, and this was not my story to take part in. Yet I felt that to leave would be to betray that story, somehow. And so those feet carried me right into the middle of it.

I was an intruder. I felt it the closer I drew to the scene before me. I gazed upon it, taking it all in, tucking each memory into a keeping place. In all the world, there should be some soul who helped her keep it. Even if she never knew.

As I turned to go, I paused and beheld the face of the sleeping woman. She was young—eighteen, twenty maybe. Face smudged, streaked where tears had mapped a course through her grief. Who was it, I wondered, buried there beside her? A husband? Sweetheart? Sister? Father? Mother? Whomever it had been, they had meant much to her, and her fingernails were crusted with the earth she had dug with her own two hands to bury them.

And how—*how*, in all the world—was she here? Her presence beside the bloody front of the war that had torn through the entire world and gouged this land into one gigantic, roping scar made no sense.

There was something otherworldly about her. In my short time in France, I had marched through many villages, passed many farms, seen the dress of those who worked the land. Her clothing, though simple, held a different air. Not fancy—and certainly very worn—but also not like the garb of the people. Her dress seemed of an era decades past, and pooled at her feet. Those feet looked cold, and I glanced away. My eyes fell on the sight of old boots, caked with mud and set with care beside the tree.

Her sleep was one of sorrow, dark brows pressed where there was no relief. The sight of that familiar place of grief planted a longing to give her something. Anything. I had no blanket to cover her form with, though the night was cold and the place where her sleeve revealed the skin above her wrist, gooseflesh standing at attention. I took off my jacket and made to spread its warmth above her—but could not. It was tainted with too much seen, and evidenced that in its smells and smudges. Not fitting for a garment meant to comfort. It offered only loss into loss.

Looking again at the mound of fresh earth, I knew of only one thing I might give. I silently skirted the clearing to gather up supplies, using my knife to clip what I needed. Then, making clumsy work of it, and pulling up all of my stealth training from Plattsburg to steal in, I left my meager offering.

First light was near—I could feel it. There was a crispness to the air before it began, before even the few straggling birds awoke to sing the sun up, if they dared amidst this battle-torn air. And I had no lumber to show for the night's work. The girl stirred, and everything in me told me I should go now. I obeyed, marking the tree in my mind. It had character to it, that tree. Aged but strong, hovered over the two bodies lying beneath it like a protector. *Sentinel*, I thought. This was the Sentinel tree.

And the girl . . . I wished I knew her name. It seemed right, to know the name of the woman whose grief I would hold the rest of my life, when no other was there to share it this night. I lingered, staring, willing that name to somehow present itself before me.

The Angel of Argonne—she was human, after all.

I stooped to straighten my misshapen wreath where it lay at the base of the tree, and turned to go, silent as the dark.

"Oy!"

No.

No, no, no.

It was George, tromping through the underbrush with all the restraint of a pig nuzzling for truffles. I waved my arms, motioning for him to be quiet.

"You've been holding out on us, bloke!" He pointed at me with his saw, his lopsided grin making to speak again. "This here is the mother of all trees. Or grandfather, rather. Patriarch, monarch, oligarch, and every other sort of arch, I'd wager."

"We know you would," Jones said drolly. George's penchant for gambling had landed him here and we all knew it.

"Shhh!" I pumped my palms toward the forest floor as if the motion could squash their banter. I looked at the girl's sleeping form. Every bone in her body had to be wrung out, to be sleeping through the chaos of George.

"What?" George hissed in a whisper. "Are there Jerries about?"

I shook my head.

"Wildebeests, then? Wolves? Other fiends of the wildwood?"

My eyeballs nearly bulged out of my head with the silent command I gave him to shut up.

George placed his saw at the base of the Sentinel tree, sizing it up. "That'll do nicely," he said. "It'll take a lot of others to get it back, but we can ask Sarge if—"

I leapt across the clearing, placing myself between him and the tree.

"No one is taking this tree," I whispered with all the force I could muster. They still hadn't spotted her.

"He's right," Henry said, lowering his voice though he didn't know why. Good man. "It's not what we need. We need pliable but strong. And it's time to get back, anyway, or—"

A frantic rustling sounded, followed by a noise that needed no translation.

The click of a rifle engaging.

I turned slowly and looked into eyes red-rimmed and blue, piercing from her mud-streaked face. And between her and me, like the dark eyes of a hungry snake sizing me up, were the gaping barrels of an aged weapon.

11

Mira

Sleep lifted from me at first light. I did not wish to wake, nor to face this day. My first, alone. Never again would I slumber beneath the same roof as Grand-père. Never again would I hear him say my name—*Mira*—he, the only one who called me so. Never again, I was coming to realize, would I see my own father, vanished long away. Loss begat loss.

Parched until my mouth burned, I finally opened my eyes. There, beside me, was Grand-père's resting place. I knew he was not there, not truly. Only his body. And yet to leave this place felt impossible. Hot tears came, and there was no blistered hand to wipe them away.

So I did. I stood. I wiped my face, my hands smudging with tears and dirt. And then I saw it.

The boughs of pines twined into a circle. Or perhaps more akin to a lopsided oval . . . but there was no mistaking it. *A wreath*.

Heart racing, I spun, spearing the trees for any sign of life. Who had done this? When none but a passing deer showed themselves, I lifted my own palms, studying them. Was it I? Had I done it in my sleep? It certainly had the appearance of being made by one in a slumber, twigs poking this way and that. Had I departed from my senses, truly? Enough that I could not recollect?

I lifted my palms and smelled them. They did not smell of pine or sap. They were rough and red from the digging, the using of new places not calloused by the wreath twining.

So who . . . ? Who was there to know of Grand-père, to mark his passing?

The old fear came rushing up my bones, my joints, my breathing.

But no. It could not be.

Pressing my eyes closed to dispel from my imaginings the face of the man I thought of, I spoke those words aloud. "*Ce ne peut pas être.*" *It cannot be.* It must not be.

It would not be.

I heard voices—and trained every sense on them. English. Papa told me, when I was young, "*Be wary of strangers, Mireilles.*" He always used my long name and made it sound like it was full of air and might float away. I made a rhyme of it when he taught me English: *My name is Mireilles, and I float away!* Papa caught me as I twirled away and smiled beneath his dark moustache.

"You have a secret strength, Mireilles," Papa said.

"I do?" I paused my spinning and laid in the tall grass, cupping my chin in my hands. It sounded like something from the fairy books. I was eight, and he was perfect. A fount of secret treasures he handed out to me in lessons, one by one.

"Many of them, yes. But one is that you know another language now. And I will tell you something else: It is even more powerful if you keep that a secret from others. Words run faster than the waters of the Meuse when people think that they are not understood. You can learn much that way." I pictured the surging river he spoke of, the splendor of such a thing. Rivers brought life in this green land. Could words do the same?

He tapped my head lightly, playfully. "If you do not float away." And with a wink, the conversation had been over.

And now that language stared at me from the end of Papa's old gun barrel, with eyes wider than this war.

"Please," the man said. "I mean you no harm." His voice was low and steady.

He raised his hands, palms in the air. They were blistered, caked with sap and soil, as if he had been tangling with my woods. I did not like that. I pulled the gun tighter into my shoulder. I might not have a uniform like theirs, but I could fire a rifle just as quickly as they, if I needed to. I was wrong to have lit Papa's lantern that night. But I had been desperate, so desperate, for him to come.

Instead, I'd summoned soldiers.

And now perhaps Grand-père would not be the only one to be buried tonight. It could be me. Or it could be these men. A cricket sang nearby, and I wished I were as ignorant as it of what this all meant.

"By George," the man behind him a few paces said. He was slack-jawed and made little sense to me. His uniform was like the others, but his accent was not. "It's the angel."

I looked at my boots beside the tree, all caked in mud. I looked at my skirts, torn and snagged. I knew my hair must be wilder than this wilderness, and I had smeared my own face with dirt to blend in with the night, hours before, only to muddy the mask of it with tears as I buried my only friend and relative. I wondered in what sort of cathedral this man worshipped, if his angels looked like earthen creatures of doom.

The third one—the one with spectacles—looked like he belonged in a library, the way he studied me. As if I were a painting or a puzzle. His gaze caught on my apron for an instant, and then his quiet eyes narrowed. "No," he said. "I don't think that's who she is."

I stared blankly at the fabric that had caught his study. Was it only a few years before that I was imagining it to be part of ball gowns? As if this world could ever have known rooms filled with light and music and slippered feet dancing and hearts weaving together. Fairy tales, all. Every one of them false.

And then there was the first man. He lowered his hands slowly, never taking those wide eyes from mine. I could not see much of him, where he stood shadowed by Grand-père's tree. His stance, though, seemed somehow . . . good. I do not know how to explain it but to say that it seemed steady and kind.

I wanted to trust his words. *"I mean you no harm."*

90

And yet I also knew Papa's words to be true. *"Be wary of strangers, Mireilles."* I knew it to my very bones. I would never forget.

I held out a hand, halting them. The one gawked, the one studied, and the one in the shadow, he stepped forward ever so slowly.

"Please," he said again. Someone had taken care to teach him manners. "We can help." He looked so sure of this that I wanted to dive into those words and find in them light and breath for my lungs and truth. All the things that seemed far gone from the world.

But then a flicker of doubt, so quick, shadowed his face. I could see his features now, in a slip of fading moonlight. Eyes of gentle blue, face kind. Ordinary, but handsome. And—tired. He looked so very tired. It was this that made me want to trust him the most, for such a one would understand this place inside of me that was too poured out, too empty for words.

"Right?" He looked over his shoulder at his friends. "We mean to help." He turned back to me and looked lost for a moment, staring at his hands as if they might somehow learn a way to translate between him and me. He nudged two open palms up in the air to show he lifted something invisible.

But my burden was so great, there was none who could help. I thought of Grand-père in the ground, of how cold and wet that dirt was, and I wanted to crumple into sobbing. But that was not who I was. My lip trembled and I bit it. My knees shook and I locked them, scolded them—*that is not who you are.* No matter that it had been weeks since I'd seen real food. Their plight was much the same, I knew.

The quiet one with the spectacles pulled something from his satchel. It was dark and round and fit in his palm. "Matthew," he said, and the one with the tired and kind eyes looked back. In a silent exchange that told us all it was meant for me, the one called Matthew took it, and held it out.

It was a potato.

I wanted to weep.

My fingers lifted from the trigger, preparing to reach. The one confused about angels licked his lips and reached out too. Toward the potato, I knew. Not toward me. Still, my instincts did not believe that, and I pulled the gun tighter, took a step back.

Matthew witnessed all of this and backhanded his comrade's reaching arm, causing it to fly and the reaching one to shake out his hand fiercely, as if he'd just been dealt a horrific blow . . . which he had not. He drew back. His pride, I suspect, wounded most of all, as he shot daggers at Matthew.

But Matthew did not see that. He was looking at me, steady and strong. He nodded, as if commending me. He held out his arm as far as it would stretch, putting more distance between us, and waited.

My fingers betrayed me. They left the rifle for the potato and I wondered dizzily if I was like Jacob in Grand-père's scriptures, if I had just given all for a mere bowl of stew.

I could smell it. It was earthy, full of promise. Suddenly the weeks of nothing caught up to me, my locked knees, my clenched mouth. All of it wound into a tight, black knot behind my eyes and swallowed me up.

The men and the trees disappeared before me and I began to fall into wretched, blessed unconsciousness.

My name is Mireilles . . . and I float away. And I did. As the world went black, someone picked me up, and began to carry me.

12

Chaplain George Piccadilly

Monet should have painted her. Or if not Monet, one of those other great men who can do great things with paintbrushes. Who was the one who painted the Mona Lisa? Monsieur Lisa, was that his name? Whoever he was, he should have painted her, and then we'd all have properly high-priced reproductions of the Angel of Argonne on our walls.

But perhaps none could capture the ethereal beauty of a creature so untouched by civilization that she seemed perfect in every way.

Perfect, I say. Oh, she looked positively savage, but beautiful all the more for it.

Matthew Petticrew, the horse groom from Harvard, of all people, carried her through the woods and I rather detested him in that moment.

"Petticrew," I hissed. "Let me have a turn."

He didn't even acknowledge me, the cad.

"Where are you taking her?" This, from Henry. Hank. Whichever one he was, and I assure you I never could quite tell which of his alter egos I was conversing with: Henry, the farm boy who seemed more soldier than story-chaser, or Hank Jones, the dimpled, bespectacled chap who America had taken under her wing as the face of the soldiers "over there."

Well, *we* were "over there" right now, and the light was dawning and we were going to miss breakfast, and if we did, it'd be hours and hours before we ate again.

Where was that potato?

A lump in Petticrew's sack answered me.

"Pssst," I said. "Where are we going?"

Petticrew slowed to a walk but refused to stop. "I . . . I don't know," he said. "I couldn't leave her there, alone like that, and—afflicted. And we can't take her to the front. "

"They have food at the front," I said.

"Imagine what the men would do. Imagine what she'd think, waking up in a place like that. She's been through enough."

"There," Hank said, pointing like he'd just released his bow, sailed his arrow, and landed a bull's-eye on his next story. "Look there!"

It was a light. A lantern, just as low on fuel as we were by the looks of it, but enough to direct our collective attention. The sky was light enough to see the outline of a small structure.

"A garden shed," I said, pointing and feeling properly valiant for it. Mayhap, if we were lucky, there would be more potatoes inside. Harris always kept a sack of potatoes in the garden shed at Winterbourne when I was a lad. Perhaps this shed was the same.

Matthew stopped just short of it and looked at me as if I'd fallen from Jupiter. "That would be a house, George."

As if I should know. "Well, we can't all grow up in the vaulted auspices of the groom's quarters, now can we? How was I to know houses came that small?"

But as we drew near, even I could sense this was no ordinary structure, whatever it was. It held the air of a great keeper of secrets.

Matthew hesitated only a moment before knocking.

"What are you doing?" Hank whispered. "We don't know who lives there."

Matthew looked around, as if trying to fortify his own thoughts. "Yes, we do." He nodded at the lady in his arms.

"How do you know?" Henry or Hank asked, narrowing his eyes behind his spectacles. That was definitely a reporter look emerging.

"Who else could it belong to? Nobody lives in these woods. At least nobody who anyone's ever heard of. We're so deep in, it'll be a miracle if we can get back out by nightfall tonight. And we just happen to find a—a woman, and a house, together? It has to be hers."

Nobody answered the knock. The whole place had an air of a waiting thing, as if it were sizing us up and tapping its garden-shed foot impatiently, the dastardly thing. Asking if we were soldiers or not, and if yes, why didn't we do something to prove it?

Hank looked over his shoulder as if the whole of Washington might rush in and apprehend him if he made a misstep. And then he plunged forward, opening the door.

It creaked, but oddly it was a merry sort of creak. Abandoned garden-shed-like dwellings with mysterious lanterns spitting to a fizzle should have a creak much more formidable.

I don't know whether it was the shelf stuffed to the brim with books, or the hearth with a rocking chair beside it and a blanket draped ready to welcome a windblown chap, or the tiny corner kitchen where morning light yellowed the floor, but the house made me rather thirsty for home, though I had no earthly idea where "home" might be for me.

No heavenly idea, I reminded myself. I had to start sounding more pious.

Petticrew laid the Angel down upon the one bed, all made up with a worn quilt in the corner, tucked partially beneath stairs that led to a loft. And then we waited. The ticking of a cuckoo clock marched seconds past, and we waited still. We were as useless as a passel of dwarves finding Snow White asleep in their forest hovel. What did one do with a damsel who had quite lost her senses? Literally, was unconscious?

"We shall break bread," I said, raising my brows and infusing my slow-spoken words with holy gravitas. There was that potato, after all, and someone had better cook it.

The others didn't hear me, apparently.

I spotted a well through the kitchen window and a pot on the stove, and went to work.

It is hard work, filling a pot with water. One doesn't like to complain, though, and before long I would be an expert at it, surely.

Back inside I opened the stove and set to work building a fire. A cloud of dust swarmed me with a vengeance.

A shuffling sounded, and Petticrew had the stove door shut just as I erupted into a coughing fit.

"Fine," I coughed. "I'm fine. No need to worry."

But the only thing Petticrew was worrying over was the fire. He turned a handle that did something or other, and the billows of smoke began to dissipate.

Pious. Sound pious.

"A pillar of smoke shall lead them," I said, gesturing at the white tendrils of ash.

"Fire," Jones said, jotting something down. I had a wish or two concerning that notepad of his and that fireplace.

"Pardon?" I sloshed the pot of water onto the stove and plunked in the potato. There. It'd be ready in no time, surely.

"A pillar of fire led the Israelites in the desert," he said. "Not smoke."

Right. "Just so."

Petticrew had gone to the window and was studying the terrain. Jones was perusing the corner bookshelf, pulling out books whose old covers appeared scrawled in French. That didn't seem to deter him, though.

Rummaging through a crock on the counter with a crack running down it, I pulled out a fork and stabbed the potato. Hard as a rock. I rather wished at that point that I'd paid attention when they'd talked at us at Plattsburg about being prepared and campfire cooking and all that sort of rot.

Perhaps if I cut it up, it might go faster. I salted the water, thinking to make a soup. That was likely how one made soup, I surmised. And as I set to slicing that spud, Jones stood suddenly, toppling the stool he'd perched on in front of the bookcase.

"I knew it," he said. "I *knew* it."

"Knew what?" I held the potato and sliced through it, nearly spearing my own palm in the process. Petticrew yanked it from me, along with the knife, and set it on the wooden counter to chop.

Hank Jones's eyes darted back and forth across the pages of the book he held at a feverish pace. "It's impossible, though."

Petticrew laid down the knife rather firmly. "What is it," he said, quieting his voice so as not to wake Sleeping Beauty, but his frustration simmered behind his words.

Jones looked at the girl. He took in the rustic chalet, more a cabin than anything so fancy sounding as "chalet," if you asked me. And again he shook his head.

"You know about the Fontinelles?" he said, turning suddenly as if he had come to life, wet rag that he was. Why, there appeared to be a beating heart within that book-brain, after all.

"Fontinelles," said I. "A family of cheeses known for their dull taste. Relatives of yours, are they?"

"The Fontinelles are not cheeses," said the wet rag, with the most disdain I'd heard from him yet. "They're people. Or were, rather. Until they disappeared."

Petticrew half listened as he checked on his patient. Listening for her breathing, covering her with a blanket. "Quite the nurse-maid, aren't you?"

He didn't even look at me. He left her side, plopped the potato chunks in the boiling water, and paced. "You were saying?"

"The Marquis Fontinelle was a remarkable man," he said. "He was aristocracy, almost fifty years ago. France has a long history of revolting against its aristocracy. But the Marquis managed to be a peacemaker among his peers and his tenants—and by daring to live outside the stride of expectations, he became a local hero of sorts. His writings have been studied for decades now. His ideas seemed revolutionary at the time, but looking back, people believe they could have spared the city a lot of turmoil, if they'd been adopted. Maybe even helped to prevent invasion. But . . . they *were* invaded. By the Prussians. And when they were, he became a target."

"Of who?" Petticrew said, leaning forward.

"Yes, of *whom*?" I said, folding my arms over my chest.

"All parties involved," said Jones. "His peers did not like the hunger for independence that the tenants showed. His tenants did not like the general solidarity of the aristocrats or the oppression of their heavy-handed ways in keeping them poor and their children hungry. And then the Prussians, who wanted to take Paris, shut the whole place in, cut off the city entirely. No way into the city, no way out. Except for one."

Jones paused as the Angel stirred over on her bed. She let out a small groan, which had Petticrew watching her like a hawk with a pained expression on his face. He was looking perpetually wounded these days.

"Do stop brooding," I said, throwing a kitchen rag at him.

He did not reply. Only glared.

"That," I said, pointing in his face. "See? Brooding. Stop it. You're not the one dying of hunger."

"I know that," he whispered fiercely. "But she'll get some food, soon enough." He jerked his head toward the potato pot.

I didn't tell him I'd been talking about me. "Quite," I said. My stomach rumbled.

Petticrew returned his attention to Wet Rag Henry. "One way out of the city," he said, signaling the story to go on.

Jones stood. "I can't believe you don't know the story," he said.

I rolled my eyes. "We can't all be walking encyclopedias."

"It's the stuff of legends," he said, unfazed. One of the greatest mysteries of our time. Or rather, the generation before us." Henry's speech sped up and he seemed nearly human and not so book-like in his growing enthusiasm. "You see, the French are an industrious people and found a way to communicate with their families outside of the city."

"Carrier pigeons?" Matthew said, looking more interested.

"Gas balloons. They began to use them during the Franco-Prussian War to steal bundles of correspondence out of the city. Launching in the dead of night, silent as could be."

"Gas balloons," I said, unable to keep the spark from my voice. My father had been a member of an aero club in London and took me to see the great race when first it began in Tuileries Gardens in old Paris. I was young then—only a boy—but well did I recollect how my soul lifted right along with the sea of orbs rising into the great beyond. My father and I had never been close, but that day was one for the ages.

"Yes," Jones continued. "The Marquis was seen one night in the middle of that siege of Paris, entering a train station where the balloons were kept. This man, once the hero of the people and well-loved of the aristocracy, now bore pauper's clothes and carried only one of his treasures."

"A diamond," I guessed. "A scepter?"

"His son. Two, maybe three years old. They flew into the night, it is presumed, and have never been heard from again. No one knows what became of them. Their Paris château sat empty for decades, his riches left to gather dust or be pillaged. The family line just . . . stopped." And Jones stopped, his tale halting as he weighed his next words. But it was his gaze that finished the story for him. He looked at the sleeping lady, then at the journal in his hands.

"At least, that's what people believed. That they disappeared in exile to another country, or perished in the trying. It's a great mystery, so much so it's almost legendary here."

"I don't like all this talk of wealthy people disappearing," I said. "First this cheese family—"

"They're not *cheeses*," Jones said.

"—then the children of the tsar of Russia—who is next? A fellow doesn't like to wonder these things, but for all that is good, is it going to be me? Money makes one a target, you know." *Sound pious.* "Money is the root of all evil," I whispered, infusing great gravity into the phrase.

The two gawked at me. This was probably one of those moments Mother was always speaking of, urging me to rein in my tongue. Well, Mother, if you think it, say it. That's what I always say.

"You're hardly one of the Romanovs," Jones said. "And besides, we're only getting the news in snatches in the trenches, and our translations are hardly reliable. Who knows what's really happened? More pertinent are the Fontinelles. They really *did* disappear from existence. Unless . . ." He trailed off.

Petticrew stopped his pacing. "Unless what?"

Jones hesitated, rubbing his eyes behind his spectacles. "I could be wrong. But that fabric she's wearing on her apron . . ."

"Rather fancy for a peasant," I piped up. Jones wasn't going to steal all the thunder.

"More than that. The French and their balloons, they were known to be extravagant. Works of art, really. The one Fontinelle escaped in was called the *Colombe de Nuit*."

I searched my rusty French. It had been acquired from an aged tutor who liked to use children's books about a zoo as his texts. I was utterly victorious in failing to pay attention back then, but a few of the words had stuck, despite my best efforts to the contrary. "The night dove?"

He nodded. "It was ornate. It had been the Marquis's, and was made of red and gold silks, with large embellishments."

We all looked together at the Angel of Argonne, at her tattered apron. It was faded and threadbare, but despite age and wear, the colors showing through were a tired scarlet and a lackluster gold . . . with a scrap of some sort of white cording looping in the corner.

"What are you saying?" I said. "She was the young tot who escaped in the balloon?"

"No . . . too long ago. That would've been . . . 1870, somewhere near there. It would have been a generation before her."

"The child grew up and had a child," Matthew said, the last piece of the puzzle clicking into place. He picked up a crudely framed painting and I craned to see it—a girl lit with sunlight and smiles, hair dark and coiling. Clearly a younger version of the Angel.

"Mireilles," Petticrew said. He could have spoken up, let us all clearly hear the name he read from the bottom of the portrait. His mouth moved around the name again, this time silently—*mee-ray*.

At the sound of her name, she stirred. Her eyes opened. We

froze, the three of us, as her blue eyes moved slowly around her surroundings and she rubbed her head.

At that moment, the potato soup, such as it was, bubbled in such a way that it sent the spoon within sliding. That served to jolt her upright and as she registered three men in foreign uniforms all gathered in what was presumably her cottage—she scrambled like a scared animal, pressing her back far into the planked corner.

"It's alright," Matthew said.

She leaned forward, gaze wary. Slowly, she gripped the fire poker next to her bed and wrapped her fingers tight around it. She was a fighter, and all the better for it in times like these, I say. Couldn't quite say the same for myself.

"We're here to help," Petticrew tried again.

She narrowed her eyes, tilting her head slightly, murmuring something in French.

Of course. She did not understand.

Me. This was for me! My time to shine. I blessed the aged tutor and his zoological handbooks, and dusted off my vocabulary properly. "*L'heure de repas!*" I declared, mentally double-checking. Yes, that was from the page with the zookeeper toting a pail of fish to the seals. *It is feeding time!* Glancing around, I saw a fork on the block behind me and picked it up, pointing it at her for emphasis.

She recoiled, aghast, and pulled the fire poker in front of her like a gate closing us away.

"What did you say to her?" Matthew hissed.

"I told her it was feeding time." She recoiled farther, even as I spoke in English.

He socked me on the shoulder. "And you're pointing your fork at *her*."

Realization set in and my face grew hot. "No, no," I said, offering her the smile that always earned me an eyelash bat or two from the ladies in Covent Garden. I gestured toward the potato pot. "For you!" And pointed at her. I twirled the fork in my hand, so that the prongs faced the pot, and not her.

Now she looked at me as if I belonged in Bedlam, with a proper diagnosis of insanity. I grinned wider, and she recoiled farther. It was as if every time she heard me speak—*me*! George Piccadilly, jolly old dunce that I am—it planted more fear. Was it my voice? My accent?

"You're making it worse." Matthew again. He dipped a ladle into the pot, poured the poor excuse for a stew into a chipped bowl, and held it out at his arm's full extension, crossing the room slowly, cautiously. A peace offering.

"For you," he said, pointing from the bowl to the young woman, and leaving it at the foot of her bed before backing up to a safe distance.

She eyed it and him, and for a moment I expected she'd fling the hot liquid at Matthew and we'd all run screaming for the ill-assured safety of the trenches. No fury like a woman's scorn, and all that. Surely Shakespeare had been speaking prophetically of this supposed lost heiress, caked in grime and curled up like a wild creature.

But she pulled the bowl toward herself and, after an instant of looking at it with suspicion, raised it to her lips and took a cautious sip. And another . . . and another . . . until soon, her hunger took over and she seemed to forget us.

Which was most satisfactory. I wasn't keen on death by fire poker. "Come on," I whispered. "Now's our chance. Let's go!" She did keep a close eye on Petticrew, but it was now or never.

I was out the door lickety-split and ready to run—and was close to the edge of the cottage's clearing before I realized I was alone. In the same moment, I turned and ran straight into the solid form of a soldier.

"Sorry, mate," I said. I offered my hand and pulled him up, looking over my shoulder to see if the others followed yet. "Did Sarge send you? I know we're late, but the thing of it is—"

A hand gripped my arm. Twisted fierce and pinned me down on the forest floor . . . where I looked up into the sunlit picture of a grey German uniform.

13

Matthew

Just that chipped bowl between her and me. She drank the broth, such as it was, and barely took her eyes off of me over the rim. It was easy to forget, standing there, that a war raged on just miles away. This place felt outside of time and reality as I stayed there in that stalemate of a staring match, each of us watching to see what the other would do.

George had barreled out the front door, and the result was an influx of peace. Even the girl—*Mireilles*, I reminded myself—seemed to breathe a very small bit easier. Jones stood at the bookshelf, absorbed in the pages, mumbling something about a family crest.

And I—I was caught. Anchored here, and yet lit by the Flame. My old friend, my old *fiend*. That driving force within. It told me to get her to safety. And yet . . . where was such a thing, in such a time? No place was safe.

As she set her bowl down, I made to step nearer, remove the bowl, show her we were there to help. But Hank Jones, the face of a thousand sons of America, beat me to it. He approached with a book open, and his expression more so.

"The book," he said, pointing at it. "Is it yours?" He gestured toward her.

She narrowed her eyes, still as a statue as she assessed him. Then, apparently finding he posed no significant threat, she gave a small nod. "*Mon* Grand-père."

I saw the way she cast a glance at a small frame that hung on the wall near me. There was such sadness in that look, in the way she bit her lip and for a moment was not a force but a wounded soul.

"Your grandfather's," I said. I touched the frame and let my hand linger as I silently asked permission. She nodded. I pulled the frame from the wall and studied the likeness of a young man, painted some years ago, judging by the yellowed edges of the paper. There was kindness about him but also the look of one who would brook no nonsense. Crossing the room, I handed the frame to her, feeling the way her hand trembled beneath mine as she took it.

Up close, I saw better how her eyes were circled in darkness beneath them, as the dirt had begun to flake off, and her pallor revealed that she had lived to the edge of all she had left, so pale and gaunt was she.

I'd seen such a look before, once. Many years ago.

She stroked the frame with her thumb, swiping quickly at her eyes with her free hand. And I knew—this had been who she had buried, hours before, with her own two hands. It was the dirt of his grave that lined her fingernails as she held his picture now.

Fingers I wished I could hold, to bring some measure of comfort. But knowing me, I'd only inflict clumsy awkward pain, somehow.

"Is that him?" Hank asked. I wished I'd thought to ask. But I already knew the answer. He pointed at the book, then at the frame, and she nodded affirmation.

He leaned in and studied the young face, his own expression registering disbelief.

"It's true," he said, speaking this time to me. "It's him."

"The balloon man?" I asked and wished the words back. I made him sound like a carnival spectacle. "The Marquis," I corrected myself.

"Yes. I'm certain. That is—almost certain."

"What does that mean for her?" I lowered my voice out of respect for her, though I knew she couldn't understand our words.

"It means—" Hank shook his head. "I'm not sure. It might mean a fortune awaits her. It might not."

He went on about "might" and "could" and all the possibilities, but I looked at her holding that picture, alone in this cabin, and knew what it *did* mean.

She was alone.

"Help!" The cry from outside was so jarring that she dropped the frame. I was at the door in a second, outside, weapon raised. Jones was right behind me. We silenced our footsteps as we'd been trained, scanning the borders of the view.

There, at the edge, was George Piccadilly. Hands raised, the bayonet of a German pointed right at him.

In an instant, Jones and I had him in our sights, weapons fixed and the cold click of gun registers bouncing off the trees. Jones was a surprisingly quick draw. Whether from taking part in our drills or always scratching away with that pen, I couldn't say.

The German looked about my age. Had a wedding band on his finger. Was following his own commanding officer's orders, no doubt, just as we were.

I hated that this war meant we so often had to point a weapon at a mirror in the flesh.

But something changed the next instant. The door creaked open slowly behind us, across the clearing. *No.* "Don't show yourself," I whispered through clenched teeth under my breath, knowing full well she would neither hear nor understand.

But sheer surprise registered on the soldier's face, showing me it was too late. The surprise was followed swiftly by interest—his eyes making free to roam over what he was seeing. Or rather, *who* he was seeing. And the roaming turned to lingering. I knew full well why, and what thoughts ran through his mind, no matter the language barrier.

The solitary good thing about his antics was that his guard was down. I made my move, thrusting my own bayonet so close it touched his throat, a millimeter away from piercing.

"Go," I said.

"Shouldn't we take him?" This, from George Piccadilly, who scrambled up and away like a crab on his back, struggling to stand. Jones thrust out a hand and pulled him up. "He's outnumbered. Surely we could—you know. Prisoner, and all that."

But I did not like the way the man's mouth curved up into a cold smile, as if he knew something we did not.

Not budging my weapon, I stared down the perimeter of the clearing. "We don't know if he's the one outnumbered . . . or if we are," I said in a low tone and waited for them to take my meaning. "We let him go, we might have a chance to get out of here. And"—I jerked my head back toward the cottage—"to take her with us."

Not in a thousand years would I leave her unattended now. There was no telling who now knew her whereabouts, nor what fate would befall a woman alone out here in the crosshairs of what General Pershing planned to be the major turning point in this never-ending war. We all felt it—this invisible unspoken something over and under and all around us, telling us we were treading on that turning point. That it was, perhaps, a months-long turning point, and the very air we breathed marched it onward even now.

It all hinged on this forest.

Her forest.

"You heard the man," George said, crossing his arms proudly. "Go on, then. And don't come back. If you please, sir."

He chose the oddest moments to let his latent polite British sensibilities surface.

The man leveled us each with a gaze so cool it was infuriating. As if he had the upper hand somehow, and we did not yet know it. With an odd smile, he raised his hands and began his backward retreat.

It was Hank Jones who followed him. The man would make a good soldier, had he not been saddled with the job of reporter. George followed suit, and by some miracle recovered from his floundering codfish ways and into a stealthy military man. He really was good, when he put his mind to it. Which he did, now. The two were near invisible, slipping into the trees and following the man.

Everything in my body told me to go, too—but something deeper anchored me there, close to the girl.

She had slipped back inside her cottage and closed the door, but I saw a slight movement at the window. Whoever she was—whether part of this fabled family Hank seemed so sure about, or

106

truly the peasant she seemed—she was used to living out here. Part of me thought she was probably better off out here without us.

At length, the door opened again, and this time she emerged with her old gun. She did not point it at me this time but instead held it in one hand while approaching warily, a cup in hand. She did not look at me but rather studied every rock and tree in sight. I watched her do it, saw how she swept it visually in a methodical grid. This was not new territory, this vigilant living.

She drew close, but not too close, and haltingly held out the cup.

I stared, unsure if I should take it.

She thrust it farther toward me, sloshing a good bit on my boot. I smiled. This girl did not need words to communicate.

"Thank you," I said. I raised it to my mouth and took a sip as a courtesy, but as the water slid past lips that stung with gratitude, I realized how parched my entire being was. It had been hours since I'd had anything to drink. She watched me steadily, and absurd as it was, I had to swallow down not just the water, but a rising laugh as well. There was no pretense here. No demurring or casting eyes politely away, and no shame in a hard and long stare. It was entirely amusing and consumingly refreshing.

I pulled the cup away from my mouth, then, astonished.

She tilted her head to the side, eyebrows pinching together ever-so-slightly as if to ask, *What is it?*

"Nothing," I said, and then truly did laugh, this time at myself. The sleep deprivation was catching up to me, otherwise I wouldn't be having a one-sided conversation like a lunatic. "It's just—I haven't laughed in . . ."

I shook my head, looked at the ground, where the answer buried itself somewhere in the mucky dark earth. I had no idea the last time I had felt that sensation.

And there she was, staring still, reaching to take the empty cup from my hand. Her fingers brushed mine, and I stilled.

Forget laughter. When was the last time I had felt a touch like that? Strong and soft, an offering to give water. Life. From the place of her own grief.

The answer was so far beyond just the horrors of this war, I could not put words to it.

I had never known a touch like that.

And then she pulled away, slowly. She held the cup up, asking, *More?*

Yes. Yes, and yes, more of this. This truth, this candid place of real and hope.

I gulped and nodded. "Please," I said. "Thank you." She turned to go, looking over her shoulder at me as she disappeared behind the cottage.

It was absurd, perhaps. That a fleeting touch and a cup of water in the woods could drive a man to such a place. But in that moment, I knew—I would get her to safety. I had to.

The men arrived back in the clearing, the look on their faces identical: one of doom.

"It's bad, mate," George said, wiping his brow with his arms.

"He wasn't alone?" I asked, readying my weapon.

"No, he was alone," Hank said, the voice of reason. "But judging by what we just saw, he won't be for long. They're moving into the forest. Readying for battle. It's a garrison, just waiting to be inhabited. Outposts, machine gun nests, rolls of barbed wire, some already spread wide. They've been digging and building for . . ." He shook his head. "I don't know how long, but we're lucky they haven't sniped us in the middle of the night yet, out here in all this."

The woods were big. Really big. This I knew and tried to believe we'd been safe until now. *She'd* been safe until now.

But we did not come to be safe. We came to do what needed to be done.

I looked at the little house that seemed straight out of the fairy-tale book Mrs. Bluet gave to Celia and me. Here it stood, right in path of the front's encroaching rumble from one side, and silent death creeping through the forest from the other.

There was only one thing to do.

"We have to tell Captain Truett."

14

Captain Jasper Truett

I dreamed of them again. Dreamed a memory. My June, and sweet Amelia, just three years old. I was home for Christmas that year, miracle of miracles. June had cut her own tree and bedecked it with diamonds. Diamonds, right there in the shack she'd moved into as a young bride. Might as well have been a palace, the way she didn't blink twice at the general cloud of bachelor life that marked the place. I'd done my best to sweep it up, wipe down walls, and do some other things that felt domestic to try and ready it for her, but I knew the truth and so did she: a two-room house in the Carolina woods was a far cry from the pristine pillared Charleston mansion she was accustomed to. God bless her, she hadn't blinked twice. Had only brushed her palms together with gumption and gotten to work, transforming it from little better than a cave into a real home.

It was only for a time, I'd promised. My girls deserved better, and they'd get it. This was just for a time. Which turned into a time, times, and half a time, as the Good Book would say. Much too long. But what did June do? Complain?

No. She disassembled a necklace and strung her Charleston diamonds on our Christmas tree. Sold a few of them, too, to afford the bright brass compass she'd wrapped in a scrap of dishcloth and tied like all the treasure in the world, leaving it beneath the tree for me. *"To find your way home to us,"* she said when I opened it. *"I checked the globe: north-by-northwest, from you to us. Panama to North Carolina. North-by-Northwest. Simple as that, and you'll find us."* She smiled, the sort of smile that'd stop a man in his tracks and take his breath, too.

In the dream I scooped up our small Amelia and it felt as real as when it happened, fifteen years ago. A newspaper with bold letters proclaiming the news from Kitty Hawk just days before: two brothers had lofted a flying machine into the air.

Men, *flying.*

"Look, Amelia," I'd said, hoisting her onto my knee and pointing to the sketch in the paper. She mimicked my gesture, tapping her little finger on the paper.

"Bird," she said, beaming at me with her proud pronunciation of the word.

I laughed and it was so full it ricocheted on my insides, on out into the world.

"Right," I said, leaning down until her tiny ear brushed my lips. "Like a bird," I whispered, then spoke low, waiting to see what she'd do. To Amelia, all the world was magic. "But this machine flies *people* into the sky. They call it a flyer."

She tilted her head, eyes wide and mouth agape.

"Would you like to fly?" I asked her.

"I can't fly," she said, smile dimpling into her plump pink cheeks and shaking her head so fiercely her curls veiled her face.

"Are you sure?" I picked her up, loving the feel of her feet kicking in excitement. "One . . ." I swung her. "Two . . ." I swung her higher in my arms, scooped around her to keep her safe and let her fly, all at once. "Three!" We launched, zooming around the tiny room as June clapped from the stove and Amelia's laughter pealed out, lighting our universe. I flew her around to the candles in the room, letting her blow them out and laughing when she declared she flew through the clouds as I flew her near the trails of smoke swirling above the extinguished luminaries.

That night as I tucked her in, sure from the way her head had grown heavy on my shoulder by the fire that sleep had long since claimed her, she fluttered her long lashes open and laid a hand on my cheek. Cupping it with trust and adoration I did not deserve.

"You fly back to us soon next time, Daddy," she said. "Soon . . ." And her sleepy voice trailed off.

I woke to the sound of planes tearing the sky open above me and to the approaching forms of two men who were about to find their commanding officer sleeping.

My face was wet.

This was why I longed for sleep but rarely slept. I could visit the good years, there . . . but I could not hide the effects of it on my face. It was as if my body knew, before my mind did, that I would awake to every bit of it vanished. My bit of paradise—a stolen piece I'd never deserved—obliterated by my own stupidity thirteen years before. And my men did not need to stumble upon a commanding officer with blasted tears on his face.

Vaguely I became aware of a presence nearby. I cleared my throat and ignored my wet face, standing swiftly and surely. This was what my men would need to see. My hand slipped inside my jacket, feeling the warm old brass of the compass and retrieving it. I opened it and snapped it shut again, letting the swift, sure *click* proclaim my presence for them, too.

Two lumberjacks—Petticrew and that chaplain—stood before me in the uniforms of American soldiers and spouted the most preposterous excuse for abandonment I'd had the privilege to hear.

I'd seen it in the face of every soldier since we crossed over the ocean: disillusionment. They'd thought they were coming to be heroes, with visions from their boyhood of valiantly riding into battle. And what they'd found was a war of machines and a cloud of poison gas. Of darkness and hunger, explosions and commanding officers asking, ceaselessly, everything of them.

Some went mad. Some adjusted. And some—well, this was a first, I had to admit.

"A regular damsel in distress," I said, dubiously.

I looked to the maps spread on the table made of crates, the yellow light swinging above us as an artillery shell hit nearby. I had no time for nonsense. I'd lost enough time sleeping when I should have been strategizing. Word had it the enemy was planning another attempt for Paris, and we'd need every last resource to outwit and outman them. The sooner I got these men back to the trenches and out of this space, the better. I needed a revelation, and fast. The maps were beginning to blur before my eyes. "You think you're knights in shining armor?"

"No, sir." This from Petticrew, who at least stood at attention, except for his hands, which were oddly behind his back instead of at his sides. He'd come a long way from the lost kid at Plattsburg. He'd been made for this. A fact that filled me with pride and dread.

"Well, one doesn't wish to boast, of course, but more than a few people *have* told me I resemble Lancelot." The Briton spoke. Every time he spoke I wondered how he ended up here, with us, and not a blight upon his own army.

"Lancelot."

"Yes, sir."

"Of King Arthur's Court," I said.

"The very same." He stood taller.

"The one who betrayed his own king and friend in the worst of ways."

Piccadilly the Briton stammered, floundering like a beached fish.

"What he means, sir," piped up Petticrew, "is that we believe we can get the woman to safety, and quickly. The next village, perhaps."

Piccadilly leaned in and spoke out of the side of his mouth to his friend. "But Jones said the family palace was in Paris."

"A palace. In Paris. This gets better and better," I said. "And at what point does the lady kiss a frog and turn him into royalty?"

Piccadilly laughed. "Well, now, no one is presuming, but I certainly wouldn't be one to object if she—"

Petticrew cleared his throat. "He means we sound like we're spouting stories."

"That's easy enough to fix, I'd say. Come with us."

Suddenly the maps on the table before me did not seem so urgent.

112

"Do you mean to tell me," I said through gritted teeth, "that you have brought a civilian—a *woman*—to the front?"

"No, sir." Petticrew. He didn't mince words and stood up to own his actions—even if they were the most preposterous thing I'd encountered yet. "We didn't bring her all the way. But we couldn't leave her alone, with the enemy encroaching on her cottage."

I considered, then nodded. It was unconventional. And yet it was why we were here: to protect the innocent. To turn the tide of this war, even if for one soul.

"Very well," I said. "Take me."

I hadn't been above ground, out of that dark hovel of an officer's quarters, in a week at least. It didn't help that it was noon and the sun had chosen that moment to emerge from its own cloudy cave.

Petticrew slowed his pace in front of me, looking at the men in the trench ahead and then back at me, and I nearly collided with him.

"Onward, Petticrew."

He looked to the side. "Yes, sir." But he didn't budge.

"Well, what is it?"

He did some kind of grim-lined smile, like he had to tell me something but didn't want to. He lifted his cuff to his face and rubbed.

I spread my stance wider, wrinkling my forehead in question.

He tapped his cheek.

"Something wrong with your face, Petticrew?"

Eyes to the side, he looked like he didn't know how to answer that. "I, uh . . ."

"Well? Spit it out, son."

Flustered, he did. "Not my face, Captain."

He let his meaning hang and pointed at the shard of a shaving mirror one of the privates had mounted in the mud.

Living in the ground left a man's face good and dusty. And if a good and dusty face went and cried like a baby in its sleep . . . my face was as mapped and dry-rivered as the papers I went cross-eyed studying every day.

113

I took my palm to my face and rubbed it good, trying not to think on how Petticrew and Piccadilly had seen it and not said a word. It was in character for Petticrew . . . and I admit, loathfully, that my respect for the buffoon-chaplain went up a few notches.

Petticrew had walked on, good man. Pulling myself up, clearing my throat, I followed. Refusing the rapid-fire blinking that wished to clear my vision, I followed the two some distance to the edge of the woods and into its boundary.

There, I found the blithering journalist, Hank Jones, pacing. I seethed.

"You brought a civilian from her home, to the front, and left her with the man who will plaster the entire United States with the tale?" My career in the military was over. There would be such outcry over this.

Maybe it was just as well. What had all my dedication won me, after all? Medals, honors, more prestigious missions—but it had robbed me of more.

"He's not so bad," Petticrew said, measuring his words. "I don't think he plans to write any of this."

"You 'don't think,'" I said. "Precisely."

Jones froze when he saw us, looking to his left furtively, where indeed stood a woman among a stand of trees. She had her palms to them and was looking up into their waving branches, watching them as intently as my boys in the watchtowers trained their eyes on low-flying planes.

"Amelia."

The low-toned word was out before I knew it. How many times had I pictured her, what she would look like now . . . and now here was the living, breathing picture of what I had so long envisioned my daughter to be like.

Same dark hair. Same blue-as-sky eyes. My thumb went to the small indentation where the compass latch lay and pressed it. *Click.* It opened, along with a crack somewhere inside of me.

"Sir?"

Petticrew's voice inserted itself into the flash of memory. I saw

114

my girl, slipping into the Carolina woods, long curls flying and laughter trailing like the robe of a queen. I saw her mother run after her, reaching back to grasp my hand, as she had a thousand times. And I saw that same hand let go, finger by finger, when I left again. Felt Amelia's little-girl lips press against my cheek to say good-bye. Laughing, still.

"Sir?"

I had half a mind to slug the man, snatching me out of the memory. But the images vanished like vapor, and before me stood the young woman.

Not Amelia, I told myself, in no uncertain terms. Amelia was gone. This girl before me, she had a faraway look, as if a spark had gone out somewhere inside. Amelia never appeared that way . . . but I knew too well how that felt.

"You said something, sir?"

I cleared my throat. "How long will you be gone?"

Petticrew's face registered confusion.

"If you go. When you go." I barked, trying to regain my composure. "When you take her. How long before you return."

"I—I don't know, sir. The next village is a few days from here, I think."

Days. That wasn't good. But what could I do? Send her off alone into a war-torn land that would eat her alive?

Not a chance.

Though the way she scanned the front, the way it all registered on her features into a strange mix of compassion and quick comprehension, I wouldn't be surprised if she showed us all up and survived that journey with more savvy than any of us.

My mind kicked into gear, working the pieces of this puzzle just like the maps back in the trenches.

I paced. Drilled the men for answers—*where is she from?* The woods. *Before that?* Nowhere, they thought. As far as they could tell, she'd lived there always. Her family before that . . . in Paris. Probably. *Where would she go?* An old family estate, perhaps? They didn't sound convinced and therefore weren't very convincing.

I wanted to send them. To get the girl to safety. Return this fabled personage to her inheritance, apparently. If we could not give France complete victory now—or perhaps ever—then perhaps this was something we could do.

I'd get upbraided from headquarters, if they were wrong. Raked over the coals and torn to bits, sending perfectly battle-able bodies on a wild-goose chase.

I said as much.

Matthew Petticrew didn't budge but didn't speak, either. He appeared to be scouring the scene beyond us for further argument. I was surprised the trees didn't burn down right then and there under the intensity of his gaze. Their leaves shivered—perhaps in relief—as that same gaze shifted to the reporter.

In a stride, Petticrew thrust his hand out. The two seemed to converse in a silent tug-o'-war staring match, and then the reporter placed a book in Petticrew's waiting hand.

Petticrew strode over to me and held it out until I took it, reluctantly. Something was afoot here that I would doubtless regret.

And all the while the Amelia look-alike was watching, her presence cinching my lungs, scrambling my thoughts and tossing them back so many years.

"What's this," I said, refusing to open the book.

Petticrew looked at the reporter, then tipped his head at the book. Pleading.

"If I may, sir . . ." the reporter said. He approached, glancing at my hand, which iron-gripped the open compass.

No, you may not, I wanted to say. His words were trouble. Always. I'd seen it in the paper and had little use for more of them. "Speak on," I said anyway. It'd buy me time to think.

He launched into a story from forty-some-odd years ago. His limbs came to life, hands gesturing. Even the girl watched him warily now, her eyes fixed on him in keen study.

She caught me watching her and averted her gaze back to the trees, attempting to look clueless.

I wanted to laugh. Amelia had done that when I'd caught her

as a tot with a chubby finger in the cherry pie and she'd looked horrified at her hand, as if it had acted of its own accord.

"And then there are her grandfather's notes, sir." Jones motioned to the book again. "Schematics and strategy—it looks like he took the whole Prussian invasion and dissected it in the years that followed. It reads like a guide for how to prevent such an invasion again. It's . . . I'm no military expert, sir, but for what it's worth, I believe this is one for the history books."

I stopped pacing. I opened the book, slowly. "History books," I said. Forget history books. If this was what Jones said it was . . . this could be the making of history right now, right in this moment. If Germany was intent on attempting invasion again—I flipped through the pages. Scanning the diagrams, the notes. Looking closer. Scanning again.

The reporter was right. And though I hated to own it, he was maybe not as useless as I'd judged him. Maybe.

In truth . . . this was pure genius.

My thumb tapped the glass of the compass. The journalist leaned in, peering at it and narrowing his eyes.

"If I may, sir, I could even show you how our present position aligns with potential strategic positions for . . ." he rambled on, gesturing at the compass.

"It doesn't work," I said, hammering a nail into the coffin of that idea fast.

He looked puzzled. "The position?"

"The compass. No need to show me."

"It's broken?" Hank Jones said, leaning forward, viewing it through his spectacles.

"Yes. Long since." And if a man like me ever even had a heart . . . that broke the same day.

"I might be able to fix it, if you don't mind me taking a look."

"There's none who can fix this, son." I snapped it closed, stuffed it back inside my jacket. By the place a heart would've beat.

"I just mean if you'll let me try . . . I'm not an expert, sir, but I might get it to where it regains some of its function."

117

"It functions just fine," I muttered. Broke it might be, but it still did its job. It reminded me.

I pulled in a breath. "Clock's ticking," I said, indicating I recognized that time was imperative in this scheme of theirs. And redirecting the journalist's thoughts, I hoped.

The-girl-who-was-not-Amelia had to get out of here. Far, far, far from me . . . from those memories. They'd bind me tight and render me useless if I didn't take care.

"Paris," I said. "Take her there." It was farther from the front. Closer to everything she might need. And far from me. "And then—if she is amenable to it—carry the book on to Provins after that." The French army headquarters was there at the moment.

"That might take . . ."

"Weeks, at least, if we're on foot," Piccadilly piped up, looking all too eager to take the full amount of time. "Do send me too, sir. I have extensive navigational experience." He pulled back his shoulders, looking rather proud of himself.

"I'm sure you do," I said. *Navigating lies and pomp.* And this was supposed to be our chaplain? It would do him good to see some of the world and be put in his place.

And get the reporter out of my sight, to boot.

The girl was approaching, slowly. Her skirts were soaked in mud, tattered in some places. She murmured something in French, studying me in a way that held me captive.

"What did she say?" I knew I needed to sharpen my ability to translate.

"Something about chickens," Piccadilly said, sounding rather pleased with himself. "Or geese."

She did not look as if she spoke of chickens. She looked as if she saw straight through me, maybe saw my Amelia, my June, both tucked down in the dark where I never let their memory away from the pounding in my chest. Not for a second.

"You three take her. Get some food, canteens, supplies." I thought of Petticrew, the things he'd suffered in the last battle. It would do him good to get away . . . and selfishly, mournfully, I knew it might

118

send him back refreshed and more ready for the next battle. Which would be, I anticipated, infinitely more intense, and much longer, than the last. We would need his quick instincts on the field. In a war of numbers, every man counted—and I fought hard against the way those numbers quickly turned into faces in my mind. Faces like Petticrew's. It was too hard.

"We need you back before three weeks is gone," I said.

I could see the wheels in Petticrew's head turning. It would be much, for them to make it to Paris and back in that amount of time. It wasn't just a matter of miles. It was the unpredictability of war-torn terrain. Roads sometimes navigable, sometimes not. Enemy and espionage tucked behind our lines. That meant every step in that journey would be on high alert and anything could happen. It wouldn't be a vacation, but it would still be time away from the trenches.

"You'll be on foot for much of it, but you might find transport by supply rail or truck for portions. Keep a look out for them."

Petticrew nodded, looking certain, but a flash of fear underpinned his stance.

"Listen," I said. "Everything you men have done up till now is impossible. Not one of you could have imagined the front a year ago. But here you are. You're doing it. And you'll do this, too. Yes, it might be impossible. But one second at a time will get you there. One second at a time is *not* impossible."

I said it. And wanted to believe it. And recalled a time I had to believe it or else I'd have given up and fallen by the wayside, never to rise again. I had been a father, and you never get back from having that ripped right out of your life. Fact is, I never did let go of it. Nobody saw that part of me, anymore . . . nobody even knew. But you never stop being a father. A part of me stayed back there, in 1904, and always will.

One second at a time was not impossible. I'd lived a decade and a half that way. These boys needed to hear it now, maybe more than I ever had.

15

Mira

The first night swallowed us up in darkness.

The English fellow, the one who had tried to tell me of their plan in broken French, snored like my old dog Gustave, who'd had white fur with big brown spots, flopping ears and adoring eyes. In a way, the fellow George reminded me of Gustave's ways, too, bounding about quite without a clue, saying things that made no sense, but making one feel as if he were a very old friend.

But I did not trust it.

The one with the spectacles—Henry or Hank, nobody seemed quite sure which—he was quiet but studious. It was hard to tell what their names were. The soldiers liked to use surnames, as if even their syllables were marching. But I was listening hard and listening to learn, and I thought I had discovered their given names. Henry or Hank Jones, George Piccadilly, Matthew Petticrew.

Henry-or-Hank seemed much more a Henry to me. Hank— what manner of name is that at all? It sounds like an illness of the skin to me. *I have the Hank*, one might say of themselves when afflicted with it. I scolded myself. Hank was probably a very fine name in America.

Yet he seemed to feel the same about it as I. He did not even respond to it, when George Piccadilly called him so. As if he'd forgot his own name. Only when George said "Henry" did he look up. He seemed intelligent and had things to say. He knew how to follow a map and draw one, too. He had not spoken any more of this idea of his that I was the granddaughter of a lost aristocrat. If he had known Grand-père, he would know it to be impossible.

Henry knew his plants, too, and had managed to brew us a tea of chamomile to drink with the tin of beans we all shared for dinner. He made one feel that he was a very trustworthy guide.

But I did not trust it.

And then there was the other one, who seemed always to be listening. To what, I did not know, for I was careful not to speak. But his eyes seemed to hear things even when his ears could not. When my thoughts traveled back to my grandfather in the ground and my heart felt like it would stop beating for the pain of it—I felt his eyes on me, and they were soft. Knowing. As if he could read my thoughts, and I was safe. I could tell he had known such pain too, and therefore he carried mine with care.

But I did not trust it. I would never trust it. Of the three men, he frightened me most. I kept my eyes on him, that he might be afraid of me instead.

So we slumbered in the dark—me by the fire Matthew had built, George and Hank and Matthew all spaced far from me and at intervals, like so many guards. Matthew, though, did not sleep. He was as quiet as the others, never moved an inch—but I could feel his wakefulness, even as my own faded into sleep. It was a force all its own. When I awoke, it was to air chilled by a nearly arrived October, and to find myself covered in a blanket that had been dusted off but still held streaks of dried mud.

They all slept but Matthew, who was nowhere in sight.

I could have escaped so easily then. But the truth was, I could have escaped at any moment. I knew the woods, and they did not. I knew how to live here, and they did not. But where would I go? Certainly not to Paris. I had no intention of going to Paris. But I did know someone. A single soul in all the world who might help me. And perhaps I might help her, too. She lived in Fontaine d'Argonne, where we would stop for supplies and rest next, according to the plan of the men. The village we so often went to for market now suddenly seemed a beacon of hope on the horizon.

These were my thoughts, woven in the clarity of fresh morning. The fog of yesterday had lifted, and it felt nice to have a plan. I did not depend upon three Americans. But they were, I knew, the better fate than many others who might find me on my own.

So I did not escape. I circled the clearing by turns, going deeper only to find more berries for breakfast.

When I returned, I found Matthew with arms full of kindling, face serious. When he saw me, his features relaxed a little but remained somber. A quick study of the clearing showed more footprints—his, for the others slept on—going in many different directions into the trees surrounding. More directions than one armload of sticks warranted.

"Good morning," he said quietly, with a nod. I returned the gesture, wary. He took a step nearer the now-cold fire, and so did I. We mirrored one another step by step, entering into a cautious dance of fire-building. He, laying the kindling. Me, stowing the berries upon a flat stone. He, laying dried leaves as tinder, searching, I presume, for the can he'd pulled out the night before that held matches. Me, standing in stubborn, silent battle with myself.

I could help. I *should* help. I had matches, even if only a few. I laid my hand upon my skirt pocket and felt the outline of my little worn cardboard box, the one Papa had entrusted to me as if it were his greatest treasure. The rattling inside it was quieter than it used to be, with so very few matches left. Four, when I had lit the lantern in the woods two nights before and brought all of this upon myself. Had it only been two nights past, truly? It felt like two hundred.

I wanted to hoard my dwindling supply. Clutch it to myself like a selfish child. As if that would somehow bring Papa back, make this all vanish. By clinging to these last matches, I held fast to a single tattered thread, attached to him somewhere away in the unknown.

"Keep the fire burning." His last words to me.

I drew in a shuddering breath, pulled the box from my pocket.

Slid the tray out and watched those four little sticks roll around, clattering like dry bones.

Something inside me hurt. It ached, so terribly. I pulled out one of the matches. Clutched it fast in my hand, fingers curled tight around it. Closed my eyes. *Please, God.* I prayed, for the ten thousandth time. *Bring him home.*

And then, by sheer force of determination, I opened my fingers and held out my hand. Offered the match to the soldier.

Opening my eyes, I saw he watched me. Studying, reading me.

Which frustrated me to no end, when I wished to clutch these embers of dying hope deep inside of me far from anybody's view.

But he held my gaze fast. Seeing, if not understanding, the great struggle within. Solemnly he accepted the match, holding it with care, lifting it with a nod to say, *"See, I will take care, I promise."*

And my fortress grew higher. *Do not trust it.*

He struck the match upon a rock and lit his dried grasses and leaves, shielding the fledgling flame with his hands as a small breeze tumbled through.

The kindling caught fire, snapping pleasant greetings of coming warmth, and a smile kindled upon his solemn face, too. He stood and stepped back, gesturing for me to step closer to it and warm myself.

Swallowing the burn in my throat, I neared the burn of the flames, tucking my last three matches in their box back into safety. Matthew's listening eyes searched mine. He knew that to ask was futile, but he could not seem to help it.

"Where did you go?" he asked. His voice was serious but kind as he scanned the outskirts of our camp. He was doing this, always. Searching. Vigilant. "Are you alright?"

Yes, I nearly said. *No*, I nearly sobbed. But I said nothing. He looked so concerned, I wished I could reach past this barricade and at least give him relief from his questions. So much weighed upon this soul, this man who said so little. I gave a small smile and could feel the relief in the way his shoulders eased. I gestured to my offering of berries, making my eyes wide to invite him to eat.

He looked so hungry I thought he might drop right there. But then he looked at his sleeping comrades. Understanding, I knelt and made three piles of the berries. Six in each pile—with one left over. I put it in his pile and picked them up, all seven, to hand to him.

He only stared. His stomach rumbled and that needed no translation. For the first time, he broke his gaze and drilled it only into the ground, embarrassed. I picked up his palm and poured the berries in. After a moment, he counted out three, closed his hand around them, and gave four back to me.

And then, the oddest thing—we smiled at one another. Less than a moment, perhaps both of us feeling the shame of a smile at such a time, in the midst of war and death and uncertain future. But that tiny smile fed my soul more than any amount of berries ever could.

It tasted—it tasted like hope.

It was that hope that carried us long, long, long through the day. When we reached Fontaine d'Argonne at last, I could never have anticipated the wave of comfort that came with it. There was the Rue de Fontaine, a street cobbled with comfort. I had not been there for over a year, and never expected the window boxes to be still splashed with color. I had forgotten the way ivy clung to the rock walls of the homes, as if it had crept down from the forest to bring wilderness and air to the village. There was the fountain that gave the town its name. As we approached, a line of women came in from the south, looking weary as they washed their arms and hands. This had always been the ritual of the men working the fields. But of course the men were in different fields now. War-torn fields, fighting.

This hour was once my favorite, here. Families would sit on balconies and front steps. There was an older gentleman who would sit and play his violin, sending the sun off to sleep. And the sun, in response, always lit the sky with colors afresh, every night. A lullaby back to the village. Grand-père and he used to talk long about the man's goat, whom he kept in a pen and who sang to

124

the man's violin with his bleating and with hay hanging from his goat beard. The goat would look at me through his funny slitted eyes and chew his hay and happily welcome my hand scratching his coarse hair.

The man was gone now. His goat, too. And his house. It was an empty space most jarring. Ruins that would have looked pretty had they been taken by time in the natural course of things, with ivy grown over to soften the hard, broken edges.

But it was all hard, broken edges. Taken in one blow from shelling, and not at all in the natural course of things. I reached out to touch the rough edges of its broken walls and felt so like it.

My eyes stung. I prayed the man was safe somewhere. His goat, too.

We approached the fountain, and the men waited until the women were done. The girls looked askance at them. I recognized one of them—a girl who used to sell goose feather pillows at the stall near ours on market day. She whispered to me, "Who are they?"

"Americans," I said back. "From across the sea. They have come to help the war." I bent over the water to splash some on my face in hopes of clearing my head. But the creature who stared back at me in rippled reflection told me I needed much more than head-clearing. I cleaned my arms and my face, like my old acquaintance did. I patted my wayward hair, knowing there was little hope of taming the mangled halo of dark curls.

"No," one of the women protested. "America has not come for the war. We have heard no such news."

"It is true," I said, my French matching hers. Papa had been right. Another language was a secret strength. I had little worry over George Piccadilly's farmstead French translations following our conversation.

"And what do they do here with you?"

To answer that would be to tell so many tales I wished to forget. "They . . . are on their way to Paris."

"And you?"

"Here. To see Aline."

The girl drew back slowly. "Aline," she repeated. Her frown sent a tremor into my heart.

"*Oui.* Is she well?"

"She is . . . she is well," the girl said tentatively. "As well as can be expected."

"What do you mean?"

She pursed her lips and scrubbed her hands harder. "You will see." She lifted her chin to gesture up the street where Aline lived.

She talked on about the village. She was brave, I thought, for seeing blessings here in this place where whole houses had been snatched away. They were lucky, she said. Other villages, like Beaulieu-en-Coteau, down the road many miles, had been ground nearly to powder. *Death traps*, she called them. But they were lucky, here.

She took her leave, and in the absence of the women from the field, the men were enraptured with the water, all three. One would think they had never seen it before, the way they drank it in from the steady running metal spout and sloshed it upon the skin of their arms, and the way George looked ready to bounce into it with his whole self.

And now how to tell the men I would take my leave to see a friend? To make them not panic and startle the village by sending them pounding on every door in search of me, their charge. I had heard their commanding officer's instructions and felt the weight of it upon me.

But Henry-or-Hank was pointing to a river that sounded through the field beyond the village, and in his discreet and respectful way, was mentioning something about "getting themselves clean" to the other two. The other two agreed, and Matthew looked to me, doubtless wondering how to tell me not to come, to wait for them. "Any chance your French tutor taught you how to say 'we'll be back and looking much more human soon'?"

George, bless him, concentrated so hard he looked like he might explode. Then, with a satisfied smile, he stumbled terribly over something that sounded a little like French and translated roughly to "The farmer will harvest the barn!"

I nodded gravely, signaling I understood. Matthew narrowed his eyes, watching the exchange.

Not wishing them to panic if they should return to find me gone, I thought to leave a symbol that I would soon return. I slipped off my apron, folded it neatly, set it on the fountain wall, and disappeared up the way toward Aline's business and home.

It was a shadowing twilight and a hush that ushered me toward the *boulangerie*. It smelled of fresh bread but was shut tight. Where the wooden *Closed* sign once hung in the window, a newer one, painted by hand with the words *Until Tomorrow*, hung in bright white.

The flat above the bakery glowed with soft candlelight, one of the windows cracked open. With no stair on the outside, I could not knock to gather her attention.

"Aline," I said in a voice that resembled a loud whisper.

No reply, but I heard her singing, the sound of pots clinking against each other in her little kitchen.

"Madame Aline?"

The singing grew louder, as if a maestro had just cued an operetta.

I waited for a rest in the music and then cupped my hands around my mouth. "Aline!"

The singing stopped. The pots fell silent. Soon, the rounded, familiar figure of the older woman approached the window. "*Peut-il être?*" She pressed her hand to her heart. "Can it be? Mon Mireilles?"

My name, cradled in her old familiar warmth—*my Mireilles*—washed me with comfort.

"Oui! How are you, Aline?"

A string of exclamations followed as she left the window abruptly. I smiled, knowing she had not abandoned me. She was only drawing away in order to draw nearer. It was her way.

True to that way, she came bustling through her shop, out into the night where a bell rang when she opened the door. A blanket of words enveloped me right along with her generous embrace.

"Mireilles!" she said, bracing my shoulders and holding me at arm's length to assess me. "You are a twig! Come. We will get you fed."

I was certainly no twig, though my face had looked wan and gaunt in that rippling reflection. She ushered me into the shop, lighting a candle at one of the two little round tables. "It is not what it should be," she said, reappearing from behind the counter and sliding a plate in front of me.

"Not what it should be? Aline! This is the feast of a king. I have not dined so well since . . ." I shook my head, uncertain. We had run out of wheat a month ago. The closest thing I had had to this was the boiled potato cooked up by the American men yesterday. A kind gesture to be sure, but in my grief, I had hardly tasted a thing.

"This is so generous," I said.

"Nonsense. It is three days old. Three! It would be bad enough if it was a day old. Never underestimate the power of fresh bread, mon papillon."

My hand froze halfway to my mouth. I had not been called so for three years. Not since Papa left.

Her hand reached over. I thought she meant to grasp mine, to squeeze it in comfort the way I imagined a mother or grandmother would. But instead she nudged it up to my mouth. "Eat!" she said. "I will not have you melt into nothing before my eyes."

I ate. Half of me feeling guilty that I was partaking and the soldiers were not. But I would rectify that. I had a little coin. I could buy them a loaf, as thanks for seeing me safely here, and bid them *adieu*.

A twinge of sadness surprised me, and it was the serious soldier's silent, sad eyes that were at the root of it. I took a bite and chewed slowly. Perhaps I should go to Paris with them, after all.

A pain in my belly told me otherwise. Where had such a thought come from? There was nothing for me there. No, this was best.

"Aline," I said. "How are you?" I repeated the question. I needed to know before I could ask what I meant to of her. I had always thought of her as a sort of godmother, like the cinder girl in the

128

storybook. And she had always had a sort of magic about her, though it took the form of flour instead of fairy dust. Even so, I did not know how to ask if I might stay, when I had nothing to offer but my own two hands and whatever work they might give.

"I am well, *mon chérie*. I am well. These are trying times, no? But as you see, the bread must be baked, and that is a gift."

"And the flowers must be planted, I see. Your boxes look beautiful." They were dripping with sweet white blossoms, and the warmth of the setting sun nudged their honey scent inside the windows she had cracked open.

I took another bite, willing the crunch of the crust to last. Picking up each last crumb from the cracked plate with my fingertip, savoring them as they melted away in my mouth.

"Just so," she said. "The sun does not cease to shine just because there is a war. And neither do bellies stop growling at supper. So, we plant our seeds, and we bake our bread, and there is life in these things. It is good. Good to have something to set our hands to. Which reminds me, it is time for me to set the dough to rise for the morning baking. Come! You remember how? Of course you do. Eat and then come. We will talk as we work. You will tell me of your Grand-père. How is he?"

I grasped my dish and followed her into the kitchen. I forced myself to tell her of Grand-père.

She stopped her bustling and turned her large brown eyes on me, cupping my face with her weathered hands. Hands that trembled. How had I not noticed before?

She spoke no words of comfort. Perhaps she understood there were no words. Perhaps, like us all, she had run out of words for the never-ending loss of the war. She only held me, and beheld me, for a very long time.

And then she handed me a bowl. "You stir," she said. She pulled down a sack from a shelf and I marveled at her strength. She had aged quickly in this war, as so many had. Her hair snow white and that hand trembling every moment. But she was strong, lifting that bag down.

Only when she set it in front of me did I see that it had perhaps not taken so much strength. It was nearly empty. "Shall I get another?" I said, gesturing to the back, where she kept her stores of flour sacks.

"No need," she said. "Or rather, no use. There is not another. But we will make do with what we have, and it will be good."

"The grain," I said. It was what was harvested here, in the fields beyond the village. Surely that was what the women at the fountain had been working on even today. "Shall I fetch you more from the mill?"

She laughed. "Only if you can beat the soldiers to it," she said. "They take it for the men at the front. They leave some, and we get by. It is just . . ." she fluttered her hand, searching for an explanation. "The way of things, now. The soldiers need to eat. They protect us."

I winced. "Soldiers." I thought of the three who would soon be looking for me. How long had I been gone? Time slowed here, and I had lost all sense of it. I would have to come to my point soon, so that I could release them of their sworn duty.

"Yes. But we get wheat from time to time and when we do—" she twirled her hand over the small room—"I bake! And the villagers come. They have been so good to old Aline. Monsieur Terret gave me his shoelaces for a loaf last week. See?" She pointed at the windows. "I am now able to draw my curtains up and keep them there by tying them with the laces. Do not worry, I washed them four times! And Mademoiselle Brodeur traded me a promised sack of wool from her sheep, when next she is able to shear them. So I shall be warm by and by, you see."

Her joyful tone, though very true, began to open my eyes. Madame Aline, my old friend, was on hard times.

"And . . . do you need help here, in the bakery?" I asked, perhaps too hopeful.

"I? Not I. But when I do, I call upon my boarder."

"You have a boarder?" My voice sounded small.

"Oui. The daughter of the tailor, you recall him. He is gone, now, I am sad to say."

"To the front?"

She hesitated. "Oui . . . and since, gone on to heaven."

The words pummeled the breath from me. A vision of my own father, of the lantern hung and lit for him, unanswered. There was hollow sorrow inside of me when I thought of him and could not—would not—put words to the creeping, growing sense of knowing that visited me often.

I knew, in some part, what it was to lose a father. And the girl, the tailor's daughter—she was much younger than I. A child, still. Aline had taken her in . . . her "boarder." Able to pay less than shoelaces and sacks of wool. And consuming far more.

Aline did not need another mouth to feed, even if I could somehow help.

My eyes were opened and my heart was crushed—for Aline, for the empty grain sack, for the girl with no home who was perhaps even now upstairs. And yes, perhaps selfishly, I was crushed for myself, too. For having nowhere to go, for the unseen things I carried with me and did not know what to do with.

"What is your question, mon chérie?" she asked me, resting from her kneading of the meager loaf.

"I—" I looked around, searching for something. I did have one thing I could still ask, though I hated to take anything from her. "I am with three soldiers," I said. "They . . . are hungry. Can I buy a loaf from you?"

"Nonsense!" Her hands flew up, scattering flour over her already-white hair. "You will not pay. Take this. Take it and be well," she said, thrusting a broken half-loaf into my arms. "And you will come and see old Aline again very soon, yes? From that cottage of yours?"

I nodded, wishing it might be so. Not telling her that my home was likely occupied, even now, by an enemy who would take everything they could from our land. Who had already taken so much.

"Go. Take that to your soldiers, and return. You will sleep here tonight. I will make you a pallet, like when you were a tiny thing."

And so I did. I took a meager broken loaf to three grown men who approached the fountain in the dark. I motioned to where

I would stay and managed to help George understand the word *dormer*. They made camp beneath a tree at the end of Aline's road. And in the safety of the boulangerie, in the quiet of the dark with tiny crickets singing through the cracked window—a miniature symphony with courage enough to play in this war—I lay upon a blanket on the floor and wept silently.

Tomorrow, I would go onward toward Paris. How, I did not know. I lay still in the dark, pain settled in my bones. My feet, my back . . . my heart. I was stuck. I could not turn back. I knew not what lie ahead. And as the night stretched on into darkness, my future unfurled into an aching dark question mark, too.

16

Matthew

Again, sleep did not come. I did not want it to. I thought of the journey ahead, of the haunted ways of the girl Mireilles. I thought of her home, her sudden loss of so much. And I remembered keenly what it felt like to have a home ripped out from under you.

I closed my eyes to rest them. They ached from the constant surveying of our surroundings. I saw the way Mireilles walked—not just on our journey, but her way of being. Strong, savvy, and yet I caught a flash of fear in her eyes every now and then. She, like me, was ever vigilant. Every sense alert, planning for any possibility.

I prayed she would rest well tonight. I prayed I wouldn't fall asleep—and that somehow I would rise with my senses refreshed. As if I'd slept a thousand nights. Mr. Haggerty used to tell me tales whenever I helped him as a boy in Maplehurst's many gardens. One of them was of a widow who had nothing, but whose supply of oil to make bread for her and her child never ran out, no matter how many loaves she baked. *"You remember that, Mr. Matthew. The God who'll do that will watch out for you just as well, mark my words. Nothing too hard or far for Him to do."* I never realized, back then, that he was infusing my soul with truth I'd need one day. That he preached to me there in the garden mud just as sure as if he'd worn a clergyman's collar and I'd sat in a pristine pew.

Rest my body and keep me from sleep, I prayed.

Pulling Chester's artillery shell from my haversack and my knife from my jacket pocket, I turned my thoughts to Mireilles and set to carving. She was a curiosity, according to Henry and his notes. I didn't like it, the way he jotted things down, watching her through his glasses. Always with respect, but always with that look on his face as if she were a puzzle and he had to solve her.

Her song wound through my memory. Her voice so pure, high notes clear and minor notes embodied with care, stepping into a swirl that reached into my chest and wrapped itself around the beating organ inside. From there it traversed my veins, on out to my fingertips and into the etching I now set my hand to.

I thought of her with her matches this morning. She'd been so deep in thought she didn't realize, I think, that her mouth moved around silent words as she counted them like her last coin: *un, deux, trois, quatre* . . .

And then she'd sacrificed one. Her box and tray were worn next to nothing. Enough print remained that I could barely make out the type upon it: *Bessette Match Factory, Purveyors of Pure Light. London.* A different design than those of the same name I'd seen soldiers light their cigarettes with. Same company, but this box from another time.

My fingers stilled. I knew, then, what to do with the artillery shell.

The song wove through me again. My voice tried to match it, and I quickly decided I should stick to carving rather than trying to hum. Then again, my pitiful off-key attempt might do a good deal to keep the enemy far from us.

The hours passed quickly, with my hands pinpricking a design and cutting metal, bending it into shape, gentling sharp edges upon unsuspecting rocks. My injured hand forgot its ache a bit, and forgot its tremor entirely, as if this new movement of bone and muscle were easing it—even if only centimeter by painstaking centimeter—away from its place of constant pain.

The shell was far from finished, but it began to take shape. I buried the excess scraps of metal in the soil as dawn broke and two foreign sounds greeted me: birdsong and kitchen clatter. I elbowed the others awake—Hank blinking bleary eyes and George mumbling off-key notes of *ta-ra-ra-boom-dee-ay* as he fumbled into consciousness. We straightened ourselves up as best we could, draping mess kits and canteens about us and approaching the bakery, the source of the kitchen clatter and—what magic was this?—the sweet smell of cinnamon.

We were swept into a universe where words meant little, but growling stomachs and the miracle of steaming pastries on plates set before us bridged any language obstacle. Blessed silence as my comrades and I inhaled, followed by a robust melody of French declarations as an older woman thrust other goodness in front of us: plums, which she packed into our sacks and patted as if to secure them there. She whisked away our canteens and disappeared, bringing them back heavy and cold. And finally, she approached very slowly, holding what appeared to be an old paper to her heart before pulling it slowly from herself and reverently placing it before us on the table.

A map.

Hand-drawn.

Mireilles looked concerned, shaking her head and giving it back to the woman, speaking something about *l'amour*. Even I knew what that meant: love.

The older woman, Aline, nodded, and slid it back toward us. I didn't know what it all meant. Perhaps the woman's true love—a husband lost, maybe—had drawn it.

"She wants us to take it," George said around a mouthful of pastry. I kicked him under the table, and he gulped the rest of his bite down. "She says it's the best way to Paris."

We had a map from Captain Truett. But well did we understand the inestimable value of local knowledge. They knew highways and byways, shortcuts and perils, far more than any foreign distant maps could attempt to. This was their home.

"Thank you," I said earnestly and hoped she understood how much I meant it.

She nodded. And with a hand to Mireilles's shoulder and tears

in her eyes, she uttered three English words, painstakingly: "Go
. . . with . . . God."

"What did she *mean*?" George said an hour later, when we had
left the village behind us and were well on our way. "Go with God."

"You're the divinity school graduate," Hank said. "You tell
us." We were spaced out, the three of us. Henry taking the lead
with Madame Aline's map in hand. George, following strides behind. Then me, and Mireilles, always a few steps behind. When
I slowed, she slowed. When I quickened, so did she. Where we
could not converse, our footprints did the talking, tracking one
another without missing a beat. Always with two yards at least
in between us, by her design.

She was paying attention every second, always on heightened
alert. Perhaps she was not so different from us soldiers, after all. I
knew the toll that took on a mind, on a body, and worried for her.

"Heaven if I know," George answered Hank and grinned. "See
that? I did learn something in divinity school. One does not talk
about the nether regions of the universe flippantly."

I rolled my eyes. "I think that applies to the lofty regions, too."

George plowed forward, kicking a pebble. "'Go with God,' the
lady said. What does that mean? How does a mere man *go* with
the supreme being of the universe? Is He not outside of time and
place?"

"Careful," I said. "You sound like a true theologian, Chaplain
George."

"See here, I'm only trying to get a handle on the things we
chaplains are meant to say, and what they're meant to mean, and
all of that. I thought I was in divinity school to work one day each
week and avoid the war. It seems I was wrong. So? What say you?"

I inhaled, thinking of our own country minister back in Greenfield Springs. How he took his sermons on the footpaths and into
simple conversations with country children like me and Celia, or
old men and women, or whomever he happened upon. By listening, first. Then by speaking, usually in truths he seemed to know

from living them and dwelling in them, not solely philosophizing about them.

"I think it means to walk as if He is right there with us."

George looked puzzled. "*The* supreme being who is outside of time and place, right there with us."

I nodded.

"Right here in a turnip field," George reiterated, incredulous. "Or—" he sniffed the air—"an onion field, more's the pity?"

"Yes." It was beautifully preposterous, the truth of it. Beside me, Mireilles had slowed her walk and seemed to be concentrating hard on each step. I slowed to match, trying to respect the space she had placed between us.

"You mean to say that though a war wages and cathedrals abound, He is here in the dust?" George kicked up a cloud for emphasis.

I didn't answer at first. I was watching Mireilles, trying to discern what thought so occupied her. She looked . . . pained.

"Yes," I said slowly. "In every place." Especially the dust.

Mireilles stumbled, steadied herself on a post at the wayside. I reached out to brace her elbow, and she recoiled quicker than I knew possible. She turned her eyes up at me, and they flashed first a fearsome warning and then softened to regret. Frozen in place, I gestured to show I meant to help her.

George rambled on, speaking in half-sermons, half-blasphemies, none the wiser that he had no congregation. To his credit, when he realized something was amiss, his concern appeared genuine.

"The angel," he said in a loud hiss of a whisper. "Is she alright?" He knelt before her. I didn't know whether to roll my eyes at his dramatics or envy his open outpouring and the way it seemed to touch her—for there, in the midst of whatever distress she was enduring, the corner of her mouth turned up.

And soon, so did she. Straightening her whole being, brushed off her dress and apron. She even took care to rather—I don't know the word, maybe *fluff*?—her skirts around her, away from herself, and I thought again how out of place her clothing seemed. The fashion of ballrooms some years ago, though decidedly worn.

Perhaps Hank's theory wasn't so farfetched, after all.

She began to walk again, this time in front of me. And though she put on a good show of bravery, and though certainly that bravery was real, I didn't miss the way she limped slightly.

What fools we were. What oafs! The three of us were by now accustomed to long marches and having trained ourselves to ignore blisters and bless calluses.

She, this woman of the woods, would not have the same calluses protecting her feet.

Ahead, I saw another ruins on the horizon. "Let's stop there for lunch," I hollered ahead, and Henry, head bent over the map, waved a hand in agreement.

But before we reached the wrecked building, the sound of something familiar tread into our hearing: feet. Hundreds of them. Marching in time with one another and with a mission.

17

Singing. The soldiers were singing, marching on to war, stars in their eyes. Was it only three months before that that had been our battalion? Like boys off to camp, some game of capture the flag. Elated at the chance to save the world, or at least a part of it.

I saw it on their faces. Ruddy-cheeked, some of them, and some smattered with freckles. All of them wide-eyed and eager. I tried to be cynical. My thoughts tried to spin words out like *if you only knew.*

But those thoughts ran up against something between them and me. An invisible mirror that acted as a time machine, too. Showing me a version of myself from months ago.

One of them, a fellow maybe twenty years old, nodded and saluted each of us, a big grin on his face. When he got to me, that grin tugged down, tempered.

And I knew. He'd seen it, too—the mirror, the time machine between us. Only when he looked at me, he was seeing a future version of himself.

And what he saw ripped the ground right out from under him.

I tried to undo it. I smiled, if you can call that mangled attempt a smile. The muscles in my face didn't really remember how to do that, and they felt like rubber and doubtless appeared so, too. The soldier looked aghast, unable to look away, and tripped so close to me that all it took was one lunge to brace him.

He gripped my arm, his uniform immaculate, a dark green that seemed to hold life. It crossed my own uniform, that same green but faded, stained, torn, as if it had lived a hundred unkind years.

He was back on his feet and had released me in less than a

second, but that image—our arms crossed, my uniform against his—was burned in my mind.

Henry had caught up with the officers and was showing them our maps, probably consulting with them to hear what they knew of the road ahead of us. In exchange, he'd tell them of the road ahead of them. The men were given leave to fill their canteens in the creek by the road and take some rest.

Mireilles hung back, and I didn't blame her. To be plucked from the quiet of the woods and then deposited in a veritable current of soldiers . . . all of whom seemed transfixed when they saw her. A living puzzle, and—none of us had to say it—a beauty. She spread her worn skirts out and eased herself into the shadow of a tree, waiting.

"What happened?" the young man who'd tripped said. He reminded me of Celia, the way he honed in on my bandaged hand. Even in those two words, I could hear the South coming through, his words as long as his lopsided grin. He'd filled his canteen and returned to me, his initial shock at the sight of us now tempered into earnest curiosity.

I shrugged. Sifted through what to tell him. "The front," I said at last, opting for the simplest answer.

"Can I have a look?"

Well, no, I wanted to say. I wanted to shove that bandaged hand deep into the ground, hide it, let them go on their way and forget about these fingers that still trembled at the strangest times, though most danger was gone.

But that would've made more a spectacle than letting the guy just satisfy his curiosity and be done with it. I held my hand out, palm up, and peeled back the dirty gauze.

He sucked in breath like he'd been the one lashed deep. "That's a nasty one," he said, eyebrows raised as if impressed. "You clean it?"

I nodded. I kept it clean as best I could, out here on the road. It was better than the trenches, that much was sure.

"What about you?" I said. I was the worst conversation-maker in all of history, but posing questions was a deal better than answering them and being under scrutiny. "You're headed there," I said. A question, but a statement. We both already knew exactly where *there* was and exactly what his answer would be.

That initial spark returned to his face. "That's right," he said. "Name's John Maddox. We're headed there to give the others a rest. Sounds like that's you," he said, his smile full again. "Got any pointers for us?"

Pointers. The only pointers there were weapons, and he'd learn that soon enough.

I shrugged. To the side of the road, a flock of sheep bleated, eating grass like all was as normal as could be in the world. The scene sliced clean away when I blinked, that green grass flashing into colorless dirt, the blue sky swallowed up by dark. How long, I wondered, would memory keep doing this? Showing up and slashing into the present?

John Maddox of the South was watching, his study of me growing serious again. "Say, you okay?"

I nodded, swallowed back a swig of water from my canteen. I looked over to Mireilles's tree and didn't see her. She was near, though, I knew.

Think. What could I give this person before me? What, when I had nothing?

"Pointers," I said, forcing a thoughtful lightness into my voice. "Whatever happens out there, I guess—just know you're not alone."

Maddox nodded thoughtfully, a bit of a joke in his eyes as he surveyed the ranks of men around. "Got it," he said. "Not alone."

My face burned. I was no good at this. "I mean . . ." How to tell him? How to equip him without scaring the living daylights out of him? Without robbing him of maybe the only day or two left of that naïve hope written broad as daylight on his freckled face?

I remembered Mr. Haggerty. *"Sometimes there's a dark so thick you just know,"* he'd told me when I'd gotten locked in a garden shed by accident. He heard my fist pounding on that door and let me out, then plucked me up when he could read the fear on my body that I wouldn't give voice to. He set me on a rock in the

141

sun and sat right beside me. *"Sometimes there's a dark so thick you just know that the God who made light with His own two hands—with just His words—is going to plunge right into that dark to find you. You remember that, Mr. Matthew."*

He always called me that. *Mr. Matthew.* Like I was somebody.

His words came to me now, pounding on the tails of those memories of no-man's-land.

John Maddox was waiting, beginning to look concerned that perhaps my hand wasn't the worst-injured part of me. And maybe he was right.

I blew out my cheeks, shaking the cloak of it all away. "Right. Pointers," I said. "When you go over the top, it'll probably be dark."

Maddox nodded gravely, as if committing my words to a permanent fixing place inside.

"Remember that light was made for dark," I said. I repeated Mr. Haggerty's words to him. They didn't sound as weighty or convincing coming from me as they had coming from the old gardener back home. It was painfully clear I was trying them on for size, slipping my feet into them and finding them too roomy for my meager faith. I sounded even less convincing than when George Piccadilly bandied holy words about.

But it was all I had to give. Words that weren't yet mine, but that I was learning to grow into. If I could learn to believe them . . .

Maddox nodded, repeating a few back. "Plunge right in," he said. "I like that. You mean I shouldn't be afraid to plunge right in when the time comes, too, right?"

I smiled, sad. And nodded. Because sure, there was plenty to be afraid of. Plenty of real, awful things. But maybe, after all, it wasn't about the presence of danger, but the presence of a God who would plunge right into it beside you.

Something in me twisted, thirsty to believe that. For the bringer of light to fling the shadows far, far from me.

"Right," I said at last. "Right."

Plunge right in.

I held on to those words like a battle cry when the fresh battalion left, leaving us all in an eerie quiet there on the road. When Mira approached quietly, her eyes settling on me. And when Henry told us, maps spread out and glasses pushed up, that the only way forward was to the village of Beaulieu-en-Coteau.

He grew grave as he said so, and even Mireilles went as white as a sheet.

"What is it?" I asked, surveying the two of them.

Mireilles swallowed.

Henry scratched his head. "It's—well, according to the captain who just left—it's . . ."

"*Piège mortel*," Mira murmured.

George leaned in, going serious. Stammering over his coming interpretation. "A death trap."

18

Mira

Coming into Beaulieu-en-Coteau was like stepping into one of Grand-père's stories. Only I am sad to say, I was thankful he did not have to see it. Much better to be walking the streets of gold than to come into a place of so much silent anguish. Surely here, the rocks cried out, toppled as they were. Remnants of homes and churches and streets and shops all tossed together.

My foot caught and I stumbled, catching myself against an oddly leaning tower. A chimney, I realized. Stones so warm that for a moment I could nearly hear the crackle of the fire its hearth once housed. Or, I realized with horror, from a blow that toppled it so soon in the past. I pulled back my hand with the thought of it and it landed on something solid.

It was Matthew. Monsieur Petticrew. He caught that hand and held it, steadying me, steadying the race of my heartbeat. It was the sun that warmed those stones. Nothing more. The sun, the sun, the sun. I told myself so with each step. What had Matthew said to the happy soldier? *Light was made for dark.* He did not look as if he believed it, but the words sank into me and made me thankful for the sun. They gave me courage to take one more step, and another after that.

It was unsettling, walking in this place. Unreal, and in some ways, too real. Too like what life felt like now.

We walked on, him releasing me once I had my balance. The quiet hung heavy, urging a soul to burrow into the lost places.

Of all the things here that unsettled me, it was the look on George Piccadilly's face that did so the most. Such a jovial fellow was he usually, the first to whistle a tune or pipe a joke into the moment. But now he looked grave. Almost green around the mouth, or perhaps his pallor was merely a reflection of the destruction around.

He caught me looking and was quick to smile that dimpled smile of his. "Be careful," he said, gesturing at the stones, and at the jagged horizon of the town all around us.

I nodded.

We turned a corner, following Henry's lead. And there, perched right in the rubble, stood a table with a white tablecloth and a tea set. Wooden chairs, a few of them splintered or broken in various places, stood around the table, and a hearth nearby testified that once this was a kitchen. Somebody's home.

Where were they now, the ones displaced? I searched the ruins as if they might, impossibly, harbor them, these invisible, homeless people, whose loss I understood.

Instead, three uniformed men bedecked in medals sat around the table, bent together over a map between them while their servants—what was it they had called them? *batmen?*—stood at the ready to pour more tea or save their lives, whichever the given moment called for. Such a vignette of finery, there in the rubble, was jarring.

Henry-or-Hank stopped in his tracks, as did we all.

"What's this?" one of them said. "Yanks in the field, is it? Well, don't just stand there, come and have a bite!"

His accent, though cheery, sent a sudden cold chill through me. It was the same as George's—but I was growing used to George, hearing the accent less and the man more. I knew it was not this new man's fault that my body reacted so. Perhaps, in time, it would not.

My soldiers, as Aline had called them, hesitated only a moment before advancing. The dining officers began to disperse a bountiful amount of food. Matthew spotted me standing still and caught my eye, motioned me over to a chair.

I sat cautiously. I felt badly doing so; I was an imposter here. But oh, did my feet ache, and my whole body, so that it stepped away from the protests in my mind and sat down despite myself.

Unpacked before us were sandwiches, canteens full to the brim of water. And somehow, miraculously—apples.

I held mine, turning the bright red of it over and over in my hand. It seemed a jewel, deeper red than rubies I had seen drawings of, here against the backdrop of destruction.

"Is she quite alright?" one of the men said, his accent striking me again. *The British are allies*, I reminded myself. They had given more to our country, I knew, than I could begin to comprehend. Still, I clenched the apple tighter at the sound of his voice. *They are just words*, I reminded myself.

Matthew, beside me, noticed my stiffness and looked concerned. He looked from me to the British men, his brow furrowed. He was a quiet man, but he saw much. I could not have that. I gave a small smile, hoping to put him off the trail of whatever he thought he was seeing.

George opened his mouth to answer their question as to whether I was alright, and I slumped a little in my chair. Here it came, the effusions of the Angel of Argonne and the exposure of this fabled history of my family's. I was just a girl from the woods who collected walnuts and pine boughs. I did not know what to do with these adornments of fanciful story.

"She's great," Matthew said. And left it at that. George clamped his mouth shut, hearing the finality in Matthew's tone. I blessed them both for it.

They talked on about the journey to Paris. The men told them of places to go and things to see there, of how it would do them good, remind them that life was still going on, away from the horrible front.

Henry, all the while, took notes with his little pencil in that notepad of his, managing to keep looking at the men even as he wrote. It had the strange effect, I noticed, of leading the men to speak on, perhaps to say more than they should.

One of them leaned in, answering one of Henry's questions as though betraying a great secret. "Look around you, my good man," he said. "This place is deserted. Changed hands between French and Germans at least sixteen times over the past three years. You'd think such a thing would do a village in . . . and maybe it will. But see that?" He pointed to a silhouette on the horizon. A spire, rising from the tower of a church. "There she stands. Holes poked in every wall, windows long blown to bits—but that is a beacon of hope. If that little church can stand through all of this . . ." He whistled low. "There's no telling what can happen."

"But remember this place isn't as deserted as it looks," one of the other men said, warning in his voice. I shivered. "Take care, young men. Beaulieu-en-Coteau is wrecked, and it's French territory sure as can be now, but the Germans haven't forgotten when it was theirs. They haven't forgotten it sits directly on their route to Paris. Their end goal. Scouting parties and snipers still come, and don't forget that."

The apple was heavy in my hand, suddenly.

A great rolling overhead snatched all eyes to the sky, looking to pinpoint its source. But for once, thanks be to God, it was true and real thunder.

I smiled. Never had I been so glad, so relieved to hear thunder.

Matthew, his face turned entirely to the sky, smiled as a raindrop splashed him right on his cheek. He wiped it away and looked at it in astonishment.

"Rain," he said, as if he had caught a diamond from the sky and not just a very plump splash of water.

The sky unleashed, then, and the batmen and officers said a hurried good-bye, packing up their mess kits and tea set, disappearing to heaven-knew-where. George hollered a hearty farewell after them, and if I wasn't mistaken, there was a certain look of homesickness on his face. "Good fellows, those," he said, his accent markedly thicker than before. "Good chaps."

"I'll follow," Matthew said. "They know this place; they'll know good shelter."

I did too, though I could not tell him so. I had never before come to Beaulieu-en-Coteau, but this was my country and finding safety in unlikely places was my homeland. As Matthew Petticrew set off, his green-grey uniform blending into the colorless ruined city, I followed.

19

Matthew

"I'll follow," I said. "They know this place; they'll know good shelter."

I started after the English officers, got three strides in, and heard a slight sound behind me. It was Mireilles, following me.

I started again, sure I was mistaken.

The sound continued, light footsteps. She blinked hard in the rain and lifted her chin, defying any protest I might give.

But I gave it anyway. "You'll catch your death," I said. "If you stay under the outcropping with those two, you'll be dry, at least."

It was at the words *with those two* that she broke her gaze, let it skitter across the rubble. In the silence, I heard her loud and clear. She'd rather traverse jagged fallen rocks and toppled buildings in the pouring rain than be left alone with the men.

"They're good fellows, I promise. George is a bit of a dunce sometimes, sure, but aren't we all?"

I knew she couldn't understand but hoped she might find comfort in my tone, my gesture toward them.

Her features softened. I remembered Celia, how she'd wake me up, tugging at my blanket whenever the wind howled through our stable loft and scared her imaginings into action. It had always amazed me, how sitting and just talking with her, telling her silly tales or truest tales or ridiculous jokes and riddles helped her remember she was home and she was safe. And what amazed me more—which I had never, ever let on—was that when I'd been

149

scared myself, the simple act of caring for another in their own fear helped me feel that same safety, too. I wondered, sometimes, if God let our fear collide in the night to shatter it away for both of us.

Mireilles, her wide eyes now in the rain and the way she seemed to calm when I spoke, reminded me of Celia, though a few years older than my sister.

She took a step closer, then another, until she had wound her way so close I could feel her warmth.

My breath hitched in my throat. The rain had soaked her fast, soaked her through, slicked her dark hair down like a veil and washed her face clean of the dust of our journey. I saw, for the first time, a light scattering of freckles over her nose and the way her lips looked red against her too-pale skin.

She shouldn't be out in this. I remembered the way she stumbled on the path today and knew she wasn't well. But I was quickly learning she had a stubborn streak to match my own, and if I wanted to get her out of the rain, it meant getting a move on and getting back to the others fast.

"Alright," I said and tipped my head onward.

She gave a small smile.

I laughed. "You'd be better off with those fellows," I said, shaking my head. "I've been known to fall irrevocably into massive holes."

It was the first time I'd spoken of Saint-Mihiel aloud. I had buried it all and meant never to speak of it. Certainly never to a stranger. And certainly never in a tone so light.

She seemed to like it. Some color inched back into her cheeks.
Keep talking.

It was a foolish notion, and I didn't know where it came from. Perhaps the way her eyes lifted, inviting more.

Well, what could it hurt. Besides dredging words up from inside of me, where they liked to stockpile and die a slow and ceaseless death, it felt oddly . . . nice. To tell someone of that night on the front.

So I talked to the only person who would keep my words safe, for she could not understand a single one.

"Did you ever see much of the battles, back at home?"

She studied me, not answering. Waiting.

I blew my cheeks out and shook my head. "I hope not. It's . . ." I shook my head again. How to put words to the ache of it all? "Well. I did, I fell in a hole, just like I said," I tried to make light of it. "Truth was, I thought that was it. I'd die there. I probably should have. There was a moment when my back hit the wall made of earth and I slid down and sat. The sky rumbled like only the earth should, and the earth bled like only people should, and people—" my voice caught—"people lived and died like nobody, ever, should."

She looked grave. I reminded myself I was talking to help her, not burden her. I lightened my tone.

"Anyway. I understand, I do. War happens. We help. It's what we do. Not one of us can fix this whole mess, but maybe we can help this one moment. You know?"

She smiled in answer, a sad smile. I began to forget she couldn't understand.

We walked on, and I talked on, telling her things of the war, telling her of Celia, telling her of home. The racetrack, the New York sunrises. The smell of spring fields. Things full of life. I told her of getting myself locked in with the goats in the barn when I was seventeen and of how Celia wouldn't come near me for days after that, swearing I still smelled like the hairy beasts.

And she, Mireilles, marched on beside me. Slowing when I slowed, plowing on when I did, picking her way around a tumbled pile of rubble when I tried to climb over it and slid promptly on my rear. She looked triumphant, beating me to the other side, and I swear I saw one of her dark eyebrows lift, a sparkle in her eye. Mireilles, this somber soul—it seemed she had a sense of humor that was as deep as it was quiet.

I would have to watch out for her.

Looking pleased, she picked up her skirts to better navigate the wet rubble and blazed right on ahead. I shook my head. This Angel of Argonne had a mind of her own.

She looked over her shoulder, pausing to see if I followed, and I caught up quick.

I ceased my aimless rambling, and in the stillness, we walked on. It was strange, the way the only sound was of our two pairs of feet, as if we were the only people in all the world, here in this lifeless place. Because we knew it wasn't true. That somewhere, hidden here, enemy or friend, people lived and breathed.

Together we scanned, paused, listened, walked on, trying to find the officers. And then, at least I presumed our thoughts aligned, we gave up on finding them and began to look on our own for shelter. Night would fall in a few short hours.

The sound of a bell ringing snatched my attention and I saw it: the partially crumbled steeple of an old chapel. I squinted, hoping to see in the distance who might be ringing the bell. A man exited the building, dressed in a dark suit. I ran to catch up to him and saw his suit, like his town, had seen better days. But he wore it with care, the priest's collar pressed and crisp, a faded yellow mark upon the white where someone had worked hard to remove a stain.

"Hello!" I hollered, and he slowed his walk, turning.

He was old, I saw, with a face marked by both kindness and sadness. "Hello," he said, wrapped in an accent thick as the hills beyond were green. He extended a hand, and I shook it gratefully. "You are come to help," he said, gesturing at my uniform.

"We hope so," I said.

"And I," he replied, looking sadly at his crumbling church.

"Is it—is it a working church?" I could feel my face burn. The audacity of that question, and the words all wrong . . . but how did one ask if a church was alive? I didn't know the right words, the holy words needed to speak of such things. What would George say? All he had was holy words, even if he had nothing to back them up.

The man studied me. "Yes," he said. "Working church." He nodded slowly. "It is empty, but it works." I was caught in the way the words settled deep in his accent, deep in his meaning.

He studied the building, as if reading the stones. And then he opened his mouth and read those stones to me. "Never could we have imagined something crushing into our walls from the clear blue skies like they did. Never did I know that our pews would be splintered by the—the—"

"Shrapnel," I offered. And knew too well what he meant.

"Shrap-nel," he repeated. "And never did I think that these walls, which have been filled with music . . . life . . . hope . . . laughing . . . tears . . ." His words slowed and rolled up and down in their own melody. "That they would be silent. But . . ." He trailed off, letting his gaze roam the outskirts of the village. "They are not silent, really."

I waited. He began to walk slowly, running his weathered hand over the jagged edges of his wrecked chapel. "They have done what they were always meant to do. Let the life and music and hope out beyond these walls. Trotted"—he let his fingers mimic the word, tripping over the top of the stones and grinned like a kid at his word choice, proud of his English—"over the hills. This town has been French, and German, and French, and German, each one taking turns taking over. This church has seen more bombs"—he waved his hand in the air—"than people over the past three years. And do you know what we have learned?"

I shook my head and hung on his coming words, my chest aching for reasons I couldn't explain. "Things may crash into our worlds and blast all we have known to bits." There was pain in his eyes, cinching his voice as he said this. "But you know, don't you, that great holes in stone buildings let the light through."

From the outside in, or the inside out, I didn't know. But the man's words felt like treasure he was offering from his near-empty pockets right into ours.

"And now," he said. "It is yours."

"Ours," I said, not following this leap.

"You need shelter, no?"

I had forgotten the rain.

"Ah, broken it may be, but it can still shelter the weary from the wet. Come."

He showed us inside. I followed, and soon sensed an emptiness behind me. Mireilles had stopped at the threshold, face upturned as if she could see the reaches of the ceiling that had once been there. As if it was the Sistine Chapel, with Michelangelo's painstaking handiwork captivating her attention.

Only there was no ceiling. The handiwork above her was that of God himself, and it came in the form of a gentling rain upon her upturned face. She stood that way for a long time and must have sensed me watching. She blinked against the sprinkling.

"You have come to help," the priest had said at the sight of my uniform. The words pounded through me and told me to cross the expanse between us, take her face in my hands, wipe the raindrops from her cheeks.

And yet—nothing seemed more natural, either, than to see this girl, so untouched, unspoiled even by the war at her own front door, washed clean by water from heaven itself.

She looked around, eyes wide, as if she'd never set foot in a church before. Maybe she hadn't. Maybe we had that in common. Mr. Haggerty, with his homespun sermons stewing in his soil-darkened hands, had brought church to me, out on those old garden plots back home. As I followed Mireilles's gaze around the room, splintered pews shining in water, I shared her awe.

"Come, sopping creatures," the priest said. He led the way to the back of the church and opened a creaking door to reveal a room with roof enough to keep a few souls dry. "For you," he said, pointing at me. "And for you—" he pointed at Mireilles and removed a ring of keys from his pocket. He slid them by and by until reaching the right one, its shape clearly familiar to him as he rubbed it between his fingers and his wrinkle-mapped face lit with a smile. "The 'holy of holies,'" he said, and unlocked another door.

For a door in a church with no walls, or not many to speak of, to be locked, it must surely hold great treasure.

I leaned to the side, craning to see as Mireilles followed him in. There was one pew untouched by war, a worn cushion that the man retrieved from a shelf and placed upon the pew, and a robe of some kind that he spread across the pew like a blanket. "There, you see? Fit for a queen."

She murmured something to him. "Ah, you speak French! Of course." The two talked in their shared language, me feeling ever more an intruder. I stepped back and surveyed my own room. To someone else, in another life, it might have resembled a bleak prison cell. Nothing but hard floor. But to me—and I knew to George and Henry—it was as good as a castle. No mud, no rats, no stench of the trenches.

"George and Henry." I winced. I'd forgotten about them. I poked my head back in toward the priest, who was taking his leave from Mireilles. She was perched upon her pew, deep exhaustion shadowed under her eyes as she ran her hand back and forth over the smooth wood. She smiled at me, this woman who was now the unsuspecting keeper of all of my words and none of their meaning.

"I'll return soon," I said, hoping she understood. Gesturing that I'd come back. Knowing I probably looked a fool.

She nodded and stood. I went to leave and sensed her following once more.

The priest gone, it was just the two of us in this holy place. "You can stay." I held out my hands in a stopping motion. "Rest. I won't be long."

She nodded again and continued to follow. I turned to try again, only to see that stubborn quirk of her eyebrow and a half-smile that told me she was coming, whatever I had to say on the matter.

"Alright," I said. "We'll be quick. You're already soaked through."

At this, she looked up and down my uniform, making a point. She was right. I was drenched. Not one to talk.

Dusk was falling outside as we picked our way through former streets. And with the dusk rose birdsong.

Looking back, I nearly blame it. Pecking holes in my defenses, tuning my ears to the sound of hope. Telling me birds only sang where war was far.

How wrong. How very, very wrong.

A single moment. Just one. I let my guard down.

There are things that will never make sense to me. Details I remember from that instant, when time slowed impossibly. The stone that I stood on somewhere in the ruins of Beaulieu-en-Coteau, how it was cracked at a diagonal, in the shape of a lightning bolt. How I was zapped with the thought—*zapped*, for there was no actual time to think it in any articulate sort of way—that if lightning had a sound, it must sound like the bullet searing toward us.

And then, in the same instant—right after the sickening snap of a sniper's bullet—the sound of Mireilles. And me thinking I must be going mad—because her words came out in English.

"*Down!*" she said. "Get down!" This time a scream, and her stricken face running toward me as if to tackle me into obedience.

I had been looking for birds.

She had seen a sniper.

And she was running at me, in the path of a bullet much too fast to outrun.

We split the air. Tangled—and dove to the ground.

The bullet collided with a ruined pillar inches from my ear and even closer to the top of Mireilles's head. She was on her hands and knees after knocking into me, her dark hair whipping as she turned to search, frantically, for the source.

But there was no time for that. "Quick," I said and pulled her around the corner of the building. I hated how fast we moved, how it surely scraped her. But it was that or death.

We sat upon a white chipped-paint sign that said *Fleurs* and listened. Sitting where a flower shop once sold blossoms, every sense aware that the slightest movement could end our lives.

She drew her knees up slowly and wrapped her arms around them, making herself compact. Whatever her tale, she knew how to hide herself.

In the silence, so many questions pounded with the rain.

Who was this woman? How did she speak English? How much English did she speak, and why had she hidden that fact? How, in all the world, had our paths crossed and planted us here together, holding our breath, sitting on a splintered sign in a pile of ruins, wondering if we would live to see morning?

But in the midst of the questions, another shot rang out. This time, closer.

I moved to cover her. To put myself between her and this unseen enemy. Desperate to be fast enough.

The same muted pulse of blood descended over my hearing.

I moved myself away from her and saw two things.

Mireilles, slumping into unconsciousness.

And on the sign beneath us, *Fleurs* blossoming blood-red in the rain.

20

"Mireilles," I whispered, fiercely as I could. "Mireilles." No response.

If my pulse had been pounding because of the sniper, it was galloping a thousand times faster now. I held the girl, slumped in my arms, rain beating down. The crimson river running into the mud in rivulets now, washed by the rain.

"What do I do?" I whispered, thankful for the downpour covering the sound of my voice. Wishing it would wash that question away. There was always a plan. Always something to do. That question, unanswered—my stomach twisted.

But maybe the rain, now bucketing, would give us some visual cover. I had to get her to shelter, to safety. That is, if she was even . . .

I pressed my ear against her dress, listening. Cursing, now, the sound of the rain. Where was the beat of her heart?

I listened harder. These were the ears that could pick out a race winner from a mile away. These were the ears Captain Truett depended on for artillery fire warnings. I shook my head, willing them to clear. How could I not hear a single person's pulse?

I had to. I pressed myself closer, willing my face to feel warmth from her breath, pounding from her pulse.

I shifted her body, thankful she was at least not aware of my touch. That my hand rested on her stomach to brace her. And that as I listened so hard for a heartbeat—something else came.

A small but mighty slam—right against my palm.

My palm that rested on her stomach.

My hand shot away faster than the bullet had come at us—and I stared.

I had to stare hard, let my eyes adjust in the growing dark. But as they did, I saw it clearly: her dress, the one I'd thought old-fashioned, was slicked against her body from the rain. And in clear relief was the gentle roundness of a stomach that looked out of place on her nearly starved form.

She was—was she? With child?

Slowly, I pressed my palm back to her stomach, feeling at first only warmth, and thanking God for that sensation. *She lived.*

And then, after a moment that stretched long, that same tiny, mighty, unmistakable ricochet against my palm.

My eyes hurt from staring so hard, and the wind that came now in place of the rain made them sting but shot my mind through with clarity.

Mireilles was with child.

I stood—or tried to, only to have my leg buckle beneath me. The river of blood had slowed to a trickle and looked black now in the moonlight.

It led to me.

I lifted my pant leg, wincing at the way the fabric tore from my skin, where it had been embedded. The gash went deep. Too big, I hoped, to be from a bullet.

Bracing myself and gritting my teeth, I struggled to stand and gather Mireilles up—but couldn't. I would drop her, I knew, if I attempted to carry her in this state. In our fast move around the corner to safety, she had struck her head against the building, best I could tell.

A cold knot cinched tighter in me with each realization. We had taken her from the refuge of her home to find safety . . . and delivered her to the lion's den. Her—and her unborn child.

Every second stretched on, settling upon my chest with heaviness that made it nearly impossible to breathe.

What do I do? I listened hard and heard no shots. Their absence sent fear drilling deeper into me than when I did hear. The man—or men—could be anywhere.

Make a plan. Make a plan. Make a plan. The driving words of my youth, pounding with my pulse.

But there was no plan.

If I moved, it could tip the sniper off.

If I stayed, the sniper could move. Spot us, pick us off. Or pick me off, leaving her alone out here, unconscious. I wasn't much to look at, knew I didn't have anything to offer the girl, but at least I could stand between her and danger. At least I could, in this moment, keep her warm. And—I prayed—alive.

There was no plan.

But there was a prayer.

"Please, God." I sputtered it into the rain. But wasn't He the one sending the rain? "Please." Voice low, so ragged it hurt, muttered into the dark. But hadn't He made the dark? How did someone entreat the God who could, if what they said was true, change all this in a second?

"Please." For the third time, the prayer uttered in a single word because it would've taken a million to try and say it all.

Mireilles was growing cold in my arms. My leg was numb from the gash. I tried to move, just an inch, and couldn't.

That's when I knew—we might die here tonight.

And that's when it came. The sound of gunfire, followed by footsteps and shouting. "Come on!"

It was Henry, rushing at us, eyes wilder than when he was in one of his writing furies. George was nowhere to be seen. "He's covering us. Come on!"

I tried. "Take her."

His eyes grew so big the whites of them would've given our location to the sniper from a mile away. "Is she—"

"Unconscious," I said.

He struggled to get her up, into the shadows. I pulled in the deepest breath I could, held it, pressed my eyes closed, and heaved myself off of an old spike. I will never forget the single moment of searing sensation and sound—and will not detail it now. It is the sort of thing so unnatural it sickens a body.

I followed. *Limping* would be too kind a word for the way I dragged my own leg by my hands, lopsided and desperate to keep them in sight.

"There!" I whisper-shouted. "The church—on your right!"

The sound of gunfire. It didn't add up. Chaplains didn't fight.

It seemed an eternity, getting into that shell of a church. I told Henry where the pew was, and he got Mireilles settled. I got myself over to her and in the blur of everything, somehow Henry went back out, bringing George to safety with him this time.

"Did you see me?" George said, beaming in the moonlight. "Of course you didn't. Good as invisible, I was. Not bad for a chaplain, eh? There were two of them up there in that old building. But we scared 'em off into the night like a proper pair of jackrabbits!"

He was right. It was a far cry from how he'd been at Plattsburg, when he'd spent target practice composing odes to the birds overhead, which he wished to see on his dinner table.

"Good on you," I said. "Thanks." I caught his line of vision. "Really. I mean it. You didn't have to do that."

"Right you are, and don't you forget it," he said. "But what's got her?"

Ignoring the throbbing in my calf, I knelt beside Mireilles. "She hit her head." I didn't tell him there was a lot more going on with her than that. A whole lot.

I was no medic. All I had was the minuscule first-aid kit issued to each of us—a waterproof package with two dressings intended for a bullet's entrance and exit. That wasn't going to do anything for a head slammed into ancient stone . . . or for her other condition, if I was right. And perhaps I was wrong. What did I know of such things?

I knelt beside her while Hank and George checked the perimeter. The journalist and the chaplain were turning out to be the heroes in this tale.

"Mireilles," I said, trying her name aloud in my full voice for the first time. It felt like one of the fine things, like how Celia used to stand at the shop windows in town and look at things she could never have and trace her finger on the glass around their shapes.

I lifted my hand and traced her cheek. It, too, felt too good.

Too good for my rough, mud-streaked hands. She was soft and true, and I had no place touching her. But I had to rouse her, I knew.

I let my hand rest on her shoulder where she lay on her side. "Mireilles," I said, a little louder.

Again, I heard the priest speak of hope. And for the second time that night, I prayed.

At first, nothing changed. But after a bit, she stirred, her breath coming deeper, her movements like one struggling to find their way to the surface.

She opened her eyes and looked around in confusion, letting her gaze land on the darkened silhouettes of the room's objects. A lectern in the corner. A chair with a reaching back, beside it. And me.

She saw me and jolted back with a force that nearly tumbled me back, too. I worried she'd hit her head again, this time on the pew, but she scrambled to a sitting position and made to move as far from me as she could.

"It's alright," I said, holding up my hands with fingers spread wide. "Nothing will hurt you here."

She stared, shoulders rising and falling, arms looped around her stomach in a protective instinct.

"It's just me," I said. "Matthew Petticrew. Remember?"

After a moment, her shoulders slumped a little, relaxing. A hand went to her forehead.

"Are you in pain?" I thought of what Celia would have done. How she had me hold a jar of fresh-caught creek water to any blow I took—and there had been many at the racetrack.

I had no jar of cool stream water. I looked around and spotted a pile of rubble in the corner. Pulling the smoothest rock I could find from it, I gave thanks that it was cold and placed it in her hand. "Hold this to where it hurts," I said. "The cold will help." I wished, rather than knew, this to be true.

She examined the rock a moment, one hand still resting on her small rounded stomach. A picture of one attempting to reconcile

162

how a rock could remove a hurt so deep she could never pull it to the surface. Suddenly aware of my observation, she quickly removed her hand from her middle.

She held it, instead, to her head. I wondered if she remembered what had happened. Her courage . . . and her use of my language.

She raised her eyes to me, darkest blue, and in them swam so many questions. Mine answered in kind, surely, with so many questions of my own. Meeting hers in the air between us in an invisible, tentative dance.

At last she spoke. Daring to use English once more, her voice rich and sweet and low in her accent. "You . . . saved me."

I hung my head. "I think it was the other way around. If you hadn't warned me when you did . . ." I let the implication trail off.

"You are alright?"

"Yes," I said quickly, forgetting my own wound and wincing when I moved my leg out in front of me. "Mostly."

"The others . . . ?" she said, looking around and not finding George and Henry.

"They're fine too. Keeping watch outside."

She nodded, her forehead pinched.

I pulled out the kit from my jacket pocket and tried to make sense of the gash. Covering it would do little but stop the bleeding, and that had already slowed. And I might need these dressings, yet, for their intended purposes. Best to let the wound heal in the open air. I rolled up the pant leg and tried hard to ignore the burn every time I shifted my position.

"And you," I said. "You are alright?" I used her own words.

She didn't answer right away.

I gulped. She didn't know that I knew of her condition. I considered, for a moment, not saying anything. It wasn't right to speak of such to her, especially when I couldn't be sure, and especially when I was an expert at bungling any words. Especially ones concerning sensitive situations.

But the weight that visibly settled on her knocked the bungling words right out of me and into the open, anyway. I could at least help carry the knowledge of it, when it seemed she had no one else to do so.

"I—I have to apologize," I said. She tilted her head, looking childlike as she awaited my explanation. "I need to say I'm sorry." I tried it in a different way, in case she hadn't understood.

"I would think you would wish me to apologize," she said. "You know that I can speak with you. That I hid that."

"I can understand why," I said. "But . . ." Where was Celia? She would know what to say. Men didn't speak to ladies about this. But then again, men didn't usually stumble upon ladies in the woods, singing and making wreaths, and end up tasked with securing their safety in the City of Light. Nothing about this was usual. Still, I thought of Celia. She had a way with words. She would say something pretty, probably.

"I felt your stomach," I blurted out. And immediately wished the words back. "I mean—I'm sorry . . ." I winced. And pushed forward. "When I tried to pick you up, when you were knocked out, I—something inside of you jolted. I felt it. Like a—a small kick."

She was beginning to understand. The look on her face morphed into horror, then shame, looking down and refusing to meet my gaze.

We sat long in the silence, rain falling outside and neither of us knowing how to move from that declaration. "I only mention it in case—that is—can I help? Is there someone I can contact for you, or anything I can—"

"There is no one," she said. She lifted her chin. It was clear she didn't wish to tell me the story behind the child. "There is me. Only me."

"You're not no one," I said.

Her look turned quizzical. I wished I could elaborate. But I knew so little of her. Yet still, I knew without a doubt that she was *not* "no one."

"You're Mireilles," I said, giving it the simplest answer I could. The only thing I truly knew enough about her, enough to speak.

"Mira," she said quietly. As if unsure whether to speak it.

"Mira." I repeated the name. It suited her, somehow. She with the long hair that whipped about in curls in the wind, her being just flowing from the shortened form of her name.

"And you are Matthew," she said.

I nodded. There was nothing more to add to that, really. I was just me.

She looked at me long and finally breathed in deep. "Thank you, Matthew."

"For what?"

"For saving . . . us. And—if I may ask—for keeping this to yourself." She folded her hands in her lap, fingers interlaced, one thumb gliding over the other nervously.

I nodded. I had so many questions. How soon was her time? Where was the man who should be here, helping her? And why did I feel my defenses rising when I thought of him, and thought of how I sat, right now, in his place?

I checked myself. For all I knew, he was a good man. A prisoner or casualty of war who would've given anything to be here. Perhaps a farmer, working the fields far away to make a life for his family. I shouldn't make assumptions. But then other possibilities came knocking. Scenarios less honorable, the sort common in this war. And my anger riled me wide awake. This was the cadence of my thoughts as they stretched on into the night.

She watched me warily, fighting to stay awake as her eyelids grew heavy. To my shame, it took me too long to realize—while I sat here keeping vigil—my presence was keeping her from rest. She was keeping her own vigil.

In the corner of the room sat a tiny chair, one meant for a child. I moved it to the threshold of the door and placed it just inside, sitting on it. Hoping she would know she was safe, both by my distance and my proximity. Far enough that I hoped the distance might instill a little trust—but near enough that I could see if any trouble befell her.

At last, sleep found her. She turned and awoke after a time, her eyes studying the stars above where the ceiling had fallen away in the corner. Then turning, slowly, to my place at the door.

"Did you not find sleep?" she asked, trying to lift herself to sitting.

"No," I said. Her wording was uncanny. There'd been a long time in the trenches where I'd searched for sleep, and searched hard—and more than that, searched for rest. But I'd given up on that.

She looked troubled, apologetic. "Not for a long time," I added. Hoping it would ease her conscience and help her know that night was familiar to me. It had become a strange sort of home.

"Many nights?"

"Many."

Her concern only deepened.

"It's not so bad." I tried to think how to lighten the mood, ease this unseen burden from her. Without telling her that when I did sleep, it was to nightmares that gutted me. "Gotta stay awake long enough to think," I said. "It's hard to get a thought in at all during the day, with George and Henry always yammering."

"Perhaps if your bunkmates were here," she said.

"George and Henry?"

"No. The smellier ones. The goats."

I must have looked one hundred percent befuddled.

"The ones who your sister said you smelled like?" She wrinkled her forehead, remembering. "How did she say . . . like 'hairy beasts'?"

I gulped. I'd forgotten. Sputtering on, half madman, half schoolboy, as we picked our way across this no-longer city, dropping stories from my youth like seeds into every crevice.

Thinking it might calm her. Liking how they cheered me, too, all the tales from boyhood I should've been embarrassed by. Shenanigans and all.

I stammered. Must have looked like a fool, frozen in the realization that she'd understood every word—and yet whatever look of horror she saw on my face, she smiled. Dropped a shoulder . . . and laughed.

"Do not worry, Matthew Petticrew. I have a goat story or two

166

myself. I think we all must. And . . . in truth . . . it was nice to hear, today."

I regained some of my senses and sat a little straighter, pretenses falling away before the woman who knew more of me, now, than the few who had known me for a lifetime did.

"Well, if you like smelly animal stories, I have plenty."

She smiled, and so did I. How, on the tails of both of us nearly losing our lives, and in the wake of me unearthing a secret she clearly wanted kept, had we ended up here? Laughing, in the dead of night. Our lives still hanging in the balance, for this was war. But learning to stand on an unexpected patch of memory of simpler times and smelly animals.

She looked so tired. I rose and snatched an old bedsheet from its place covering an ancient instrument in the corner, shook it out, wrapped it quick around itself, and carefully slid it under her head.

"A pillow," I said and felt ridiculous.

But she looked at it and ran her hand across it like it was gold. "Thank you." She laid her head down, dark hair coiling in strands behind her that looked softer, much softer, than the makeshift pillow.

I swallowed, embarrassed. I would never watch a girl sleep in any normal world. Just sit here and watch like it was alright. As if it wasn't too close, as if it didn't matter that I hardly knew her and she hardly knew me and I, somehow, seemed to be the only living bearer of her greatest secret.

So I retreated from Mira's chamber, this time to the outside of the door, lying down, and checking in as the night wore on, just to ensure she was still sleeping peacefully, more times than I should have.

But it was her face above mine, checking on me, that I awoke to at first light the next morning.

21

Mira

When I was young, I followed Papa into the woods one day. He was hunting for us, winter soon to come. I saw him spot a fox, so red against an early snow. He had it in the view of his weapon and was ready to pull the trigger.

"*Stop, Papa!*" I yelled at him. He looked angry for a moment; how many times had he told me to be as silent as the snow when we were hunting? But even my shouting did not send the animal running. For I had seen what Papa had not: the fox was wounded. Asleep, perhaps, or near unto its death, but I remember how I thought I would explode from the ache inside of me, thinking of the little thing becoming someone's dinner.

I ran to it and saw such sad eyes. It was an animal and I was a girl, and I knew there was a natural order to things and the way of life, but still—I could not fathom killing it.

Papa knelt beside me. He laid one hand upon my back, and one hand upon the fox.

"*Créature torturée*," he said. *Tortured creature.*

His voice was soft, so strong and kind, and I did not know whether he spoke of me or the fox. I only know he sent me home and never told me what became of the little fox. I named it Pierre and invented many wonderful tales of a happy fate for it in the days that followed, chattering each of them into Papa's ears. He only smiled, sometimes sadly, and laid his big hand on my small head.

"Mon papillon. *Si plein de vie.*" So full of life, he called me.

I wonder what he would call me if he could see me now. Sitting in a holy place destroyed. Kneeling beside this sleeping man—he himself a créature torturée. And I was, yes, full of life—but not the kind Papa spoke of. The kind that would make me unfit, in the eyes of some, to be in such a holy place as this, ruined though it might be. Ruined though I might be.

I turned my attention toward the American soldier. Even in his sleep he looked tired. An ancient sort of tired that went deep into his bones, no rest upon his face as his dark eyebrows pressed toward each other like they meant to hold the world together.

I laid a hand upon him, just as Papa had done for me.

"Si plein de vie," I uttered Papa's words, this time as a prayer. "So full of life, Father in heaven. Make him so."

If God above would hear a plea of one such as me, I would spend it on this man. For he was spending his life on me, though I knew not why. Perhaps it was this that had caused me to tell him my name, the name I had thought lost forever with the passing of my grandfather.

I heard a sound, repeated like the steady ticking of a clock but softer. Looking up, two shadows stretched over us. George. Henry-or-Hank. And an apple, flying up and down, up and down in George's hand as he tossed it like a ball and smiled like a child.

He held it out to me. I took it, nodding my thanks. These men did not yet know that I spoke their language.

Matthew Petticrew stirred, that ancient tired way of his easing, just for a moment, into the fleeting look of a little boy. I wondered what it would be like to have a little boy. If he was like this man . . . something in me squeezed in a happy way at that thought. I had not often had such a feeling, when wondering about this baby. Indeed, it was very hard to think of, sometimes. But I knew that the time for thinking and wondering would soon come to an end.

I took his hand and pressed the apple into it. Summoning him awake to something good, after the night he had faced.

"I say," George said, offended. "That was for you, Angel of Argonne."

Matthew stirred, sitting up slowly. Bleary at first, then astonished. Confused. At the apple in his hand. My presence by his side.

"Was I asleep?"

"Yes, you slacker," George said, taking an impossibly loud bite of his own apple. I did not know this word, *slacker*, but at the way Henry elbowed George in the middle, I guessed it was not good.

"Slacker," Matthew repeated, as if the word were ridiculous. He pulled his face into a smile. Up close like this I saw the way his cheek near me—imprinted by the seam of stone floor he had slept upon—etched into curves around his mouth when he did so. It was—it was nice. "As I recall, one of us did try to outrun the war, and it wasn't me."

"And yet here I am." George spread his arms low and wide, turning his face up to the roofless sky beyond. "Chaplain George, at your service. And a hero, what's more, if you'll kindly recall last evening's escapades."

He came near and I felt myself tense. I did not mean to be so. I knew in my head that the man meant me no harm. It was not his fault that his accent reminded me so of another.

"That fellow never sleeps." He tipped his head at Matthew. "Surprised we caught him catching a few winks at all." He chewed on his bite of apple and seemed to remember then that he was, by his own claim, my translator. "*L'âne ne dort jamais.*" He shook his head and pushed his mouth to the side.

I worked very hard not to laugh. *The donkey never sleeps*. I nodded gravely.

He pulled another apple out of his satchel and handed it to me. We all breakfasted so, the men speaking of plans to leave soon and which route to take to Paris. Madame Aline's map was a treasure, but as Hank-or-Henry said, it was not her fault that it had led us into the den of the enemy last night. We needed "more current intelligence," he said, and they agreed to find such along the way.

Stepping outside the church felt different, somehow, from when we first set foot inside. I had felt an intruder, then. But somewhere in the night—somewhere with my head pounding so hard, and

170

waking in the dark to find I was watched over by someone very kind, distant but near. Even in the smallest act—of eating a bright red apple for breakfast and feeling the little one inside quicken in response—it felt like a safe place. A healing place. And I left a little bit of myself behind, there.

The journey through the rubble was a breathless one, each of us with our senses standing tall and our figures crouched low. But where words did not come, neither did gunshots, and birdsong ushered us out of the clutches of that place, back out onto the road.

22

Henry

WAVES OF COURAGE
For column "Your Boys, America!"
By Hank Jones (Or Henry Mueller)

We passed an entire battalion of your men on the road a few days back, America. The valiant American Expeditionary Forces, on the road to the front. We knew they were yours by the way they beamed courage. Back home on the farm, when the wind would come sweeping through, we'd all marvel at the way it took single stocks of wheat, set them to motion, and blended them into wave upon wave of movement. It caught the light and gave us all hope for a life-giving harvest in the months to come.

Well, America, your men do the same but a hundred times more. Let me tell you, watching a battalion of them take up the whole width of a muddy road, watching the way their marching moves their legs in sync and seems to set the ground to trembling—why, it makes me stand in my tracks and salute.

These men were fresh off the trains. You could feel their eagerness in every footstep. You could see it in their eyes, the way they were fixed on the horizon ahead. They were bringing force and life to a downtrodden place.

[News Editor: I know you may cut the following. Please consider leaving it in. The courage is highlighted by the whole story, not defeated by it.]

My comrades and I, on special assignment, stood to the side and let them pass. The fresh faces, the eager ones, passing by the somber few who accompanied me, was a thing to behold. Since we're speaking of wind, have you ever heard wind blow through a place? Picture it: It kicks up dust and debris, making its presence known and formidable. But then somewhere along the way, it passes an open pipe—the thing that will catch it, recognize it, and sound a hollow, mournful song right back to it with its own force. Or maybe you've seen children do the same, blowing air across the top of an empty soda bottle.

That was what the passing men were like. The fresh soldiers, so full of anticipation and life. Singing "Let's All Be Americans Now" and saluting us as they marched. But you could see it as they read on our faces—particularly on the face of the soldier who stood next to me, who has seen battle more than any man should—how those smiles melted into flat lines. How a few of them looked from him, back to their singing comrades, torn between two realities: their present, and their future.

My soldier friend saw it, too. I saw him see it and saw him conjure up a grave but valiant nod of respect for any who looked his way. Though he could not smile at their anticipation, he could yet respect it and instill some hope and courage in them, from one soldier to another.

It was as if he was extending an invisible hand to their shoulders. He would not give false hope to the men. He would not willingly send them into battle with masks pulled over their heads about the atrocities they might face. But he would, with all sincerity, say to them, "Your courage is good. Your fortitude is right. You will need them both, and who knows but that we were born for such a time as this? It is a brave thing that you do. Go, now, and do it well." In that fleeting exchange with no words, he sent them on their way armed with candid purpose. He harnessed the wind and sang their song right back to them.

These are times such as the world has never seen. We all heard of it back home for the past years before our country entered the war, but being here on this war-torn soil itself has opened this reporter's eyes more than I wish to own. I am a farmer by trade. I sow fields of hay and plow them come fall with my trusty mare, Mabel. We use new machines to aid in our harvest at times.

I am not the only "farm boy" here on the front. Too many of us have stood wide-eyed as we see that here the war sows fields of blood. The trusty steeds are used to pull cannons and great guns larger than any machines I've ever seen for farm duty. The harvest is one of men.

Simply put: It is awful. It is atrocious. It is abominable.

And yet—we believe hope is at hand. This country so deeply scarred by trenches and terror is beginning to feel its wounds stitched together by Allied forces, battlefield by battlefield, salient by salient, victory by victory.

America, it is a brave thing that you do. Go, now, and do it well.

———

There was more to the story, things I couldn't put in, for the safety of the soldiers. A new route we needed to take due to a flooded road. On this more northern detour, we found a German salient—a bulge into French territory long held by the enemy—that had been recently abandoned by the enemy, by all appearances. And a warning that "all appearances" were usually wrong, which explained the sniper from the night before.

This, and the carefully chosen words given by Matthew Petticrew about what awaited these new men. "It's fierce," he'd said. "But you can do it." He was very aware of the many listening ears. Men of few words, I was realizing, said much with their silence over here.

As they conversed, I finished my piece and in the next town found a hotel from which to wire it to the paper, with a prayer that hard truth might bring truest hope. As I exited the hotel, none other than the reticent Petticrew stood at a postbox, slipping an envelope in and flushing red when he turned to find me there.

"Good to keep in touch, eh?" I said, slapping him on the back and, I hoped, letting him know he didn't need to explain any letters to me. That was his business. As for me, I'd had my fill of the written word for the day.

And as for him . . . well, if my editor wanted these pieces written "like America was my sweetheart," maybe they should have gotten Matthew Petticrew to write them. Judging by the way he watched over the French woman, he might know a good bit more about that than I did. I considered, briefly, writing of our mission in my installments. America would take great interest in a lost heiress discovered in the shadows of war. But I did not know if it was my story to tell.

23

Matthew

Time is different in war. I knew very well that only six days had passed since we found Mira. I knew very well that it had been twenty-seven days since Saint-Mihiel. I knew, now, that shells and artillery would echo in a mind and shake a body well beyond the twenty-seven-day mark.

And I knew that in only a handful of days on the road in this treacherous, beautiful land . . . a lifetime could insert itself. Carve time clean away until the snipers, the washed-out roads, the battalions, the comrades, the growling stomachs filled out those meager days and made them feel like weeks. Months. Years, even.

But nowhere did I see this more clearly than in Mira's dark eyes. I worried for her.

We were between villages, and far—at least I hoped—from the enemy. You never knew, and you never ever settled that within yourself. You let your guard down, you'd die. And if you died—then those in your care died, too.

And the ones they carried.

"There," I said, spotting a barn up ahead. Built of stone, built to last. It would be a place to shelter for the night.

Henry was with me, and Mira just behind. For once, he didn't take out his notepad. I felt for him, truth be told. He had fight in him but wasn't allowed to fight. He funneled all of it into his pen, and I did respect him for it—but I couldn't pretend I didn't wonder what he was writing. Or who he was writing about. The last thing Mira needed was a light shining her into the newspapers, broadcasting her story to an entire country in between ads for cigarettes and liberty bonds.

He was a good guy, though. He nodded, looking at the large barn and shaking his head. "Gone from sleeping in trench stench to roofless cathedrals to sleeping with the cows all in the space of a few days. Could you ever have imagined?" He smiled and shrugged, and I liked that there wasn't a shred of disdain in his voice. "Looks like home to me," he said. "I've slept in my fair share of livestock stalls before. Let's go."

I felt Mira's gaze on me, saw a wink in the barely there smile she gave. A look that spoke clearly of a seventeen-year-old boy who smelled of goats. I refused to acknowledge the look and heard a silent laugh in return. We had a private joke, it seemed. Secret livestock stories, binding our souls.

Henry tromped the way up the rise and showed us how to live like farmers. He disappeared for a bit and came back with a sack, careful to hide its contents until it was roasting golden and savory over a fire. A goose, it was, and you'd think we were all kings, the way we dined that night sitting on the dirt floor.

In the night I studied the map, the places we'd drawn in our new route as if we knew where things actually were. Over on the left edge stood this one word, shining like a beacon: *Paris.*

But as I looked at my comrades, weary from the journey, I wondered if we'd make it.

Mira groaned a quiet, pained sound in her sleep from the hayloft. The others slept through it. As rustling sounded above, I made my way up the old ladder and saw her sitting, arms looped around her knees, head bowed.

She was silent, and the look of anguish on her face made me think she was forcing her body to absorb whatever sound, whatever groans were trying to find escape.

I remembered that sound, from long ago. And I remembered what had happened to my mother.

I knew I shouldn't do so, but I drew near and sat beside her. "Are you alright?" I said, making my voice as low as I could.

Slowly, she raised her head, her body stiffening at the realization that she was not alone. She swiped tears quickly with the backs of her hands. "Yes," she said. In a flash, she bit her lip, features compressing in pain again. "I am alright," she said, as if speaking the words would make it true.

I looked around for something—anything—to help. The bones in my fingers ached to take hold of something, to vanquish this foe she faced.

Only straw, a shovel, and—I narrowed my eyes to see in a shadowed corner—an oil lamp. Retrieving it and returning to her side, I sat. Reached inside my jacket for my matches and realized they were down in my haversack. I felt her watching me and cringed that I'd failed to give her this one small thing again.

With the lightest touch on my shoulder, she offered out something. My eyes fell on the small box.

I laughed quietly. Matches. I accepted the box and lifted it. "We're making a habit of this, aren't we? I'll have to keep better track of my matches so that I don't use all of yours." I slid her box open and saw the way she watched the three thin sticks roll around.

"You're sure it's alright to use one?" It didn't seem so, looking at the way she bit her lip, as if this cost her greatly to offer.

She hesitated, then nodded. "Oui."

I waited. Releasing a breath that relaxed her shoulders a little, she began to tell me of her father. Him leaving for the war and her promise to keep a lantern lit for him.

"The lantern in the woods," I said. The one that had brought me to her.

I struck the match, moving toward the lantern. Again, she nodded. "The matches . . . they are hope."

They are hope. The three words socked the air from me. Bringers of hope . . . creators of light from dark, when struck on hard places. And her supply, dwindling. Near gone.

Heat neared my fingers as the match burned itself nearly out, and the oil lamp surged to life. It hissed and sputtered and set a gentle glow between us, sending shadows dancing.

I hated to ask the next thing. It crossed into forbidden territory, it revealed my absolute ignorance, and it put her in an impossible place. But it was the only thing I could think to ask.

"Is the child coming?"

She froze in place. I'd just extracted her deepest fear and placed it directly before her to confront.

I wished I could pull back the words. Wished I could catch her in her free fall into that question.

"I do not know," she said at last. "I . . . do not know very much of such things."

The silence stretched tense between us. "That . . . makes two of us." I didn't tell her I knew some. I didn't tell her of the night I sat beneath my mother's window, out in the night, and heard the same sort of cries.

We had spoken of some things, in the days since the church. The night had become ours. The only place she chose to speak in our shared language, the only time our companions slept. We had spoken of growing up, of her grandfather. She told me of her father, vanished into war many years ago. But never had we spoken of the child.

Oddly, it was my confession that seemed to break the straining silence between us.

She made to rise, stiffening halfway up. I reached for her elbow to steady her, and she didn't withdraw, as she had other times. "It is my fault," she said. "I was meant to ask Madame Aline. I had determined to do so. But . . . when I saw her, I could not." Her cheeks flushed. "I was . . . I had . . . I just could not."

Her face flushed. I reached for something to say but found nothing. My arm stretched out, gesturing toward the doors that opened the hayloft into the night. Perhaps footsteps, the simple act of movement from this place of anguish, might help in some way.

She studied me a moment before I felt her relax and realized my other hand still held her elbow. As she straightened, her arm slipped into mine like it intended to live there, to rest there always. We walked the few steps to the doors. Carefully, I pushed them open, wincing when one clattered on a loose hinge. When no sound came from below and it seemed the others still slept, we sat.

She seemed burdened, so burdened. I could feel the weight of what she carried pulsing upon her. If I could but lift some of it . . .

"Is there anyone who knows? Did your grandfather . . . ?"

The questions felt so personal, they could have been weapons— or stitches in an open wound. Both hurt, I knew. But one healed. I hoped for the latter.

"No," she said, and there was fondness in her voice. "I did not want him to know. It would have killed him. He was already so sick. I confess—" She stared at her hands, clasped together in her lap. "I did not know for a long time what was happening to me. We had heard people speak of a sickness in the world, and I thought I must be growing ill with it."

I nodded. The influenza was another war, just as great as the one we fought in the trenches, and greater by the day.

"And then when I realized . . . I could not tell him."

There was another question. A blaring one, one that begged details she should not be forced to speak. It was a question I couldn't bring myself to speak. *Who?* Three little letters and a universe of hurt. I would be no gentleman, if I spoke it.

So I waited, and let her own words decide what to tell and what to conceal.

"There was much shame, Matthew Petticrew." She said my name as if to seal a pact between us. A question, a pleading that I would hold this between us. I nodded. "I should have known much sooner. I grew up in the forest with the animals," she said. "It is no great secret to me where life begins. But, I confess, I did not imagine life coming from such a—a lifeless act."

She was asking me to read her words. To understand a story, without her telling it. I had to listen hard, listen past the pounding in my head, the clenching of my jaw as I began to understand.

"When I was a girl, I became lost in the woods. Very close to home, but it was growing dark. I heard a pack of wolves about and took shelter inside of a very tall, hollow tree. It was like a house, its outside hiding its inside until you looked at it just so, and saw the opening. I called it *le cœur*, for the way the hidden inside was like a heart. A safe place. All the life and branches around it protecting a perfect hideaway, and all the life of the tree coming from inside. It was my fortress that night, with the wolves prowling. I spent the whole night there, finding solace in that refuge. After that, the forest always felt safe to me, though I knew there was danger. But . . . there are those in this war who are more monster than man," she said at last. "I do not know if they came to war that way, or if the war made them so. It was my—my—" she stumbled over her English, and she winced as she chopped up the coming word—"un-for-tu-nate fate to meet one in the woods. He appeared wounded. I approached him to help." She let the statement hang. "He . . . did not need help." I imagined two unseen worlds playing out into the night from the loft doors where we were perched, one from each of us. From hers, a world of brokenness and betrayal, spinning like blue threads into the night. From mine, red searing ropes of justice.

Hers found mine, there in the black night, and silenced them, blue threads coiling around boorish red vengeance with what she spoke next.

"But it is not mine to change what has happened," she said. "I cannot. It is mine to walk through what will come."

She said it so simply, with so much resolution, it smote me. How many times had I woken in a sweat from scant sleep, visions of Saint-Mihiel tearing my mind to shreds? And how many times had I boarded it shut and closed my eyes to what was ahead?

And yet here was someone who had faced her own war. Alone. And who was choosing life, and life, and life again, with every step she took, though it cost her all she had. Choosing not to live in the moment that had to be seared into her memory. Choosing not to pry her own eyes open against sleep, lest she find herself flung back to the scene in her dreams.

It was very clear, then: One of us was a warrior. And it was not me.

My instinct was to gather her up, carry her through, protect. But watching her now, crowned with moonlight and courage, I saw clearly that she had already placed her care in the hands of another.

"You have been a gift, Matthew Petticrew. But you know—you know that the things you are trying to do have already been done?"

I studied her. Wanting to understand.

"There are none who can undo the past. But there is one who will carry the pain of it. He knows too well the sting of injustice. No, more than that. The blood of it. But with it, He bears the scars of his own injustice with the same hands that carry me now. And the same hands that have made this little one."

With so much tenderness it made me ache, she rested a hand on her stomach, swollen somewhere under the folds of her dress. The gesture of a mother for her child.

What would my own mother have given to be able to live on and show that love to Celia? Bitterness ate at me like acid—for Mr. MacMannus and for Mira's attacker. But here Mira sat—the one who truly had every right to be bitter—and in her steady, quiet way, with her steady, wide eyes . . . she wrapped something so fierce and pure around that bitterness, it smote me again.

"Do you know how I know these things?" she asked.

Throat throbbing, I shook my head.

"I know because He sent you. You picked me up and carried me to my home. I suppose you never stopped carrying me. It is what you are doing even now."

"Not doing a very good job of it, am I?" I said, rubbing my temples with my fingers. "If I was, I'd have you home by now. To Paris." And to someone who would know what to do if these pains of hers kept on, and led to the inevitable event. This, I didn't say.

She looked out to the night. "Perhaps I am home," she said. "I do not know this place that Henry speaks of. The story he has told." She wrinkled her brow. "It fits, like a piece of the puzzles my

Papa used to create. But I do not know it. This château he tells of, it is no more a home to me than this barn is." She laughed softly.

"If this barn feels like home to you, maybe we're more alike than we know," I said.

"Yes?" She waited, her heels knocking softly against the stone wall outside as her legs kicked, keeping cadence with the frogs singing their night song.

"I lived above a stable pretty much my whole life," I said. All it took was a little tilt of her head, an invitation, and somehow I was telling her all of it. About Mrs. Bluet and blueberry buckle, and Mr. Haggerty and his garden sermons. About Celia and the racetrack, the way she flew and pulled the old bedsheet behind her, looking like a muddy angel running around and around.

Mira smiled. "I think I would like your Celia."

"She'd like you," I said, and smiled thinking of my sister. Truth was, if she showed up here, she might just scare Mira out of her wits with her bounding ways. But it was those ways that had gotten her through our toughest years. And now she was in Paris, the very city we were headed for. I'd written her a few days back, hoping against hope that she'd meet us there.

A breeze tumbled in, waking the creaky hinges of the hayloft doors, and sending a shiver through Mira. She rubbed the heel of her hands in her eyes, and I kicked myself for keeping her awake. She, more than any of us, needed to rest.

But there was something hovering, still, over the two of us. A wondering, and while I couldn't cover her with my jacket or build her a fire to keep her warm, lest it alert our location, I could at least tuck this assurance about her. Lay that furrowed worry on her forehead to rest. Assure her that I would hold fast to the secrets she had told me and hold them with care. That what she'd confided, her voice so laced in shame, served only to astonish me the deeper at her strength.

"Thank you," I said.

"What thanks do I deserve?" Mira's head tilted, listening.

For so many things. For the way this war and all its horrors, its atrocities, the things that plagued me, parted like the Red Sea as she walked through with a courage so bright I could nearly feel it, driving me like a militia man's drumbeat.

That was what I should have said. But the drumbeat drove words away, and all I could think to say was, "For telling me."

She stood slowly, as if each joint in her body felt every movement keenly, and returned to her pallet. "It is good that someone knows," she said. "For the child, I mean."

I nodded and waited. She seemed ready, if reluctant, to say more.

"You . . . are a man to trust, Matthew." She pressed her eyes closed, as if doing so both sealed the statement and sent it into the cosmos as a desperate wish. It cost her much.

That night, sitting in the old hay of an empty horse stall and pulling out the scrap of metal to occupy my hands engraving, I made a promise. As the rest of the barn slumbered, its creaking beams and hinges bore witness as I swore, in the stillness, that for the rest of our journey, come what may, I would do anything in my power to try and make her claim true.

24

George

"Welsh rarebit," I said. The four of us approached Épermay—not a village, praise be to the heavens—but a true town, with a train depot and all manner of civilization. *And restaurants.* As George the Fifth is my king, and as surely as the day is bright, this town must have food. It must. Food such as Welsh rarebit, more's the glory.

My belly ached at the thought of a hot meal, and I intended to plant great aspirations in my traveling mates.

"Pardon?" Hank the Wet Rag said, and adjusted his spectacles higher on his nose.

"Ah," I clutched my chest. "Get your pen out, mate, for here at last is something noteworthy for you to record."

He obeyed, warily, keeping step.

"Now. Welsh rarebit. You take the bread—and you'd better be sure it's crusty and fresh. None of this nation bread they've been trying to sell us in the other towns."

"*Pain national*," Hank said. "National bread. It's the law."

"It *is* a pain, yes. Law be hanged. None of that. Get some real bread. Toast up a slice or four. Then get your chef to spread this divine stuff on it—a mix-up of cheese and mustard and some sort of spices or another. Slather it on and don't be shy. Then, it gets blistered beneath a flame until it's golden and melted enough to bring a man to his knees. That is what we're going to find in Épermay, my good man."

"Hate to break it to you," Matthew said, bringing his stride up to walk with us. "But I don't think Épermay is populated by an abundance of British pubs. Or illegal forms of non-ration bread."

"Just you wait," I said, adding a good bit of brow-waggling to boost the fellow's confidences. "Just you wait."

As it happened, Épermay *was* populated by something glorious, but it wasn't melted-cheese pub bread. A corps of nurses flooded the streets and with them a scent most heavenly. Lovely faces every which way, and did we remember, up till now, that uniforms could be crisp and clean and not drenched in mud and varying unmentionable substances? I elbowed the others, making sure they saw. Hank was busy staring hard at the ground, bashful fellow that he was. Matthew stood alert, scanning every face as if they might hold answers to a piercing question.

As we drew closer to the train depot, another wave of people disembarked. These, the trench-weary. They looked like walking skeletons, gaunt and haunted. Or in some cases, not walking at all, but borne on stretchers. Some flooded into a delousing tent. Others to a hospital set up in an old bank.

And among them, the civilians, the townspeople who tried to carry on with some semblance of normalcy while feeding and housing the soldiers.

In a vineyard, worlds collided as workers plucked grapes from a harvest, while a stone's throw away a division performed drills, and I was thrown back into our days at Plattsburg.

Come evening, before curfew, the soldiers would be able to attend theatres, hole up in libraries, play cricket with local children, or whatever game the French liked. Croquet, I suppose. That sounds rather French. In short, they would be allowed to do other normal-life things to try and remind them, between trench shifts, that they were still human.

It was the wounded that jarred me. I had seen plenty, said prayers and holy-like words over many, at Saint-Mihiel. But seeing the wounded here, away from the front, against a backdrop of stony buildings and blooming flowers, drove question marks into

186

me in ways I did not entirely know what to do with. Forcing me to see this clash of worlds. How so much good and so much bad could be alive together in the same universe. Which was terribly somber of me to think, and it spoke of things deeper than I knew how to handle.

I wished, fleetingly, that I had a wise and holy man I could pose these questions to.

And then I remembered, I was that wise and holy man. Supposedly.

"It's me!" I said. "It is I." Hank looked askance at me. He was always looking askance. Why did he not look reverently at me?

Perhaps I should find a real reverent and holy man while I was here. I had much to ask and much to learn. But first, we checked in with the AEF tent and were assigned to a local billet. A farmhouse that would lodge us for a night or two, feed us.

As we approached it, following the sound of geese squawking in the yard, I wondered briefly if the mistress of this manor knew anything of Welsh rarebit.

She did not. She fed us a midday meal of salted potatoes, after which Hank the bookworm disappeared to the local library—"for research," he said, and I shouldn't wonder if the word was stuck somewhere in the bridge of his nose. It earned him free passage, though, and Matthew the maddeningly ambiguous soldier tasked me to "stay with Mireilles," while he went off to do something or other in the town.

The town where the nurses were. The shoe-shiner. The bands playing and probably pastries flowing and I knew not what.

So I sat with the Angel and thought perhaps she'd sing me a tune or two if I tapped my foot in time, but she and the woman of the house took to scrubbing things. Scrubbing!

I did not entrench myself in a war and come all this way to watch scrubbing take place and feel the dry taste of potato skin push away all hope of Welsh rarebit.

So. I took my leave of the ladies, seeing that Mireilles was well situated and seemed cheerful enough. *"Au revior, les poules!"* I said, rather proud of so resourcefully commandeering the French word for *hens* in the absence of one in my repertoire for *ladies*. Hens were ladies, after all. It might be I could use the same tactic to charm some of the American nurses with my command of the local language.

Thus, I took myself back to Épermay.

The sun was shining on the road, and the vineyard workers had disappeared. The soldiers who'd been drilling were vanished. All signs pointing to a grand *soirée* surely taking place in town.

And yet when I reached the heart of the city, the place where flats above shops, a steepled church, and completely un-cratered streets made one feel as if they had touched into a war-less land, at last . . . there were no pastries flowing in the byways, nor music piping, nor nurses chattering away.

"Hello?" I said to the town.

Quiet, you, the town seemed to stay back. A moustached man poked his head out of a door and prattled something that I had no earthly hope of following.

"Yes," I said, nodding and grinning. "Oui!" And then, "Where is everyone?" I gestured at the empty square.

He prattled something again, gesturing at the buildings, the sun beginning its slow decline from afternoon into evening. He raised two looped fingers from a flat hand, mimicking the drinking of tea. "*Le Goûter*," he said.

This, I understood. Tea ran through my veins. And if I was not mistaken, this good man was extending glorious hospitality and inviting me to enjoy this French version of the auspicious pastime. This explained the absence of any people in the town—they were all busy partaking in tea time. At least something was still right with the world.

"*Merci*," I said, jubilant, and started toward him. But he pulled his door closed, holding out a hand to wave me off from inside his window.

I hung my head. Alone and hungry in this town that had felt so full of promise, with all hope of tea removed by a bearded stranger.

So, I wandered dejected into the square, a tree-lined patch of green. And that was when I spotted them.

A man and a woman, sitting on a bench, their voices low. He leaned toward her to hear what she was saying, and she gestured greatly as she spoke. She was of the sort who spoke with her hands, I thought, and when she turned her head, I caught sight of white-blond hair and punch-red lips. I stopped in my tracks. Why, she was beauty itself. And, more than that, with the spark of life in her wide green eyes and a naïve sort of innocence in the joy behind her smile, she was life. *Life* itself! The essence of Diana, Aphrodite, Athena, Juliet, Cleopatra, Guinevere, and all those other timeless sort of names. I didn't know one from the other, but I knew that surely all women of might and myth must be rolled up into this singular being before me.

I pounded with the pulse of a man whose breath and heart have been irrevocably stolen. I took a step forward, thinking surely, any moment, she would lock eyes with me. Be summoned to my being, as I was to hers.

She moved. Even her movement was grace. All thought of Welsh rarebit flew into the wind, for what cared I for pastry and cheese now? *This is it*, I thought. She was shifting, her grey jacket belted neatly against her figure, an arm cuff declaring her a part of the Red Cross.

And then—she embraced the man. I saw his face.

It was Matthew Petticrew.

The mongrel.

"Hallo, what's this?" I hollered, feigning a friendly laugh and hurrying their way. The woman pulled away from him, looking shocked either at my appearance or at my timely presence in rescuing her from this fiend.

"Chaplain George Piccadilly," I said, bowing before the wondrous creature.

"Piccadilly," she said, trying the name out, perhaps with matrimonial thoughts.

"Has a certain *ring* to it, don't you think?" I flashed a broad smile.

Matthew mumbled something about a circus and its monkeys belonging back there.

"For the last time, Piccadilly is not that sort of circus," I said.

"Well, I was just thinking how uncannily like our name it sounds," the woman said.

"Our name?" I inclined my head. She looked to Matthew. Surely she did not mean he was her—why, her *husband*, of all things.

And him, making friendly with the Angel of Argonne, all this while. With a woman like this looking at him so adoringly. "What's this?" I said, making my voice as grumbly as he was wont to do. "Eh, Petticrew?" I clenched my teeth and clenched my fist, ready to bring justice down upon his sorry head. "You never mentioned you were married." I pulled back my fist. Waited for him to rise.

He did, at the slow speed of treacle.

I released my fist, full force, letting it fly right at his blastedly set jaw. The lady's gloved hands flew to cover her mouth.

Time slowed, my fist still moving toward its mark. Pride surged at her reaction. She was about to see what a true man was made of.

Just as my fist made to land a glorious blow—Matthew stopped it. Raised a hand, expressionless, and deflected my arm.

"She's my sister, you idiot," he said. Offering his arm to the woman, he made to walk away.

"Matthew!" she said, looking back and tearing herself from him. Stubbornness ran in their family, it would seem. "You've hurt him!"

I hadn't known I was shaking my hand, attempting to rid my knuckles of the crunch they'd suffered. She clasped it, examining it and pressing it between her two hands.

"He's fine," Matthew said. He hesitated, less sure, and added, "Right?"

"What happened?" This, from a third voice, as feet pounded up the gravel path. Stuffy old Hank Jones, a book and a paper tucked under his arm. "You alright, George?"

"I'm fine," I said.

"He's fine," Matthew said.

190

"He'll be fine," said the lovely lady.

Hank Jones appeared to notice her for the first time and dropped his book, tripping over himself to get it. Poor sap.

"Fellas . . ." Matthew said, sounding like he'd rather not say it at all. "Meet my sister, Celia Petticrew."

25

Mira

The men came clattering in like a herd of goats, all noise and knees. Something seemed different about them, about the tone of their conversation. Our hostess, Marie-Agnès, whose silver hair escaped in wisps from beneath her red kerchief, had pulled out a tiny packet of sugar while they were away, saying she had rationed her own rations. That any visiting soldier might have something sweet to send him off to battle.

The effect was that when they smelled the plum tart baking in her wood oven, silence fell over them like a blanket.

"What's that heavenly smell?" The voice of a woman, so cheery. I peered around the stone column of the small kitchen to see who it might be.

"*Votre fille?*" I asked Marie-Agnès if it was her daughter.

She shook her head no, looking as puzzled as I.

Matthew Petticrew stood beside her, lifting a hand to the young woman's elbow. She was lovely, I thought. She was young, unsullied by road travel and wide-eyed with an innocence that made me ache for something I had once had. It was silly of me, I knew, to feel so. When I was as she, I did not know what a gift such a time was in this life. And she looked—she looked just right, standing beside Matthew. The ache grew deeper.

"Mireilles," he said quietly, his voice running gently over the raw parts of me that threatened tears. "Marie-Agnès. This is my sister, Celia."

"Sis-ter," Marie-Agnès said. "*Sœur*," she spoke again, for my benefit.

Matthew Petticrew's sister. I breathed relief and then stood straighter, startled by my own reaction. I saw it, now, as they stood smiling side by side. So happy to be together. It made me happy, too. They were alike, though his hair was as dark as hers was light, and his eyes bluer. Hers were green like my forest in springtime, and she seemed full of that same new life. She approached me and clasped my hands in hers. "Mireilles," she said. "Mira."

Something fluttered inside me, to hear that name. Matthew had told her something of me, then. I knew not to wonder how much he had told, whether he had betrayed my secret. I knew I was safe with him. But—the thought of him, speaking of me to his family . . . it was like someone opening a door on a cold night, letting light and warmth from inside spill over me.

I did not know what to do. I wished to thank her for the light, the warmth. But all I could say was her name, without giving all way. "Celia," I said, lifting my chin and nodding, hoping to convey delight at meeting her.

The rest of the afternoon and into the evening was spent in so much happiness, all around, that I hardly knew what world I had landed in. Was there truly a war outside these four walls? Could there really be winter on the way, with such a warm fire snapping in the stone hearth? What were rations and hollow stomachs, when ours were full of Marie-Agnès's sweet plum tart, and even roasted chicken for the evening meal?

This house, and the people in it, seemed an offering from heaven. A reminder of hope.

Celia had not much time before she needed to return to her duties. I learned she was aboard a hospital barge on its way to Paris—or at least very near it—through the canals. There, she and the other nurses would tend to men wounded and transport them back to field hospitals and beyond, where they could heal or die. We all knew of the latter, though she spoke only of the healing.

"May I see your quarters, Mira?" she said, gesturing up the

ladder stair to the attic, the place I was to sleep. Marie-Agnès translated and shooed us out of the kitchen. I led the way, and once we were alone, she hesitated only a moment before facing me. "Mireilles," she said with familiarity and an inquisitive tilt to her head. "I visited with Matthew a long while today."

She was speaking as if she knew I understood. No gestures, no stuttering attempts at French. I swallowed.

"Please don't be upset with him," she said, her face melting into a plea. "He . . . thought it had been a long time, that you've been subject to travel with three bumbling men." She laughed musically. "His words. And he just thought you might like a bit of a break from all of that." There was such kindness in her, in Matthew. That feeling of a door spilling warmth, stretched closer to me.

Celia continued, "He thought you might like a chance to talk to—well, someone like you. So he confided in me that you are an excellent speaker of English. He's so impressed, Mira, and truly would never have betrayed your secret if—"

I could feel the warmth from that cracked-open door turning to consuming heat. How much had he told her?

"Well, if he didn't think it would help."

I did not know what to say, without knowing how much she knew. The way he had spoken of Celia before, I felt as though I knew her. I wanted to sit with her, to know her as a sister, as he did. The one who had brought him so much joy in a dark time. But I did not know how to just—*poof*—be a friend to her and speak of the thing I had only first put words to a few nights before.

But perhaps she did not know that much. Matthew would not betray that trust. And yet . . . he had told her my other secret, of language. My confidence wavered.

Celia waited, and the silence grew uncomfortable.

I closed my eyes and pictured Matthew. The concern that ran so deep, so far beyond words, when he looked upon me.

I could trust him.

Though there were no others in this wide and widening world

that I could say such of, I could thank the Lord above that Matthew was a man of honor. He had meant this as a gift.

So I spoke. Three words reaching across worlds and oceans, I laid down the next plank in the bridge between us. "Thank you, Celia," I said, my words tumbling clumsily in my accent.

She nodded, and looking around, spotted a spindly rocking chair in the corner. She directed me toward it and took the crude straw mattress for herself. She sat upon its edge in her nice coat and skirt, making it look more throne than relic.

"Matthew thinks very much of you," she said. Her smile was sweet. Dimpled and pure, and I wondered for a moment what it would have been like to have a sister.

"Does he?" I said, my surprise very real. "He must think much of strange women who do not know where in the world they belong, if that is true."

Celia laughed. "He thinks very much of one woman who knows how to think quickly and sing like a lark and face down journeys of great peril."

I warmed at the mention of the singing. I had not known he had heard me. I wanted to ask more but clutched another phrase she spoke instead. "Journey of great pearl," I said. "This is a phrase I do not know. A gem of the sea, yes? I fear I do not take the meaning, though."

Celia's laughter was kind. "Per-il," she said. "It means . . . great danger, much risk to one's well-being. It means one doesn't know quite what will happen but faces the unknown with courage and fortitude."

Her words sounded like very good words, but my tired mind was having trouble following the way they rolled out so fast from her. Her brother was a thoughtful speaker, one who weighed his words and chose few of them to speak, ones that seemed always to carry so much in their depths. His sister seemed to do just the opposite—speak her words, then catch them and consider them, then say more words to explain. As if she were swimming in them, and happily so.

"It means you are brave, Mireilles," she said, growing serious. "Matthew said as much. He said it was not his story to tell, and that you would choose what to tell. But he hoped I might be able to help, somehow." She paused. "Are you ill, Mira? We have the hospital barge waiting at the canal. It's for the soldiers, but I'm sure I could convince them to let you aboard, if we can help you."

Was I ill? My body felt so, sometimes. My soul felt it much more, when I thought to all that had happened. And yet—I carried life, too. That did not make me feel ill. It made me feel . . . frightened, small . . . and sometimes so full of awe that I knew not where to put such feelings.

I swallowed, wishing for words. For this courage she spoke of, enough to tell her. She was a nurse—she could help. She could tell me what to do, what to expect. I had never known my mother, who breathed her last when an illness came in the months after I had arrived. Would that be my fate, too? I did not know. I had never had the influence of a woman in my life, beside Madame Aline every few months. What would it be like, to take a sister— someone else's sister, if not my own—into confidence?

I opened my mouth. Closed my eyes. And prepared to speak the truth to a stranger. Whether the horrible story, or the wonder-filled thing it had led to. I was learning that perhaps the only way forward was to separate the two things. This little being inside of me, its flutters and jolts, its tiny little hiccups—it knew nothing of the dark incident that had begun it all. The incident that did not erase the way my breath caught when I thought of this: a life grew within me. *Me.* The girl of the forest, who did not even know her own origins until a stranger came with tales of balloons and wars.

I looked at my skirt. I had chosen it from the attic a few months before, when my middle had begun to grow. My grandmother's old dress, I had learned. Grand-père's eyes glistened with nostalgia when he saw it, never imagining the reason for my donning it.

"I—" My voice scraped over the truth. "I am—"

With child, I was about to say. But the sound of the door closing firmly directly below us made me jump in my seat, jump right out of the words unspoken.

We both whirled our heads to the window, where darkness had begun to fall.

"Who can it be?" Celia asked, standing and approaching the window. I followed her lead, and we both stood there at the chilled pane with its bumpy, blurred glass and watched a familiar figure stride through the little brown picket gate.

"Of course," Celia said. "Matthew. It's his way."

"What is his way?"

"Keeping watch," Celia said. "I can't begin to tell you the number of times we did just this, as children. Me, hearing him slip out in the night. Him, keeping watch. Back and forth he would walk, or rather 'round and 'round, in our case."

"At the racetrack," I said, smiling. I liked to picture it.

"Yes." She smiled, too. "He told you?"

"He said you—how did he say it? You had the wind inside of you, and you needed to run."

"I remember desperately wanting to run over the hills and away from our situation. Wishing I could meet our mother. But the only place to run was the racetrack, and if we pocked it up with footmarks, it would mean our hides the next day. We'd run—*oh*, would we run!—and then he'd send me off to bed after I'd exhausted my legs enough that even my mind would turn off for the night and let me sleep."

"But he stayed out?"

"That boy would take a rake and walk the track, dragging it behind him, covering over our footprints. Every time, without fail. All so I could get a little distance from my fear." She shook her head, and I have never seen someone look so filled with joy and filled with sadness all at once. "That's just Matthew. He breathes justice like other men breathe air."

We watched him now, walking circles around this little billet farmhouse as his friends reclined by the warmth of the fire downstairs. His solitude didn't last long, though, and neither did our silence. The door opened again, releasing George and Henry into the gathering dark. With our window cracked open, we couldn't help but hear when Henry's voice lifted on the wind. His words were unremarkable. His tone was even, as he always seemed to be. And yet the message—it sent my pulse into its own race.

"We need to talk, Petticrew," Henry said. "It's time . . ." He blew out a breath. "To take our leave of Mireilles."

26

Matthew

My jaw locked. I swallowed, hard.

"What." Statement or question, I didn't know. Much more a declaration of impossibility. I shook my head. "Why would we ever do that?"

Henry looked over his shoulder at the house worriedly. I did, too, and noted the windows were empty, where moments before Celia and Mira had been silhouetted in the attic. At least they weren't hearing this.

"She's not well," Henry said. He pinched the side of his spectacles and pulled them up, as he always seemed to do when that brain of his was going ten thousand miles a minute. "Perhaps you haven't noticed, but the journey's been hard on her."

I scoffed. "Of course I've noticed." There were days when she looked as though her legs were ready to buckle beneath her. Though she tried to hide it, her hands often went to her back, rubbing low where she felt pain. I had caught myself, once, reaching out to do it for her. Thank heavens I came to my senses before she noticed; my touch would have sent her jumping out of her skin, the way she reacted to unexpected moves from the three of us. And the truth was, I had no right to touch her, to help her, though my chest fairly beat itself to smithereens, caging that desire.

"Right-ho," George said, slapping me on the shoulder. I had half a mind to flick his hand off like a flea. "You've seen, too, then, eh? The girl's pale as a sheet, while the rest of us grow toasty and golden in the sun."

George had an interesting definition of "toasty and golden." Had he seen his reflection lately, he might know he was the very definition of "pale as a sheet," the way his skin refused to budge from its translucent state.

"All the more reason for us to get her to Paris," I said. "To safety. Security. Right?"

"That's just it," Henry said, clutching a book I hadn't seen him carrying beneath his arm. "See—what will we do once we get her there? We were to help her find her lost estate, but I'm beginning to see it was a very ill-planned venture. No one I talk to, in any of these villages, knows what became of the family home of Marquis Fontinelle. Some say it was grown over and remains empty to this day. Others say it was commandeered by the government earlier in the war for use as offices. The point is, without knowing what we're bringing her into, we could very well be hurting her more than we're helping. It got me thinking— maybe the legacy we should be seeking on her behalf isn't that of an inheritance. Maybe it's a person. See . . ." He flipped pages in that book as I attempted to harness my racing thoughts, syncopated with protests.

"According to this account I found at the library in Épermay, when the Marquis escaped the city, it wasn't only his riches and home he left behind. He also left a sister"—he ran his finger down the page—"Sophia Fontinelle. She was younger than he was, away at school in Switzerland at the time of that war."

Family.

The breath went out of me.

For the girl who had lost everything and was about to face the greatest challenge of her life. It sounded . . . too good to be true. I shook my head. "How could we ever find her, now? In the middle of a war?"

"We don't have to." He held up an article. "From the news office, here. The archives. Sophia Fontinelle wed a mayor, and according to this, they relocated to Bordeaux when the Paris officials evacuated four years ago. They have remained there since."

"Bordeaux." The word seemed bitter as I mapped it in my mind. "That's . . . far."

George sputtered. "Far! Far's putting it mildly, mate. It's entirely across the country! Why, if you tripped, you'd land in Spain!"

"Bit of an exaggeration, don't you think?" Henry scratched his head. "It's far, yes. A good bit farther south and east than Paris. But also a deal farther away from all this—" He thumbed over his shoulder, as if we could all see through the night, miles away to where battles raged even now. "And it's not all that far for a train. There's one leaving tomorrow from here, and it would have her there faster than we would complete our journey to Paris. She'd be off her feet, in a train—"

"A target for the Boche. A cesspool of the influenza." Never.

"Now hold up, mate," George said. "We're all a target to both of those foes, wherever we are. Did you forget the sniper? She'd be leagues safer on a metal beast of a machine racing through the countryside toward civilization than she is with a lot like us."

It . . . made sense. I hated that it made sense. But they didn't have all the information. "So we just—what? Pack her off to the other side of the country without a friend in the world? Feeling like she does? To a relative she never met, who possibly doesn't even know she exists, and even if she did, who might not be inclined to let a—"

I bit my tongue. It wasn't mine to say.

"What?" Henry said. He held his blasted article and his awful book out with open hands, like an offering.

They both were trying to help. I tried to remember that. I took a deep breath.

"Better for us to stick to the plan," I said, willing the resolve in my voice to somehow build a path forward. "We'll see her safely there, connect her with good care. We—we have to anyway, right? Get to Paris and then on to Provins to deliver the book."

I wasn't making sense, and I saw it on their faces. We could skirt Paris entirely and get to Provins, and do it in less time. *It'd be better for everybody.* The thought socked me like cannon fire.

I tried a different tack. "What if this great-aunt won't take her in?"

"Ah, but what if she does?" George folded his arms over his chest.

"She married a government official, you said."

Henry nodded.

"A politician."

Again, a nod.

"Someone in the public eye."

"Quite so," George said.

"I could do a piece on it," Henry said, pulling his pencil out from his jacket.

I reached out and grabbed the pencil. Snapped it in two, tossing it on the ground.

They gawked at me and I wished I could undo it all. Make sense of it for them while keeping Mira's confidence. Find a way to keep her with us.

And not let her go.

But then . . . *a home.* A family. What if the husband was a good man, who didn't care what people thought if his wife took in a lost niece who could undermine his wife's inheritance and whose present state outside of wedlock could sink their name?

I looked back over at the house, still vacant of any sign of the girls. Rubbing my pounding temples I stooped to gather up the pencil shards. I fit the splintered pieces together, feeling how they completed one another, filling the cracks and broken places. I gripped them so, willed them to stay that way and handed the thing to Henry. "I'm sorry," I said. "I shouldn't have done that."

His mouth went grim. "What's going on?" he asked. Ever the journalist. Digging for truth.

Well, maybe it was time he had some. Maybe it was time these fellows understood the gravity of the situation. That life was on the line. *Lives,* plural.

I hated myself for it before I even did it but couldn't stop the words. I had promised not to speak them. And yet, if I kept that promise, would it not lead to her abandonment? To her being suddenly alone again? And with no guarantee of safety on the other end.

I told myself she was more important than a promise.

I told myself she could hate me if it meant that she would live and be well.

"You are a man to trust, Matthew." The memory of her words stopped me. I had vowed, in the wake of them, to prove her claim true.

But if I let her go—if I did as they suggested and left her to face it all alone—was *that* the act of a trustworthy man?

No.

I told myself these things and shoved the words out before I could tell myself I didn't believe any of that.

"She's going to have a baby."

The words dropped with too much force, driven like bombs from the black night and flung like shrapnel right into the men. I saw it sink into George, the way he unfolded those arms and stuck them in his pockets, hanging his head. I felt it click into Henry's consciousness, watched his face draw somber. The tension across my shoulders eased its grip a little when he put his pencil back into his pocket and didn't write a word on that notepad of his.

And last—I heard it. In the approach of light footsteps. In the way they halted, suddenly. And in the breaking dark between her and me when I turned to see it: complete betrayal, written on Mira's face.

203

27

Captain Jasper Truett

The land mocked me. It blurred past from where I sat on the slip-shod train. One second, all was green and growing. The next, the scene held crumbled buildings and rising smoke. Smoke that had me thinking of Amelia. I willed it to be the memory of flying her, laughing, through swirls of extinguished candles. I willed it not to be the other memory of her and of smoke.

Blue eyes flashed, her girlish smile, and I closed my eyes around the thought as if that might keep her. Catch her and anchor her to reality, where I might embrace her once more.

But my thoughts betrayed me. Too soon, they left the happy moment and went to the other one. Me, sitting in hot Panama under a clump of Poor Man's Umbrella, rain falling on the larger-than-life leaves, the leaves earning their name twice-over. A steep drop-off that I hung my feet over, the sound of a river below.

We'd be leaving the country soon, heading home. I shined my compass with the best cloth I had—a scrap of jungle-soiled handkerchief—and studied the directional notations. "North by Northwest," I said, repeating June's words and picturing the way her long hair caught the wind atop our little Carolina hill when she turned to smile at me. "I'm coming home," I said, then clamped my mouth shut when another soldier approached and delivered a letter.

I knew before I opened it. The writing was not June's. It was more formal, no traces of June's windswept loop at the bottom of the *p*'s just to bring beauty to something plain.

I opened it, swallowing.

Words scrawled on a paper. Stupid letters, just sticks and curves with dots. My finger flicked a torn corner back and forth to the cadence of those large sheltering leaves in the wind above—and I read.

The sticks and curves and letters arranged themselves into words that shattered my world. I closed my eyes, pressed them tight, and willed the words to rearrange into something different.

But they did not. My compass slid from my shaking hand, clattering onto a ledge halfway down the drop-off. Numbly and dumbly, I climbed down to get it, my chest pounding with a desperate plea to get them back, too.

When I picked it up, its tinny rattle told me it was done for. Its innards just scraped to a halt, its homing magnet jarred loose with no home to point to. It broke that day. And if a man like me ever even had a heart . . . that broke, too.

The train lurched, vaulting me from a cliffside in Panama to a train in France.

June and Amelia . . . they were gone again. Gone, still. But the girl—Mireilles—was not, and neither was Matthew Petticrew. Them, I could help. And perhaps if I could catch them, intercept that book they carried, we might help more. Far, far more.

The train chugged, the metal screeching of its many parts grinding into me. Into Épermay, where it spilled ragged passengers out like so many rats, me right in the thick of their current. It was jarring, never failed to be, when one left the front and saw that somewhere in the world people still walked streets, ate regular meals, meager though they might be, and endeavored to be human.

Even here, where being a railway hub meant the town was in constant danger, a target to the enemy. The oldest war tactic around: cut off the wheels of the operation, cut off the supply line. Cut off the supply line, stop the flow of soldiers, food, ammunition, medical supplies. Dry up those things, and victory is yours.

But Épermay, by all appearances, had escaped unscathed thus far. I prayed that good fate would continue. Rumblings were that

Germany was on unstable ground back on their home front—and all the more desperate to make one final push toward Paris. Towns like this were not yet out of danger.

Yet life went on here. Across the way, a café hosted a handful of soldiers and a violinist playing. I scanned their faces and saw none of my men. I hoped they'd be here, that I might find Petticrew and get him back. Things were gearing up for the next offensive, and we had need of his skills. I needed to get back on that train and on to headquarters for orders and to get that book to the General's men there, but first I wanted Petticrew on his way back, posthaste.

This was the likeliest place I'd find them, based on my calculations of their pace and where they should be by now. But I saw no one familiar. Truth was, they could be anywhere. Taken a different route, or made camp along the way.

I looked instead for the girl. She'd be easier to spot in this sea of uniforms. The girl I'd blockaded from every thought, cursing the way she'd presumed to look so like Amelia. It was the sort of thing June and I would have laughed at together, both of us knowing just what the other was thinking.

But it had been a heap of years since I'd looked up from a meal to catch my wife's knowing glance, see her tipping her head for me to look at Amelia before I missed some remarkable something. Years since she'd begged me not to go again, saying I'd miss all remarkable everythings.

And years since I turned my back and took the step that changed it all. It followed me, that one step. My blasted black boot falling on that old dirt path, a cloud of dust swallowing it up. A cloud of regret gulping us all down, never to release us back to one another.

"Why must you go, Papa?" Amelia's eyes, so round, imploring me to stop buttoning my uniform jacket, stop packing my things.

"Because I must," I'd said, ruffling her hair and wishing I could say it better. That I must go to protect her and her mother and our country and others like them everywhere. That though my service wasn't required, it was requested. I had never said no. Could not imagine starting then.

So I said *no* to the ones dearest to me instead.

"Because you're brave?" she'd said, patting my cheek with chubby fingers that I held as long as I could.

I'd nodded. I didn't feel it, but I let her believe it. *"And so must you be, my little lightning bug."*

And while I was off being "brave," protecting lives in the middle of a war in Columbia, my own family slipped away at the hands of a senseless house fire.

I had seen my share of fires. Played my part in putting them out, even. And yet it was the one I never saw, the one I should have been there for, that burned inside of me still. Burned until I was hollow. The Incredible Hollow Man, they should call me. Who lived and breathed though his heart stopped beating long ago. Who became so mechanical in his existence and movements that he was very convincing as a soldier. A hollow tin toy soldier, the ideal vehicle for giving heartless orders and moving on, over and over again.

But that was in the past. Far, far, far in the past. I'd boxed it up and nailed it tight so long ago—and yet somehow that box had found me here in France and opened irrevocably like that old legend about Pandora. Try as I might to shove it all back, to put Amelia and June back into their safe and silent space and close the door on them, they followed me everywhere in this war.

I turned. Ignored them, knowing adding ten thousand more apologies to the million ones I'd spoken over the years wouldn't change a thing. I set my foot on a dusty path again. Found the billet office who told me what I needed to know, and off I went.

It was dark already. I should've made camp, waited until morning. But something drove me on, down a too-quiet road through a vineyard where I wondered who, one day, would drink the fruit of these vines, decades from now, and whether they'd give thought to the soldiers who walked these roads, whose shoulders were touched by the reaching leaves of the grapevines like sad farewells.

A humble farmhouse rose in silhouette and I checked it against the description given me. *Brown picket gate. Sheep in the yard. Stone house.*

This was the one.

I approached the door and was ready to knock when I heard raised voices and knew immediately that it was the sound of soldiers and anger. My men.

I rounded the outside of the building and there they stood. The Brit with his arms crossed, proud as a peacock. The reporter leaning forward, taking in every word spoken by the impassioned speaker. And that speaker, the very man I'd come for.

I was tired. Tired of the journey, tired of this war. Tired, so tired, from life. I knew I should have walked right up to them, given Petticrew his new commands, and taken him along with me that instant.

But if this tiresome life had taught me one thing, it was how to pause. Listen. Even—*especially*—when my instinct was to charge in and take action. So I did, taking one step at a time closer in the shadows, until I began to be able to make out their words.

The girl—Mireilles, if I was remembering right—approached from the direction of the house.

With her soft footsteps came the impossible sound of my own heart. Rising up from black soil and trying so hard to beat. A rusty sort of sound from inside me, the Incredible Hollow Man. The shriveled heart, coming to life. I ignored it—all of it, and her—as long as I could. Until the beating within grew louder, ordering me to look at her. To see what my daughter could have been like, had she lived.

She looked so broken. And yet so full of hope. Something lighting her young face as her eyes fell on Matthew Petticrew. And the cracks of brokenness seemed to sear the light of that hope right through her whole being, right out into the night until it was palpable to this clumsy, rusty old heart of mine.

The men climbed the steps of Petticrew's words, ascending toward that moment when everything froze.

"She's going to have a baby," he said. And in his low, breaking voice was the very shadow I see on all my men's faces just before they're about to go over the top and into the thick of the battle. It is everything good in their lives, gathered up for strength, rallied around them to drive them on. It is everything impossible ahead, looming in sheer, terrifying dark. It is the collision of those two things as they explode over the top, charging into that unknown. Some come back. Some do not.

In that instant, Petticrew locked stares with the girl. She froze in place, the searing light of hope snuffed out completely. Her chin lifted. Her shoulders rose and fell in measured defiance of what had just happened, in absolute war against the flash of utter destruction I'd seen on her face the instant Petticrew uttered those words.

I'd seen that look before.

The one of hope betrayed.

It had stayed with me for years. Foot in sand, swallowed in dust.

It was a moment that was fleeting and eternally branded into a soul, all at once. One of those that can never be forgotten.

Until a bumbling British chaplain speaks up and shatters it.

Piccadilly pointed, flabbergasted. He pointed at the girl, who was most assuredly wishing she were anywhere but there, anywhere but the subject of a buffooned point like that.

"Did you see that," he said incredulously. "She understood. She understood! You understood every word of that, didn't you, Angel of Argonne?"

I rolled my eyes.

"I am . . . a genius," he said, spreading his hands wide in emphasis. "I have been translating, you know. Tutoring her along the highways and byways of the intricacies of the English language."

"If you think expounding on Welsh pastries is tutoring." This, from the journalist.

George looked offended. "It is. It *is*, and it's worked, and she's just understood every single word we've said." He took a step toward her. "Haven't you?"

She took three steps back, stumbling into another young woman, one who'd gone white as a sheet and was looking between Mireilles and Petticrew.

"Matthew?" this new young lady said. All concern, very earnest.

"I—I—" he stuttered. Poor fool. He looked around, looked for some bit of help, maybe a way to undo what he'd just done. Poor kid. He'd know, now, that there was no undoing.

Only maybe for him—unlike me—it wasn't too late to mend the tear, jump the chasm.

"Petticrew," I said, stepping into the reaching ring of light that encompassed them from the glow of the farmhouse. As I stepped closer, Mireilles stepped farther back, disappearing beyond that same ring of light.

There was a pang in my chest as she vanished. *Stop it*. She was not mine. Not my daughter. Not disappearing again.

And yet . . . she was somebody's daughter. What would her father give to be here? To guard her? To bring her back into that ring of light and vanquish whatever she faced?

Anything. Her father, if he knew what was well and good, would give anything. I'd wager my life on it.

"Petticrew," I said again, and this time he registered my voice. There was a lag, for this boy who was the quickest among them, to stand at attention. But when he did, and saluted, I could read it in the stiffness of his determination: He was fighting every impulse to turn and run after her.

"A word, please. At ease," I said to the others as an afterthought, watching the chaplain fumble into salute too late.

Petticrew joined me, and I lowered my voice. "Explain to me why one single week after I sent you on your way to Paris, you are standing in a cornfield, blithering about something that is no concern of yours?"

My words were too harsh. I knew it. Saw it in the way he winced.

"The men thought it better that we send her away from here tomorrow," he replied. "By herself."

I waited.

His jaw twitched.

"They . . . did not have all the information needed to make an informed decision," he said, sounding terribly unconvinced.

210

"Petticrew. Listen. Think of the trenches. That dark room with the swaying light and the maps where I go cross-eyed trying to make plans. Do you think I might receive highly confidential information in that room?"

"Yes, sir."

"And is it my duty, then, to go running after every one of you soldiers to explain that confidential information? So that—what, you'll do your duty better?"

"No, sir."

I bit back words stronger than the ones that came. "Right. Because, Petticrew, sometimes the whole truth would just plain kill you all." The whole truth nigh on killed me every day, though I wouldn't say so. "Sometimes it'd be too much for you to carry, when you've got so much on your shoulders. And sometimes, a man's gotta trust that his men are just going to do their duty for duty's sake. Top secret intelligence be hanged."

Petticrew looked to his comrades from the corner of his eye, as if he wasn't so sure.

That made two of us.

His face burned red, even in the dark. It was a fearsome hard thing to come face-to-face with a calamity you caused and could never undo. I could feel the weight of it on him. Crushing him. Wished I could've shouldered the pack of it for him, for my muscles knew the burden well. But this . . . this was a burden only undone the hard way.

By facing the one harmed.

"There's a girl out there in the dark, son." He winced at the word *son*. "Alone. Now I could go get her, any of us could, but something tells me she'd have none of it. Probably wants nothing to do with us. And truth is, there's only one man who has anything to say in the matter that might begin to make it right. That is, if he's got his brain screwed in right."

Heaviness descended upon him like a stone until, finally, he nodded. He turned to go, but then stopped and faced me.

"Captain?"

211

I waited.

"How . . . are you here?"

A question I'd asked myself in this life more times than I could count. *How am I here?* How was I the one who remained?

But that was not what he meant. "You know that top secret intelligence I mentioned?" He nodded gravely. "Something to do with that. Reporting to Chaumont for directives. I tracked you down on the way because we need you back."

"On the way," Petticrew said, and I could see him etching out a map in his mind. "But isn't that . . . south?"

Yes, and I'd come due east to find Petticrew. "Sometimes a detour is worth making," I said. "And I'll be taking the book from the reporter with me. General Pershing's men have need of it there."

He looked behind him at his companions, who were bent over some book together. "And you need us back?"

"You, son. We'll need our chaplain soon, but he can wait. And the reporter—" I spat the word and stopped myself from saying *good riddance.* When I forgot that Jones was the man behind the empty-word articles, he wasn't a bad fellow. Not at all.

"We don't need a reporter just now. But we're heading into an offensive that . . ." I looked around. This country was crawling with spies in every form, uniformed and civilian, both. On all sides. "Let's just say it's a big one. We need your—your special skill set. Not to mention Chester Hasenpfeffer won't quit asking about you all. He's like a lost puppy, that one."

I tried to lighten the moment with mention of the kid who had become a bit of a mascot. But the gravity remained in my voice. It was going to be big. It was going to be important. And—I dreaded, but knew it to be true—it was going to be devastating. We would lose men. Too many men. Which made me want to send Petticrew packing to the hills, tell him to take that girl and run for safety.

But he never would.

"Things . . . hinge on this offensive." I leaned in. He needed to understand. "It's the beginning of the end. It has to be."

He swallowed. "Sir, if I may . . ."

"Speak freely, Petticrew."

He filled himself up with air and courage, standing straight to face me. "Permission to carry out the mission you assigned first, sir. To completion."

"You wish to see her to Paris."

"I do."

"Yes," I said, so quickly it nearly gave the fellow whiplash. "Stay on your feet there, Petticrew. Do the work and return to the front as fast as you can. Once we get moving on this, it's likely to go faster than you can imagine."

"That's what they've been saying since the beginning of the war, sir. Four years ago."

"It's gotta be true sometime."

It had to be.

28

Mira

When Papa left, I lifted my chin and put on a smile, for his sake and Grand-père's.

When I found I was with child, I bit back tears at night and replaced them with a song. My anguish was not what I wished to swaddle this child with before it was yet born. I took that song to the soldiers, then, the thousand lost boys in the trenches, in defiance to the lies that told me they were all like the one who took from me what was not his.

When Grand-père closed his eyes and did not open them again, I dropped myself on his grave, the last bit of home that I knew, and picked myself up to carry on when the soldiers came, when these three men offered a path of life.

Lifted chins and put-on smiles, bit-back tears and songs in the night—all of it imploded upon me now as I ran. On and on through the vineyard, shedding each one of those things like bits of myself left far, far behind.

I knew not where I went.

But what did it matter? At least one thing hadn't been taken from me: the life within, and the secret thereof.

But that was all dashed now. Even that was no longer mine. What did I have but the feet that carried me?

And so I flew. Stumbling into branches, cradling my stomach as my movements came much more difficult than they once had. I do not know when the tears started. I only know that they stung, and the stinging felt right. Everything stung. Everything was cruel. Everything but the stars above, and they, in their gentle, fearsome light, blinked down on me as if they wished to sing a song to me. To remind me of a strength outside myself.

I did not wish to hear it.

Blindly I went on until I could not anymore. I felt myself losing strength, losing the ability to see where I went through my swimming eyes. I should have stopped then. But I did not, not until my foot caught upon a root and sent me stumbling to the earth. Catapulting, full-force, into a dark and sharp place. I hit the ground, my palms scraping against gravel as it embedded itself in me.

And finally . . . I wept. I wept for Papa. I wept for Grand-père. I wept for the thousand lost boys, and for the babe within. I pleaded with the God of those gentle stars to spare the little one—for what if my fall had harmed it? Tears fell for the fall, and for every buried thing that had surfaced in that fall.

I tried to wipe tears from my face, but the salt of them stung the wounds in my hands, where little rocks had dug themselves in.

And then, suddenly, I was not alone.

A presence, steady and true, sank down beside me and lingered a moment before reaching out like I was made of glass and taking my wounded hand in his.

My fist curled tight. I knew, without looking, who it was. By his touch, by his presence, which felt as familiar and steady as time. I had thought I could trust him. I knew better now.

I did not wish him there.

He held my bleeding hand in his, waiting. Covering my aching fingers with his own, as if to help them unfreeze.

And they did. They betrayed me. They melted into his coaxing stroke, which opened them and let the night breeze blow over my wounds.

He did not speak. He only held that hand, bringing it close to his face, so close I felt the warmth of his breath as he studied it in the moonlight and began to remove the pebbles.

I tried to take my hand back. Anger twisted through my veins, my limbs, urging me to retract everything I could from this man. He released his grip, showing that I was free, but letting his hand stay there, telling me he was not going anywhere.

My hand throbbed.

My heart ached even deeper. It was much. Too much for me, all of this, all of the loss catching up to me. Chasing me down in the night and pinning me, digging in to me far deeper than the intruding rocks in my palms.

"Mira," he said, his voice rough with regret.

I winced at the sound of his voice around my name. A name only he knew.

And he had no right to. I had given it to him that night in the ruined church. My lost name, the one that had died with Grand-père. I had given it to him, and with it, an invitation into my world. All that I held dear. All that I was.

This . . . *this* was the hand that had betrayed me.

The battle inside burned, part of me seeing him as my friend. A good man, a brave one, the one who'd been locked with the goats as a gangly youth and raked racetracks beneath the moon to set his sister free.

And part of me seeing my betrayer. Burning all the deeper because my betrayer *was* my truest friend, this man who had come upon me in the woods and gathered me up and held every bit of my life close to his heart ever since.

"Mira," he said again, voice deepened with anguish. He held out his hand, silently imploring me to let him help. Until, finally, I laid my open palm back in his and let him continue.

The work hurt. The dislodging of grains of sand and hard bits of rock from human flesh, where they were never meant to be. He was gentle, but it did not change what had been done.

"Mira," he said a third time. This time in a near-whisper that seemed to hold within it an entire universe.

It was too much. I turned away, ashamed to hear my name on his lips. Why, I did not know. It felt so, so strange—to be known.

To be seen. To have a gaping part of me held in hands strong and kind. Hands that had fisted in passion as he'd spouted my great secret to his friends not half an hour before.

He shook his head slowly. "I'm sorry."

I winced, keeping my eyes shut, turning away from him. Wishing for darkness, for the stars to quiet their light and let me dissolve into the shadows. The night—it had become our homeland, his and mine. The place where all the rest of the world slept and our hearts found each other in the dark. To sit, to talk, to be heard—and to see that the darkness was created and held by the same God who had spun the sun and all its golden light.

"I should never have said that. I—it wasn't for me to say, and I just—they wanted to send you on a train alone away from us, and I just—I couldn't—"

He was saying *I* very much. It seemed to fall upon his ears as sharply as it did upon mine, and he shook his head.

"*You*," I said. "*You* thought? *You* could not? This—this did not happen to *you*." His name belonged at the end of that sentence, but I would not speak it. He looked pained by my words, as if the gravel had embedded itself in his heart.

Good, I thought. And loathed myself for it. I turned away again.

"You're right," he said, his voice flat. He took a deep breath and started again. "I would give anything to undo what's been done to you. It's true, I should never have told what wasn't mine to say." A long pause. "With everything in me . . . everything I have . . . I am sorry."

Everything I have. He ran his thumb gently over the heel of my hand, which was unharmed. As if to say—*everything I have is just me.* He did not have much, perhaps. But he was offering all of himself, every bit of heart, in this moment.

"There are other things that you deserve. Apologies—and so much more. They, too, are outside what I can give. But—I would like to try. If it's alright."

I did not know what he meant. Perhaps all his nights with no sleep were addling his mind. A pang of compassion swam through me.

But he waited, so I gave a simple answer. I could not speak the simple yes, so I turned to face him instead.

"I am sorry . . ." he said, brushing an embedded grain of sand from its place in my palm. "For your father and your grandfather."

I winced, not liking that he had done what I could not: grouped my papa together with Grand-père. Among the dead.

I still held hope.

"I am sorry . . ." He gentled his stroke around a larger pebble, coaxing it out as tenderly as he could. "For you having to leave your home—your whole world—behind." I had hardly allowed myself to put words to this loss. I had not thought that anyone else would, either, for why would they? But his care, his *seeing*, set the tears to a steadier flow, until one dropped upon the back of his hand.

"I'm sorry you've been stuck with a sorry lot like us," he said, pulling his mouth into a half smile. A laugh bubbled up inside of me. Oh, what a gift, to laugh when the world seemed so dark. Like a spark igniting, washing the place with light. But I felt betrayed by the laughter, for I was still angry. I snuffed it out as swiftly as it came, not ready to forget.

"And I am sorry," he said, serious again. Lifting his gaze to mine at last. Lifting his hands to my face. Searching my eyes for permission to linger there, letting his thumbs run over my cheeks to gather my tears into his hands. "I am sorry for what was taken from you in the forest." His voice grew ragged, like the wind when it blows through the trees in the dead of winter, clattering twigs around, looking for life to soften the blow and not finding it.

People did not speak of these things. Even I, tucked away in my wooded world, knew that. *I* had not spoken of it, not ever, until this man had come along and somehow I had found myself with him at my side as I lay in a pew of a demolished church, with holiness and destruction everywhere. Within me and without.

And so his words were chosen with care and pain, so much so that they entered into my own pain and locked into the broken places there.

218

"I . . . wouldn't blame you if you want to get on that train tomorrow. I think you heard what Henry said about your family."

I nodded.

"If you want to go, you will go. We'll get you there. But if you want to go to Paris—and if you can put up with me a few more days—I'll see you home, Mira."

It was those words that broke into my storm that night and sang me to sleep: *"I'll see you home, Mira."* It was the sort of thing a man might say to a woman in one of the stories I'd read, if he were courting her. Walking her home for the evening in the midst of evening birdsong, perhaps gathering a fistful of wildflowers to present her at the end of their stroll.

But this was no peaceful stroll home in the twilight. That was not to be my story. Not with Matthew Petticrew, not with any man. It sank with heaviness in me, as I thought of clutching pebbles and blood in place of wildflowers, and high-sailing shells in place of birdsong on this very long walk "home." He was not courting me. He was endeavoring to save my life and the life of my child.

But those words, they sang me to sleep in the little billet attic with a slow current of hope that night. *My name is Mireilles . . . and I float away.* The old familiar refrain misted me from wake to sleep and right into the words that would never be ours: *I'll see you home, Mira.*

29

Henry

YOUR BOYS, AMERICA!
October 3, 1918

By Hank Jones
~~America, your boys press on.~~

~~Your boys are courageous~~
~~fierce~~
~~brave~~
~~strong, America!~~
America, the truth: this is hard.

———

I paced the empty aisle of the vineyard, trying to beat the sun. It was early morning, and I had a piece to send over the wire before we left Épermay today. But the words would not come. And when they did, they fell flat and beseeched me to cross them out. The only thing I could do with decisiveness.

My brain was clouded over, the effect of a late night spent arguing with George and Matthew, still not knowing what to think myself.

And here I was, charged with writing an inspiring piece on brotherhood and camaraderie to kindle hope and courage in the hearts of Americans everywhere.

I had no such words. Maybe I needed to get the other ones—
the clouding-over ones—out of my brain first, clear the pipeline.

So I scratched them down on the notepad.

YOUR BOYS, AMERICA!

*Your boys, America, are ripped in two. Half of them wanting
one thing, half of them another, all of them wanting the right thing.
I have been writing to you long of your sons, your brothers, your
fathers. But what if I told you there was a daughter here in need of
everything good our great country has to give?*

*She needs medical care. She needs family. She needs, frankly, all
the things your boys at the front need, only she doesn't have letters
and treats coming in packages from home.*

*We could walk her to a train this very morning, set her securely
on her way, and have her off the roads, off her tired feet, headed
toward a bright future. Well, potentially bright.*

"*Potentially disastrous.*" I heard Matthew's voice from the night
before reminding me. He was correct, but wasn't any path we
chose potentially disastrous?

*Your boys, America, are just that: boys. We are not men. We have
reduced ourselves to schoolyard squabbles, only instead of fighting
over croquet and football scores after school, we are fighting over the
life of a woman and child.*

*What's that, America? You know of another daughter of France
who now belongs to you? Who, crowned, stands upon an island in
New York and declares,*

> *"Give me your tired, your poor,
> Your huddled masses yearning to breathe free,
> The wretched refuse of your teeming shore.
> Send these, the homeless, tempest-tost to me,
> I lift my lamp beside the golden door!"*

Yes, America. A resounding yes! She, that Statue of Liberty, like the daughter of France I now speak of, shines a bright future in a weary landscape. And we, it seems, are dooming her to the path of the "homeless, tempest-tost, the tired and poor."

Ah, it's a good thing we came here, America. See what good we're doing.

The words were bitter, making my fingers hurt with how I clutched that pencil and willed it to move faster.

I didn't know which was more absurd: the fact that it was my job to converse with a country as if she were a person, or the fact that I was reduced to spelling out my frustrations to her in a letter I'd never send.

How had I come to be here? How, when all I'd done was hop on a train, a farm boy on a mission to a library to save a cow?

I ripped the page out and crumpled it, tossing it on the ground. Started anew. I'd write something patriotic. I'd tell of the training we'd witnessed, the men running drills in the vineyards, the way Épermay treated them with gratitude and honor. I'd tell of the jazz music playing in the streets from our bands, the way it lit the faces of the weary locals, those "huddled masses yearning to breathe free," and how the brassy sounds seemed to infuse them with hope. If I had to wager a guess, I'd bet such music would have a long and lasting future here in this fertile, hope-starved country.

I sat and started again.

The morning went on, with a few billet chores to occupy us. Matthew's sister, Celia, spent a very long time with Mireilles, the two of them speaking in hushed tones. She, a nurse, and Mireilles, soon to be in need of a nurse's knowledge. I could only hope Mireilles had some magical process to follow when the time came, to get her through. Who knew where she'd be, or who would be there to help her?

Celia spent an equally long time, then, with Matthew, who looked equal parts embarrassed and grave, soaking in every word his sister spoke. If one didn't know better, from the way she gently advised him, it would seem Celia was five years Matthew's senior, and not the other way around.

All I could hear were snatches of her voice, this sister of his. Bits of her face, haloed in golden flyaway hairs that coiled around her rosy cheeks. My pencil moving, I looked down to see I had taken to sketching her.

She turned my way. Instinctively I ripped out the page that held her sketch and crumpled it in my hand.

When she approached, head tilted and smile offered, I could barely look her in the face. I heard, in her gait, the cadence of a story—some might call it a limp, but it was more. A part of her that told a tale, and in the voice of her ways, it came out as a melody.

I nodded a greeting, waiting for her to pass.

"I'm no commanding officer, Mr. Mueller," she said, her voice cheery. "You seem ready to salute at any moment. At ease." She laughed, and the muscles across my shoulders obeyed her command. *At ease.*

Celia took up the crumpled paper from the ground and before I could think, I lunged for it, thanking her for it, face burning. In the process, I dropped something, and she stooped to retrieve that instead.

Another crumpled paper. I froze. She unfolded it and studied it, then me.

"I thought you were a journalist, Mr. Mueller."

"That's . . . debatable. I've never seen any articles by Henry Mueller," I said, scuffing my feet. "Just some guy named Hank Jones."

She smiled at that. "Oh yes, I know all about Hank Jones."

"You do?"

"All of the nurses do. All of *America* does, if you want to be precise. But all of the nurses are particularly interested, and there are many who've laid claim to nursing him back to health, should he ever encounter peril to such an extent that he finds his way to the hospital barge."

The heat in my face returned. Words were my currency. I knew what I was supposed to say here. Something like, *"Oh, yes? And have you put your name in the hat, pretty lady?"*

I cringed. The words would sound as natural from my mouth as piano music from a trumpet. I'd botch them a thousand ways and hate the artifice of it all. But to the point: I knew the words I was supposed to say in a situation like this. George Piccadilly would've tripped all over himself by now and proposed marriage thrice, spouting such talk. And who knew? Maybe Hank Jones, if he was real, would go around flirting and winning hearts.

But I was just me. Just Henry Mueller, who wanted to laugh at those sort of words.

So I spoke different ones instead. "I'll, uh . . . I'll pass the message on to him," I said. "But I'm afraid they'd all be sorely disappointed in the conversation partner they'd find. I can write a thing or two, but it's my editors who shape it into a shiny 'love letter to America.' They have created Hank Jones out of thin air."

This was where she was supposed to brush me off, lose interest, by all good logic.

But she didn't. She looked at the paper. "Seems you can draw a thing or two, as well," she said and closed the space between us to hand me back the picture. "I won't tell the subject of your picture that you saw fit to crumple her up and toss her aside, though." She was jesting, I knew, but she shouldn't have to think that.

"I didn't mean to do that," he said.

"Which? Draw it, or toss it?"

"Both. Sometimes my pencil just runs off on its own and draws something that—" I gulped—"something that catches its attention. I . . . hope the subject of the portrait doesn't mind."

"Oh, well, I know her, and she says she'll think a while on it before deciding." This, she said with a smile.

"Please tell her I didn't mean any offense. And that she's deserving of a much better artist."

She nodded and waited. In the silence, words began to come back to me, one by one. As well as the situation at hand.

"Can I ask you, as a medical person—what do you think should be done?"

"Ah, now there's the journalist."

"It's a mess, is all, and you might be the only one here with any sort of insight into what's best for Mireilles."

She looked off toward the house, where Mireilles tossed grain to some hens, who ran about pecking as if there weren't a war on. Oh, to be oblivious. And to not have to be the one to destroy the rare oblivion of others.

"I think Mireilles might have a much better idea what's best for her than I do." She inhaled. "She's remarkable, really. But to answer your question, if I were in charge, I'd put her on the barge with us and keep her by my side until we could get her to a proper home—a midwife, or a doctor, someone to help her through this. But . . ."

"You're not in charge?"

"No one is, truthfully. We've got our orders and our chain of command, just like you do, but the truth is we're at the mercy and whim of a war and a fever."

"The influenza," I said. It was beginning to make more head-lines than the war did—and to take more lives, too.

"Yes. So, in that way, it's best if she doesn't hop on board our barge. So many of the soldiers are contracting it." She looked at me directly then, scrutinizing. Assessing for symptoms. "I've already given my brother a proper inquisition over any possible symptoms. Do you need one, too?"

"I'm just fine, I assure you."

"How about Hank Jones, then? Has he encountered the flu?"

"If only." I spoke the words before I could stop them—and was met with quick, warm laughter.

"You're funny, Henry Mueller," she said. "Dry wit. I like that."

I smiled, the dry wit leaving me wordless just now. Didn't know what to do with a person sitting long enough to have a conversation with me, much less laugh at my quips.

"So, no influenza for Hank Jones. You're certain?" she said, her face growing serious.

"Yes. But he is up against a difficult fate. A deadline."

"Well, tell him, if you would, as he writes to his sweetheart, America, that she can take a bit more of the whole truth. If he doesn't mind."

"He doesn't." And I wouldn't mind sitting and talking longer with Miss Celia Petticrew, either. But she had a barge to catch, and Mireilles, I hoped, had a train.

"And tell him to let Henry Mueller have a turn with the pen. It's a good, strong name, and I've a hunch he has some good, strong things to say. This is a war, after all, and you know what they say."

Her eyes were so large, so clear as they waited, her silence kind as it shaped the question mark between us. "The pen is mightier than the sword, Mr. Mueller. Or the bayonet, as the case may be." She smiled, the corners of her mouth dimpling in sadness and hope intertwined.

She turned to go and was nearly trampled by the arrival of our hapless chaplain.

"Ah, good, there you are," he said.

"Me?" Celia tilted her head, beholding George with curiosity.

"I do believe I've been looking for you my whole life, my estimable Miss Petticrew. But sadly, no, it was the other one I was addressing."

I looked around. There was only me. The other one.

I tried to bite back a sarcastic remark. Celia Petticrew might think me witty, but she wouldn't like that wit when it was pointed like a weapon, I was sure of it.

"Come on, then," George said and started to walk away.

"Where?"

"Just come, you'll see."

My eyes met Celia's, and she looked as befuddled as I. She shrugged a shoulder as if to say, *Why not?*

So we followed. We skirted the small farmyard, a cackle of various feathered outcries heralding our approach. Wonder of wonders, I had to really work to keep up with George. I hadn't seen him drive on with this much purpose in his step since—well, ever.

226

"Where are we going?" I asked.

"Just here," he said, rounding the back of the horse barn. "I've discovered the whereabouts of the single most broody man to ever walk the face of the earth."

"Broody," I said, molding the word downward in tone. "What on earth are you getting at, Piccadilly?"

"There," he said, pulling up so that I collided straight into his back. He waved me off and pointed at something a ways in front of him. "That." He whispered. "Behold, Brooderly Broodman in his natural habitat. Crossed with shadows from lifeless trees and watching his future rush off in the currents of a river cold as ice."

It was just Matthew. Sitting beneath a dead tree by a creek. And sure, he looked a little downcast. Petticrew was a bit on the somber side in general, but that didn't warrant us making a spectacle of him. Even if I did disagree with him most emphatically about Mireilles and a certain train. I shook my head. "Is that what you dragged me over here for? To make fun of—of that?"

Matthew hung his head, unaware he had spectators.

"I'm leaving. And you are, too." I turned to go. George gripped my elbow and darted in front of me.

"No you're not," he said. "Not till you go fix that." He tipped his head at Matthew.

"I didn't do that," I said, too forcefully. Matthew looked up and saw us. Closed the gap between us, standing there and waiting.

"Well?" he said. "What is it?"

George jabbed my arm with his pointy elbow. I grimaced, shooting him a look that said, *what?*

Somewhere, a barn owl hooted. "Who-who," it said, taunting us, as if to ask who'd speak next. "Who-who!"

"Shut up," I said to the owl.

"Shut up," Matthew Petticrew spat at the owl, too. We glared at each other, waiting.

George Piccadilly stepped back, crossing his arms over his chest and looking awfully satisfied.

Matthew lifted an arm at him in question and let it drop back against his own leg. "What is this?" he asked.

"This"—George raised his eyebrows—"is a meeting of the minds. Neutral ground, a place for reckoning and reconciling. Drawing up treaties. Armistice," he said, raising his hands in the air near his ears as if he held the grand word between them and meant to loft it into the heavens.

He pointed between us. "Look here," he said. "Whatever happens next, we're in it together. We started it together, we'll end it together, and though you wished to wring each other's necks like a Christmas goose just now, you'd better leave that notion behind you posthaste, if you see what I mean."

"No," I said.

"I don't," Matthew Petticrew said at the same time. Couldn't seem to learn how to wait his turn to speak.

"Blast it all to smithereens, you fellows are as dense as they come. Make peace!"

"There's nothing to make peace over," I said. "We've just gotta come to some conclusion. And the answer is clear."

Matthew's stance eased, just a bit. "Agreed."

"Mireilles must go," I said.

"Mira will stay with us," Matthew said at the same time.

George looked grim. For the first time in his life, possibly, the indomitably optimistic George Piccadilly looked ready to explode.

His fingers fisted. His fists began to shake. His face reddened, and I wondered if I should take cover. Matthew, too, leaned back with wary concern.

Judging by the increasingly lobster-like hue of him, George Piccadilly would explode in approximately five . . . four . . . three . . . two . . .

"Adversity!" He spewed the single word. Mount Vesuvius, in human form. And we were Pompeii, the wrath of his word falling on us like molten lava, freezing us in place. Not petrified, as was Pompeii, but—stupefied, to much the same effect. Stumped, as it were.

"Huh?" Matthew said.

I let him do the talking, this time. Profound as he was.

"Adversity, I say! A brother is *born* for adversity. So saith Psalms. Or Platitudes, or Proverbs. One of the P-books, anyhow, and—"

He halted, so suddenly the silence nearly knocked us into one another. He spun, to see that Celia had approached from behind and was tapping him on his shoulder. She whispered something at him behind her hand.

"Proverbs," he said, nodding. "Just so. Thank you."

He seemed to be reeling in his own deliverance of this speech, all tangled up in it. "Now, where was I?"

"Proverbs," Celia said, clearing her throat. "The seventeenth chapter, if I'm not mistaken." She stepped back, watching on in amusement. I couldn't help noticing that the light slipped through the branches far above, playing across her features. She caught my gaze. Smiled. And shifted her eyes toward George, redirecting my gaze silently.

"Now, see here. A brother—" he took a deep breath, calming somewhat "is *born* for adversity. And what are you? *Adversaries*. I cry foul! I say nay. Did you cross the world, survive the battlefield?" He pointed at Matthew. "Did you write in your book"—he pointed at me, spinning his finger like a crazed pencil—"survive a sniper, and encounter a veritable forest angel, all to cut each other away and toss each other out like so much rubbish?"

He waited.

So did we. But oddly, a bothersome heat began to creep up my spine. It felt like, well . . . almost like shame.

I swallowed.

George saw it. He saw it, and in an entirely uncharacteristic swoop of insight, he caught it. Gave me a knowing look. "You know it. You know this standoff must end. That whatever happens with that poor—" he inhaled, whether for dramatic effect or from true feeling, I couldn't decipher—"poor Angel of Argonne, you had best put aside your differences.

"Because I'll tell you something. It's not about you. It's not even your decision. So, put yourselves aside. Put this foolish"—he winced at the word, shaking his head and breaking a sweat, this man who wouldn't even fetch his own olives—"*foolish* disagreement behind you. You were born for this, I say. Born for times of adversity. To—to—why, to *band* together, not to be adversaries!"

Even the owl was silent, as George waited.

Matthew's mouth was grim. Brooderly Broodman, indeed. But he gave a solemn nod.

And so did I.

He put out his hand.

And I took it.

George gripped our hands and gave a solid pump, releasing us all away from one another and stepping back, looking on us with the affection of a wise grandfather.

A wise grandfather who couldn't get his boots on the right feet most of the time but had somehow managed to broker a peace treaty between two warring nations, right here behind an ancient barn.

George closed his eyes and tilted his head up to the heavens.

"Don't look now," I said to him, and he opened one eye to squint at me from his place of holy repose, "but I think you just preached your first sermon, Chaplain George."

Both eyes flew wide open.

He looked from me, to Matthew, to Celia, to the yellow-eyed owl who watched from a barn window above.

"You don't say," he said, true disbelief in his every word. "You don't say! This . . . *this* calls for a christening."

"Don't get carried away, old bloke," I said. There's no one here to christen. We all have names."

"Our brotherhood-born-for-adversity doesn't have a name."

Matthew rolled his eyes. But then he froze, looking sideways at George. Looking a little like a hopeful kid, even though he tried to keep his words very nonchalant. "You mean . . ." He stuffed his hands in his pockets. Shrugged a shoulder. "Like the Rough Riders?"

"Just so," George pointed. "We'll be the—Brave Battalion!"

Matthew grimaced. "I don't know. Does it feel sort of . . . cheesy?" He used the word the other Plattsburgh and Harvard boys bandied about when giving each other a hard time.

"Definitely an element of cheese in that," I said solemnly. Maybe in the whole notion of naming us.

George's hackles rose. "Now see here," he said. "If we're speaking about cheeses, may I remind you that you, *Hank*," he spat the *k* out like a weapon. "You were the one so keen on 'finding the Fontinelles.'" He made his voice so nasally on that last bit it had to hurt.

I'd had about enough of him. "For the last time, the Fontinelles are not *cheeses*!"

"Brave Battalion," Matthew said the proposed name and tried not to cringe. But he raised his hands to make a point, to do his part to keep the peace. "Cheesy or not, there are too few of us for a battalion. A thousand or so too few."

"The Courageous Company, then."

"Couple hundred too short for a company, sorry to say," I chipped in, grinning at Matthew. I wondered how long we could keep George going.

We volleyed the joke on past his suggestions—Proud Platoon (answer: no), Successful Squadron (answer: absolutely not), Dastardly Division (negative: to an exponential degree).

He threw his hands up in the air, letting them fall against himself in exasperation. "What, then? Is there no name under God's glowing orb of a sun that will satisfy the two of you?"

Celia raised a finger, stepping again out of the shadows. "If I may . . . ?"

George let his face hang slack, along with his defeated posture. "Please," he said. "Anything."

"Something . . . simpler, I think. You're a band. Yes? Banded together, against all odds. And usually, these groups—battalions, companies, all of them—they are numbered. Shouldn't you be also?"

I leaned forward, the gears of my mind clicking into her words like they were meant for each other. "Something memorable," I said.

"Three, right?" George said. "Have I guessed it? Clearly I'm no good at this, so please put a bloke out of his misery, if you'll be so kind. Are we to be the Band Three? Because it doesn't precisely have that ring to it, that elusive something—"

"Seventeen-seventeen," I said.

George rolled his eyes at me. "It's *1918*. Or have you forgotten? I know time on the road moves in a waggly sort of way, but—"

"From your sermon," I said, backhanding his shoulder. "Seventeenth chapter of Proverbs . . . seventeenth verse. I think."

"Right. Yes. Of course. Precisely," he said, as trying to convince himself. Or us. "The One Thousand, Seven Hundred and Seventeenth Band."

"The Seventeenth Band," Matthew said, shortening it.

Silence fell. Blessed silence, assured answer.

We were together, we three. For perhaps the first time since we'd set foot into the Argonne Forest, we were truly, deep-down, together. Even if we disagreed.

The Seventeenth Band. Sorry lot that we were . . . we had a name.

And we'd need that name to hold us together. Because the subject of the chasm that had tried to divide us—she approached, footfalls soft. We all turned to face her. Mireilles, cloaked in quiet assurance but shaking as she exhaled, spoke.

"I . . . have decided."

30

Mira

The sight of the waiting train rattled my heart inside of me. Was there ever such a creature as this? Not since I had seen the great iron beast rise from the canyon beyond the forest had I beheld such a thing. Unseen churning caused billows of smoke to exhale from the creature like a great dragon. The dragon meant to convey me away from these men and into a blind unknown place so very far away. When they spoke it—*Bordeaux*—I could feel the strings that tied me to the Argonne tightening around my chest until I feared they would snap and take me with them.

Matthew was quiet beside me. "You're sure, Mira?" His sincere eyes asked me to hear another question beneath the one he spoke.

"No," I said. "I am sure of nothing."

"You—you don't have to go."

The great dragon was receiving passengers into its creaking metal belly. Its door stood open, like a mechanical hand beckoning me. *Come*, it seemed to say, its voice very cold. *I will ferry you to where you belong.*

Behind me lay the quiet road, the one I could walk with the men if I so chose. I could find help in Paris—Celia had told me of a sisterhood of nuns who were nurses and would help me. "*Jour de Soleil Sisters*," she'd called them. *Day of Sun.*

For a moment, I had let myself believe it. I could stay with these men, continue to Paris. Find this home that Henry spoke of . . . and perhaps make a life there, for the baby.

But what if I did stay with the men, and they became targets of men armed with guns, once more—or worse? Bombs, bayonets—so many perils required of them to face, to see me to a home that might be there and might not. What if it kept them from the true war, the one they had come for?

I would be less a burden this way. Surely. The pains that had come in the barn loft had stopped some days before, and I hoped this meant I had more time.

I took a step and stopped. I felt Matthew's gaze before I turned to meet it. How did he come to be able to say so much when saying so little? He had the sort of face that could not hide anything. Especially not when he was searching your eyes, deeper and deeper, his face that of a man harboring a very deep sadness. And a very deep hope.

"Mira . . ." he said. I waited, wishing I could say something to help. But he seemed determined, quite so, to say what he had to say, his jaw working and those deeper-and-deeper eyes lifting to mine.

I could not look away. And would not have, even if I could. In our many footfalls beside one another in this land, in our words spoken through moonlight. In the look he gave where I caught laughter in his eyes over a joke I understood but his companions missed. In every story he had entrusted to me—first without knowing I could understand them, and later, costlier to him, I knew, when he knew I understood every word. In all of these things, he had given himself to me.

And now, I was taking it, every bit of it, away.

I reached out and laced my fingers into his. He was a stranger, I reminded myself. A man I had only known a matter of days. But my fingers laced into his like they had always been meant to be there—and my heart followed.

"You are full of courage," he said. "Full of peace. And you give those things to others in their darkest times." He did not seem finished, but he paused.

I shook my head. "I am not any of those things, I fear."

He laughed soberly. "A whole line of men in the trenches have a song trapped inside of them that would say otherwise. And it comes to them at the darkest of times, when they need something good. You gave them that. You gave them hope."

"I only sang because I was afraid. I only sought peace because I did not have it. Those things—they were given to me. I was parched, and I was given water. All I did was share with other parched souls where to find it, too."

He lifted a hand and tucked a strand of hair behind my ear. The smallest gesture, but it began a great ache within me. "I wish you could know what it's meant," he said.

I raised my hand to his. "I do, Matthew Petticrew. You have shown it to me, too."

Inside of me, my chest constricted, and the thought flew into my mind and nearly knocked me over: I might never see this man again. He, who had entered into my darkest grief and stooped down, carried me home. Who had been carrying me home ever since. *I'll see you home, Mira.*

Something tore around my heart. I raised his fingers to my lips—those hands that had combed through my secrets and held them close. I pressed them to me, closed my eyes, and fixed the warmth of them forever to my memory.

And then, because there were no words to make it all better, nothing to do but ride the current of this tearing inside of me, I turned and boarded that train.

Again, I felt it. His stare, from the platform, watching me through windows. I clutched my carpetbag and took a seat, feeling light-headed.

"Are you alright?" A voice beside me—a man. But I could not look, for the tight pain of the days before returned to my middle, and below. I winced around it.

I forced my breathing to slow, praying the pain might leave my body as my breath did, too.

"Miss . . . Miss Mireilles," the voice said beside me. My eyes flew open, alarmed. Who would know me here?

Every thought of pain flew from my mind as I saw beside me the

captain who had come last night. The man who had been witness
to Matthew's revelation to the others about me.

"Shall I get help?" he asked, making to stand.

"No," I said quickly. Afraid. I was not ready. And more than
that—thankfully, I realized—the pain was easing. "No, I will be
fine." The concern on his face drew deeper, and for a moment he
looked a little like Papa. The way his dark hair was flecked here
and there with white, and the way he disbelieved me when I said
I was fine.

I smiled. "Thank you for your concern."

He nodded and set the newspaper he had been holding on the
seat between us. He gestured for me to place my small carpetbag
there, too, and I did.

I searched for something to say, to ease his concern. "You are
going south, too?"

He nodded. "Headquarters," he said. "Chaumont." A man of
few words. "And . . . you are going south." He said it as a statement, but he seemed surprised.

I looked out the window beyond him and saw Matthew watching on. He had his hands in his pockets, looking like someone had
taken him and tied up all the passion that gathered like a growing
storm, and he was bound and determined not to break the ropes
and free himself.

"Yes," I said absently. "South. To a relative, it seems."

"Family is important," the man said, and I nearly didn't hear
his words, for the quiet tone of them.

"Yes," I agreed again. "Do you have family, Captain Truett?" I
liked his name; it sounded full of honor.

He looked out the window, too, away from me. But his sight
landed instead on my reflection, and I saw his beside it. Tormented.
He hung his head. "I did. Once."

Outside, Matthew straightened from the pole he had been leaning on and looked like he was attempting to read our conversation.

"I suppose you still do, then," I said. I recognized in him the
voice of loss. I knew it well, for it keened about inside me, when

I thought of Papa and Grand-père. "One does not stop being family when they dwell in eternity." I hoped the thought might comfort him.

He looked at me then. Stricken and silent, like I'd crashed into a wall and torn it down when I had no right to. But as he studied me, his defenses shrank back, a small tenderness replacing them.

"If I . . . had a daughter," he said, breaking past the thickness in his voice. "I would be mighty happy if a good man found her and looked at her the way Petticrew out there looks at you."

"And if . . . if my father were here . . ." I could not bring myself to say *alive*. He could be a prisoner. A soldier still. There could be many, many reasons I had never heard from him in all this time— despite what the hard knot inside told me. "I would ask him what I should do. Where I should go."

He seemed to weigh that heavily. As he did, a threesome of young men in British uniform jostled down the aisle, taking up the row of seats across from us.

"Hallo," the one in the middle said, leaning forward to tip his hat at me. I gulped, dipping my chin in the smallest of nods. Hoping not to be rude, and hoping he would leave me be.

"Your father," Captain Truett said, clearing his throat and giving the boys across the aisle a look that silenced their chatter, "I'd wager he might turn the question on you. A father and a daughter . . ." He shook his head. "He'd want her to be safe."

I nodded. "To go and find a relative, and see if she might take me in, being family?"

He tipped his head back and forth slightly, weighing, unconvinced. "Or to go with the family she already has."

"But I don't—"

"Maybe it isn't my place to say, Miss Mireilles. In fact, it most definitely is not my place to say. But for whatever it's worth, there's a young man out there who's among the finest soldiers I have ever . . . *ever* had the honor of fighting alongside. And not just in this war. He's single-minded. Loyal. Just as bad as the rest of us when it comes to denying that he's shaking in his boots. But he is a man who will see things through, and more than that, he's a man who puts his whole self into the mission before him."

"I am a mission," I said, not liking the way the word weighed upon me.

"Well, no. That's just it. No one has given him directives or orders here. He's the one who's come to me, twice now, and asked to be allowed to go with you, to help you find safety." He whistled low. "Heaven knows we need him back at the front. He's got ears like no other and can tell us all to hit the ground long before anyone else can. But . . . he hears you, too. He sees you. And if you don't mind a stranger saying so, you're not leaving that boy's mind any time soon. You might pull away on the train, but you'll never leave him. Not really." He spoke as one who knew such from his own life.

An attendant approached, taking tickets. The engine chuffed to life, and my heart along with it.

I looked at my reflection again. At Matthew, beyond. The two melded together for an instant.

I stood.

"Ticket, miss?"

I looked at Captain Truett. Matthew outside. And the waiting man, ready to take my papers.

"No, thank you," I said, and moved to step around him. I stopped halfway up the aisle and turned, happy to see a smile on Captain Truett's always-serious face. I smiled and nodded. "Thank you."

His chin dimpled as his mouth pursed in, showing he'd caught my meaning.

"Madame?" The train attendant followed a few steps, his words cracking into the cloud around my thoughts. "If you've no papers, no ticket, what is your name? Perhaps we have record of you."

I walked on, giving him an apologetic smile. "My name is Mireilles," I said quietly. *And I will not run away.*

Two steps off the train and onto the platform and I paused, locking eyes with Matthew. We each of us stepped toward each other, the space thick with meaning—and froze as a creeping, looming shadow stole over us from above.

31

George

"Épermay, you tragic siren of a town." I scuffed the path with my boots, and thought how they looked rather like a real soldier's boots, all scratched and caked in mud. What would Mother think, to see it? Her son, packed so safely off to America to avoid this war. "Well, I've at least got a talent for avoiding Welsh rarebit and sweethearts, Mum, if that's any comfort."

Even the local bakery, this morning, had informed me that Brioche was forbidden. "Brioche is forbidden," I muttered. "Brioche! Betrayed by its own motherland! The crown of golden buttery breads. How you wound me!"

I saw a picture of myself, walking the countryside and wringing my hands. "It's come to this, Mother."

I laughed. And then I laughed at myself for laughing aloud, here on this rise above the town. Petticrew had gone to see the Angel onto the train. Henry the bard had gone to send his latest saga over the wire to his adoring public. Captain Truett was taking his cold, assessing eye off us all and leaving for headquarters, thanks be to the heavens. And the heavens were as lofty as ever, away up there beyond the blue.

I tugged at my shirt collar. I had no cleric's collar; I was not entitled to one as a mere chaplain, it turned out. But even so, I felt its phantom presence there, squeezing my neck whenever I came up against my own unholiness. I had, in essence, lied my way into the clergy. Was there a very special place in the eternal below regions reserved for such an act? It seemed, even to me, that there should be.

"Lord," I said, attempting a prayer. "What a fix I am in."

A sheep bleated behind me and I jumped. "What? You can do better?" It looked at me from its flossy white fleece, chewing slowly and daring me to go on. I lifted my face to the sky. "Lord," I said. "It's me, George. George Piccadilly. The third, if you were wondering. I know it's a rather ridiculous name. One of the soldiers from Georgia told me it sounded like a garden vegetable that belonged in a jar in the pantry. But it is my name, and I am at your service."

The sheep bleated again. I turned to glare. "I'm speaking to the Monarch of the Universe, if you don't mind terribly."

The sheep didn't look impressed.

"I don't blame you," I said. Truth was, I was in a bit of a no-man's-land myself. Metaphorically, of course. They didn't let me go up into battle on the real no-man's-land. Not a chaplain's place. And so here I was—too holy for battle and too heathen for holy work.

And yet—hadn't Henry the Wet Rag told me I'd preached a sermon? Me! A sermon. The mind boggles.

"Lord," I tried again. The sky was vibrant blue today. My theology wasn't what it should be, but I wondered if that meant He was indeed up there listening. A few clouds scuttled past. "Could you teach a fellow how to be?" I asked. It was a simple question. But it got right down to it. I didn't know how to be, who to be, and was just wandering the world aimlessly. I could say a pious word or two, but I didn't know what any of it meant. Matthew spoke of the "sermons" his gardener friend gave him back home, and they seemed to give him life, here, out in this land of destruction. Words of life to fill him and fortify him. "How do I find that, Lord? How do I get it, and how do I bring it here?"

I halted in my tracks.

I turned back to face the sheep.

"Did you hear that?" I said. "Who am I, and where has George Piccadilly gone?" I wanted to *do* something? Not just survive and

get on to the next thing but to . . . I don't know, find *meaning* in
it all? This ticking organ inside my ribs—it seemed intent on finding . . . *purpose*. Me. Purpose. It was as foreign a thing as Welsh
rarebit to this forsaken land.

I shook my head. "I could use a sermon right about now."

I approached a battlement, a small rise in the ground grown
over with grass to camouflage it and porticos through which to
aim machine guns and I knew not what. The town had them all
around, from the beginning of the war. They were used, now, for
training, but the soldiers were drilling a quarter mile away at least,
marching infantry marches. I'd passed them on the way up the rise.

It was eerily still. A harbinger of peace, one might hope.

The clouds above scudded more swiftly, stretching a long, long
shadow over me. It felt nice, to be shielded from the warming sun,
and I raised my gaze to salute them.

"Good heavens," I said, and quite believed it to be an extension
of my earlier prayer. For there, above me, casting the shadow over
my being and half the county, was a whale of a beast in the sky.
Grey and stretching, a zeppelin in the flesh. I had seen an airship
once before I left London, hovering over its skyline and dropping
bombs in the distance. I rather believe that was when Mother
hatched her plan to Harvard-ize me and send me away to a land
that knew nothing of *Luftschiffs* instilling fear into its citizens.

And here it was, creeping over the skies as if it had tracked
me down from that moment. *Aha*, it very slowly seemed to say
as it crept across the sky, pushed by its propellers and preparing,
it seemed, to deploy two planes from its clutches. *Aha*, and *Be
Vanquished*.

I didn't fancy being vanquished. Not now, when I was finally, it
seemed, beginning to understand what it meant to live.

The planes dove like a dance of angry hornets, and that's when
my dense skull began to comprehend. They had come for Épermay.

"Oh, Épermay," I groaned. "You tragic siren of a town!" My
feet were off, then, carrying me to the battery where weapons lay
hidden beneath that grassy green knoll.

The soldiers, I knew, would not be far behind me, dashing up from their drilling to arm these guns and prevent disaster.

But I was closer.

I watched as the planes, and the zeppelin, both made for the train station.

"Angel of Argonne," I said above my pounding footsteps. "And blimey serious Matthew Petticrew!" I could picture it. He'd be sulking on the train platform at the departure of his lady love, and the shadow would eclipse him most fittingly. He would narrow his eyes, thinking he could bring down this threat with his superhuman power of brooding.

No amount of brooding would stop these mad hornets.

Flinging open an iron gate beneath the gunnery, I stormed in, trying to remember the artillery training from Plattsburg and cursing the fact that what I remembered most from the camp was the cheery sound of the gramophone I'd smuggled in and the tangy taste of olives.

What would the journalist say? He could do something with that.

"Olives taste like justice," I said out loud, doing my best Hank-the-Wet-Blanket impression. "And justice will save the angel and her child!" I gritted my teeth like Captain Truett would. He would grunt, too, more like a growl. I tried it. Oddly, the words infused me with a burst of energy that chased me up hard grey stairs into a lookout. My limbs sprang to action, remembering. After loading the cannon, I took aim at the easiest target—the zeppelin. Behemoth of the sky. I sucked in a breath—and let the cannon fire.

The force of it knocked me to the ground with such power that it blew the air from my lungs. Was I dead? Had I died? And if so, had I at least taken the behemoth down with me?

I scrambled to see through the porthole and grabbed the binoculars stationed there. Scanning the airship, I spotted it: a hole. I jumped in the air, making to repeat the process. A little hole in a big creature like that would not a victory make, but by golly, it was a start! And perhaps enough of a distraction that it would slow their progress toward the train station. Even I, thickheaded though I was in matters of war, knew that would likely be their target. Stop the coming and going of arms and men and all that.

I repeated the process until my bones were surely obliterated inside of me. I had no hearing to speak of and when a sharp jab poked my shoulder, I nearly jumped out of my skin, shrieking.

Soldiers. Real ones. The ones who knew what to do, thanks be to God above! They took charge, and I helped to load the cannon, and they soon had one of the planes on the run, buzzing in loopy demise until it crashed well and good right into the zeppelin.

My ears still rang, but I could feel through the absence of vibrations that all went silent. As if the world held its breath. We all scrambled to the grass roof to watch an allied plane give chase to the remaining enemy plane. And the airship—an inferno glowing through the many holes in its grey flesh—sank slowly and ember-filled to the ground below it.

Right atop the train station.

32

Matthew

A churning inferno descended from above, shining through holes in a grey vessel overtaking the sky. It floated down upon us like a wounded giant, lopsided and spectacular in his fall.

Mira. I jolted to find her. She was frozen, neck craned, watching with sheer horror on her face. She, accustomed to seeing only eagles and falcons in the air, about to be swallowed by a German airship afire. My own fire lit—the Flame—and launched me into movement.

I ran for her. And she, perceiving my movement, ran for me. Our hands found each other mid-stride and we ran. Ran. Ran.

It was chaos. The train lurched forward, its conductor acting quickly to save every passenger aboard. I gulped. Captain Truett was aboard. Fear for him washed me. It looked suddenly minuscule, that train, with the mammoth-sized fiery frame falling above it.

If I knew Jasper Truett, he was in there somehow commanding that train with his iron will. It lurched forward, barely escaping the zeppelin's collision as it nicked the tail end and set the car to rocking. Sparks flew as the track and the wheels grappled before settling, blessedly, into steady action behind the retreating train.

Truett was safe. But there was no wash of relief—that would have to come later.

Soldiers jumped from the airship, opting to fling themselves into a fall that would, without a doubt, crush bones and twist muscles, rather than go down inside the ship. I did not blame them. To collide with the earth was one thing—to collide with the earth and be still aboard as its gas-filled pockets inside exploded and surged, was another. It was that thought that sent me running blind to all but the sight of Mira, eyes afire, keeping pace beside me. We passed stone planters of bright flowers in a blur. We ran past the spot where the violinist had stood just moments ago, past the town that had been shelter to us and witnessed the cleaving of our souls together by shattering words the night before.

As we rounded a cobbled corner, a flash of motion collided straight into me, its source crumpling.

A girl. No more than eight years old, chattering in a muddle of French and panic, pointing at the sky like it was coming for her. Which—a quick glance confirmed—it was. I knelt to help her up, noting the way she cradled a small box with great care.

Mira looked at the looming airship, still coming down, and she knelt beside the girl, amid a fall of floating bits of ash and embers. Leaned in, eyes wide with a pleading for trust, as she infused her voice with calm for the child.

I did not know what they said—only a mention of a *mama*, as the girl gestured away toward the hills. Mira's gaze followed, and she, too, searched the hills.

"We have to go," I said. "Will she come?" If she wouldn't, I'd carry her. Anything to get her out of here. But I didn't want to scare her more, either.

Mira translated, and everything in me heaved relief when the girl took Mira's hand.

We ran until Épermay was behind us, a billow of black smoke rising above it like an umbrella.

We ran, still, until we drew up at a crossroads, where the road was rutted and muddy, and a towering cross rose from the sludge like so many across France did, marking waysides and journeys of both foot and heart.

The girl detached herself from Mira, her smile dimpling as if they shared a secret surprise. She pointed at the box and down a winding path.

"*Venez!*" she said, gesturing for us to follow.

Mira looked between us, translating. "She wishes for us to follow," she said. "Her aunt has just been married, and they are gathering to celebrate. A—I do not know the English word."

A reception. I didn't speak it, but I knew it. Recalled it well, from Mr. MacMannus and the new Mrs. MacMannus's evening of celebration, and how Celia and I had watched on from the barn. She, dancing about the creaking boards, and I, wondering what it would be like, for once, not to be on the outside looking in. Always a window or a wall between me and the others. Mother bearing Celia, departing from this world. My father, opening his home in celebration of his wedding to the whole of society, but not so much as blinking our way.

And now here stood a young girl, poised on the path before us, gesturing us in.

I nodded. "We should see her home to her family, at least," I said. We needn't intrude upon the event itself.

The girl understood something of my answer, for she gave a small jump of celebration and started on her way.

Mira's gaze fixed fast on the horizon behind us. Now that the girl was a little ways ahead, Mira seemed to register the events she'd kept so calm in. She trembled slightly, and I placed my hands on her shoulders.

Not that it did much good. My own hand was shaking again, too. I clenched its muscles, willing sinews to still. But they would not. They were in another place, on another battlefield, pulling my thoughts back there, too.

But I would not go. Not to the place that lived inside Saint-Mihiel. That memory with its own pulse, its darkness eating slowly away at me in images of fields of red drenching the land. Encroaching on me now in my waking hours, as well as in my sleep. I heaved an invisible door—a heavy, thick one—shut on the thoughts. Fixed my attention on the moment before me now.

"Mira?"

She shook her head, torment in her eyes. "What *was* that?"

That was war, I wanted to say. But war she already knew. More so even than me.

"A German airship," I said.

"Why did they come?"

I didn't want to fill her world with more worry. But she valued information, I was coming to realize. I could see how she latched onto each bit like a puzzle piece, moving it around and sifting it into place in that mind of hers, to see a picture of this strange world outside the Argonne.

We walked, following the girl at a distance. She seemed to have forgotten us, until she stopped suddenly and turned, tilting her head as if she'd had a sudden realization. She said something and laughed. She opened her corner-crumpled box and reverently removed something. Lifting a hand to reveal her treasure, she pressed a finger to her lips and said, "Shhhh." She giggled.

"Is that—"

"Brioche," Mira breathed, her eyes wide. And it was. Brioche. A mouthwatering roll, baked to glistening golden-brown perfection. I could picture George rending his garments and releasing a mournful cry when he learned of this.

The girl turned, breaking off the smallest pieces and placing one each in our palms, face alight with expectant glee.

It was no more than a crumb. But I knew it was the treasure she treated it as, in these times. Exchanging a glance with Mira, who looked as if she knew something I did not, I placed the crumb in my mouth and let it sit there as long as possible. Savoring the buttery flakes, the way my stomach came alive and remembered it was made for more than hard tack and old tins of meat.

The girl chattered happily, gesturing for Mira to take her turn. Mira's cheeks grew pink.

"It's good," I said, raising my eyebrows. "Go ahead."

She did, hesitantly, and I watched the sheer joy of the way she closed her eyes, long eyelashes against her pale skin, and gave meaning to the word *savor*. Suddenly remembering she was being watched, her eyes flew open again and she smiled sheepishly.

The girl pointed toward a farmhouse where people were gathered. Clearly the wedding reception she'd spoken of, a small clutch of family and neighbors gathered beneath the open sky among leaves and laughter, both of them gold.

She spoke something and giggled—I only caught the words *merci* and *l'amour*. And then she was gone, dashing down the slope to her destination, leaving Mira's cheeks growing pink.

"What did she say?" I asked, curious.

She shook her head. "It was nothing."

It wasn't nothing, judging by the way Mira blushed. I waited, and Mira looked at me with a tentative smile.

"She said it is like the French wedding procession." I must have looked confused. "That . . . *we* are like the French wedding procession. Children lead the way for the new bride and groom as they approach the celebration."

Which, in this scenario, made us . . .

I swallowed.

Mira's smile dimpled as she pursed her lips. "The people have each brought a roll or small cake and will stack them into one big cake," she said. "Just as it was done long ago. Hers was baked especially for the bride and groom in the village *boulangerie*. Very secret, such a delicacy in a time of war. She said—that it was right for us to have a bit of that one, in the procession." Mira looked away, her smile bashful. "It is only her game she is playing, of course."

"Of course," I said, letting my eyes dance over Mira in amusement.

"I played such games many times when I was young," she said, her voice easing into its musical depth, more normal.

"Oh?"

She laughed. "My papa would catch me pretending to dance at balls, right in our woods. I must have made such a sight, all alone, with no music but my own silly humming. Twirling about the meadow like a lark gone mad."

I listened, transfixed. Even her stories felt musical, transporting.

"I once imagined this old scrap"—she lifted her apron—"to

have been a part of a beautiful lady's ball gown." She laughed. "Can you imagine? What would Henry say to that?"

"Henry would proclaim with great conviction that the balloon it came from was indeed a fine lady. And then he'd wax eloquent about how that symbolized liberty." I furrowed my brow and spoke gravely in my best Henry Mueller impression.

She laughed at my quip. "He is a good fellow."

As we neared the bottom of the hill, snatches of music drifted into our conversation. Happy bits of accordion with a lilt and quirk about it.

"And what do you say of my imaginings, Matthew Petticrew?" She paused, laughter in her eyes. She lifted her apron, fingering a fresh tear from its run-in with a floating inferno. The smell of smoke still in the air. "I was very wrong, thinking it part of a ball gown, was I not?"

I swallowed, my throat thick. She was entirely captivating, cheek smudged with dust. "You were very right," I said, meeting her eyes. "A beautiful lady's gown."

The words were out before I could stop them. I didn't know how to say these things. I was such a buffoon I couldn't even come right out and say what I meant so that she'd take my meaning.

But the flush on her face had returned. She had taken my meaning. Every bit of it.

If I could have completed her childhood imaginings for her, I would have. Some other fellow would sweep her into a dance and never look back. But I didn't know the first thing about dancing. I knew marching. Farther back than that, I knew galloping. I knew running a track in the middle of the night.

I did not know dancing. The closest I'd ever even come was seeing the couples dance through those glowing windows at Maplehurst, so far in the distance.

But I'd do anything to give her what she dreams of. Such a small thing when she'd lost so much, and I had so little I could give.

So, I slowed my march to a walk.

I offered my hand. And I waited.

It would be no waltz. But this stroll through a field, hand in hand if she'd allow it . . . it was more a dance than any other this world has ever played witness to.

Her fingers found mine. Tentatively, at first. And then, like they knew they'd discovered a safe place, they relaxed into the warmth of my own. My hand, still trembling, had a mind of its own. Holding hers tighter, and gentler, found in that gesture the home it had been searching for all its life.

The accordion music stopped, and so did we. It picked up again in a moment, and I felt her fingers stiffen.

"What is it?" I asked.

"The musette," she said. "The accordion music. I had forgotten . . ." She studied our hands, intertwined, a slow smile spreading over whatever memory she now held. As if a lost hope had been found.

And I filled with it. There was no window between her and I. I was not on the outside looking in. I didn't know what the next days would hold or how I would ever leave her once we reached Paris. . . . But in that moment, all I could think of was the rightness of her hand in mine.

A few stray flecks of white ash drifted on a breeze from the direction of the town. Remnants of the destruction, masquerading as snow. She held her other hand out, letting a piece of ash fall on her upturned palm, and closed her hand around it. Her bag was gone—left behind somewhere in the fray of the day. But even empty-handed, she sought to give. So like her, taking something broken and wrapping it in safety.

I looked at her other hand, holding mine.

And I noticed, then—my hand had stopped its tremors.

She released the ash into the field, watching it drift down over some late-blooming poppies, crimson in the gathering blue of night.

"Au revoir!" The girl was in the distance now, waving her farewell to us at the fence of an orchard where the music played and couples danced among the branches, bride and groom weaving through them.

Mira waved back with a sincere smile.

"The airships," she said as we walked on. This time—for the first time—with no destination. "What do they do?"

I told her of the zeppelins, the way they hovered above London and dropped bombs there, the way they traveled to the western front, the eastern front, floating high above the reach of any planes. And of the rumors of a push for Paris, which Captain Truett had confided.

At the mention of Paris, her presence grew heavy. Burdened. "Don't worry," I said. "We'll get you on another train to Bordeaux. Maybe back in Épermay, if the railway still stands. Or—or from Paris." It was occurring to me how close we were to the city now, at least according to the map. It may well be the next place a train was possible.

And suddenly the very thought—Mira on a train—seemed the most preposterous idea in all of history. This heart, carried away from mine by a heartless machine driven by coals and steam and seven thousand tons of metal. No locomotive would dare.

There was mud on her cheek. Sun on her hair. I watched as she, in burdened silence, knelt at a spring and cupped her hands. Scratches and scrapes from the night before screamed angry red. She gathered clearest water in them, bringing it to her face.

It was the simplest action. The sky did not rend. The ground did not shake.

But I rended. I shook.

Standing there on God's green earth, beholding something pure and good and true—it was air to my scorched lungs.

I crossed the grassy rise and knelt opposite of her, that spring running between us. She looked up in that wide-eyed, studying, unhiding way, droplets of water clinging to her lashes.

I swallowed. Every muscle in me ached to gather her up. Hold her close, right up to this chest that pounded with a homecoming cry.

But I did not gather her up. The apparition of the locomotive that would dare to carry her from me plowed invisible between us—and those blue and watching eyes pierced right through it. Seeing me.

I willed the pounding inside to fall quiet. I schooled my arms, the yearning to pull her close, and instead I reached out. Slid my palms beneath her upturned hands. Traced the angry red of her wounds and lowered them once more into that clear flow of water, where currents ran about her fingers like liquid silk.

The blood ran with it, red mixing with the water, until all was clear and all was clean.

I lifted her hands again into the air. Pulled a ball of bandage from my sack and began to wrap them, binding her wounds like she had bound the rawness of my heart.

In the distance, strains of that music set merrymakers' feet to dancing. In the far-off distance, the sound of shells set soldiers' feet to pounding.

And right here—her hands in mine, her eyes fixed on mine, the sound of the water wrapped us until surely, surely she felt my very pulse.

But this could not be. She needed more. She needed what I could not give: a home, a person who would not leave her in the coming days, weeks, months. A soul that was not already claimed by the bleeding trenches of the front.

And so, requiring the strength of at least a seven-ton locomotive, my words came out ragged. I hated them as I spoke them. Plans to send her away, to do as she had decided. And yet, as the words tumbled out, my hand that held hers pulled her close, until she leaned against me, her shoulders falling into mine. Her form crumpled close, my entire being holding her, telling me to shut up, that I would never, ever, ever let her go.

The words stopped. Her head tucked beneath my chin, her hair smelling of lavender and soot. Her shoulders trembled as if the strength she wore like a cloak had finally dropped away, snatched and singed by a flaming zeppelin. It was as if a dam broke within her, and all the grief, betrayal, heartache, loss—the gentle, lilting, somber way she held memories of her grandfather, her father, her forest home, and the budding sense of wonder for the child within her—moved like currents and set her to shaking. She stood upon an invisible crossroads.

And I held her.

This is it, I thought. This was the place—this moment, this nameless field in the middle of France where I didn't know which way was up—this was why I had come. What I had been born for. *Who* I had been born for.

I'd combed racetracks and picked Harvard horse hooves and saw Plattsburg sunrises and tromped into another world in a forest far away . . . all for Mireilles.

Please. I prayed. A plea with a thousand endings. *Please let me stay, God.*

It seemed a forward prayer. And to own the truth, I didn't quite know all that I meant by it. Let me live? Let me be a part of her life? All I knew was that those currents, as they churned, showed me the tangle of her battle. I yearned, with a pounding of my pulse and a conviction of my being, to stand in that battle. To fight alongside her. For her. *With* her.

We stilled, the grass reaching up tall around us, sky gentling above where only a short time before, it had been torn in two by fire itself. From where we stood, we could see that in Épermay, smoke had settled and all was quiet. We could see the road in the other direction, winding around a stand of trees, off toward a river in the far distance. Beyond, though we could not yet see it, awaited Paris.

And in between . . . there was us. Frozen in time, right there in the soft grass.

She looked at me, searching. She did not speak for a long while. As if she, like me, feared that words might shatter the elusive peace of this moment. She pulled in a deep breath, her exhale shuddering a release of so very much.

Heaven help me, I ached for her in the depths of my soul. It was more than wanting to kiss her. More than a lonely soldier enjoying the gentle presence of a woman. It was—it was everything. Encompassing. Asking to be in her world. A world so broken, so much taken from her. A yearning to somehow be part of the unbreaking. Or to sit amid the rubble with her, to feel her lean against me. To give something of myself—my own broken, incomplete, imperfect self—to her.

In the distance, the sound of glasses clinking together, toasting beneath the evening sky, sounded. A gathering of souls, knit together to launch a husband and wife off into their life together.

Unbidden, the vision flashed before me: Mira, a bride. Mira, happy. It was so clear a vision, it would be engraved upon me for the rest of time. There was no coming back from this place. From her.

Evening wind lifted her hair, blew it back from her face. And wouldn't that be her way? To have the wind for a veil, the grass for a gown. Beholding her here, so slight in stature and too lovely for this world, I wondered if she would blow away, too. Just be scooped up in the air and carried away somewhere good, somewhere with sun and silence, no curtain of shrapnel falling always, everywhere.

That wind came under and around me, too.

We did not have that land of sun and silence, nor absence of shrapnel.

But she was here.

And I was here.

Her shoulders released from a locked hold into something easy. Like she was recalling, after a long while without air, how to breathe again.

She did. She breathed in the wind. My arm brushed hers. She didn't stiffen or move away, as she so often had on our journey. I wanted to hold her. But it would be too much, I knew. And I—who was I, after all? To wish myself upon this wind-driven creature? My own boyishness burned itself into my lungs. I had never so much as danced with a girl.

Mira. I thought, and realized I spoke it, too. Her eyes were worlds, searching mine.

My free hand lifted to her face, knuckles brushing a dark curl from her cheek. Ever so slightly, she leaned into me, my palm opening to cradle her.

So soft, she was. She, whose life had been chiseled by the elements and framed by tragedy. Whose home had been ravaged—whose very self, too. Whose life was also changed by the trenches, the dying of men, the destroying of life.

I cannot account for it now. Why I leaned in, when all logic told me not to. Why she, too, drew in as if made to fit there. How my lips met her dark hair, first, and then her forehead. Gently, for she was treasure. Meeting her, discovering her, my chest pounding. How warm she was, how true. And how I lingered there, and with a wave of longing—to protect, to be hers, to be known by her—I met her lips. Soft, and sweet, and lingering. So like her song in the night. So pure it cut through agony and dared me to hope again.

She leaned into me, head upon my shoulder, her curls against my face.

I didn't know how long we stood there. I knew her train was to have left at midday, and the sky above us was slipping into corals and reds to rival the poppies at our feet, as if it, too, had caught the embers of the zeppelin.

She finally pulled back, and we stood long in the silence. "Matthew Petticrew," she said at last. "May I stay with you?" She pulled back and paused. "May I go on with you and the others?"

Yes.

Yes.

I had to get the word out, an intensity that was gathering the longer it was trapped. I had to keep her from blowing away.

I took a deep breath. Cupped the gentle curve of her face in my hand. And spoke it as simply, as purely as I could.

"Yes."

33

Henry

YOUR BOYS, AMERICA!
October 4, 1918
By a humble observer

What if I told you, America, that at the crossroads of a nondescript corner in the middle of France, you would see a singular story unfold? What if I told you of a village descended on by a flaming zeppelin? What if I told you of me, emerging from the dark recesses of the little library there, blinking in the blinding light of two suns: one blazing from a blue sky a million miles away, and one in the shape of a long airship, crashing into the train station and the street before me?

Well, I will. I will tell you all of that, and I'll tell you how your boys, America, poured from every corner and cranny of that town. Some on leave, some in training, some in transit—all of them jumping in to the conflagration. Squelching fires, capturing enemy soldiers, and taking a catastrophe in hand in order to bring peace. They, shoulder to shoulder with the brave people of the village and vineyards, did a great work today.

I will tell you one more tale, too. When all was extinguished and everything put to rights but for the metal skeletal corpse of the burned-out airship—which, even as I write this, perches upon the train platform it tried to consume—I witnessed two further astounding incidents.

One was a previously floundering fellow who singlehandedly altered the course of that ship and the course of that day. He rose up, the good man, and found courage he hadn't known he was in possession of. And with it, he walked into a village given over to chaos. That soul found that his uncanny way of lifting a scenario with jovial words and an emerging honesty that seemed to astound even himself was apparently, astoundingly, made for just such a situation. Characteristics that stuck out like odd limbs on a person bumbling through the corridors of life, until he found that they weren't odd limbs at all, but rather the carefully crafted shape of himself, molded to fit like a puzzle piece into this moment. His purpose. He poured himself out: helping children up, stopping to ask after women searching frantically and men driving on in blind and dumbfounded purpose.

He begs the question of me, and perhaps of each of us—what if what we believe to be our shortcomings, our oddities, are actually purposeful quirks that suit us for the moments we were made for?

He accompanied me, after that long day, out of the village. It was there, at a crossroads, that we saw a sight we will never unsee. A soldier, one of yours. Standing beside a woman whose entire universe has been upturned by this war. It was a simple image, but beneath it is the truth of a man who crossed the world to find her, and enter into her brokenness, and ask to carry her to safety.

Just one person, giving everything he has for another.

It's why we joined this war, America.

And it's a story that reaches far, far into each one of us.

"What's that?" George Piccadilly snatched the paper out of my hands as we made camp near the crossroads, in the trees.

I yanked it back to safety. "Nothing that concerns you."

And maybe nothing that concerned the *Washington World*, either. But at least I could try. The thought of Celia Petticrew telling me to let Henry Mueller have a chance had urged my pencil to keep scratching out words. There were stories worth hearing, and in order for them to be heard, they had to be told.

I needed to try.

But I didn't have to let George know what I'd written about him. It'd send him flying higher than the zeppelin he'd brought down. Today had changed him, and was changing him still. He was still his knuckleheaded self, but all that nonsense was tempered by something more.

"Where d'you suppose they've gone off to?" he asked, gesturing up the small hill where we'd spotted Mireilles and Matthew. "Gone to fetch some beef broth and soufflé, do you suppose?"

Perhaps he hadn't changed so much after all. I dug in my haversack and shoved a carrot at him.

"Mmmm. So much better than soufflé," he said and snapped off a big bite of the carrot, chomping with an incorrigible grimace and prodigious volume.

It was dark before the two pilgrims returned, something different about them. Like a spell woven thick but invisible, though neither would speak of it. We all sat around a small fire, shielded enough that it would not be easily spotted from the road, and talked long about the events of the day. The sky had fallen, quite literally, and we'd lived to tell. All of us were scratched and banged up, plenty of scars to bear tales. But all of us oddly light, as we began to realize we had survived something so horrific.

The next two days carried us on in like manner, following the course of the Marne River. It would take us nearly to Paris, and soon. The farther we got on our journey, the less we talked, each of us registering that this brotherhood—and sisterhood—had an end in sight. Mireilles, especially, grew quieter with every step. And so did Matthew, who watched her—watched all of us, really—with growing concern. I wondered if he was thinking as I was: that the end of it would lead us right back to the beginning . . . where it might end us for good.

34

Mira

I remember well the tale of the girl and the road. How the sun spilled over the pages of Grand-père's book as I would lay across the floor and run my thumb back and forth over its planks, smoothed by our footsteps over the years at home, and wonder when my feet would carry me out into the wide world.

And now here I stood, the road stretching far behind me. I had taken a journey. I had, I suppose, sought treasure, like the girl in the pages. And now, rising before us in the distance, were the city walls of Paris. My treasure was not of coin or gem. It was that of life.

I felt the little one quicken inside of me and wondered if she or he could also hear the raging river before us. It was all that stood between me and our destination now. The only obstacle left for us to cross.

I turned around, forsaking the roar of the river, to hear the men. They stood scratching their heads, pointing at different places in the river, and studying Henry's map. Trying to find the best way to cross the waters of the Marne.

I smiled. The soldier who could outwit an entire clutch of Germans, Matthew "Catch-a-Crew" Petticrew, as the others had told me. The journalist who held the heart of a nation but was too bashful in person to speak to a girl. And the awkward, buoyant chaplain who had traveled all this way and stumbled upon his own faith during the journey. They were good men, the three of them. And they had come a long way from the bickering trio they had been when we began. As I watched them study the river and join their ideas together to build a bridge of ideas where the true one had been washed out . . . I thought that they were like friends, but so much more. They were brothers.

Fondness for them each warmed me and set my heart to swelling. They felt like brothers to me, too.

Matthew caught my eye and let his gaze linger. Reading me, as he did. My heart quickened, too. Perhaps . . . perhaps he was like something more than a brother.

Brother, friend, or anything more, it was for this reason I knew I had to set these three companions of mine free. It had come upon me slowly the past two days, this realization. I had taken them for too long . . . and taken more of Matthew Petticrew than I ever should have. I had made it harder for him. I knew it to be so, and it twisted something inside of me and made it difficult to breathe.

I approached them, picking up my mud-drenched hem. "It is alright," I said, clutching the map and pressing it gently toward Henry. "I will go on from here alone." I infused a lightness and assuredness into my voice, though I did not feel such. I felt only sorrow and trepidation.

Henry looked puzzled, pinching the side of his spectacles and bringing them closer to his eyes. George looked quite as if he did not catch my meaning, grinning his dimpled grin. And Matthew . . . Matthew was stricken.

"It is alright," I repeated. "The Marne, she is much like the Meuse." I named the river that snaked past and within the Argonne. "I am watching her currents; I can see where to cross." I narrowed my eyes, forcing myself to look away from Matthew and to gaze downstream, where the wide expanse grew wider and the currents spread out to a calmer pace. "There," I said, shielding my eyes from the bright reflection of the sun. "I can cross, and then go on to the city, and I'll be—" *Home* was the word that fit there, but it did not feel true. "I'll be in the great *Paris*!" I opened my palms, showing all would be well, that the conclusion of the story was at hand.

I said nothing of how the thought of the city—of all the people, the buildings, the noises and smells, and a château I knew nothing of—made me ill inside.

They took turns protesting. We had come this far, they all said in their own ways. They would see it through.

Matthew's words from the night at the billet, when he pulled the bits of earth from my open palm, rolled over me again. *"I'll see you home, Mira."*

I had known, then, that would never be our story. My story was already written. I ran my hands over my stomach to remind myself of such, and I started out toward the Marne. If I stopped for goodbyes, I would crumble.

But I should have known those stubborn boys would not go easily away. They followed me, protesting. George put himself between me and the river, swearing he would lie down and allow himself to be a bridge before he'd see me tread these waters alone.

I laughed gently. "But don't you see?" I beheld each one, lifting my hand to their cheeks, one at a time. "That is just what you have done. You have been the bridge from past to future. All will be well." My voice wavered, betraying me.

Henry dropped his gaze. He did not pull out his notebook. He—why, he lifted his hand quickly and swiped beneath his eye. Quiet Henry, who felt so much more than his printed words let on. "Continue to write," I said to him, gripping his hand for a moment. "This is a hand that is changing the world. Do not give up, Henry Mueller." He met my gaze, at my use of his full, true name. "Hank Jones will step aside—I feel it."

George made a show of trying to lie down and be that bridge he'd promised. "Do not dare to lie in that mud, George Piccadilly," I said. "Wherever you go, there are those who will need a voice of hope. You will not want your mouth to be caked over with mud from the Marne. You will need it to speak." And I believed it. He had stumbled into faith in the unlikeliest of ways and told us it all had to do with a sheep he'd had a conversation with just before the zeppelin took the skies. He said that if a donkey could speak in the Bible, surely a sheep could be "a divine instrument of change in a thickheaded chaplain's heart. Miraculous creatures, in point of fact."

And then there was Matthew.

My Matthew.

So much a part of me that when I opened my mouth to let the words come out . . . they would not come. He already had them, just as he already had all of me. Just as those words he'd spilled on the streets of the ruined village, before he'd known I understood a bit of it, had begun to stitch us together. Just as my story, spilled into his heart and held there, so securely, so tenderly, had caught me forever.

I only squeezed his hand. I could not, for all the world, have offered any words right enough to this man.

So I spoke the hardest ones I would ever speak to him. And the last.

"Good-bye, Matthew."

I dared to look at him and knew in that instant I should not have. The depth of those dark blue eyes, his desperation to understand, to change my mind—it would be the end of me.

"Thank you," I whispered. "For every moment." Every moment had changed everything. Had changed me.

I tore my gaze from him and felt the beginning of the tearing in my heart, too. I stepped into the Marne.

35

Matthew

The waters rushed cold around me, but I hardly felt it. I followed Mira as the others watched on. I knew they were concerned for her. I knew that they knew, somehow, that I would be the one to go after her.

Even the river seemed to know it. The currents were shallow and gentle at first. Mira, remarkable Mira, did know how to read the waters. She was fast in traversing them. Too fast.

"Mira!" I said, tripping on a root or a rock halfway across the expanse, trying to catch her. She was far ahead of me, the distance growing swiftly. It hit me with a fierce blow that this could be it. I really could be losing her. She, stubborn, determined, strong soul that she was, could be across to the other bank in a matter of moments and disappear into the bustling city beyond before I could stop her.

The thought shot straight through me, and a fiery surge followed. My old foe, the Flame, come to my aid this time. Catapulting me into those currents, the bottom dropping out of my lungs when the bottom dropped out of the river, right there in the middle. The water grew deep and strong, slowing Mira enough that I could catch up.

"Mira, please!"

She turned, her long hair floating upon the waters in dark ribbons.

"You have done it, Matthew," she said, looking me full in the face. "You have delivered me to Paris. I can go the rest of the way—I have done harder things. And you, you will go back. Away from—"

Her words were cut short. I watched in numb horror as she disappeared, swallowed away in an instant from my sight. The river current had her, its icy fingers gripping my Mira.

Gone. Her absence socked me hard, the suddenness sickening.

It took a single second to realize what was happening. It took another to shout her name with more force than I knew was in me, and for that voice to be engulfed in the roar of the river. And it took an eternity before I saw it—a hand emerging. Just a snatch of a moment, downriver.

It was impossibly fast. I dove in, unseeing of the boulders and branches that moments before seemed absolute barriers between us. White foam blinded me. A churning roar deafened me.

"Mira!" I shouted again and faintly heard the others shouting, too.

God in heaven, help her. I prayed the prayer I hadn't prayed since I was a boy. Over and over and over as the currents slammed me into a rock, speared me with some shard of a fallen tree, stirred in me desperation.

I took hold of the same boulder that sliced my arm. All went silent as I clung to it and turned, scanned painstakingly, not missing a single inch of that river.

Too much time had passed.

Or was time even alive here?

Was she?

I gulped. Whispered the prayer aloud, letting the river carry it away to heaven or to oblivion. "God in heaven." My breath came ragged. My words sputtered. "Help her."

I would not close my eyes. And I dared to believe—to beg—that the God I prayed to would not close His, either.

And then . . . there she was. Bursting to the ruthless surface. I don't know how I reached her. I have no recollection of diving beneath frigid water and swimming to her. I only know that she was in my arms, then, some primal force driving me as I pulled her toward the bank that seemed impossibly green. The air was colder than the water, and I knew only to keep her warm—and pulled her to myself as we stood with the river flowing on and on around us as if we were just an afterthought. Nuisances in its frantic force.

I cradled her and strained, with the ears I'd once used to name horses from afar, with the ears Captain Truett was so eager to get back to the front to hear shells and incoming bombs. I strained, instead, to hear her breathe.

But I could not hear a single breath.

I could not see if she breathed. If she lived.

"God in heaven, help her," I whispered for a third and final time.

I had no thought in that moment but to plead for her life. Later, I would look back and be able to wonder things like—how much time had passed? How cold was it? How could anybody survive a battering such as the river had given her, bruises already showing on her face and arms?

But in that moment I looked only at her—at the way her scrap of apron, that piece of balloon that had delivered her father into the safety of the woods so long ago, untangled from its river-hewn twists and swirled about her ashen face there in the water. The faint outline of an indefatigable matchbox still in the skirt pocket. Bringer of light to impossible places.

All went silent around me as I heard, in my mind, her voice. The lullaby that found me before I'd ever laid eyes on her. "*It was the only thing I had to give,*" she'd told me. "*To bring a small bit of life to a lifeless place.*" It dug into me now, rooted in my chest, and began to climb, as if each note were a handhold, up through my burning throat and out of my mouth.

I . . . sang. To Mireilles, the Angel of Argonne. It was downright ugly, this song in my voice, when it should have been hers. It was choked and raw, drug from the trenches to this moment. Wordless, only haggard humming. A desperate prayer that was far beyond words.

But perhaps it did not matter how haggard and worn a lifeline is to the person drowning. Perhaps, in her kindness, she heard only the heart behind it. The heart that split right in two, holding her so still in my arms.

And perhaps by some miracle, those horrific notes, that desperate prayer, played some part in what happened next. I do not know. But her eyes fluttered open ever so briefly.

Her chest rose ever so slightly.

She sputtered, and what followed was a tangled blur of embracing and speaking and trying to keep from crushing her as I pulled her close, until at last she stood, collapsed into me. Releasing everything she had held in. All of it, resurrected from the depths of this river, its currents pushing her full force into me. Depositing her, body and soul, into my arms until they did what they were created to do. They held the Angel of Argonne. My Mira.

When she pulled back to search my face, I prayed she could read the message pleading to be heard from every speck of my being. I feared my gaze would swallow her up, so deeply did I need her to understand. With the roar of the river around us, I pulled her close so that she could hear. Pressed my mouth to her ear to be heard.

"Never make me leave," I said. "Please, Mira." And then, with all the force of that river and more, all the rugged, battered foam of being drug over the boulders into this very place . . . "I love you."

She did not stiffen at my touch. She did not pull away.

"I—I love you," I repeated, the words gathering strength from the raw scrape of my voice, the words gentling around the feel of her next to me. "Won't you let me, Mira. Let me love you. Always."

She was holding me, she was holding the babe within her, a hand cradling her middle. She turned to the sky as if it held her answer.

"Be my wife, Mira," I said. It was reckless, maybe cruel—for we were in the middle of a war. I knew—we all did, though none spoke it into words—that my life would likely not extend beyond the next month.

But I could not fathom not being Mira's. Her not being mine. We'd crossed a world and found one another in the middle of the forest, all of our pieces and stories locking into each other, fastening us together.

I had no more words to say. Only the pulsing silent plea between us, only my fingers threading through hers.

"Yes." I saw the word but did not hear it above the river.

I dipped my head forward, eyes wide, a silent question. Unable to believe. Ready to be carried away myself on these currents if it was true. *Yes?*

She nodded. "Yes, Matthew Petticrew."

36

George

"George!"

By heavens, Broodman lived! And shouted for *me*, following his harrowing tangle with the river, good man! It was clear from where we stood that he'd rescued the Angel, who now stood in his arms on the bank of the river.

Not that any of us were surprised by the sight of them together. It had been only a matter of time. And had taken only a near-death experience with a raging river to finally get them there. There he was, the fulfillment of all his gaping hole-in-his-soul dreams in his arms, and he shouted for me. Me! The fellow gave a care for my well-being? Would wonders never cease?

"Not to worry," I shouted, giving a wave. "We made it across and all's well!"

A sharp jab to my side, and Henry, who really was quite literally a wet rag now from his journey across the Marne, jerked his head their way, leading on.

"Ow," I said, sucking in a breath.

"You ford a river on foot and nearly crack your skull on the way, and *that's* what you say 'ow' to?" He rolled his eyes.

We reached Matthew and the Angel.

"We're fine," I reassured him, out of breath and teeth beginning to chatter. A silence hung as they all studied me, as if stupefied.

Right. *Right.* It wasn't about me. I was beginning to see it might take a good deal of time for me to remember that quite naturally. But I was determined to reform my admittedly George-centered ways.

"That is to say—" I cleared my throat—"everyone alright? All present and accounted for? Bones, toenails, various limbs and noses? Shall I offer a prayer?" I pulled out my pocket prayer book and opened its sopping pages. Surely there was something in here for the consolation of souls recently subjected to harrowing experiences. I flipped to the table of contents. What would that be under . . . ?

Henry removed his jacket and, awkward though he was, poor chap, placed it upon the Angel's shoulders. He had gotten wet from the waist down, the mongrel, and had the only dry garment between us all to offer her.

She nodded gratefully, offering him a smile. He ducked his head in response and set to work gathering wood, building a fire.

What was happening to me? Ever since my conversation with the sheep, it seemed I—why, I was seeing things I never had before. These kindnesses among strangers and friends alike, and I wished to be a part of it. Very much a part of it.

George's fire snapped into action, its warmth and popping sparks a welcome presence in the October air. I carefully turned the wet pages of my prayer book. What could I say?

"You're a chaplain," Petticrew said. Had he taken leave of his senses and forgotten so simple a thing?

"Yes," I said, drawing out the word slowly.

"Chaplains can . . . perform ceremonies."

If ever a moment called for the furrowing of brows, it was this one. I furrowed. Taking in the pair, drenched as river rats. Matthew guided Mira closer to the flames.

I looked between the two of them.

They looked at each other, then back at me. I furrowed. And in that chiseling of forehead lines, I began to sense they were communicating in cautious, wordless petition for me to understand. They held up their wet hands, which were woven together, that I might calculate the rest on my own.

"I see what you're getting at," I said, raising those furrowed brows into a look of shared understanding. I spoke with solemnity, with an air of gravitas, as such an occasion called for. "You wish for a ceremony."

Relief flooded. Petticrew faltered, looking to the Angel to confirm. She bit her lip, and did I detect the beginnings of a hopeful smile upon her face? She nodded.

"If you would," Petticrew said.

"Here and now?" I eyed the river. The two of them and their wet forms, side by side. It all began to make sense. It seemed a tad—well, spontaneous. Rather sudden, in point of fact, but who was I to deny such a holy rite?

"Here and now," Mira said.

"Very well." A shiver of purpose ran down my arms as I peeled the wet pages of my prayer book to the appropriate page. This one was easy to find. Henry watched on from beneath a tree to my left, wide-eyed and reverent, notebook tucked solemnly away and hands clasped in front of him. All of Paris looked on in the far distance beyond. Paris! Witnessing this momentous occasion!

This was a weighty thing. Me, a part of something true and good. I uttered a silent prayer of disbelieving thanks—and uttermost cry for help.

I began to read. My stomach twisted, and not for anything to do with rarebit. I, George Piccadilly the Third, was about to tread upon holy ground.

"Well-beloved," I began reading. Putting feeling in my voice, with all sincerity. "You have come hither desiring to receive holy baptism. We shall pray—"

A shifting, as Matthew and Mira looked uneasily at one another.

Grasses crunched behind me. A tapping on my shoulder, and Henry spoke very quietly, as if to preserve my pride. "I don't think that's quite right," he said, voice very low and lifting his spectacles as if I should somehow take his meaning.

"Well of course it's not 'quite right,'" I said at full volume, full of conviction. "But who among us is perfect? Who among us, I ask, will cast the first stone if they desire to be baptized *after* being submerged? Even I know it goes the other way 'round. They might've gotten it mixed up, and I might not know much, but I'd dare to suggest that the grand Monarch of the Universe who created that river and fashioned their souls won't mind one bit if they—"

"George." It was the Angel. Mira. Mireilles. She stepped forward and laid her hand on my arm. The effect was the same as her song on me—inexplicable calm. "We wish . . . to wed."

I gaped. "Wed." I turned the word over in my voice like the curiosity it was. Glinting and mythical. "Now?" I looked sideways at Petticrew, attempting to ascertain his level of sanity.

"Ah," I said, pointing. "I see. It's a joke. You're—you're joshing me. You've hit your head, I saw it happen. It's a funny joke." I smiled a congratulatory smile. It was well-deserved, this man of great gravity having achieved something humorous. The joke was on me, I understood, but what had I just been telling myself? Not everything was about me. Hang my pride; they could have their joke, and well did they deserve it after their harrowing waltz with the River Marne.

"I can die having lived a complete life, now that the stone-faced Matthew Petticrew has told a joke. We saw it here first, gentlemen! Did you get it down for the newsmen?" This, directed at Henry. "Earth-shattering stuff, this!"

Mira spoke again. "It is no joke," she said. "Please, George." She smiled, giving a small shiver. "If you would."

"This instant," Petticrew said. The fellow looked positively— well, I don't know what—but the beginnings of a smile started to turn his mouth upward. No small miracle for him, and I thought his whole body might buoy up and float away with it. He looked at Mira as to engrave every last detail of her in this moment onto his very bones. "Please."

He'd said please.

I pulled in a breath. "Right-ho," I said. The words very George Piccadilly, but the tone very somber. "Wed, you shall be."

The prayer book felt like a forever thing, then. Knowing that these words I spoke would be laid down as stepping-stones joining two separate paths into one. They were not my words, nor was theirs my life—and yet the simple act of speaking, lending my voice to the words . . . it was a humbling honor. I felt very small in it. And—why, it felt so very right, to feel so very small. Odd, that. That in the midst of such a humble and lofty thing, I was fuller than I'd ever been. And grateful, by golly.

I began to read. My stomach twisted. Once again, I, George Piccadilly the Third, was about to step onto holy ground.

"Well-beloved," I began solemnly reading. "We are gathered together here in the sight of God, and in the face of this company, to join together . . ."

37

Mira

Paris. So often had we spoken the word in these last days that it had
seemed to become an assured part of my future. So very—usual. Less
a fable from Grand-père's tales and more a part of the true world.
It rose before me now, stone upon stone, stretching wide and high.
And now . . . it would be the place I first journeyed with my husband.

It was a breathless thing, a secret held between only him and me
and the river and our two friends. It felt too beautiful to be real. It
was not, perhaps, what I had dreamed of my wedding day being
when I was younger. With only wind for a veil, the rush of water
for a hymn, a fire in place of a reception, giving the very best wedding gift: a drier, warmer version of ourselves. A ceremony with a
bit of a stumbling beginning but with all the strength of the ages.

Like us. We two, who had crossed worlds to find each other in
the solitary depths of the Argonne Forest. I looked at him now.
He looked at me. Taking my hand, we stepped into a world very
strange and enormous: the city.

I closed my eyes and saw it as Grand-père had. A place clothed
in stone, from street to building. I wondered if my story would
become a part of those kept here, seamed into the mortar.

"Ah, Paris," Grand-père used to say. *"La Ville Lumière . . ."* His
voice held a fondness as he spoke of its streets, of the strength of
such a city, of the River Seine flowing through it like a messenger
of life. *"The stones, they tell stories."*

"Happy stories, Grand-père?"

He grew somber. *"Every kind of story, Mira."*

It had seemed immovable when he spoke of it. It was strange—the feeling that I knew this place but had never seen it. In his stories I had not heard the chatter of the people, some hushed, some hollering. The creak of trains and the play of music, the way churches spilled souls into the street, holding close the prayers they left behind them. Prayers of mothers, sisters, soldiers, doctors, street sweepers, all of them together.

I wrinkled my nose, trying to place something.

"What is it?" Matthew asked.

"Something is missing," I said. "Grand-père—he spoke of church bells. Always, the church bells."

Henry dropped his gaze.

"You know of them?"

"You may not like to know this," he said. "But they've gone silent, for the war. They only ring now when a warning is needed."

The silent bells seemed to cry to me as I fixed my eyes on the form of the great Notre Dame on the skyline. My foot caught something, and Matthew gripped my elbow, keeping me from falling. Too late, I saw what I had stumbled upon: the beautiful stones of these cobbled streets, wrinkled into a pile, surrounding a dark crater before us.

My hand flew to my heart. This was not what I had meant when I wondered if my story would become one of those kept by the city.

"Paris will swallow me whole," I said, trying to laugh.

Matthew smiled, but I saw the concern deepen around his eyes. He was a kind man, this man of few words. This man who was my husband.

My husband. How strange to think it so. How good.

We walked on for a time that disappeared into the city. As if we had stepped into the pages of Mr. Hugo's *Les Misérables.* I had borrowed the book from Madame Aline some years ago, and it came back to me now, this city of frozen time, of fierce hope, of war after war after war. Only instead of street barricades with Marius standing his ground, a tower like a great triangle of metal lace rose on the horizon, its long neck reaching into the sky. It was laden with cannons and gunfire, as if it could see far beyond the walls of this city, see all the way to the men who would march toward it, fly their zeppelins over it, and drop unthinkable destruction within.

Henry's pencil would surely catch fire at any moment, he was scratching notes so quickly into his notebook. He paused, looking up and up at the tower, shaking his head in wonder. "Eiffel Tower," he said. "They've turned it into a radio tower for the war, too," he said. "Weapons all over it, bunker beneath it, antennae sending invisible messages all over the front."

As we walked on, I started to distinguish sounds and movements, and the cacophony of the city began to sort into a symphony. In my forest, I would hear a rush of wings overhead, a shuffle of pine needles underfoot, the chatter of squirrels, and Papa whistling in the distance. It was music to me. The city, too, was music. Or rather, it could be, if I learned to hear it. So many languages, people come from faraway countries to work in the war factories, Henry told me. The sound of pigeons as they ducked about in their funny bobbing way. Children giving chase around a postbox, a ball bouncing, the hooves of horses pulling carts, the engines of motor cars tripping into life.

We passed narrower streets, with homes stretching each length in grey stones marbled with light and dark with age, iron-laced balconies holding life, so much life, inside. I breathed out slowly, the number of people swimming about in my head. So many, so many, all in one place.

"Here it is," Henry consulted his notes, written after asking an officer on the street. He looked up and down the narrow way to confirm. "Jour de Soleil Motherhouse," he said. He shuffled his feet, unsure. "You . . . want us to come in?" He looked dubious, unsure whether a sisterhood of nuns would want them in their midst. Though from what Celia had told us, they made it their business to help the sick, the soldiers, and everyone in between. To bring care to those who needed it.

Henry looked over his shoulder. "I was going to stop in at the land registry office to see what we might find out about your family's house. . . ."

I smiled. There was a twinge of hope in his voice for this academic mission, but that he was even willing to step so outside of his realm here at the motherhouse made me smile despite the tremors inside of me.

It was a humbling thing. I had come from a place where all the world, it seemed, was mine to roam. To live off the forest, cut wood, light fires, cook meals, plant and harvest food. A good life with Papa and Grand-père, we three believing it was up to us to care for others.

And now, here I stood upon ground of cement, where I could harvest not a thing. No forest for wood, no food to cook. I was the one in need of help.

I swallowed. Matthew met my eyes and took my hand. "All will be well," he whispered. And then, to George and Henry, he spoke of a plan to meet, after we finished here and they at the land office.

I wished to believe all would be well. I prayed to believe it. The kind woman inside, in her dark habit and gentle smile, welcomed me with such warmth. She surely must have had ten thousand questions of this pair who showed every mile of their journey by the dust of their clothing. Who spoke words such as *husband* and *wife* with so much tentative wonder they sounded spun of glass. But she only wrote down the address Henry had found for the château, lighting up and declaring we were nearly neighbors with one of their lodging houses.

We left with the promise of a Sister Marion who would come the next day to assess my health and help me prepare for the *bébé précieux*, and who would check in very often with supplies while Matthew was away.

She spoke it as if she knew he would only be gone a short time. As if this were only the beginning of our story.

And I left with hope in my heart.

Hope that carried me into the young evening as we met back with the other men and journeyed on, the streets growing less crowded in this new area. More trees, less people. More birds, less talking. Henry, offering in his quietly assured way what he had learned from the *cadastre* at the land registry: the chateau belonged, officially, and in wording he had learned was sometimes customary, to "heirs of Franz-Christophe Fontinelle." A great-great-grandfather I had never known. Whether that was me or this great-aunt Sophia, or perhaps someone else entirely, I did not know. It seemed that nobody knew. But it was our family home, come what may . . . and for this, I was thankful.

And then we stopped. Henry flipped backward in his notebook, looking to a pen-and-ink sketch he had copied by hand from a library book in Épermay, and up to the sight before us. The sketch showed a grand villa, bedecked in brick and pillar, with precisely trimmed shrubbery, women with parasols, men in top hats strolling down the path leading to it.

The sight before us . . . was not so. It was a rusted gate, grown over with ivy and flanked by trees.

"Right!" George said. "Looks like she's been waiting for us. Shall we?"

I swallowed as he creaked the large iron gate open.

Matthew made to step through, his being on high alert. He did, and after making a circle around the outside he reported back that all seemed quiet—all was empty.

The emptiness he spoke of unfurled tendrils reaching out, wrapping around me like the ivy that clutched its walls. Drawing me in. All three men waited for me to take the first step.

And I did. Into a world far apart from the city we had just traversed. A place full of hush and memory, sleepy and weary. As if it had been waiting, just as George said, to be awakened.

I approached with care, making my feet fall silent, just as I had done in the forest. Just as I had when I had approached the injured soldier to help him. Just as I had before everything had changed.

I stopped. Felt my breath come quick and short. *This is not the same.*

"Everything alright, love?"

I startled. The accent. Pulse skittering.

Turning, I saw George's kind face, the way he smiled like a buffoon. *This is not the same.*

The sickness came over me as I remembered. *Please, God. Deliver me.* From the memory. From summoning it in sleepy houses and well-meaning friends.

The child kicked within, reminding me. *Life.* Life had come from that darkness.

I took another step, and another. Willing my lungs to open. To take in breath. For my child. For me.

Matthew was beside me, wordlessly stepping with me. Not saying a single word and understanding too much. I felt that, in him.

Soon, the château stood before us in full view, unmasked of the growth at the gate.

I could see it: the way such a place must have glowed at night, with strains of music slipping from its windows. I could picture Grand-père as a young man, dressed as the proper people of Paris many years before, brass-buttoned and top-hatted. Perhaps chasing after my own father, so young then, he would have toddled through hedged paths and jabbered nonsense.

What would they have thought? If they could have stilled time, skipped decades, and found me here? Bedraggled of the journey and holding them in my heart, staring here into a happy place.

A place they had left. To find a future, a simple life, a safe place for generations yet to come.

I cradled my middle. Desires I knew so well.

The front door hung off its hinges. Henry looked at me for approval, then pushed it open. It scraped against something—rubble, perhaps, from years of neglect.

"It's a wonder," he said.

I stepped inside, and in that, felt the marking of something momentous. The beginning of something, righ here in the echoes of a past I'd not known of.

Henry was right. This place . . . the frozen glass of the windows, the pale yellow upon the walls that seemed to offer fragrance of aged sunshine. "A wonder," I echoed.

"A place like this . . ." he continued. "The way most structures like this are going, it should be full of soldiers."

"Soldiers?" I looked around at my three sojourners. "I suppose we have remedied that, then, haven't we?"

He laughed. "Most structures like this have been commandeered for quartering or taken over for hospitals. They've even done so with an old abbey outside the city."

"Ah," I said. "You mean *very* full of soldiers."

"Quite!" George chimed in. He plinked a few keys of an old piano in the corner, releasing a woefully hollow off-key sound in addition to a cloud of dust. He picked out a tune and beckoned Henry over, who set to examining the instrument. I could nearly see the gears in his mind turning, finding how to tune it, thinking up a way to write of it as some bit of metaphor to his adoring readers, even as George tromped on with a jolly song. They would be occupied for hours if left to their own devices. Which they should be. They deserved it, after everything. The gift of a broken piano—something they might fix—to hearts weary of a war they could not fix.

There was only Matthew, now, who had not spoken.

"And . . . what are your thoughts, Matthew? What is running through that stormy mind of yours?"

The grave look vanished a moment, his mouth pulling into a smile. "It's . . ." He shook his head. "Amazing."

Tucked into his pause was something more, but this man who hid so many of his thoughts would not speak it, I knew. Unless invited to.

"But?"

"You see too much, Mira." He laughed, and the slow roll of it tumbled through me. I tried not to think that soon that laugh would have to leave. Along with that smile, and the grave look, and the unspoken thoughts that ran so deep. I tried not to think that all of those things, held in this man, would be headed into battle.

"Well?" I said, trying to keep my tone light.

"It is amazing. But . . ." He looked up into the vaulted space above us, where light shone through and fell upon a chandelier that held no candles. And he looked to me, then, as if all of the light from those once-upon-a-time candles had landed inside of me instead. Lifting his hand, he fingered a piece of my hair with tenderness. "Not amazing enough."

I looked around. Plaster fell from walls in patches, cobwebs draped corners as much as my own bedraggled hair draped me, after drying in clumps from the river. But though the place was worn and forgotten, it was unmistakably grand.

"I think you are puzzled," I said.

He tilted his head. I had the wrong word.

"Confused," I tried again. "Yes, I think you are confused. I am barely fit to be a maid scrubbing the floors in such a place." I laughed, the sound bubbling up and lifting my spirits as I pinched my torn skirt and held it out as proof. "This . . . is a palace." Falling apart and showing the wear of years empty and abandoned, perhaps. But a palace, still.

"Mira." He bent close, his voice low. "You have always lived in a palace. One with leaves for a roof and branches for walls. Fresh air as a cloak and sunshine for your crown. Nothing could ever hold a candle to that."

His words made me ache for my little forest house. My home. I had not been able to give words to it, but he had. I had *le mal du pays*—I was homesick.

Matthew, my wordless Matthew, looked amused. "Come," he said. "Let's see your palace."

He offered his hand and I took it, the two of us stepping onto the wide stair that narrowed and then split into two branches halfway up. He stopped there, at the landing. "It branches, here."

"So it does."

"When you're missing your own branches, maybe you can come here. See?" He pointed to where one of the windows was broken, a straggling branch reaching in from the outside. "It knew you were coming."

We turned, he to the left and I to the right, climbing the separate wings of the stairs. Slowly, eyes locked, taking each step together and yet apart. I could nearly feel his heartbeat across the expanse between us. It pained me . . . and filled me. This would be our lives soon. Apart, yet together.

My hand easily found its way back into his as we ventured down the hallway. This place, so broken, filled through its cracks and missing panes of glass with the sounds of slow evening breeze and birdsong. The hallway was strewn, its chinked marble floor a scattered carpet of leaves, twigs, and dust. A forest floor, laid down like a carpet for a queen.

"Not so very different from home, after all," I said. At the end of the hall, one door stood open. Or rather—the door had long ago gone missing, somehow, and we discovered the source of the leaves that had summoned us hence.

Before us was a round room with shelves upon shelves upon empty, empty shelves. Many a broken window, one of them in colorful shards of stained glass.

"A library," Matthew said.

"Once upon a time, yes?" I said. The books, but for a scattered few, were long gone. I approached a shelf and ran my hand along it, stopping when I came to a single volume, ruffled by time and raindrops blown in from passing storms outside. Yet even in its aged, bourgeoning state, it was familiar.

As if it had been waiting for me, always. Faded blue spine with once-gold letters.

I picked it up, holding it. Finding a lost part of myself that I had never even known, returned in full to me. The book grew heavy in my hands, and that heaviness wrapped me in safety.

"This is it," I said. "Grand-père's book." I shook my head slowly, running my palm over a page petrified in rumpled form, knowing just how it felt. "*Incroyable*," I whispered.

Matthew leaned in to see.

"It is . . . it is incredible. Out of all of the things that have been taken from this house since he left it so long ago, with only his courage and his son. That *this* would somehow be waiting for me."

"You . . ." Matthew said, sliding his hand beneath mine, to

help support the book. "With all of your courage. And with your little one."

I do not know what it was. I do not know if it was that picture in my mind— Grand-père leaving, driven by war, son in his arms, for a chance at life. Or the way it made me see a picture of myself, as if I had watched from above as I approached this château, driven by war, baby in my womb, for a chance at life. I do not know if it was because he was gone—buried in quiet peace beneath the wreath Matthew had created. Or if it was because of those same wreath-laying hands now holding mine. Or if it was because of Papa—Papa always, always in my heart and in my mind, never willing to pry my fingers loose of their hold on him. Never willing to let him be a memory and not a hope.

Perhaps it was one of those things—or perhaps it was all of them. But there in this room, with a book in my arms that had waited for me since a lifetime before I was born . . . I finally fell. Right to my knees, right in the forest floor that was there upon the marble, and right into the arms of the soldier who had seen me. Listened to me. Learned me. Dared to know me, right down to the shadows of life. And I wept.

I do not know how long we sat that way, me wrapped in him and him with arms that felt as if they had been searching for me—little me, in this big room, in this wide world—all his life. But it was dark when the current of tears slowed to a trickle and the trickle slowed into uneven breaths raked over my ribs and grief and hope.

The moon was high, the house silent. Matthew stroked damp strands of hair from my face, behind my ears. His hands all the gentler for the calluses they bore, and the care they took with me because of it. It made me think of another pair of scarred hands that had given all to hold me.

And so it was that in a decrepit mansion where all fell apart on the obscure outskirts of Paris, I fell into the sleep one only finds in the safest, dearest of homes.

I fell into sleep in the arms of my husband.

38

Matthew

I meant not to sleep that night. I meant to drink her in, imprint every bit of her in my mind. Most soldiers carried a picture of their wife or sweetheart with him to remind him why. To bring him comfort, offer hope. I would have no picture. There wasn't time, I knew, and even if there was, I wouldn't want to invite some stranger into it. I would blockade the world away and soak in Mireilles for as long as I could, if she would let me.

And so I determined not to sleep, knowing that would be easy. A man falls out of the habit when he's gone so long without. But tonight . . . tonight it would be different. It would not be keeping eyelids open until they hurt to avoid nightmares that hurt far worse. It would not be evading screams and scenes emblazoned on the mind, memories that pulsated only in darkness, when my consciousness could not keep them away.

Tonight it would be to savor. To etch her onto my being the same way I etched landscapes onto a spent shell, hoping to redeem some shred of beauty into vessels of destruction. I knew too well that I was a vessel of destruction. And in the searing pain of catching her tears, I wondered if God was etching some semblance of goodness onto such a soiled canvas as me. And the source of that goodness . . . was Mira.

And so I watched her. All through the night, holding her. My wife. Aching for her, for her courage, for the little life who dwelled so safely inside of her, kept from this war and its atrocities by her willingness to bear them instead, for both of them.

I watched, and etched, and blinked, and fought those blinks until I could fight no more, for the goodness of it all. Until finally those etchings grew deep, into trenches I would refuse to dream of . . . and I slipped into sleep.

There is a darkness that is so complete, it is pure rest. Absolute nothing, as if all the sleep one has been missing for all the weeks before has been gathering, mounding weight to cover you with when you finally find it, there in the land of oblivion. It covered me that night. And in it I knew, for the first time since coming to the shores of France—and probably a lot longer—*peace.*

But it was not to last. Somewhere in that velvet black cloak of deepest rest, in that place where dreams vault up and mimic reality to perfection, up shot a star shell. The sort of shell meant to illuminate no-man's-land and expose whatever transpired there, so that artillery fire could soon follow. That life could soon be pierced.

The star shell, in the thick of my sleep, did its work. Shot straight up into that beloved darkness, that peace, that dreamless place where all I had was reality and the girl in my arms. And as it did, it illuminated all the hidden places. The sounds I had long buried. The sights I could not unsee. All of it, kept here in a living museum that only opened at night, only in my sleep, only for me.

I saw Chester. The child soldier from Saint-Mihiel. The kid's young face, so like a younger brother. His zeal for battle, his innocence crushed. Did he live, still? I did not know. And why did it trouble me? Why his face out of all the thousands? Because, I knew—he was them. Me, eight years before. He was all of us, just a boy in a war too dark for him in a world too big, trying to do his part. *Please be alive.*

In waltzed Celia, flying down that midnight path of racetrack, me raking over her footsteps. And now she was off—closer to the frontlines than me, making footsteps I could not and would not undo, completely out of my reach. *Please be alive.*

The window of Maplehurst, Mr. MacMannus watching us

284

leave, the only time I'd seen a hint of uncertainty in his posture. He walked away.

The comic strip from the *Herald* I'd had pinned to my wall in our home in the barn, typeface worn, bottom corner crinkled, nothing comic about the way the young Jasper Truett was depicted riding in that volunteer cavalry so long ago, alongside Theodore Roosevelt. He came alive from the page. Aging into the very real and fierce Captain Jasper Truett standing in the flesh as the fire, smoke, the muck, the blood of the battlefield played backdrop. He walked toward me.

"You'll be alright!" he was saying, but I couldn't hear his voice. Only see his grime-streaked face, his mouth moving, desperation in his eyes as he shouted those words. Desperation even beyond that of the battlefield, desperation that lived so deep, it was as much a part of him as the air he breathed. It seemed to pulsate as he said those words again and again—*"You'll be alright!"*

Engulfing me, now, were trenches. Deeper, and deeper, everyone out of my reach. I saw her—the Angel of Argonne, walking the graves with bare feet, laying wreaths. Singing music too pure for such a place. Too good for me. And I saw her look down upon me, that face smudged and kind. I saw her smile, could feel it land on me way down there, soft as a feather, warm as a kiss.

And then her face—it broke from the smile. Crumpled into deep anguish as she bent over herself, grasping her stomach. I saw her lips move, but could not hear her. Not above the gunfire. *It is time, Matthew.*

No. I writhed in the stifling heat of this place, clawing at the ground to get up, climb to her. *No.*

Mira. I spoke her name and could not hear it. *Mira.* I watched her leave and could not follow. *Mira . . .*

All went mute. Black. Me, alone, in that trench. No Celia. No Chester. No George, Henry, Captain Truett . . . and no Mira.

I could not get to them. Could not protect them. The Flame— that old sense of burning justice—twisted and writhed in me with nowhere to go. Wrangling, strangling. I would give anything—

everything—to help these ones who lived in my heart closer than its own pulse.

But I could not.

I had nothing. I was nothing. I could offer them nothing, and there on the battlefield, there in the aftermath, there in the moment a child would come into the world and Mira would be alone no longer—I was absent.

Oh, God. It was prayer, and grief, and defeat. *Oh, God.*

I was five years old again. Crouching beneath my mother's window as she cried out. Helpless to do a single thing. Losing her. Trying to hear her, as she spoke my name, sounding so far away. *Matthew . . . Matthew . . .*

"Matthew."

A sweet voice—real. I woke in a sweat. Jolting up, shoulders heaving. Black all around. Was it real? I jerked, trying to see the trench walls.

And then I felt it. Gentlest touch, there in my writhing. And the song. The one I had loved before I had even seen its source. The one that had entered into my own inferno before she even laid eyes on me.

She ran her hand down my forearm, lacing her fingers into mine. Her song continued, haunting notes in clearest tone, dropping comfort in lilting time all around me.

My breathing slowed to the song's gentle movements. The shaking in my hand lessened but did not stop. It was cradled there in her hand, with fingers stroking so gently I forgot the always-there ache of them.

I bent my head. Ashamed, relieved, all of it at once. I had slept. And she had seen the reason I do not sleep.

She bent her head until it touched mine, her song falling silent.

We sat that way a long time, the sound of crickets coming from the broken window, heedless of the shells in my dreams and the shells hundreds of miles away. Miles I had crossed with this woman.

I should say something. Explain it for her, this horror she had witnessed. Here, the first and perhaps only night we would spend as husband and wife. It was not a honeymoon, not the night of lovers wed at last.

It was—in some ways—more. And yet so far, far from what she deserved.

Dumbly, I could think of only one question, my voice ragged from the nightmares. "What does it say?" I said. "Your song."

She ran her thumb over my palm. Part of me didn't want to know what it said. Words were just words, and none could ever be put to what those notes meant for me.

"It is what my mother used to sing to me," she said. "I . . . remember little of her. But the song, it has always kept."

"I wish I could give her back to you, for this." I winced at how direct my words were, bookended by two unchangeable things. Her mother gone, her baby soon to come.

But Mira, as was her way, heard my heart in it and held my hand closer.

"What . . . do the words mean?" I asked. "Did she write them?"

Mira pulled her head back and shook it, her long hair brushing the backs of my hands. "He shall neither slumber nor sleep," she said, her eyes wide and steady upon mine.

I swallowed.

She went on. "The day is yours, the night also is yours. You have prepared the light and the sun."

They were vaguely familiar, these words, though the way they pounded at my chest to be let in, you'd think they had been searching for me through the same dark trenches I'd just emerged from in the dreamworld.

"They speak of sorrow, and they speak of hope," she said. "They speak of the God who does not slumber nor sleep. Like another, who I know." She traced my jaw, her touch tearing into the fortress I'd hidden these things behind for so long.

"They are from the scriptures. David's Psalms. They speak of you, Matthew."

My hand rose up, covering hers, keeping it there against me. I shook my head. "That doesn't describe me, sadly."

She laughed, a gift. "I mean—my English fails— they speak
to you, Matthew. That the night is not to be feared. For the God
who fashioned it did so with care. Knowing these days you would
not sleep. Promising to draw near in the very midst of that night.
When you do not slumber, neither does He. You are not the only
one holding the world together in your wakefulness, Matthew."

It was my turn to laugh.

"But He is."

And now she was the one being direct. Her words cutting, making their mark. Searing away the illusion that my wakefulness did
any good in all the world.

"The only one," she added, for emphasis.

The words, they hurt. Tipping over a row of backward domi-
noes in my memory. Mira. Celia. Chester. Mother. That all my toil-
ing, all my concern, anything I did—perhaps it was well and good,
but any notion that I could create their safety was sheer illusion.

That terrified me. Shot me down to the core with cold realization.

"I can't leave you, Mira." I said it, knowing the dawn was im-
minent. That the day would come, and when it did, I would fear
it more than this night. For I would leave my wife, and this child,
in a strange city without a friend in the world—and doom myself
to a very likely future of not being able to care for them.

The air seemed thin, suddenly. Who would care for them?

"We do not have a choice," she said.

"I can't. I won't. I won't leave you. I won't do to you what's
already been done to you."

Gracious though she was, those words hurt her. I wished them
back immediately.

She pulled back, tucking her hands into the rumpled folds of
her skirt.

"I'm sorry, Mira. I didn't mean—"

She met my gaze with sorrow in her eyes. Eyes so wide they
looked like they had taken in this whole war. And perhaps—in
many ways—she had.

288

"No, you are right," she said. "I will tell you a truth, Matthew Petticrew, that you can fix to the armor of your heart. That lullaby—it is as much for me as for you. As much for this child, as for every one of those boys and men in the trenches. I am facing a night. At times, it has been cold and dark. Unbearably so. And at times . . . it has been more beautiful than anything I could have dreamed of." She squeezed my hand.

The sky grew grey outside, letting first veils of light in. I saw her by the first light of day, an heiress in a peasant's dress, right in her own castle. She spoke on.

"In that forest, terrible things happened. But in that forest—because of those things—wonderful things happened, too." She lifted my hand to her stomach. The intimacy of it tore through me. The last time I had touched her so, she had been unconscious. It had been an accident. And the little one had announced his—or her—presence to me by sending me a kick I would never forget.

"The God who does not slumber—the same God I questioned, and railed against, and sobbed to, and ran from, after He seemed not to see me or care—He brought me you, Matthew Petticrew. And it is because He brought me you that He has reminded me He can do anything in all this world. He can see me through what is next. And you, too. He can bring this child into the world. And—I pray—He can bring us together once again. He crossed you over oceans and years and brought you to my door in the middle of an isolated wood. If He has done that, then I can believe He can do anything."

The light was dawning in earnest, now, slipping over the windowsill and creeping up behind her. Crowning her and cloaking her, as if to prove all that she said was true.

It was too good. And the goodness was too terrible against the backdrop of this moment in time.

"That is—if you wish to be brought back together," she said, her brow furrowing so endearingly I could not help but lean in and kiss it. Inhaling her. Hands upon her shoulders, willing this moment to last forever.

When I drew back, her eyes were shining with such joy.

"You don't know what you're saying, Mira," I smiled. "You hardly know me. You may well regret the moment you agreed, in the middle of a river, to marry the crazy American."

"Hardly know you," she breathed. "You speak with many girls in haylofts, and carry them from snipers, and keep watch over them in ruined churches, and marry them at rivers, and tell them of your horse Gulliver, and introduce them to your sister?"

"You're a wonder, Mira." I laughed again. "And you're right. I've never done a single one of those things before I met you." *And never will again.* Not with anyone else. There would never be another. She had entered my life with that song and in every moment since, she had voided every alternate possibility of any other *something* that might ever happen in this life.

"This . . ." I said, letting my thumb stroke the sleep-rumpled dress over her gently rounded stomach, letting my gaze fix immovably upon her face. "Is all that could ever be, for me. There is only you. Only this. Always."

The coming light spun a spell about us as we lingered together. She shivered. What was I thinking? She should have a roaring fire in every hearth in this house. And something . . . even if it was such a small thing . . . from me.

From my pocket, I pulled out what had become of Chester's shell casing. The large metal cylinder had been left behind in Fontaine d'Argonne, all but the small bit I'd carried and carved throughout our journey. A smooth rectangle, sitting humbly in the palm of my hand. I thought of the many nights along the journey I'd twisted a nail, over and over, into its metal surface. Engraving but not piercing. Dot by dot, until the image unfurled.

A tree in the forest. The Sentinel tree, the one that had stood curving and aged, watching over Mira where I'd first found her. Etched in metal that had fallen from the sky in a war that had launched me into her world.

Unfolding her fingers now, I wrapped them about the small brass offering.

She sat up, with expectant delight on her face. She held it, and the morning sun set a sheen on the dull metal. She traced the image of the tree with her fingertips. "It's beautiful," she whispered. The spell of the morning light deepened as her presence soaked in the meaning of it.

"It's . . . from a shell," I admitted sheepishly.

She tilted her head, cradling it with care. As if she meant to heal the whole broken world in doing so. "Something so beautiful, from something so . . ." She let the sentence trail off.

I gulped. She deserved diamonds and sapphires, not metal from destruction.

"It is . . . the tree at home," she said. "Yes?"

"Yes."

"Matthew," she said. "You did this, by your own hands?"

I dipped my chin. "It should be more. But—I hope it will protect something you hold dear."

She studied me. I reached to where her apron was folded neatly on a wobbly chair, matchbox perched atop, and retrieved her letter. Her only remaining possession from the forest, save the apron and clothes on her back. *The matches . . . they are hope,* she'd told me. That seemed like a lifetime ago.

I slid her matchbox into its new home, the brass cuff encompassing it like the cover of a small book. She had lost so much. . . . this was the battleground I longed to stand upon. To fight for hope. For her.

"Mira," I said. "I wish I could promise I'll come home. I wish I could find your father, promise to bring him home. I wish—I wish you didn't have to do what's coming alone." I slid the matches back out and held one up. "But I can promise I'll fight for this." It was she, now, who reached out and rested her hand on my jaw. Her touch so gentle and true. "I'll fight for light." I swallowed, my throat aching and thick. "For hope."

She bent her head until our foreheads touched. "I know you will, Matthew Petticrew," she said. "It is who you are."

My chest pounded, ready to crack open wide. How long we

stayed there, I didn't know. Time . . . we were outside of it. Until somewhere in the house, a plucky and horrifically off-tune piano melody began to play.

"Seems we aren't the only ones awake," I said. I held her still, not ready to leave this moment. But the piano grew louder, the two-man chorus more boisterous.

We retraced our path from the night before, this time gilded in light. At the bottom of the stairs, we followed the growing sound through two oaken doors standing wide, welcoming us.

It was a ballroom, I guessed. Or once had been. The vast open floor where George was running in stockinged feet, gliding across as if on skates over ice. Henry plinked away at the tune, and when they saw us, they stopped. Rushed to greet us, taking a serious stance facing one another to create an avenue in between them.

"What's this?" I asked warily.

They bowed, and George cleared his throat. "Whereas the heiress has come home to reclaim her throne," he said, then waited.

And waited. And scowled at Henry, raising his eyebrows expectantly.

Henry tilted his head in reluctant acquiescence. "And whereas she is to be lady of the house from here on out . . ."

"We have brought her home to her!" George pointed a finger in the air, punctuating his declaration. "Come, if you please."

He led the way to the far end of the ballroom, where a wooden platform took up a fraction of the room. Dark, tattered curtains hung akilter, made of what looked like once fine fabric. A vestige of times when it shrouded an orchestra or troupe of actors, I imagined.

"My lady," George said dramatically, bowing once again. "May we present to you . . . your home." With measured ceremony, he pulled back one curtain, and Henry the other.

The room fell silent as Mira stepped up into what can only be described as a miracle. It was as if they'd tromped right back into the heart of the Argonne, each of them hefted up an end of her forest chalet, and tromped back across France to plant it for her here, in the middle of this grand empty tomb of a home.

To the left, a bed, just where the one in the forest had been. A rick-ety table, planted in the space that would have been a kitchen, the window looking out into an overgrown garden of some kind—so much green, we could pretend we were indeed far from the city, if we fixed our eyes only through that ancient glass.

In the corner, just where the crammed bookshelf had stood in the Argonne, was a stack of splintered milk crates, with four books spread out to occupy as much of it as could be. In the same place where George and I had boiled water for her potato "soup" stood a dented copper pot, perched on a stand over what looked to be a fire ring beneath it.

"Probably best if you don't actually light that," Henry said, looking bashful about what was presumably his contribution. "But if you do . . ." He pulled something from his pocket and stepped forward quickly, placing it in her hands and retreating before he could take it back.

A potato. With garden soil clinging to it still. She held it as if she had the crown jewels in her palm. "Where did you find this?" she said in hushed reverence.

How I loved that she could utter hushed reverence over a dirty potato.

"Out behind the manor," Henry said, standing a bit taller. "There's the remnants of a potager garden out there. Potatoes, onions, radishes, carrots—all gone wild and scattered with no rhyme or reason, but they can at least provide something more than our measly old potato for your soups."

"A wonder," she said. "Probably the descendants of the veg-etables Papa and Grand-père once ate."

I could see it, then. How a potato, of all things, was knitting a cloak of security about my Mira. A sense of belonging and family. *Thank you, God.*

"How did you do all of this?" she asked with eyes wide. Not in ridicule, as some might have done when taking in the homemaking efforts of two bachelors. It didn't have the touch of comfort that a home dwelled in did—not blankets, or flowers in vases, none of that. It truly did resemble more a fort built by kids, or a bachelor apartment. But the similarities to her home in the forest echoed the better for it.

Henry shuffled his feet. "We just moved a few things around, is all."

George gawked at his friend. "If by 'moved a few things around,' you mean 'moved heaven and earth to assemble this grand scene by staying up late into the night and scouring the corners of this cavernous château,' then yes. You are correct."

Henry shrugged a shoulder. "Anyway. It's a little bit of home for you, we hope."

Mira was walking each inch of the perimeter, letting her hand run fondly over each of the worn pieces of furniture. "It is remarkable," she said, eyes shining. "Thank you," she said to them, and then to me. "For bringing me home."

39

Henry

October 1918

"The pen is mightier than the sword."

Celia Petticrew's words, cloaked in the sweetness of her voice, carried an edge to them, as if they had been the sharpened weapon of which she spoke. Cutting through the slough of words I'd written since landing on the shores of France. Slicing away the fog of propaganda. Carving out the shape of something true in this landscape, and inviting me—no, *urging* me—in.

"We bivouac here," Matthew said in the fading light. His voice was quiet, and whether the life had gone out of it or had come into it so much he could not contain it, I could not tell.

Earlier in the day, after having shown our papers to a convoy en route to the Meuse-Argonne, we were pulled into a truck of men. Slapped on the back in instant brotherhood and deposited here once the river turned and our route diverged from theirs.

In silence, we made camp beneath a clump of trees. And in that silence, this night, worlds swam in and between us. The pulse of truth: This might be the last moment the Seventeenth Band would ever see one another, alive or dead.

The morning would find us back at the front—the sounds of warfare in the distance told us we were close, as did the map. Reports of the Meuse-Argonne offensive were many and varied, but they all resounded with an ominous common thread: The battle was intensifying. The end of this endless war was near—for better or for worse—and the soil of this land unequivocally soaked in the blood of its allies and enemies, ever more so as its end approached.

There was finality in the air.

A country across the sea, waiting to hear.

I took up my pen.

Your Boys, America!
By a Humble Observer

It is time for something different, America. I have asked much of you in these letters. This war has asked much of you. The unending war, the "war to end all wars," the "Great War."

Great War.

You may wonder, from the hollow ache of your heart, how can it be called "Great"? What mind, attempting to describe it as far-reaching and all-encompassing, landed so ironically on a word that also implies something good?

Tonight . . . I have no tidy words to offer. No grand orations or inspiring prose of courage and daring. I have been sent here to observe and report. Perhaps, if we are being honest, to put a gloss on this unimaginably hard place. But tonight, I have none of those things.

I have something more. Something much, much better.

I have something truly great, in all senses of the word.

It is simple and true and tells a thousand stories in the space of a hundred yards. It is the scene unfolding before me, here on the eve of battle. May I invite you in? May I wrap these images around words and deliver them to your hearts as the scene unfolds?

Four men are making camp. They have just been on a journey that's spanned a handful of days and many lifetimes. As you know, in order to protect the safety of the American Expeditionary Forces, I am not permitted to give specifics. By order of General Pershing's office, the men are not even permitted to keep journals. But if you'll lend me your ear and your imagination, I can give you more. I can give you their hearts. A captain, a chaplain, a sergeant, and me.

After you read this, close your eyes and envision: It is October in France. The air is warm for an autumn night. In the distance, the rumble of war. The incessant shelling, bombing, shooting, marching, digging—and the earth has been trembling with it for four years now. Trembling so that she is tired near unto death. She is scarred deep and forever, this swath of earth stretching north and south, jutting east and west in ever-changing salients, breeching country borders up into Belgium and down to where Switzerland meets France. Scarred and drenched with the mingled blood of allies and enemies. She will never be the same.

The captain, who intersected our path on his own return to the front, looks grave. An army of shadows haunts him, even as he seeks to lead an army of living men into victory. He has taken a lantern from his haversack, and if we watch, we may find out why. This is of interest, for as you must know, men do not light so much as a cigarette by night, for fear of drawing enemy fire. There are patrols whose job it is solely to watch for such from ten miles away, and trust me: they do. They ensure the lights—and those who hold them—are extinguished by force of sniper or bomber.

As the captain retreats and disappears into the edge of the woods, our attention shifts from him to the chaplain. This younger man is pacing, wearing his own trench into a six-foot span of earth as he squints and holds a book of prayers so close, in the dying light, that his nose is literally stuck in the pages. He mutters, making out the words, and once he has a handle on them, he repeats them again and again, each time with growing conviction. I have rarely witnessed somberness descend upon this typically jovial man, but it has cloaked his entire presence, this night, as he speaks,

"'O God of Might, we implore Thee: help us that our arms be strengthened against our foes . . .'"

At the far edge of our little camp stands the platoon sergeant with his back to the warfront, facing a Paris too far west to see. His story is not mine to tell, but I think I can say this, and I think you will understand: He has left his heart there. Wholly, deeply, in a love for the ages to rival the tales of old, his is a heart completely given to and for another. He faces her now, through a night whose end may mark his end, too. Beyond that, I cannot say more of the story, but there is more. Very much more, dear America, and it would break your heart if you knew it. Lend them yours, this night, and your prayers, too.

The chaplain reads on, his prayers weaving back into the moment. His voice grows thick and hoarse. It wavers, trips over a dry patch. Whether dry in throat or spirit, it is impossible to say. His words run out.

At the silence, the platoon sergeant raises his head. He tears his gaze from distant Paris. Stoops to pull a worn canteen from his small heap of earthly possessions. A tin cup, too. Approaching the chaplain, he pours what little he has left into the cup, the melody of water gathering into a void filling the silence. He offers it to the chaplain. Pushes it gently but firmly toward the man when it is first refused. And that water, the gesture of a broken man giving the last of his own so that the prayer might go on, seems to infuse the chaplain with strength.

So, he keeps on:

"'O God of Might, we turn to thy most loving heart as our last hope. O King of Peace, we humbly implore the peace for which we long. Dismayed by the horrors of a war which is bringing ruin . . .'"

Dark is coming. The captain returns, and in the last veil of light on this last day— perhaps the last day— I see that his lantern is full. Not of light . . . but of bracken. Leaves, twigs, grasses.

But there—quick as a breath—a flicker of light. And another, and another.

It's the trench trick of the glowworms. Their light is small enough that it won't draw fire, but strong enough that it can make way for sight. Just enough to spear the darkness, transform its oppressive weight into hope.

A reminder that the God who created the light also created the night.

There is nothing to fear here.

The captain, without a word, sets his insect-filled lantern amid a swath of tall grasses. He begins to outline a ring of rocks around it, as if it is a bonfire to gather by. Stones thumping against ground, clacking into one another. In like silence, the others draw near. One by one, they sit.

I join them. For these men—though they are soldiers, battling against both militaries and principalities—they have allowed me into their brotherhood. I count it the deepest honor to be among them. None of us speak it, but each of us know: They live to die, and die to let live. Dear countrymen, tomorrow comes their battle as they arrive again at the front and press forward.

Inside the lantern, the glowworms shine steadily on, one or two of them in a dance of flickering life. I think on them—the way they have burrowed into muddy chambers beneath the ground. The way they wait then on wings to grow, wait to take flight.

I think on the men   the way they have burrowed into muddy trenches beneath the ground. The way they wait now on morning, wait to take flight.

I ponder sharing this with the men—"The Seventeenth Band," an unofficial moniker they have claimed, for brotherhood is a hidden gift of war. I ponder sharing this with the Seventeenth Band. Attempting to inspire them with such comparison—for when glowworms become fireflies, fire flies . . . light takes to the sky . . . and anything is possible.

But I recall the end of the story: when the glowworm's transformation into firefly is complete and the wings take to flight, an invisible clock begins to tick. The small creatures, who ascend from dugouts of mud into victorious flight—they will live only days, perhaps weeks.

But while they live . . . they live to light. They shine. And because

299

of it, they cause life to go on and on, giving way to more of their kind, time without end.

I look in silence on these faces: the captain, the chaplain, the platoon sergeant. I think of my own unremarkable face, sitting here beside them. Any one of us, America. Any one of us, flawed as we all are, could be next. And any one of us would go forth into that destiny, if it means life might go on for others. The captain with his army of shadows and broken compass—he holds it in his palm, as if it might give him an answer he has long sought. The chaplain, with his prayers wrung from a place so deep that none of us knew he was capable of it. And the sergeant, who is the invisible thread binding us together, showing us what it means to buckle down and live. Truly, truly live.

He shifts, turning to cast one last glance westward, where he has left his heart. As he does, his boot shifts, and jostles the lantern just enough to slide its lid akilter.

A flash of light skitters loose, circling the lantern once . . . twice . . . vanishing away into the night. A solitary firefly, leaving the safety of this place.

This is what it was born for. To rend the darkness.

It rises above a land scarred with the footprints of armies. A land tattooed in trenches, gouged in graves, running with veins of wires that carry electrical impulses through them like blood to the heart. Beneath villages, underneath weddings and battles, orchards and bakeries, cobbled roads and rivers that dare, in their indefatigable currents, to hope for a life after all this. Into war offices where telegrams are transcribed into words, and men are thence sent to battle, to live or to die. The little light ascends over all this, a topography etched in lives. Flits with a force even the "war that will not end" cannot extinguish.

An invisible clock begins to tick.

The chaplain's words descend with the night's utter darkness:

"'O God of Might, give me strength to die a true and valiant soldier.'"

Amen.

40

Captain Jasper Truett

October 1918

The sun rose again today. I looked down the trench and saw the boys—"green-gilled college boys," I used to call them. Well, maybe some had Harvard degrees stuffed in their brains, but their education these past months had been the hardest kind of all. The kind a man should never have to receive. The kind so bad I never, in all my life, imagined war to be this way. Not in any of my campaigns till now.

It made me think it couldn't get much worse.

And that scared me senseless. Every time I thought that, I was proved wrong. These boys . . . any one of them could've been mine. If I'd been a better husband, a better father. If I'd been there for my family.

But I wasn't.

So I'd be here for these boys now.

I searched the trench and spotted Petticrew. First time I ever laid eyes on him at Plattsburg, he looked like a giraffe, craning his long neck to find the stables. He'd left here on his journey a broken man, weary. They'd made good time to Paris, had been delivered back from the city to the front by a transport unit coming with ammunition. The best weapon among them being the man who had checked all the boxes:

Constantly aware of his surroundings. Petticrew was on high alert now. Determination driving his awareness farther than ever.

Keen insight into geography and terrain. I watched as he circumnavigated a clutch of soldiers and caught a roll as someone dropped it.

Calm in a crisis. So calm it was eerie.

Able to command respect without belittling his charges. Truer than ever, as evidenced by the way the men in his platoon approached him with respect but not trepidation.

Yet in all this, there was something more about him now. Behind the determination . . . there was light. Fierce, the sort that wouldn't be easily extinguished.

He'd need it.

Soon we would take the Argonne. Or begin to. One of the last places in this once beautiful country to be untouched by war, at least in parts. The Boche had been laying traps and wire, digging trenches for weeks now, but my scouts had it all mapped.

It was a wreck. All those roots and trunks, mangled branches above and below. Slick hillsides, deep pits, sharp cliff's edges. A death trap, layered into dastardly perfection during its last hundred years of undisturbed rest. It had been preparing for us all this time, and we'd only had two weeks to prepare for it.

I thought of the girl. The one who came out of that forest. Maybe there was good in there, after all. And maybe if she lived in such a place, was born in such a place, grew life in such a place—maybe there would be good there for us, too.

I shook my head, pulling myself out of this cloud of thought. This wasn't my job. I was losing my edge. And if I lost my edge, I'd lose lives. These boys would be the ones to suffer.

I blew a whistle. "Men!" They gathered, received orders. I saw those telltale signs I'd come to know as the pre-battle silent symphony: pulling pictures of sweethearts out, kissing them. Twisting wedding bands on their fingers. Muttering silent prayers. One or two retched. Two or three slept. This was what they did as they prepared to live—and die—all in the same space of time. It was a heavy silence, thick and vibrating with erratic pulses of a thousand men. One of them, Private Schulman, muttered a word over and over. *Hineni. Hineni. Hineni.*

I asked him what it meant. "It's Hebrew," he said. "It means—something close to 'here I am.' It means you are listening. You are ready. You will live into what comes next, with everything you have."

I nodded. The man had conviction. It was serving him well.

I watched the sky. I watched my clock, chained to my being.

"We are close, men. This war has been turning, these past months. There's hope on the horizon. And that hope is you."

I meant to buoy them with these words, but they settled with grave realization. They were—in essence—the hope of a world so war-weary it had forgotten how to hope.

I knew the feeling.

"Captain?" A voice pierced my recollection. It was George Piccadilly, British chaplain to the American Expeditionary Forces.

"Chaplain," I said.

He looked at me more serious than I'd ever seen him. "Send me up, too."

"Chaplains don't go over the top."

"This one does. That is—this one wants to. Go over the top, that is. Sir."

"No."

He hung his head. "With respect, sir, if I may."

Exhaling, I nodded.

He raised himself to a proud stance, spreading his shoulders wide and lifting his chin. "You cannot afford to leave me behind. I have extensive experience in—in—" He seemed at a loss for words, for assuredly the first time in his life.

"In arguing your point?"

"Just so, sir. But also . . ." His stance muddied a bit, shedding its clamped-on pride. "This is what I'm here for. These men are going in. Facing . . . death." He fumbled over the word. I could tell such a serious subject felt foreign in his mouth. But important to him. He took a breath to fortify himself and repeated. "Facing death, injury, all the lovely things this war is known for. And—that's why I'm here."

"I thought you were here to dodge the war."

"So I was, and look how that turned out. I can't help but wonder . . . perhaps I was meant to be here all along. I don't know a great sum of things."

I bit back an affirming answer. Too easy a target.

"But I know a chaplain is likened to some kind of shepherd. And I know a shepherd goes in when his sheep need him. Frankly, sir, I'm more sheep than shepherd. But at least I can show up. At least I can stand with them. Pray with them. Do all the things a chappy's supposed to do. Right in the thick of it."

He had a point. My boys could be in there for days, at least. War was a snarling, growing being, which had a way of splintering maps, oozing into tactical plans, engulfing everything in a thick swamp of dark. Anything could happen in those woods. And the way Piccadilly twisted the corner of his jacket in his hands betrayed vulnerability in this soul full of bravado, for the first time. I couldn't help but respect that. And yet . . .

"Orders are orders. Chaplains don't go into battle."

I turned to go and could feel the complete crushing of the first show of courage this man had mustered. The very first—and offered from the very depths of him, into the greatest heights of courage.

"But . . ." I stopped, hand clasped around my wrist behind my back, not turning back to look at him fully.

"Seems this is a place where unlikely things happen. If I were to see a chaplain go over the top, I'd be privileged to live to tell about it."

I walked away, letting his stunned silence sink into himself. Maybe I'd see him up there. Maybe I wouldn't. But one thing was certain: the rollicking Briton who'd come to Harvard to tunnel out of a war had emerged into its heart as a man of courage and substance.

These fires of war, they were something to be reckoned with.

I skirted a group of men telling jokes and knew their laughter for what it was: a desperate play for some sense of normalcy. An act of collective defiance against the curtain of despair that would take them in their clutches so easily, if they did not fight it by whatever means they had.

That curtain swished its way into the shadows, following me as I turned down a small side trench. I could feel its heaviness overtake me, almost hear it kick up the dust around me.

But it would not take me. And not because I would ignore it. But because I would face it.

There in a dugout so small, tucked out of sight and notice of the others, I sat. Drew myself into the earth and prayed to its maker.

I prayed for that girl of the woods. For her baby.

I prayed for my own girl—or rather, thanked God in heaven for the sweetness of her in my life. Like honey poured upon mud-caked hands had been Amelia's love in my life. She had deserved better than me . . . and I thanked God that she had had better in Him. That He held her now. And He held her mother, too.

Then I prayed no more, for the words liquefied. They seeped through the walls of my being, until I began to shake with trying to hold them back. But then—a crack. The same one that opened all those years ago on that Panama cliff—it widened. Quaking waves rolling up from that cavern, across the miles, through the war-torn soil of France, and out of me. Silent, choking my breath into shaking sobs so deep they tried, and failed, to find voice.

If not for the cover of shells falling, machine guns firing, earth shaking already, I surely would have set these trenches to trembling. My own fingers trembled, fisted tight and pressed to my eyes. Roots, exposed when some soldier dug this hole for unearthly respite, clung to clumps of soil and rained them down on me as if they, too, cried.

It was wretched. It was right. This mingling of mud and tears, a man no better than clay, laid bare before One, and only One.

I prayed. Not words, but this continued strain of wracking

sobs—and somehow knew that God in heaven was here, too. Here in the mud. Hearing my prayer-beyond-words. *Wretched man that I am.* So many faces swam before me, faces of soldiers I'd lost, should have done better by. And that silent sob turned into a heaving shudder . . . a relinquishing of myself. As if someone had reached inside my ribs cracking under the weight of these memories, these souls whose blood was on my hands . . . all the way back to Amelia. As if that invisible hand had taken a key and opened a rusted-over lock—and let every bit of it out in a rushing current. At the back of that lineup, the bottom of that river, there was one more face.

Mine.

I could see it as I must look. Lines from years, lines from unspoken lives that lived within me because they lived no longer. These ghosts that followed me. I saw them sometimes in my dreams, always silent, eyes wide as if asking me, *What would have happened? If I'd lived?* Innocent eyes, like children.

And in my wordless prayer, I saw this wordless answer. My own face—the last straggler from the shadows—was the one whose eyes were filled with torment. These others . . . they had lived. They had died. They—I hoped, and knew for some of them to be true—dwelled in unending comfort and safety now.

It was I who was still on the run. I who was the living skeleton, a shell of a man who could bark orders and orchestrate battle but couldn't bear to face up to the battle inside his own self.

Come.

That was the word. I didn't hear it so much as feel it pulling me, a desperate invitation born in blood and bought with life. I knew what the holy scriptures said, I knew how many of my men lived, carried by hands that knew the same battle as I, but had given His own life instead of watching others fall all around Him.

Come. As if I, too, could know such a way. I could be one of the ones who reached into that nail-scarred grip and took the life offered.

Come.

"Captain Truett!"

Two callings. One of heaven, one from Sergeant Steerforth, right here on earth.

Two realms colliding, there in the clash of my own breath.

"Here," I said. "I'm here." *Here I am.*

The words slammed me. What was it that Schulman had said? That word . . . *Hineni. "It means you are listening. You are ready. You will live into what comes next, with everything you have."*

I was ready. Ready to be seen—scars, sins, and all. To be known by the God who perhaps knew me all along and used that airship crashing into my train car to bust down my walls and show me.

I pulled my compass out, the old familiar companion. Gave it a shine on my battle-stained jacket, the only thing I had to offer. And when I opened it to see that sorry old familiar broken needle, my breath caught in those ragged lungs. There was that old needle, bent and tired . . . but it buoyed back and forth, homing in on its purpose: to point the way.

I thought of the night before, our camp. The chaplain uttering his prayers. Petticrew pining after Paris. And the journalist—the good-for-nothing journalist I'd tried and failed to be rid of—studying us all. Seeing me. Watching that compass too close.

A smile tugged at my mouth.

Maybe he was good for something, after all.

For the first time, I was going into battle not to run. Not to drown out the hounding pursuit of my own mistakes. But to fight for life.

41

Matthew

History repeats itself. I was here, with all the men, living yet buried in these trenches. Waiting for the whistle that would send us over the top and make us heroes or cowards, let us live or render us corpses.

The wedding bands twisted. I did not have one, but for the invisible one that cinched my heart and bolstered my soul. Collective breath was held. Sweethearts' pictures were kissed—and though I did not have a picture, I had a love engraved deep onto my being.

Twenty-three days since Saint-Mihiel. Eighteen days since arriving at Argonne and hearing that song. Ten days since we left with the Angel . . . and she, through waking nights of shared survival, embedded herself irrevocably in my thoughts, in my heart. My bride of only four days.

So short a time, back home. So long an eternity, here. Enough to change everything, for always.

"Fix bayonets!" Captain Truett yelled. The metal-domino sound all up and down this planked subterranean corridor *click-click-clicked*, metal registering readiness where our hands did not. I followed the sound with my eyes and saw them: scores of men, capped in identical metal helmets and muted green uniforms. Every one identical, and every one cloaking a vastly unique universe inside him. I wished we could see them—the memories, the hopes, the hearts they held within their own. Surely the sheer volume of past and future, hope and possibility, would explode this entire war.

But we could not see them.

I closed my eyes and envisioned the finish line. It was not the sifted-earth soil of Maplehurst. It was not the enemy trench of Saint-Mihiel. This time . . . it was the forest. Mira's forest. Branches twining, ground soft, magic held in its dark. And now . . . enemy.

I pressed my eyes closed harder. This was where I was headed. To take ground for our country and for France. To drive back the enemy. To end—as the murmurs from headquarters and trench-hovels alike were saying—this war to end all wars.

I released my breath.

The whistle blew.

And the mad scramble over the top began. Our voices drove us on with feigned courage or animal instinct or sheer determination, one great collective battle cry. Ushering one another inward and onward, onward and upward, across this gouged land.

It was strange. In all the hollering and battle cry, the skirting of craters and plunging into clouds of midday night, brown dust . . . it was Celia's voice I heard. Asking me, as she did when she was only ten, if I thought men would ever visit the moon.

We'd lain on our backs in a haystack watching a moon so bright it hurt to look at, though it had no light source of its own. Only reflection of a sun invisible to us in that moment.

"No," I'd told her. "No man can do that."

No man.

No-man's-land.

This place between trenches, unclaimed and fought for with blood and life. I was here, ready to cross that impossible moon.

God above, give us light.

The journey across was familiar, and I hated it for being so. The same as Saint-Mihiel, the same as a thousand other battles fought by a million other men before me. All to take a few inches of ground, perhaps then to lose that same ground the next day or the next week. Lines in territories, shifting like tides. But we pressed on. And on, and on, until we reached it. The edge of the forest, standing there like a fortress we did not know if we could trust.

We slowed, me and the others, slamming into the ground when machine gun fire erupted, creeping forward when it fell silent.

And then we were in.

The hush was heavy. Our movements slow, knowing that in this place, where shell fire behind us turned to distant echoes of thunder and stillness before us belied the danger that lurked here, our mission was simple: Push the Germans back. Win the war.

And the execution of that was impossibly complicated. Every hill, tree, creek, reach of overgrowth, nest of undergrowth—all fodder for poets who came before us centuries ago to write of the peace of such a place—every corner of this forest could hold our enemy, and our end. It shivered up my spine and hollowed me out, causing me to shift my eyes in every direction, constantly. A haunted forest, in tree-bark flesh. It did the same to every one of us.

On we went. Up rises. Into thickets. Dodging a spray of bullets, having our hearts ripped from us when those bullets hit a fellow soldier not two inches from us. *Why him and not me?* It was a question that would keep, and haunt. For now, we left that question to swirl over the ground as we tromped forward.

We spread out among trees, following the officers' gestures to stay low and keep quiet. Captain Truett was near me, kept looking back at me. Was I doing something wrong?

A sound erupted beside me—Chester, sucking breath through his teeth and wincing like he'd just been pierced through. A look at his foot told me he had. He'd stepped on something, dark liquid already seeping through his boot. His foot jerked and knocked something down the hill behind him, ricocheting with a sickening noise that may as well have been a giant arrow in the sky pointing out our whereabouts to any who might be listening.

As he tried to silence himself from his body's reaction to the searing pain, we all heard the telltale *zip-click* that informed us he was too late.

The Boche had heard.

"Potato masher!" Captain Truett hissed. A grenade. Where it

would come from and where it would land and who it would erase from this earth, we would learn in a matter of five seconds.

A quick look around and most men took cover—but two did not. Chester, limping and trying to find shelter, and the captain, eyes alert as a deer's, rifle at the ready. To our left was a wide tree. I pulled Chester to it, into its overhanging branches, which reached low to the ground. Dashed back out and silently nodded the captain over. We had three seconds left if we were lucky. Maybe two . . . one . . .

He tore himself from his position and dove to join us, none too soon.

Searing explosion. Billowing cloud, dust swallowing us. Bark, twigs, bits of tree and earth. Deafening sound that set off silence, punched through with the pounding of my own pulse.

I looked at Chester and Truett, and they looked at me and each other. Each of us scanning for one thing: wounds. Shrapnel. Of which there was none.

A blessing and a curse . . . for that meant one thing.

"Concussion grenade," I said, hearing my own voice stifled and swallowed up by the ringing that pinged around my head.

"What's that mean?" Chester shouted.

"It means they're coming," Captain Truett said, silencing him. "They've stunned us, and now they'll want to finish us off with bayonets. Stay put. Stay low."

But Chester's foot was gushing, still. "Captain," I said, tipping my head at the wound.

His mouth was grim. He'd seen worse, and so had I, but we both knew if the kid lost too much blood, he'd be a goner. Unconscious, unable to move, and a sitting duck for the Germans.

As it was, we were barely shrouded by the veil of leaves and branches. I looked around, inched as quietly as I could around the tree to see if there was a better place—somewhere I could fix him up with what little I had in my pack.

It was much the same. Branches blessedly low, but good for little more than a curtain in the way of protection. A favorite hideout for children, under different circumstances. But not a fortress by any means.

And then my hand, sliding along blindly as I scanned the woods through shaking leaves, gripped something. An edge. I followed it, discovering a wide gap in the trunk, hollowed out and weathered to smoothness and complete darkness.

It was familiar. As if I had gripped this very place in my hands before, though there was no way I could have.

"The tree was like a house," I could hear Mira's low, captivating voice, rising and falling thoughtfully as she described her tree. *"I called it 'le cœur,' for the way the hidden inside was like a heart. A safe place. All the life and branches around it protecting a perfect hideaway, and all the life of the tree coming from inside."*

Surely this couldn't be it. Of all the trees in all the woods, we wouldn't now find Mira's hideaway. But whether or not it was hers, one thing was true: it was hollow and dark. Safer than where Chester was now.

I inched back around and managed, with Captain Truett's help, to pull him in. All the while, a nagging thought swam just beneath the surface of my still-clouded mind. Where were they? The Germans? If that had been us—if we'd been the ones to launch a stun grenade, we would've seized the moment while the enemy was still stunned to rush in and take them while we could.

But a glance outside our green-leafed fortress showed not a soul in sight. It should have been a freeing realization . . . but it was just wrong enough that a sickening heaviness rolled in instead, along with a distant roll of thunder and the hanging scent of coming rain. Something else was afoot.

In the dark, I ripped into my supplies and strained to see. I got Chester's boot off, got him wrapped, and waited.

Captain Truett was gone. He'd known it, too—I'd seen it in the hyper-concentrated look on his face, the way just a slip of madness threatened to surface in the not knowing.

But he was a professional soldier. Nothing rattled him into

incapacity. He was what I aimed to be, as long as I was here. And he slipped back out wordlessly, motioning for me to hold position.

I don't know how long he was gone. Long enough for the thunder to grow louder, closer, and for rain to begin. Long enough that Chester bled through the thin excuse for a bandage—and long enough for me to realize his heaviness, laying against my shoulder, was suddenly speaking on his behalf.

The pit in my stomach twisted. I jostled my shoulder a little, hoping he'd stir. Nothing. I nudged him harder, and his head only rolled back. His name burned silent in my lungs, held where it couldn't be spoken, lest it give us away—and I leaned in to hear a verdict from his own lungs.

A beat with no breath. And another. But there—so slight I almost missed it—he breathed. *He lived*.

And then, as if they'd heard it, too, came the voices.

"*Jetzt! Loslassen!*" I didn't know the words. But I knew the tone of a command, of something critical on the edge of that voice.

The *zip-click* of another grenade. Another explosion somewhere beyond our tree.

Weapon readied, I strained to hear, praying the captain would come.

But no footsteps fell. In their place, a silent visitor came instead. Green like the leaves and yellow like the sun and sinister in its combination, creeping along the ground like a predator on the prowl.

Gas. *Phosgene. Chlorine. Mustard. Tear.* My brain rattled off the types of gas that had been drilled into us back at Plattsburg, and it didn't do a lick of good. I couldn't remember which was which. Which needed the masks, which didn't; which smelled of moldy hay and which had no smell; which would kill us right away, which would take its time.

So my hands sprang into action to make up for my lagging brain. I reached for my mask and buckled it on, fumbling with the straps. Reached for Chester's to do the same—and found none.

No mask.

The green-yellow monster crept closer, entering our wall of

leaves. It'd be in here soon, filling up this tree cavern and filling up his lungs, taking what little life he had left.

I thought to when he fell. The tumbling object down the hill. *His mask.*

The realization knocked into me.

I looked at him. Fifteen years old. That worn picture sticking out of his jacket; two parents, two sisters, kid brother, and Chester grinning like his muscles weren't worn out waiting for the camera's shutter to release. The picture was torn at the corner, patched up with a label from one of the tin cans of apples.

His mother waited at home for his medal. Would she instead receive a death notice? I knew what it was to lose a mother. Could not imagine what it was for a mother to lose a son. My own mother, God rest her, would know no loss if I never returned home.

I looked at the gas. It was at my ankles now, wrapping and swirling as if it had waited long for this moment and was savoring food after long hunger. There was no escape. No place to outrun such a pursuer.

I thought of Mira, of the baby. What would become of them if I died? Time didn't allow an answer. But I saw her kind eyes, the strong set of her jaw, the softness of her hair. I could see the picture of a babe, safe in her arms, just as she had been safe in this tree when the wolves had come. Would I cross France by foot in order to give her the safe arrival of her child, and turn around and deprive the same to Chester's mother? Would I leave my own child a legacy of a hypocrite father? Would I now forsake this child before they were even born? The child had changed me before it had even taken its first breath. Given me the barest, most fragile lens of a father through which to see the world. What if it was my child in Chester's place?

Mira had been entrusted to my care for a time, to get her to safety. Away from this very moment, which could have been her fate. Poisoning her home.

And I . . . I knew, more than that, that I'd been entrusted to her care. Her hands, which held the ragged beating organ inside of my chest, chose to love. We had journeyed together—and it had been more a gift than I ever deserved, or ever could deserve. It was enough. More than enough.

I had one last bit of me to give.

My hands flew, unbuckling straps, removing the mask, lifting Chester's head. Hearing his wheezing. Holding fast to the vision of him offering me his hard tack as a peace offering, bringing me a spent shell like a kid with a trophy. Offering everything he had to me.

And I prayed the old prayer, the one that marked me for all the life that was to follow, the first night I prayed it. One last time . . . *God in heaven, help him. Help them.* I wanted to pray to see my own son or daughter. To hold them.

Instead I held Chester, repeating that prayer over him, again and again. Silent words swirling up among the gas, head bowed over the kid.

The prayer burned into my mind as the air burned into my lungs. I laid Chester's barely alive body safely in the same peat that once blanketed Mira away from the wolves. Hung my head between my knees.

Darkness came. Breath did not.

And then . . . utter black. *Night.*

42

Mira

I loved the ballroom cottage the men had made me, and though I tried to sleep there the first few nights, I gave up upon the third night and wrapped myself into a knit blanket, climbing those stairs to a trail of leaves, making my way to the library. It was here that I found rest at last, in the corner where I fashioned a palette of long-forgotten blankets that I'd laundered in the garden and dried there, too. The scent of the sun upon them sang me to sleep, to dream of *le cœur*. The safety of that tree back in the forest. And to dream of my Matthew.

I awoke to the memory of his arms around me, to the sun cresting that library window as leaves danced in an early morning breeze. They were odd little companions, the leaves—I swept them away during the day, happy to have work to do. Wishing it would sweep away the war, too, and praying it might help in some small way. Savoring their spice, the way they spoke of the woods so far away. Wondering at their color, the way they lit the earth as they faded away.

The windows, though, still had gaping holes. I loved them, truly—the way they let in the sound of birds during the day and clean air at night, and how they ushered in these spinning waifs, fallen from trees, as if depositing them at my feet to make me feel at home.

I had gone to see the Jour de Soleil Sisters today. As the woman at the Motherhouse had said, they had a lodging house for some of the sisters very near to the château. We soon learned that they shared a fence with me. Part of a fence, rather. A little corner in the back of my garden, and they laughed to say at last, someone was here to pluck away the sunflowers in the fall, which kept planting themselves in their kitchen garden.

Their company, I was finding, was a gift. The company of women was a world I'd never known. Women who knew how to be industrious, who let me learn alongside them, and who made it their purpose to help people, especially in wartime.

They insisted on sending over their grounds keeper, Michael, who was brother to one of the nuns. He came every morning, sporting a groomed grey moustache that curled at the ends, and a wooden box full of tools. He was boarding up those broken windows one by one. I knew it had to be done, but with each one shuttered, I felt something shutter inside of me, too. Less light, less air.

It was getting colder, these October nights. And the moon seemed brighter. The night seemed a land to live in, not slumber through. But exhaustion was heavy upon me, so much so that I wondered if I was ill. I had spent days in much harder work back home in the Argonne and felt far less tired than this. This exhaustion—it was so heavy, it was a presence. The city swirled with horrific tales of the influenza sweeping the world. Of how it would steal your breath, and then your life, so swiftly.

My child's life.

It was enough to drive a person quite out of a sound mind, the wondering and worrying. At night, the worrying grew shadows that stretched and devoured—so I pushed back. Filling the dark with memories of a hearth in the little forest house, memories of a loft along the journey to Paris, the moon so bright. And memories of Matthew and his kind touch . . . the rest and depth and strength in it . . . and at last, I slept.

I dreamed of him. I dreamed of him in my forest, laying that wreath, finding me, dirt-streaked and wild. I remembered him watching with such care I might have been made of glass, when I had been hurt at the ruined city. I dreamed memories I didn't know I had stored up—and woke with eyes wet, grateful to my Father in heaven for creating memories, and minds able to hold them.

I did not have him. Nor the promise of a future with him. But I had these memories, and I had the currents of a river, wrapping us and our vows together forever. No one could take that. And no one could take my prayers. I prayed, when I awoke, for whatever he faced in those woods. They were such a good place—and so much bad could take place there, as I knew too well. But they were also a place of bad turning to good again.

I awoke to sunlight. To more leaves to sweep, and an empty house full of memories of those who came before me, all dressed in ball gowns and feathers. I laughed so often, looking at portraits, wondering who they were, wondering what they would think of a forest waif now presiding over their grand château. I hoped they might like me, if they had known me. A portrait of Sophia Fontinelle as a young woman peered kindly on me from one of the large rooms. She had a sparkle in her eye, eyes of dark blue like my own, and I thought we might have been friends. I wondered about her, and allowed that wondering to drive me to letter-writing. With the help of the sisters and a wartime office in the heart of the city, I found an address in Bordeaux, posted it in the mail, and tried to keep from wondering every moment whether I might yet find family.

I swept and scrubbed floors, and Michael pounded more planks on more windows. Light was leaving this place. I scrubbed harder, as if that might bring it back. As the layers of dust and dirt and time chipped away beneath rivulets of muddy water from my rag, I saw the white marble begin to shine.

In it, I saw my reflection. I looked a stranger in this place. And I looked small, with the ceiling so high above me, the walls so wide around me. I was surrounded by a great emptiness.

Emptiness was meant to be filled.

I stood, the beginning of an idea quickening. Tightness gripped my stomach and my hands flew to where the child lived.

It was not time. Celia had told me it should be a month yet, or more. She had also warned that early pains might come and might mean nothing.

I pinched my eyes shut, as if that might usher the feeling away. The ache subsided but left a shadow behind, a lurking fear that it would grip me again.

It did not.

I scrubbed more, the idea taking form with each splash of my rag, until I had it formed enough. There would be much required to make it work, but . . . it could work, I believed.

After I'd pinched a few late berries from the overgrown garden and pumped water from the kitchen into a chipped teacup, I sent a prayer to the heavens and slipped between the hedge to see Sister Marion. She was Michael's sister, she was brilliant, and she hailed from Ireland and brought the vibrant green of that place here with her strong spirit. She had also become the closest thing I had to a friend.

"Our soldiers, they are coming, yes? Needing care?" I asked.

She nodded.

"And the hospitals are sometimes full. Yes?"

She looked tickled by my statement. "Sweet Mireilles," she called me, with only warmth and no condescension. "There is no 'full' or 'not full.' We find room, or we make room, or we go to them in the streets or tents or homes because we must. We will not let one slip past, if it can be helped." Her words were kind, but I saw the shadow that fell upon her as she thought of untold scenes she had witnessed.

"And if you had a large house, a large, empty house with nobody to fill it—could you make room there?"

Now she beheld me, lines around her eyes softening into understanding.

I was so full of the idea, thinking of those great gaping rooms serving a purpose, saving lives, that the ideas nearly bubbled up inside of me. And as they did, the pain gripped me once more around the middle.

I flinched and looked away.

"Mireilles?" Sister Marion was up and at my side. "Tell me what you feel."

I told her.

"Has this been happening long?"

I shook my head. "Only twice. It is nothing, I know. I have a month or more still." I had to. Though I had come to stand in wonder at the thought of the life inside of me, I was not ready. I was not a mother. I did not know how to be one.

"So," I said, brushing the episode away like my broom to the leaves. "Will you use it? Château Fontinelle? I will help. I can clean, and though I am no nurse, I know some of tending to wounds, and I can learn. If you'll let me."

"Not so quickly, my dear." She laughed. "It is a grand idea, to be sure. Excellent, truly. But you cannot be sweeping and scrubbing and transforming a—forgive me for saying so—a *tas de déchets* into a hospital ward. You need to rest, you know. You are already very busy building a person!" She laughed with joy, and I tried not to be hurt that she had called the château a heap of rubbish. I knew it was true, but in its own way, it was home—or the closest thing I had to one. I did not like to hear it called so. The more reason to change it, fill it.

"We will send some sisters to clean."

"I did not mean to make more work for them," I rushed to say.

"They live for this! To transform. To make room for more wounded, that they may make room for more healed. 'Tis the work of life." She furrowed her forehead. "It may not be a proper hospital ward—that would mean doctors on hand, and inspections from the military and medical people to a greater degree than we may be equipped for. But perhaps a place of rehabilitation for those on the mend. No surgeries, but the changing of dressings, the feeding of body and soul. A safe place to heal."

I smiled. So well she had put to words what I felt as I did the simple work of sweeping leaves. *The work of life. A safe place to heal.*

And it was settled. The next days were spent in a flurry of scrubbing and dusting, fixing and moving. I did not know what would become of my letter to my great-aunt, but I trusted that she, with the sparkle in her eyes and the years of this place gone empty, would not mind such a thing here. Château Fontinelle was not the dazzling show of riches it once had been—and perhaps never would be. But by the simple act of working hands and willing hearts, the gaping, rotting state of emptiness had been transformed to a far simpler one: that of waiting.

And so we waited.

Word reached the Paris hospitals and field hospitals and beyond very soon. Perhaps even the hospital barges in the canals, far and away into the reaches of the front. Perhaps these men who began to arrive had been sent by Celia. Perhaps they knew my Matthew.

We filled the ballroom with them. Then the foyer, then the drawing room, dining room, sitting room. Nurses came, dotting holes into the heavy decades-long silence with the efficient *tap tap tap* of their shoes, carrying them from one patient to the next, and with their quiet murmurs amongst themselves.

The men spoke, too. Sometimes the noises were not pleasant—sometimes they were war, held captive in a man's body, escaping only in pain. But the sound of those comforting, tending, healing, wrapped those guttural cries like a cocoon, into transforming safety.

I quickly learned how to clean wounds, stitch them, soothe burns. I watched, always, for Matthew. Listened for his voice. Felt the chasm in my chest grow wider each day he did not come and each day he did not write to me—but thanked God for it, too, for perhaps it meant he was well and fighting. That surely was the reason.

The pains kept coming, every now and then, and Sister Marion kept a close watch on me, insisting on sleeping nights in the library.

"Oh, dearie, bless my soul if that's what you've been sleeping on." She bustled over to my corner and rolled in a cot, starting to stretch my blankets over it.

"But that will be needed," I said. "For the soldiers."

"Aye, and what do you suppose you are, up at all hours doing battle to save people? A soldier in her own right, that's what."

She wasn't right. I was just me, just Mireilles, just the forest girl. But I slept on the cot that night and will forever be grateful for Sister Marion's presence. That night, the pain found me. It found me fast, and unforgivably. Waves upon waves of it. I thought of the soldiers, of what they faced downstairs. Amputations. Infections. Worse.

"It is your time, sweet Mireilles," she said, her red hair streaked with white, her face lined with compassion.

"But it isn't," I said, inhaling sharply. "It isn't."

"Alright, then, dearie. You just lie back, and let old Marion tend to you." Her voice was melodic and calm as she put a hand to my hot face and crossed the room to the window. "Your self is working hard," she said. She always said that to the soldiers. Not *your body*, but *your self*. It was singular to her; I had never heard anyone else speak so.

"Then my self is terribly confused," I said, mustering a laugh. "It is not time."

She opened the window, turned, and tilted her head. "Why not?"

"It's—it's impossible," I said. A bushel of ways to explain tried and failed to appear. And I was, perhaps, embarrassed to say that of all the hard things, all the impossible things in the past days, Matthew had been there for them each. Taking my hand. Seeing me. Setting his jaw against injustice. Running his hand upon my face in tenderness.

Sister Marion waited.

"It is silly," I said.

"I like a good joke," she said. "But I've an inkling that what you have to say is anything but silly. Why not try old Marion? Tell me what burdens you."

I did. She had known only that my husband was away at war, nothing more of my story, until I unburdened it all before her, ready for her to draw back in shock or walk away entirely. I told her of Matthew, of our journey. Of the man who came before Matthew. Of the Marne River. And of how I would give anything for my husband, my friend, to be here now.

She did not draw back in shock. She did not walk away. Sister Marion drew near, instead, and picked up my hand.

"Brave girl," she whispered, eyes glinting with a sheen. She looked as if she wished to say more, then shook her head. "Brave, brave girl," she said simply, voice thick with a depth of understanding. She breathed a deep breath and found a smile. "Your Matthew sounds like a very good man."

I nodded, unable to speak for the pain. Pain in my middle, pain in my heart.

"You think of that river," she said. "And I will pray that it might bring him back to you soon. And when he comes"—she leaned forward, her voice lined with hope—"what a surprise you shall have to show him!"

I did. I thought of the river through the watches of the night. Wrapped my heart around the hope of it, as thunder blew in through that open window, off in the distance. Clung to the image of it as rain began to fall for the first time since the ruins of Beaulieu-en-Coteau, lacing the air with a lullaby. And wept with the promise of it as, hours later, I held in my arms the one I had carried beneath my heart so long.

Château Fontinelle stood silent that night, as if it, too, listened. As if every soldier waited, breath bated, for that first cry. And when that cry did sound, so Sister Marion would tell it later, every broken body and wounded soul inside of those walls hung on the little cry that tumbled through the white-marbled corridors and into their hearts as if it were their life's breath. Their medicine. Their hope and their reason.

But one soldier did not hear.

43

Henry

Dear Editor,

When I agreed to work for you, you said you wanted America's sweetheart, the boy next door.

Well, I don't know that I'm any of those things, but I will say this: A sweetheart is one thing. A true love is another. And a love letter is something entirely different from what you've been printing. You've taken my words and turned them into preprinted valentines, sold for a dime a dozen or less. I understand. Truly. Papers must be sold, people must be bolstered. They need a face for the cause their sons and husbands have given themselves to. A valentine.

However, if I may be so bold . . . could it be that at such a time as this, what they need even more than a valentine is a love letter? It may not have the shine and luster of its dime-store counterpart. But it has heart.

A love letter is cherished for generations, read until it's yellowed and crumbled, and remembered long after the lives are gone. A love letter tells truth, even when it's hard.

The following is not a valentine. The following is a love letter.

Please. With respect, I ask of you: Deliver it to its intended, in full.

America: Your Men
By Henry Mueller
(Not Hank Jones. Please.)

Dear America,

You have known me, America, as Hank Jones, your trusty war correspondent. I come to you today, hat in hand, to say that the man behind these words is someone far more ordinary. Henry Mueller, the farm boy from Virginia, who got his book learning from the village library and read Homer while milking cows.

You might say I fell off the turnip truck.

That may well be. And maybe I hit my head a time or two in the fall, but I landed smack-dab in the middle of the War of the Nations.

I don't have much to offer in a place like this . . . but I have my pen, and I have the truth. I will give you both, and beg your ear to hear and your heart to understand.

Imagine the earth. The most beloved patch of it that you've seen or known. Perhaps your beloved patch is Manhattan, with brownstones rising and the smell of fresh-baked bread in the air. Perhaps yours is a bungalow-lined street in sunny California, where you can hear the ocean and taste the salt spray. Perhaps, like me, it's an alfalfa field where you're glad to rise early and glad to hit the hay "tireder than dirt," as my father likes to say, because it's a good and honest life that means something. Wherever your most beloved patch of earth is, fix it fast to your mind's eye.

Now, gouge that patch of earth deep and wide with trenches. Have you ever seen an ant hill in a jar, the sort that schoolchildren study? The way the tunnels are networks, crossing and bridging, taking up the whole of it? Do that to your patch, but sized for men instead of ants.

Now, strip away the trees, for in our imaginings, the shell fire of France has come to your beloved patch. It obliterates the greenery. It buries life-forms of every kind. Dogs, horses . . . men.

Now, imagine the best man you know. Husband, brother, son, friend—whoever he may be. Imagine him in that earth. Imagine him clutching all that he holds dear, examining it against the backdrop of that shell fire, and deciding yes. Yes, it is worth it. To go over the top. To risk all for the sake of what and whom he loves.

This is war. This is a gentle comparison, harsh as it may seem. I will not tell you of the sights, the sounds, the smell, the sickness. Your boys, America . . . they have borne it for you and would not wish it upon you.

But I will tell you of one man. One of the best men I know. We nearly lost him last week in the depths of a forest. In truth, we know it is only a matter of time before we do lose him to the effects of what he faced. I will not tell you where, or this will be censored . . . and you deserve to know. As much as he deserves to be known.

He was a man of few words and great passion. But though he will soon be lost, he will not be forgotten.

America, I ask of you: Will you remember him? This moment, wherever you are, will you stop and give thanks for him? When his time comes, very shortly now, he will have died the one way he would have desired to: in helping someone. Giving his life for theirs. If you want a man to represent your boys, to show you courage and deepest sacrifice, don't look to Hank Jones, Uncle Sam's nephew. Look to this man who gave all in the woods.

America, we talk a lot sometimes. We've got a lot of war posters and war songs and war efforts. Sure, maybe it's how we do our part and get through and help our fellow man. But, America—we are broken, too. Let us not pretend we do not see the open wound that this war is in each of our hearts. The shadow of fear it casts, the ravenous hunger for lives that it feeds but can never fill.

But in that shadow, I wonder if I could cast some light, too. It is men like my friend, sacrifices and stories like his, that take the dregs of destruction and redeem them into hope. This present time—the machinations of war, the ravaging of disease, the never knowing what will happen next—it would have us believe that there is no hope.

But it overlooks a man who will give everything in order to offer another man life.

It is the oldest, truest story. And I see it—we see it—more often than we can say. This present time—the giving of life, the mining for light in the darkest trenches, the never knowing what will happen next—it whispers to us of a love given to us each, long ago, in the ugly dark of Golgotha.

The place of the skull, reclaimed to be the place of life.

We are one step closer to coming home. The battalion I am attached to pressed through, at no small cost to them, and we will continue to await and fulfill orders. I, with my pen. They, with their rifles.

Your boys, America . . . this is it. This is their moment. For better or for worse, if they rise or if they fall, your boys are strong in their brokenness. You have much reason to be proud.

I reread it before wiring it. It wasn't what they wanted. It wasn't even yet what I wanted, could not do them justice, though I'd tried with everything I had left. It would be censored and changed in a thousand different ways. But it was real. I prayed a bit of that truth would find its way to the paper. And that the man it spoke of would be seen and honored the way he deserved to be.

I thought of Celia Petticrew. *"Let Henry Mueller have his say."* Her last words to me before we'd parted. I cringed, thinking that this might be the first true thing of Henry Mueller's that she'd read. Would that it could be much better news. Would that it could comfort her. She deserved it.

Still, her words gave me the courage to wire the article and launch it with a prayer that its recipients would find hope in it.

The Argonne had changed us. Perhaps someday I'd write more of that. But, for now, to share more of it felt like opening a place to the world that belonged to no one but us. Sorrow would be our companion long, long after this.

44

Mira

November 11, 1918

The city was afire with joy. On this, the eleventh hour of the eleventh day of the eleventh month of the year . . . the war would stop. "Cease fire," they call it. *Armistice.* My home, my Argonne, my Matthew—whatever happened there, it had led, at last, to an end.

I wanted to plunge into the joy, too. I wanted to line the streets of old Paris, wave flags with the rest of them, and search the faces of the soldiers who were to march.

But just as much as I wanted to, I wanted *not* to. For as long as I did not know, there was hope.

There had been no letter from Matthew. No news of his being. We had heard bits of the Argonne. Many, many fallen there. But when I closed my eyes, I could only see him there, crouched over Grand-père's grave, those somber wide eyes looking at me.

"Come back to me," I whispered. And with it, with a desperate plea to heaven to stitch our two bodies back together the way our hearts were stitched already, I left Château Fontinelle. I forced one foot in front of another, again and again, to see the river of soldiers flowing into the city. Medaled and proud, wounded and well, all manner of men from all of the allies.

I bundled my wee one next to my heart in a sling of muslin borrowed from the nurses. "Come, *mon papillon.* We shall meet your papa."

Please, God. I prayed that I spoke no lie.

Paris was alive with a bubbling, flowing current of jubilee. It was a fool's errand, I soon realized, to try and behold the face of every soldier who passed by. They were swept up in the thanks of the people, French girls looping their arms through the men's by the handful. And these, just the first wave of soldiers who were to come, returning triumphant from the front.

But no Matthew. Not in the marching lines, not in the grinning faces of soldiers riding atop cars, not in the throngs that moved like one great being. There was something so beautiful in the joy that seemed to infuse every stone and every bone in this city. It came, I thought, from living what they could not bring themselves to believe. A walking state of wondrous disbelief. Never have I seen such a thing before.

A man bumped into me and after righting me, he braced my shoulders like we were old friends. He, with his cane and white beard and fisherman's cap, speaking so quickly I could not understand. He spun us around in a dance, right there in the streets, patted my wee one's head, and skipped off with a laugh that I would never forget.

Bounced between shoulders and pressing on to the Pont Neuf bridge, I made my way to the Île de la Cité. It drew me, this river-island, to where the Seine parted around it like an ancient, immovable ship. The river sloshed up onto the walkway as if it, too, could not contain its joy this day.

On quieter days, I could stand at the stern of that ship—a little patch of grass with trees bundled in. They called it the *Square du Vert-Galant*. I made my way through the throng there now, slipping into my willow fortress beneath a looming tree whose branches fell like rain into the currents below. Downstream, at this end of the island. Flowing on into the unseen in a way that made me believe, even for a moment, in the future.

As the water tugged and pulled and let the willow branch tips meander upon its surface, it tucked me into a wall of leaves. I closed my eyes, as I always did there, and inhaled the scent of them.

Soil. Bark. Leaf. Water. I yearned for home and could imagine myself back in the Argonne, back in another tree-refuge.

The willow was not my refuge tree, the one that had protected me all through the night from the wolves, but it shared a kinship with it. Today, though, even when I closed my eyes, I could not summon the picture of my wooded home. Others pressed in, too, eager for the shade. There was noise—everywhere, noise. Accordions piping happy tunes, sudden choruses of men breaking into song. A symphony, cacophony. I loved and loathed it all at once. For this—this was sheer joy. Liberation. Freedom! Life that these people had never dared hope for.

The city rejoiced and my soul betrayed them, mourning for the forest home that was forever lost. I made my way past the arches of the old bridge, where ancient faces carved in stone watched my journey to the other end of the island. Up the streets to where flying buttresses soared from Notre Dame, where bells rang free and melodic, pealing with abandon, a song held captive for years released at last. The awful faces of gargoyles, crouching there like guards, seemed to hiss at the distant, fading war.

The island and all its bridges bustled with parasoled women and brass-buttoned policemen. A little dog yipped as a boy held a biscuit and stooped to break off a piece for him. Everywhere, joy.

But still, no Matthew.

I crossed back over the Seine, walked the streets until I could walk no longer, and returned in a daze to the Rue de Arbre. It was eerily quiet, here, all the people gone to be a part of the celebration.

I slowed, not wishing to arrive back on the steps of the château. It felt less a home every time I came back and had no word of Matthew. A few remaining leaves twirled down from oaks, my quiet companions dancing their slow dance in the wake of the frantic flurry of Rue Royale, where the revelers were. No lamplighters tipping canteens as they lit their beacons, no brassy triumphant bugle tunes but for those in the faraway echoes.

Hearing the singing so far away, now, it was much like my hope.

330

There, but . . . fading. The babe stirred next to me and gave a tiny whimper. It troubled me, that sleep came so fitfully to such a small creature. With all of the noise, it was understandable, but the wee thing seemed always to be this way, even from birth. Claiming rest here and there in little snatches, but never deeply.

I wondered sometimes if it was because of me. This land of unrest that I lived in, which sent me into pacing, dreaming up too many different endings to our story. The little whimper came again, a reminder that I must not continue to live in the shadowlands of not knowing. I knew that we may never find out about Matthew. I had heard stories in buckets from the nurses—of soldiers they could not identify, deaths they could never send word of because the families were unknown. And how would anyone know to send word to me, but for Henry or George?

My heart twisted at the thought of Henry's quiet ways and George's smile that made you love him and roll your eyes at him in the same breath. What of them? Had they come out of the forest? What of the kind captain from the train in Épermay?

My footsteps became heavy with the thoughts, the singing fading into the quiet shuffle of my feet, alone, upon stone steps. I placed my hand on the doorknob and hesitated. I knew what I would find inside: more joyous sounds, men bolstered by the news of the victory. It was good! It was very, very good. I told myself so. They needed this and deserved it.

But when I entered at last, the creak of the door hinges echoed in eerie quiet.

Something was wrong.

Hushed voices, somewhere upstairs. Two soldiers in bedraggled uniform, each seated on one of the square pillars at the bottom of the stairs. So much like those gargoyles I'd just left behind at Notre Dame, standing guard in their grotesque appearances over something good and true and beautiful. These men were like them. Like statues, that is. Still in stature and grey in pallor, bearing the marks of this grotesque war.

One of them lifted his face toward me.

My heart nearly stopped. "George?"

He stood, and I crossed the room to see if my eyes, indeed, deceived me. For this somber-faced man could not be the jolly, grinning Englishman who had taught my wounded mind not to run at the sound of that accent.

He took my hand but would not meet my eyes with his.

The baby stirred, lips parting in slumber in the sling. George looked at the child, wordlessly, stifling a sound within him that I did not wish to know the reason for.

Henry had risen from the other pillar and joined us. He, breaking silently out of his reticent ways, ran a bandaged hand over the child's back.

Neither spoke.

"Tell me," I said. "Please. Say something."

For the longer they did not speak, the heavier my spirit grew.

Steps on the stairs above stopped their words before they came, and I looked up. Sister Marion saw me and froze. "Mireilles," she said. "Good. You've come. Follow me."

I know not how I came to be there, at the top of the stairs. Nor how the long hall vanished away, depositing me at the threshold of the library.

We did not house patients here.

Everything had been speaking truth to me since I entered the château. In the absence of words, I knew their actions were meant as considerate kindness. The hush of the house. The somber respect of the men's postures. Sister Marion's usual flow of chattiness curbed into tender concern. All leading me here, to a private place in this very public house.

It all pointed to a truth I did not want to know.

Still, I dared to beg God, in that silence, for a miracle.

I entered the room. Two cots were tucked against the far wall, each one positioned so that their occupant's head would see out the window.

The cot on the right was empty. But a man lay very still on the cot nearest the bookshelves. His head bandaged, along with his leg. I stopped in the middle of the room, watching to see if his chest rose and fell.

It did. Barely, and in intervals so irregular my eyes begged to look away, to unsee him. But my heart drew me nearer, desperate to know at last.

The man faced the wall. I could not see his face, and my eyes swam. I lifted a hand, hovering it over his shoulder. Summoning my courage and a thousand prayers.

45

I laid my hand upon his shoulder. The man did not stir.

"Matthew?" I said, my voice a near-whisper. Sister Marion approached, laying her hand on mine.

"Mireilles," she said. "It is not . . . this man will not . . ."

I shook my head. I would not hear the words spoken. "Matthew," I said, a little louder this time.

Noises sounded behind me, but I did not register them. Not beneath all the pounding from my soul.

And then came a voice. I didn't dare believe it. "It should never have been him." The voice—surely, surely it was Matthew's—came from behind me.

I spun. And there he was. Bandages wrapping his face about his eyes, round and round. But the set of his mouth, the frown that was somber but gentle—it was, undoubtedly, him.

"Matthew," I breathed. "It is you." The words floated from my mouth and sounded so very silly and so very far away and yet they kept coming. "It is you," I said again, dumbly, as I crossed to meet him. I picked up his hand in mine, just holding it. I needed to feel him, his fingers in mine, and even when I did, I could not believe it.

No amount of blinking could have held back the tears, then. It only sent them cascading down my cheeks silently, where his hand lifted and caught them. As his fingers touched my face, his chin—so strong, always—trembled. A very deep battle waged within this man so dear to me.

It was then that my thoughts, muddled as they were, finally cleared enough to put questions to words. What had happened to him? These bandages—what were they? And what of the man on the cot?

"Matthew," I said again, universes of words aching from those two syllables. They asked—*What has happened?* They poured over him—*You are here. You are safe.* And they begged of him—*You are safe, yes?*

The man on the cot groaned, and Matthew's expression fell.

Sister Marion bustled to the cot and helped him shift. In the doorway, Henry and George stood, hats in hand. Faces grave.

I was standing right in the middle of a tangled tale, and I did not know what it was.

"What has happened?" I said at last.

Matthew, unseeing, lifted his other hand to find my face until his warmth cradled me. His fingers were rough and torn by the war, by the woods, by all that had brought him to me. I lifted his fingers and kissed them, forgetting a moment that we were not alone.

The clouds shifted outside, sending a slice of sunlight through the broken stained-glass window, setting us in a kaleidoscope of broken color. Together, we approached the man upon the cot.

The man groaned, speaking something indecipherable. He shifted, slightly, his face now toward us.

I stilled. I knew this man. I had seen him only twice, but they were the two moments that had altered the course of my life. First, by sending me from the Argonne with my three brave guides, and later, by helping me to gather my courage to leave that train in Épermay.

Captain Jasper Truett.

46

Captain Jasper Truett

A woman spoke. Muffled and far away, sweetness in this dark. June? It had to be June. Amelia was too small, forever a child. Unless—unless by some miracle it had all been a nightmare, and she was grown and well and hadn't been taken too soon. She was born too soon, that much I remember clearly. I'd paced our floorboards like a madman for worry of her. When was that? It seemed so close it could have been this morning, and so far it could have been twelve lifetimes ago.

I could picture my wife's smile as I paced. She had a smile that could rival the sun for lighting up a man's world. Her name matched the dawning of summer, and it fit her. I saw that June-smile now, her holding Amelia, all swaddled in white like a tiny little bride. *"See, Jasper? See, I told you all would be well. How could it not be, with such a soul in the world?"*

The memory snapped away, and I floated over it somewhere, watching Amelia grow, seeing June's smile. All my imaginings, the ones that have haunted me this decade and more, had grown faces and voices and I watched them turn, page by page, before me. That smile that lit the world, how it continued brave and true, even when I was gone. Amelia, dimpling cheeks the same way, twirling in gold like she was made for sunlight and it was made for her. Writing letters to her daddy by speaking them to the clouds, thinking I'd catch those words she tossed into the sky, wherever I was. Her mother, transcribing the words to paper so that I would, indeed, catch them.

I didn't write back. I never wrote back. She couldn't read, I told myself. And what was more, I was an idiot when it came to words. Never knew what to say. But I could gather her up in my arms and hold on tight, and so I'd save my embraces for when I saw her and could wrap her up like a father should. Afterward, I'd kicked myself until my heart bled for my stupidity. How hard was it to pick up a pen? It was infinitely harder not to. Or at least to live with the consequences after.

The picture snapped into flames. Hot flames that made me swim in sweat even as I dreamt. I knew I was dreaming. I knew this was not real, though once it had been. I heard Amelia's cries, saw June dashing through fiery rooms, and I wanted to yell at the fire to stop. It was as if the sun had come down and trapped itself in our home to have that showdown with June's smile, and June had rushed headlong into the inferno to pull out our tiny little Amelia, that tiny little bride. Only this time, she was swaddled in bedsheets, arm splayed into the hot air and hair hanging down as June took her out.

I suffocated with the scene of it every night and every day, just as the smoke suffocated them. They made it out—but too late.

And I'd been wandering in the wake of that fire, a trail of smoke, ever since. I was full of vengeance for a long, long time. But how does one fight smoke? How can a man pin it down and claim retribution?

He cannot. It only chokes him more, the futility of it, and drives him mad.

It was in the depths of a forest in France that I finally met that smoke face-to-face. Gas, yes, but I knew it for what it was. The hand of death, just like what had come for my girls.

It was headed for Matthew Petticrew and Chester Hasenpfeffer. And when I saw it there, yellow-green and sickening in the way it crept in a slow, silent dance of toxic mist, I knew.

I saw Matthew take off his own mask. I watched him lock his own death sentence into place as he locked his mask around Chester.

He went down, there behind that green curtain of tree branches.

My own pulse pounded with the battle cry that had sent me into these dark woods: *fight for life*.

Everything slowed as everything sped up. I was there in a split-second, diving for the boy. The new groom, the father with a child soon coming, or maybe already here. He would go to that child, the way I had not gone to Amelia.

My mask was on him. Barely. And none too soon. I went down, slamming the ground as pine needles and old leaves softened by winter flew up in response, confetti in the air between us. My compass tumbled out into the debris, resting atop the ground. A gut-blow.

Fight for life. It was the plea of my own life. And I would close my eyes around the image of a young man starting where my own life had once ended: on the beginning edge of fatherhood.

I felt my breathing slow. I turned my head with the last strength I had left and lay face-to-face with the old brass compass. Tarnished and tired, its needle moving in the blurry darkening vision before me. North . . . by northwest.

"Simple as that, and you'll find us." My June.

And while my body entered a desperate struggle, something else happened. Above the gas, below it, around it—however it came to be, something else swirled in and through me. As if a Good Father, somewhere, tucked me in. I, a child; He, the silent, valiant vanquisher of anguish.

I knew only one thing in that moment.

Peace.

And now I laid in limbo, that same peace about me. It wouldn't be long now. Time had no place here, and I was close, so close.

The voices grew clearer.

"See?" that sweet, low voice said. The Angel of the Argonne. None could forget that voice. "Because of you," she said.

I felt something, then. Someone picking up my hand, my arm along with it, and moving it to my side. Something was placed upon it—something with that same warm peace that shrouded this place.

338

It stirred. A tiny sound, that of a baby. A pure song in this great dark. Like its mother. The great peace grew thicker.

This, then, was what I had missed. The coming back, the being there. The holding of a young life that was meant for holding.

"Papa," Amelia had said to me, that last good-bye. *"Papa, come home soon."*

I could picture her. My Amelia. Held in the arms of a Father . . . arms that now reached out to me.

The spent old battle-worn body that held me was parched of air. Fading, fast. I summoned that metal courage one last time to push out last words. . . .

"I'm coming."

Matthew

"Tell me," Mira said that night.

We were in the garden behind the château. She had been spending time here, tending the wilderness that it might stay wild. A refuge to life in this place.

Wind brushed over the tops of the growing things. Some lifeless, clacking together lightly. Some supple, a gentle whisper. I was learning to see with my ears, and though it felt foreign in some ways, it also felt, oddly, like putting spectacles on over long-nearsighted eyes. I had always heard before I'd seen. Now, the sense was sharpening.

She leaned her head against my shoulder and smelled of honey. Had she always smelled so? She waited. *"Tell me,"* she'd said.

So I did. I told her all. Of the Argonne and Chester. Of awaking in the forest to find a mask secured on me . . . and Captain Jasper Truett—the very same one I'd studied in the papers as a boy—beside me, barely alive. Of the field hospital after, and the journey here.

And then I asked the same of her. Holding her hand as her hand held the baby's head. "Tell me," I said.

She did. Of the coming of the child, of the night shrouded in thunder and the air "laced in rain," as she said.

I knew that sound, that smell. I remembered it well, and how the gas crept in beneath it. I had thought I was breathing my last . . . and a world away in an old château in Paris, a little life was breathing its first. It had been out of thick darkness that I had gasped unexpected breath and returned to the land of the conscious. I was in a mask—but did not know how. I was alive—but could not think how. And the sights before me, they were beginning to blur. I thought I saw the Captain, then Chester. I uttered a prayer before darkness reclaimed me, and I did not wake again until the field hospital, where I learned three things:

Chester lived.

I was blind—whether forever or just for now, I did not yet know.

And Captain Jasper Truett was on death's door.

Celia found us in that hospital, and in that happy authority of hers, arranged for us all to come to Mira, to this house of healing. She knew that one of us would not leave that house alive, if he even made it that far.

I count it a miracle that he did. And I pray his home-going, this night, was the miracle he had been awaiting for so long.

None of us had spoken since the captain had truly breathed his last. There was stillness here in the garden, bursting with untold things between me and Mira, inviting us in.

I didn't know much of hearts. I was only simple Matthew Pet ticrew, the kid who used to lie on his belly in the dirt to hear the hoofbeats of horses. But maybe those hoofbeats had taught me something of heartbeats, after all. Mine, just now, was not so much beating as it was bleeding with longing to hold Mira and to hold her child. But—was it my place? I had clung to the thought of the child, but was that fair of me? To consider myself a father?

As if she heard this battle flowing from within me, she slipped her hand beneath mine, letting the baby's head rest in my palm.

"Your son," she said. Two words, breaking the silence. Breaking the dam within me, ushering in a flow of utter inadequacy, of gratitude that swallowed me up. And the crippling realization that this child in my hands was an entire life, waiting to be lived.

As the world outside these walls raged in the wake of a war that had taken life upon life upon scores of life . . . as it reeled in the face of a sickness sweeping the lands and snuffing out breath

. . . as each new gust of wind picked up spent ash from fires and rubble even as the soldiers marched home . . . here was something good. Pure. True.

I didn't know what to do. I hadn't held a baby since Celia, and even then, Mrs. Bluet had laughed, though kindly, at my awkward young boy-sized arms and their attempt to cradle her. I'd hardly dared to imagine what it would be like to hold one as a man. And certainly had never imagined doing so with bandages wrapped about my eyes like a mummy. I would scare the poor creature to pieces.

But he did not seem frightened. And the sky didn't split open and rain down a sudden burst of knowledge of how to do this, how to be here. That palm, holding that sweet head with the softest tiny patch of hair atop, did not brand me *Father.* I had the sudden conviction that I would surely drop him. I could carry live ammunition over miles and not falter, but a human child? Weeks old, and in these hands, with unseeing eyes?

He was doomed.

Seconds crept on, and my thumb stroked that little head, sleeping soundly. I had never felt something so . . . soft.

"Am I doing it right?" I said, clearing the catch in my voice.

Mira's laugh was soft. "Yes," she said. "He looks as if he has been waiting for this." Her voice took on a strain of wonder. "He has never rested so deeply as this, Matthew. It is as though he has been waiting for a part of himself."

My throat burned.

"Waiting for you," she said. She sounded happy.

Something strange happened, then. I had never felt it since I was five years old, digging dirt-caked fingers into the windowsill and watching life through a golden window. And I had never thought to see it again. But as I sat there between the child and Mireilles, I could so clearly imagine a picture of all that I heard and felt:

A mother, happy. A baby in her arms and mine, all wrapped up in a worn scrap of blanket—or rather, a scrap of a certain colorful balloon, my fingers attested, running over rows of stitching softened by time.

And her smile—deep as the Marne and wide as the Argonne, falling right on me.

We sat there a long time. I couldn't see the stars' movements in this eternal night of mine. But when even the frogs and crickets began to tire of their songs and Mira shivered beside me, I knew it was late.

I leaned forward, over the still-slumbering child. "What's his name?" I asked.

There was a long quiet, and then that voice that had come to me in another darkness, in what felt like an eternity before, spoke. "I named him for his father," she said. "I named him for you."

I sputtered my own name out, clumsy as all get out. "M-Matthew?"

"Well, the proper French, you know. *Matthieu.*" I could hear the smile in her voice, gentled soon into a serious tone. "I want him to know of the man who gave his life to him. Who chose him."

My throat burned. It was so much. Too much. To be spared, to be here, to have a human life placed not just in my arms but in my very life. "And—and his second name?"

A pause. "I do not know what that is," she said.

"A middle name? First name, middle name, surname."

She laughed again. "You Americans are funny creatures," she said. "Is one name not enough?"

"I thought the French had long names. Even more than us, sometimes."

"Perhaps sometimes," she said. "Aline once told me of baptism names, of stitching on the names of ancestors and godparents. But no—what did you call it?—middle name." She shivered, and I shifted the baby into one arm, so that I could wrap her in my other. She seemed to sense the thoughts weighing on me. "Would you like him to have a middle name?"

I felt odd speaking it. As if it might disrespect what had transpired in the hours before. But the thought would not leave. The picture of a man who'd give anything to be there for a child. Who had made it possible for me to do so.

"I was thinking of . . . Jasper."

It was probably sacrilegious, somehow, giving a name so soon after the namesake had passed on. My face burned, and I made to move my arm so that she wouldn't feel trapped, somehow, by my idea.

But she caught that arm, and held it fast. "It is perfect," she said quietly. "Matthieu Jasper Petticrew."

48

George

"By George, I think they've got it," I said, peering out the window. The lovebirds sat in the garden like some old Paris scene in a painting somewhere. If someone were to paint them now, they'd probably be hung in the Victoria and Albert like a tribute to this dreary old war.

"Get away from there." Henry crumpled up and tossed a paper at me from across the study. "Don't you think they've earned a little privacy?"

"No such thing in this war, mate," I said. "Besides " I sniffed. Blasted tears. I'd made it into the woods and back without so much as a tear and that scene of the lovebirds was going to be my undoing? "Better take what you can get out of a time like this. Not much good to come out of all we've seen."

"Maybe," Henry said, his pen stopping for a blessed half-second.

"What's this?" I asked, snatching up the paper from the desk in front of him. "Another 'Dear America'? I thought you'd said your piece."

Henry was up in a flash, lunging for it. He snatched it back but left a corner of it in my hand.

I cleared my throat. "'Dear Celia,'" I read.

"Quit it." Henry strode to the window, a tangle of history books and heart.

"Now who's the one spying on the lovebirds, eh?" I elbowed him and handed him back the corner. "Who's Celia?"

Henry looked at me like I'd banged my head on a crowbar somewhere.

"Ah," I said. "Yes, that's right. The nurse. Sister to the soldier. You and she have an understanding?"

He set his chin, not answering.

"Well, good. She seemed a peach of a girl."

Henry muttered something.

"Eh? What's that?"

"Nothing," he said. He drew in a deep breath, crossing his arms over his chest.

"I saw they ran your last letter," I said. "That took some courage."

He shook his head. "Can't believe I sent that in," he said. "But it's a fitting way to go out."

"Don't tell me they gave you the boot, old boy. Did they kick you out?"

Henry laughed, his whole expression amused. "Would you believe they want me to stay on? Said I'd found my voice for editorial, and they'd never had such a wide response to a piece."

I nodded in exaggerated approval. "So, you'll be moving to Washington, then."

"Not on your life."

"What, then? New York? Chicago? You've got offers from all the big papers, do you?"

He looked at the floorboards. "Well . . ."

I picked up a book and whacked the Wet Rag's arm but in a good way. "You do! You do, and you'll be the next Pulitzer, and I'll be able to say I knew you when you spent all your time abroad buried in bookstacks in dusty old village libraries."

He shoved his hands in his pockets, and a smile tugged at his mouth, wonder of wonders. "I . . . I've got to see a farm about a cow," he said. "That's how this all started. I'm going home."

49

Mira

December 25, 1918

"You're sure you want to go back." Matthew's voice was tender. He'd been quiet for most of this journey back to the Argonne.

It was Christmas. Little Matthieu's first. And though we had much—*so* much—to fill us with joy, there was also much that we mourned.

Grand-père, who lay buried here in the depths of these woods. Jasper Truett, whom George and Henry had brought back here before their home-goings, to be buried among the men for whom he had given so much. His grave was unmarked but for a simple cross, like so many others. But still we wished to honor him, somehow.

And Papa. If I closed my eyes, I could see these trees as they once had been: tall and alive, strong. Like Papa. And if I closed my eyes, I could tell myself what had driven me here—it was time to say good-bye, once and for all.

Little Matthieu wriggled against me where he was wrapped so close to my heart. A comfort, in this difficult day.

We were very close, now. It had been a difficult journey, Matthew's sight only just beginning to emerge. He could see shadows and light, sometimes a little more, when close enough. Colors, the blurred outline of a person. But nothing more. *"And you,"* he'd told me. *"I'll always see you."*

He was seeing me now, understanding me as we stood at the

edge of the woods. Or rather, what was left of the woods. It smelled of cinders and the air was heavy with the story of what had happened here, those weeks of the Meuse-Argonne offensive.

And now it was empty. Splintered remnants of trees sticking into the air, crisscrossing in grotesque fashion. As if a giant had stooped down to lay kindling for a great fire.

"We don't have to go in," Matthew said.

"No—it is alright," I said, infusing my voice with lightness. "That is—unless you do not wish to?"

He was silent for a moment. Searching the horizon as if those blue eyes could see it clearly. Much weighed upon him, here, and I wished I could lift that burden.

"Let's go," he said at last.

As we walked, he told me of his first trips into the woods. How he had named the trees as landmarks—the arch tree, the chorus, and of course the Sentinel, which was etched upon my matchbox holder. I laughed, picturing them well, for I knew the trees he spoke of like old friends.

We neared my old clearing, and through a few still-standing trees, I saw it—three walls standing, one broken into bits. Looking wide-eyed and forlorn at me through windows whose glass had been blown in, as if it asked, *What has happened to me?*

"It will be alright," I whispered to my little chalet. My heart ached. I knew something of what that felt like. "You will see."

"Did you say something?" Matthew asked. What would he say to me talking to a house?

"It was nothing," I said with a small laugh. "Only nonsense. Here," I said, guiding him. "Here is the lantern tree. At least—I think it is. It is difficult to say, with so many of them gone."

He reached out and felt the bark of it.

He knew what I wished to do here. I'd told him my hope one night, in the château, knowing it was perhaps silly. But he had only said, "It's perfect."

I reached into his haversack now, pulling out three items: a small lantern; a candle to set inside of it; and my brass matchbox, its lone wooden stick tumbling about inside, awaiting its moment to shine.

"It is time," I reminded myself, feeling the ache in my chest begin to burn. I had not thought it would be this hard, after so long since Papa had disappeared.

"*Mon papillon.*" He had called me. "*You keep the fire lit now, yes?*"

I had promised . . . and so I was here. With the final match, ready to lay that hope to rest, ready to let him rest in peace, wherever in this war-torn land he had breathed his last.

My hand shook as I plucked up that last match. My heart rent to the sound of it scraping against its box, so worn from its journey, so safe in its brass cuff.

I would light the candle. We would linger and let it burn down. Speak of memories. Tell little Matthieu of his own grand-père, my papa. Let my Matthew know of him, too, this gift of a good and wonderful father, the sort of father I could already see in Matthew. Sadness choked my words at first, but soon the warmer thoughts came, and with them, it was easier to speak. Of Grand-père and Papa's nightly battle over who would sleep upon the floor. Of Grand-père's carvings, of Papa dancing with me in the clearing, of the way he stirred the coals of the hearth fire three times in a circle every time he took up the poker, like the habit was an old friend.

I watched the white candle accept the flame of the match, surging into life against the white winter sky. Its small trail of smoke twirled up to mingle with the puff of breath from little Matthieu, and I thought, *How good. Light, and life.*

Tears came. There was one thing yet to do.

I unwrapped Matthieu from his muslin sling and settled him into Matthew's arms. "I will return very soon," I said. He knew where I was going and sensed, I think, that I needed to do it alone.

It was hard to find green for the wreath. Most of the trees were obliterated or singed. But a few very old trees remained, and a few very new saplings, as well. It took long, for I had to travel farther out than I had thought. When I returned, my boys were gone, and the pleasant smell of chimney fire summoned me to the cottage as it had so many times in my youth.

I did not know if I wanted to step inside. It felt—too hard. And something felt strange in the air. Matthew had managed to build a fire somehow—it did not surprise me, for how clever and quick he was in learning to work around his limits. If he could do that, then surely I could find strength to enter my old home.

I approached my little chalet that had for so long been a place of magic and hope, dreams and good things. Even now, in its broken state, it offered curls of smoke from the chimney, and if I tried, I could imagine it was like old times. Coming home on Christmas Day with an armful of firewood, warming my hands around a bowl of soup, laughing and singing with my family.

But when I stepped inside, it was not laughing or singing that met my ears.

It was a long string of French, in a low but firm voice.

I froze, listening. Had gypsies or soldiers left behind taken up residence? Refugees, perhaps?

Matthew spoke, then. "Sir, I'm afraid I don't understand your words, but—" The sound of the old fire poker, or perhaps a stick, raking agitatedly through the fire's coals. Around and around and around.

I could not see who did the raking—it must be Matthew. The raking stopped, and so did his speaking. I knew that way of his. He stopped himself just so whenever a sudden idea took hold. I could hear his mind turning. "You know, I once was told of a man who told his daughter not to let on if she knew another language. English, for example."

Me. He was speaking of me. What was he about?

"He told her it would give her great power, a secret like that."

The man did not speak. I ventured a glance around the wall that blocked my view and saw a tall man, clothes plain and worn but clean. His back was toward me, and he held what was left of the old fire poker still.

He listened.

350

As if he understood every word that Matthew said.

And Matthew, my Matthew, still cradling the babe—he understood it too. I saw it in the way his mouth tried to smile, but he stopped it. His own masquerade, just to be sure.

My heart pounded in my chest.

If he was right . . .

"I wish I could meet that man," Matthew said. "I have much to thank him for. And much to tell him. Such as . . ." He glanced my way, and his smile, warm and gentle, broke loose. "Such as where his daughter is."

The man dropped the fire poker altogether, letting it clatter to the ground. Reaching out, as if to convince himself that what Matthew said was true, he laid a bony hand upon Matthew's arm and uttered a single, husky word.

"Where." Choked, nearly, in desperate need to know.

Matthew reached out a hand and pointed.

The man turned.

Our eyes met, mine brimming with hot tears. His, lined in memories he would never speak. Creased by war, brows lifting upward in desperate defiance to see the one thing he had traveled years for. *Hope.*

And I fell into the arms of my Papa.

Here in a room where I could introduce him to his grandson, to a son by marriage . . . and where we would talk long into the night, telling him a tale of hope in the darkest of nights.

Together, in the morning, we four left the little chalet. We walked past an empty lantern, where only a pool of spent wax testified that light had burned long into the night. We left the forest, arm in arm.

Out of the shadows . . . and into the reaching light.

Matthew

Four Years Later
October 24, 1921
Chalons-sur-Marne, France

It was George who had cabled us. He addressed it to Henry and me, going on and on—on a cable, of all places—about the ceremony that was to take place back in France.

BLOKES COME. YOU MUST. OR ELSE. I WILL PAY.
RICHEST SORRY PAUPER OF A CURATE WHO
EVER LIVED, BEING INDEPENDENTLY WEALTHY
IN MONEY AND ENTIRELY IMPOVERISHED IN
SPIRITUAL MATTERS THAT I CONTINUE TO LEARN
IN. ONE OF THEM IS: WE GATHER FOR IMPORTANT
TIMES. I BROOK NO ARGUMENT. I AM PAYING.
YOU ARE COMING. BRING WIVES AND IMPS TOO.
SEVENTEENTH BAND!

They had taken soldiers from four unmarked battlefield graves and placed them with care in caskets. One would be chosen by a fellow soldier, transported with great solemnity and care, aboard the USS *Olympia*, back to Washington. He—the fallen, unknown soldier—would lie in state in the rotunda of our nation's very capitol until the eleventh day of the eleventh month: Armistice Day. And then he would be entombed and honored, forever, in our national cemetery. Any could visit. Any could pay honor. Any mother, father, widow, child, brother, soldier, friend—and wonder, *Is he mine?* The question mark a gift to grieving hearts. A tribute to the thousands and thousands of lives given.

None of us spoke it. But we all thought it. *Is it him?* Jasper Truett had been laid to rest in a battlefield, alongside his men.

So we came. We gathered, as George the Unlikely Curate had said. We watched in somber respect as the rose bouquet was laid upon a casket, the soldier chosen. We would never, ever know the true identity—but just the possibility that it was him was enough. Just the knowledge that whomever it was . . . that life would continue to bring solace. Healing. Hope. And to be a symbol to receive a nation's gratitude. Guarded, always. Protected, no matter what.

It was somber, weighty. I saw a thousand faces in my memory as we witnessed the ceremony, and so did every soldier there. We would never forget.

George took us to a café afterward that served olives, Welsh rarebit, *and* Brioche. By special arrangement, we later learned.

Mira chased the little ones—Matthieu and our son Franz, named for her Papa. They led her in a chase around a fountain in the village, and I recalled another fountain, the first on our journey. Before she had spoken a single word to us in English, looking haunted and alone.

How far she had come. How far each of us, how different from the men we had been.

Henry, writing volumes of books from his farmhouse after he finished long days of haying, urged on by his wife, a certain plucky nurse who was mother to my niece and nephew, home with them now.

And down the hill from Henry and Celia's Virginia farm, a man whose sight had returned slowly, if imperfectly, found his way back to his beginnings and began a small horse farm. Mira and I walked in our field each evening as the sun slipped down and the moon rose. This homeland of ours, the night. Where our souls had met and mingled, where we had learned the gifts of the difficult places. We loved to watch our boys race their cousins in our humble arena and never once thought of raking over the tracks of such joy. Here, their grand-père gave chase, whenever he was not otherwise occupied with his own garden and woodworking, in his home that was built onto ours. He had seen years upon years of war. He and I—we were grateful, I think. To be understood without needing to speak of these things that would never leave us.

George happily served a small village chapel, St. Thomas's in East Sussex, where he'd recently engaged himself to a farmer's daughter by the name of Sally Rivers, whom he extolled incessantly as "the Princess of Pevensey Bay" and who adored him with a boundless affection that rivaled his own. He liked to say his most faithful congregants were the sheep of the fields, the caves in the cliffs, and a handful of friendly fisherman and farm folk. He had found his calling, he said, and was devoted to it with everything he had.

Chester Hasenpfeffer had arrived at the ripe old age of eighteen, at last. He currently served, to his family's great pride, and thanks to a "good word" put in by a certain former employee, at Harvard University. He worked in the kitchens, cooking up stews and sitting in on classes, smelling of onions and carrots and peppering the professors with approximately two thousand questions per day. He was going places, according to the general consensus in the auspices of the faculty room, where "Hasenpfeffer stories" also provided happily humorous atmosphere whenever needed.

All of it—every bit—we could trace in some way to Captain Jasper Truett. To that dark night season and the way it, in all its awful brokenness, gave birth to a light so rare and precious we would never take it for granted.

After the ceremony, we ventured to the place it all began—the hush of the Argonne. Mira and I, we took the boys to the cottage, which was little more than an empty shanty now, bits of it broken by war and by time. I watched her for heartache but saw only magic spark in her eyes. She was seeing it as it had been . . . and seeing where it had led, for each of us.

And we three, the Seventeenth Band, we clipped pine boughs from young growth and twisted them up into two wreaths: one for the resting place of Grand-père, and one for the hollow tree that had been the site of the giving of life.

We would venture once more to Paris before returning home. Stop to see Sister Marion and the Château Fontinelle, which Mira and her papa and her great-aunt Sophia had given in trust to the Jour de Soleil Sisters and their good work. They reserved a single room for us, if ever we should want to come and stay. The library.

It swallowed me up, sometimes, the reality of it all. My hand still took to trembling at times. And Mira—who had been through it all right along with us—she spun that song of hers into the night, reminding me . . .

There was life, there in the dark.

author's note

**In the centennial anniversary year
of the Tomb of the Unknown Soldier**

Perched on a hill overlooking our nation's capital, a sentinel walks. Steady and sure, day and night, rain, shine or hurricane.

Twenty-one steps. Pause, twenty-one silent seconds. Measured turn. Twenty-one steps in the opposite direction. Repeat.

A constant patrol meant to echo, endlessly, the twenty-one-gun salute . . . the highest honor rendered in military tradition.

At the Tomb of the Unknown Soldier in Arlington National Cemetery, the tomb guards take meticulous care in preparing their uniforms: brushing, sanding, shining each element until it reaches perfection. Pleats pressed, medals measured meticulously. It can take up to twelve hours just to prepare for each shift.

And then, their watch begins. With each turn, the rifle is shifted to the outside shoulder, the guard always placing themself between the weapon and the soldiers, who have known enough of weapons.

I witnessed this richly symbolic ceremony in fall 2019. It was just me and the tomb and the guard, at first. And then, people began to filter in to witness the changing of the guard, the laying of the wreath. I had begun research for this book, and as I watched the utmost care play out before me in every painstaking detail, I couldn't help thinking of the trenches. What the soldier of the Great War endured. Could he ever have imagined, in his darkest moments, such a resting place as this? Untouched by gunfire, mud, or gruesome things . . . a place marked by quiet, white-marbled peace? Sentinels who've sworn a creed to "walk my tour in humble reverence," their very lives dedicated to honoring their brothers in arms? Were ever there two more opposite places than the death-laden trenches and this final resting place?

Echoes of that stark, beautiful contrast live in every part of his journey to Arlington: When he lay in state in the capitol rotunda, crowds lined up, four abreast for blocks, to have a chance to pay respects. When it came time for his procession from the capitol all the way to the cemetery, people lined Pennsylvania Avenue, "they flowed like a tide over the slopes about his burial place; they choked the bridges that lead across the river to the fields of the brave," according to Kirke L. Simpson's Pulitzer–Prize winning coverage from 1921. These same crowds—people in the thousands—joined in reverent recitation of the Lord's Prayer, a resounding-yet-hushed benediction over this "forgotten" man, then in the words of the faithful hymn:

"Rock of Ages . . ." They sang of a strong place, unshakable. Far from the mire of the trenches.

"Cleft for me . . ." A savior broken, laid down, for this one who knew sacrifice, too.

"Let me hide myself in thee . . ." Refuge. Safe and secure, eternal.

The hymn washed over all of Arlington that day in an air of still, hushed reverence.

Artillery. Cavalry. Marine band. Choir. The rare bestowing of a Congressional Medal of Honor and Distinguished Service Cross. A procession led by the President, General Pershing, Supreme Court Justices, and members of Congress. Dignitaries from England, France, Italy, and more bestowed their respective country's high-honor medals. And perhaps the higher honor: flowers from war mothers who would not see their sons again.

When all the speeches were made, all the medals laid, all the songs sung and prayers prayed . . . he was laid at last to rest there in the place that had been prepared for him, upon a bit of soil brought from France, and within walls etched with these words:

Here rests in honored glory an American soldier known but to God.

As dark fell over the capital city . . . the lights began. Illumination of a jeweled arch ignited by search lights, the Washington Monument lighted to give the effect of strands of light from top to bottom, search lights from its top as well as from the Capitol building crisscrossing in the night sky.

All this *light*. Blanketing one who had known more darkness than we can imagine.

It strikes me so deeply. For the symbolism of it all, for the lives lived and lives lost and redemption so present in the honor shown. And, I think, for the way it echoes our own stories, too.

Places of dark, being pulled from the mire, being carried away to a place of safety and peace. Like the soldier. Like Mira, Matthew, Jasper, Henry, and George, each in their own way. Each coming to be known, and to be held. The shadows of the past never glossed over, but treated with such care, the scars allowed to tell stories, but cherished in a healing way, too.

And always, the light. Searing through the night.

In penning this story, I have meant no disservice to the courageous World War I soldier entombed at Arlington. This book never aimed to fictionalize him; in fact, it aimed to avoid fictionalizing him at all costs. His life is true. His anonymity allows him to represent the countless ones who never came home. The tomb is a place of grief, hope, healing, closure, promise, and so much more. I hope that only respect, gratitude, and a fierce guarding of the real soldier's true story—untouched by this imagined one—is found in these pages.

In this year that marks the 100th anniversary of his final burial, it is an honor to remember, and to learn.

acknowledgments

In *Yours Is the Night*, there are countless lives and people who have inspired the journey as well as those who have made the writing of this book possible. I owe thanks to so many. . . .

Always, to my family. You are the story of my heart. Thank you for sharing this journey and putting up with my randomly wrinkled brow whenever a story idea hits.

To my Ben, who this book is dedicated to. None of this would be possible without you. We've been cooking up journey ideas ever since we decided in our high school library to tie our shoelaces behind our ankles and revolutionize the world. Can't imagine why the trend never caught on, but it was the start of a great many laughs and an even greater many adventures with you, and I'm so thankful.

To the courageous publishing team who helped to wrangle this manuscript: Raela Schoenherr, Jennifer Veilleux, and Elizabeth Frazier, and the entire wonderful Bethany House team. Agent Wendy Lawton and the Books and Such Family. I am grateful for the honor of working with each one of you!

To Erika Hays, who eight years ago showed me pictures of the Tomb of the Unknown Soldier—it planted the seed of this story. Thank you, my friend!

To Allen. I believe your name was Allen. In January of 2019 you were kind enough to let me and my baby sit in your row on a flight from Dallas. You worked at the Pentagon and shared about a small museum you discovered quite by accident beneath the Lincoln Memorial while out on a run. I shared about a story idea I had, pertaining to the Unknown Soldier at Arlington. You told me more about the tomb, and spoke of your courageous friends who were laid to rest at Arlington. Ten months later, I got to go see that hidden museum beneath the Lincoln Memorial. I got to go to Arlington to pay respects to "the Unknowns," as you called them. I thought of your friends, and thank both you and them for your service. I hope this story finds you, someday.

To my sister April, whose history-loving heart takes her on many adventures, from which she comes home to tell of things like the garlands and trench art. Your footsteps have guided this story in a thousand nuanced ways, and your friendship in my life has done the same. Thank you.

To Danielle Esquivel, who graciously checked and corrected my usage of French. Any remaining errors are mine alone. I thank you for your generous help and for your friendship over the years. What a treasure it is!

To the real lives that inspired many of the people and events in this story: General Pershing, Major Charles Whittlesey, Sergeant Alvin York, Colonel Hayward, and Lieutenant James Reese Europe, to name a few. Also from my research: the officers who took tea at a table amidst rubble. Couples who met and wed within days or less, on the brink of shipping out. The soldier who marched a whole line of Germans, unarmed, into captivity. The composer whose musical ability equipped him to hear and identify the direction of incoming artillery more quickly than others. Ernest B., whose pocket-sized volume of soldier's prayers inspired George's prayers. The men of the preparedness movement, who gave of their own time and money to train at Plattsburgh long before America entered the war.

To the real places depicted or echoed in fictional versions, particularly Épermay's (fictional) location, so similar to the (real) town of Épernay. Beaulieu-en-Coteau is based loosely on the village of Fleury, the "village mort pour la France" ("village that died for France").

The ceremony in the prologue, depicting the choosing of the soldier for the tomb, did happen as described.

And now . . . a sincere note on the shadowed forces Matthew and Mira each faced. War can bring unthinkable things. I deliberated long and hard over Mira's circumstances brought upon her by the stranger in the woods. My hope is that it has not been treated here as a mere story element. It's sobering that such attacks were heartbreakingly frequent during the war. But beyond the staggering statistics lies the hearts of the women who were so real and so deserving of the utmost care. In including echoes of that here, I deeply hope it holds their stories with even a little of that care they deserved. I've sought out voices who have shared their own experiences in this realm, hoping that by listening to what they have shared, their hard-won hope might also be present in this story. If this is your story, too . . . may I offer my prayers? Coming before the God whose heart rends over every mistreatment, every tear. May the aching places be gathered up, held close, defended, and cherished.

In similar manner, it is my very deep prayer that the effects of war upon body and mind—"shell shock," as they called it back then—are handled in these pages with respect and care. Matthew is the primary character who takes us a little into the world of what we now know as PTSD, and Jasper to some degree as well. To those who have experienced PTSD or have loved ones who have, please know that any small reflection of this reality in this book was included in hopes of holding this experience with care and respect, and never to exploit it for story's sake. Your very real sacrifices have been deep and lasting, perhaps more than we will ever know. For what you have given, I offer you my very deepest thanks and prayers.

And finally, to my Lord. The day I finished this book's nearly final read-through was the day I sat, heart entirely spent from the story, and heard a song on the radio speak of your pursuing, rescuing love. Sending out an army, rescuing from darkest night. How the tears spilled. How thankful I am . . . for your rescue, for your pursuing, rescuing love. Thank you, for owning the night—and for the light you infuse into it, too.

Amanda Dykes is the winner of the prestigious 2020 Christy Award Book of the Year, a *Booklist* 2019 Top Ten Romance debut, and the winner of an INSPY award for her debut novel, *Whose Waves These Are*. Her second novel, *Set the Stars Alight*, was recognized as a Historical Novels Review Editors' Choice and received a Library Journal starred review. A former English teacher, Amanda is a drinker of tea, dweller of redemption, and spinner of hope-filled tales who spends most days chasing wonder and words with her family. Find her online at www.amandadykes.com.

Sign Up for Amanda's Newsletter

Keep up to date with Amanda's news on book releases and events by signing up for her email list at amandadykes.com.

More from Amanda Dykes

Reeling from the loss of her parents, Lucy Claremont discovers an artifact under the floorboards of their London flat, leading her to an old seaside estate. Aided by her childhood friend Dashel, a renowned forensic astronomer, they start to unravel a history of heartbreak, sacrifice, and love begun two hundred years prior—one that may offer the healing each seeks.

Set the Stars Alight